PENGUIN BOOKS

SWEET THAMES

Matthew Kneale was born in London in 1960, the son of two writers. He studied history at Magdalen College, Oxford, then spent a year in Japan, where he began writing fiction. His first novel, *Whore Banquets*, won a Somerset-Maugham award. *Sweet Thames* won the 1993 John Llewellyn Rhys Prize. His most recent book, *English Passengers*, was shortlisted for the Booker Prize in 2000 and is also published in Penguin.

When not writing, Matthew Kneale travels, and he has visited eighty-two countries and seven continents, walking in mountains from Ethiopia to New Guinea.

Sweet Thames

Matthew Kneale

PENGUIN BOOKS

PENGUIN BOOKS

Published by the Penguin Group
Penguin Books Ltd, 27 Wrights Lane, London W8 5TZ, England
Penguin Putnam Inc., 375 Hudson Street, New York, New York 10014, USA
Penguin Books Australia Ltd, Ringwood, Victoria, Australia
Penguin Books Canada Ltd, 10 Alcorn Avenue, Toronto, Ontario, Canada M4V 3B2
Penguin Books India (P) Ltd, 11 Community Centre, Panchsheel Park,
New Delhi – 110 017, India
Penguin Books (NZ) Ltd, Cnr Rosedale and Airborne Roads,
Albany, Auckland, New Zealand
Penguin Books (South Africa) (Pty) Ltd, 5 Watkins Street, Denver Ext 4,
Johannesburg 2094, South Africa

Penguin Books Ltd, Registered Offices: Harmondsworth, Middlesex, England

First published by Sinclair-Stevenson 1992
Published in Penguin Books 2001
2

Set in 11/12 pt Melior
Printed in England by Clays Ltd, St Ives plc

This book is dedicated to
HENRY MAYHEW,
Victorian journalist of genius,
without whom it could not have been written.

Author's Note

Readers of this book should know that, though fiction, it is no historical fantasy. Far from it. The more strange, painful or ludicrous an incident may seem, the more closely based upon actual occurrences it is likely to be.

Note on Names

Those interested in the history of the mid-nineteenth century may notice that some fictional figures and institutions in this novel bear close resemblance to those actually existent at that time. I found this a useful means of avoiding becoming too directly tied to the daily narrative of 1849.

Thus the fictional character of Edwin Sleak-Cunningham may have more than a little in common with Mr Edwin Chadwick, important figure in the Victorian sanitary movement. The same closeness is true of the fictional Metropolitan Committee for Sewers to the Metropolitan Commission for Sewers; the fictional Association for the Promotion of Health in Cities to the Health of Towns Association; and the fictional National Council for Health to the actual Board of Health.

Acknowledgements

I would like to thank Dr Angus McIntyre of Magdalen College, Oxford for his help in setting me in the right direction in my researches and his careful inspection of the manuscript. Likewise I am grateful to Dr John Davis of Queen's College for his advice and thorough scrutiny of the text. Also to Nicky Young for her reading suggestions. And, most of all, Vicky Egan, who proved equally invaluable as editor, adviser and friend.

Chapter One

The glory of a London unobstructed by effluent. This was the vision of the future that flashed into my imagination as I stood above the sewerage outlet on the north Thames bank. Our metropolis free from noxious odours affronting the nostrils, from unsightly deposits, from the miasma cloud of gases hanging above the rooftops. I grew lightheaded at this dazzling prospect. Until I realized, surprised, that juices were stirring in my loins.

'Thirteen inches deep here,' Hayle, my assistant for the morning, called up from before the sewer where he stood ankle deep in the current of effluent.

I noted the quantity in my field book.

'That enough measurements yet for you, sir?' In his voice there was a detectable note of complaint. 'We don't want to overdo it, do we.'

I knew the cause of his grumbling well enough; we had been at work since half past five in the morning, on this, Easter Monday, when most of London was in holiday mood, perhaps out for a spree at the Greenwich Fair. Not that this was an unusual state of affairs for me; the urgency of my task had required that every spare moment be put to good use, including – to my own shame – more than a few sabbaths.

Half past five. My lack of sleep gave the morning a dreamlike quality. Still I felt no sympathy for my servant. After all, nothing had forced him to work so early except his own eagerness to earn my shillings.

'Mr Hayle,' I told him, 'if you don't mind, I'll be the arbiter of when we're finished here.' As I peered down at my notebook I was sure I detected, from the corner of my eye, quick movement of his fingers, as if he were making some obscene gesture. Looking up, however, I saw nothing except a faint smile on his lips.

'Whatever you say, sir.'

I had never liked the fellow. More than a few times I had discerned in his manner a sarcasm, as if to work for me were beneath him. Even for a servant – a class I especially detested – there was in Hayle much 'I know better though I will not say it clear'. He was quite a crone, having served in some lowly rank of soldiering in the war against Bonaparte, and probably it was there that he had learned to treat his masters as a snide nanny might her charge. Frequently I had discerned in him sneering. Sneering at my mere five-and-twenty years of age. Sneering that my drainage scheme for London had found no supporters in the world of engineering. Sneering at my humble background – my father had been a repairer of watches – and my having grown up into the world without Hayles of my own to direct.

But it was he who was stood in the shit.

'Try over there,' I suggested, watching not without satisfaction as he wobbled against the current into a deeper part, and the liquid nearly overran the top of one of his boots.

'Mister, mister . . .' The street urchin tugged at my sleeve. He had been following us for an hour or more as we toured the sewerage outlets into the river, regularly demanding a shilling. A sadly vile creature, he resembled a torn sack poorly repaired with string; string, indeed, seemed the greater part of him, holding together what remained of his rags – shiny with grime – with bulbous knots bulging about his wrists, ankles and waist. But at least, in the furtherance of his own cause of begging, he displayed a lively perseverance quite absent in Hayle.

'I'd keep an eye on him, sir,' the servant called up. 'He'll have your watch.'

'That's not so, mister, never so.' The urchin's face was wizened into resemblance more of an old man than a boy. Framing his forehead with a kind of sad exoticism was a red 'Wide Awake' hat, brim long since lost, so that it resembled a filthy fez. 'I just wanted to ask a question, didn't I. Just a question.'

I was curious. 'And what was your question?'

'Why's 'e jabbing that stick into all that filth?'

It was a not unintelligent enquiry considering the source. 'He's measuring the depth,' I explained.

His face screwed itself into a fist of incomprehension. 'Wha's he want to do that fer?'

'So a fine new system of drainage for our city may be planned.' I studied the lad's face, wondering if the quickness in his eyes represented interest in my words or mere alertness for opportunities of theft. 'We must know how much liquid pours through the sewers, you see.'

Hayle glanced up from his work. 'Training him as your assistant, are you? You'd be better off leaving him to turn into the nat'ral grown murderer he's intended for.'

'You should show a little Christian faith, Hayle, rather than condemning the boy.' I returned to the urchin. 'What's your name, lad?'

'Jem.'

'Well Jem, is our work interesting to you?'

'Oh yes, certinly 'tis.' The creature bolstered his reply with a kind of smile, half-toothed and hungry, the effect by no means reassuring.

'Then you shall learn more of it.' I glanced at Hayle, yawning extravagantly in the stream of effluent. 'My servant here shall act as demonstrator of the methods we are using.'

The yawn abruptly died.

It had not been the best of mornings. Throughout I had been uneasy, agitated by a dream. Absurd, I reasoned, to be so alarmed by a mere imagining. One, moreover, whose subject I could not so much as remember, as all recollection had slipped from my grasp on the instant of gaining consciousness – at that quiet, early hour – eluding all effort at recapture. But still the nightmare clung to me, troubling my thoughts with its aftertaste; something of a smouldering panic, almost as if I had committed a crime.

I was dimly convinced it had involved my wife.

'Over there, nearer towards that boat,' Jem ordered. Hayle obeyed his new master with visible sulkiness, petulantly splashing through the flow towards the skeleton of a rotted skiff. He planted the measuring stick sharply, as if hoping to impale unsuspecting submarine vermin.

'Twelve inches.'

The urchin peered down at him with seriousness, not at all playing a game. 'Now do the bit with the wood.'

With a glare at the lad, Hayle held the measuring stick just above the level of the liquid, plucked a red-painted wood chip from a sack on his back, and dropped this into the flow, regarding its speed of progress past the stick's markings while also observing the watch in the palm of his hand. 'Two seconds and a quarter.'

'Thank you.' I noted the figure in my field book.

'Wha's'at strapped to you?'

The child had observed the case attached about my waist, and I opened it up to extract the handy portable sextant it contained. The instrument – which I had had little enough need of that day – was new and shone pleasantly.

Jem's eyes widened. 'Gold, is it?'

'Listen to him,' called out Hayle. 'No mystery what studyin' 'e's bin up to.'

'The boy's showing no more than a healthy interest in the science of the device,' I retorted. I held the object before the creature, without actually releasing it into his hands. 'It's brass.'

He touched it with his finger, leaving a small greasy smudge.

'Will you remember what you've learned today?' I asked him.

'Oh yes, mister.'

'Then you shall have a reward.' I replaced the sextant in its case and took from my pocket a shilling. The lad stared, clutched towards it, then, when I released the coin, darted back some yards – doubtless lest I change my mind – and despatched it into some recess of his rags with the swiftness of one well alive to the danger of letting silver see the light of day an instant too long. Without a word he scampered away along the river.

'Waste of good money.' Hayle looked put out. He would have liked the shilling for himself.

'Don't be so mean-spirited,' I told him. 'Probably you are wearied and agitated by your exertions – you're no longer so young, after all – and this has made you so.' I glanced at the columns of figures in my field book; ample now. There was no sense in detaining the servant longer. 'Pack up the things and that'll be enough for today.'

He trudged from the sewer to a street handpump close behind, where he began cleansing his boots and the measuring stick, subjecting them to angry belches of water.

The charitable exercise had, of course, been partly to taunt Hayle for his sneerings, but not for that purpose alone. I had also been fired by a genuine hope that the lad would somehow be won over to the importance of sanitary change. It was a notion very much in the spirit of my passions of that time; I was caught by an urgent wish that all – however lacking in usefulness they might appear – might be won to the brave cause of drainage reform.

It was still only quarter past eleven. I had promised my wife I would be home by one o'clock, as she had planned a small luncheon party; though I had little fondness for the guests invited, it was so unusual for her to suggest such an event nowadays that I felt I should give every encouragement. Who knew, perhaps it might help set her upon a brighter course.

An hour and three quarters. It was quite an amount of time. I stared out across the river, pondering what useful task I might set myself; one that would not take me far from my route back to Pimlico, yet would also be attainable without the help of a servant.

It was low tide and beyond the marker-less mire of Thames mud the river seemed little more than a ditch in the ooze. A black Thames barge crept warily along its surface, heavy brown sail flapping in the light breeze. To the west four figures were advancing along the water's edge, silhouetted dark against the grey sheen and, idly watching, I studied their progress nearer, until they were close enough to observe in detail.

A strange party they were. Each carried a pole that was taller than himself, with a hoe attached to the end, and had a sack strapped to his back. All were shoeless, and wore similar coats: long and greasy, with objects dangling from the breasts that seemed to be lanterns. Lanterns? My interest grew as I realized they were not passing by, but seemed to be making their way towards the very sewer entrance we had just investigated. For what possible reason? They had reached the place where Hayle had stood only a short while earlier, when the tallest chanced to glance up. Seeing me, he let out a cry.

'Spy.'

In an instant they were off, bare feet producing a faint squelching in the mud as they dashed away eastwards, towards Wapping.

I turned to ask Hayle what manner of men they could possibly be. But he had already gone.

Foreign sunlight shines in between the slats of the shutters, bright and hot even in the late afternoon. Through the distance of miles and two full years I see that London summer in a remembrance strangely focused. It is as if it were not me but a different man who lived through those months of fearsome discoveries. I can almost see him thus, as a soul separate from myself.

There. Still puzzled by the sight of the four men with poles, he steps forward to cross the Strand, watching for horse dung, picking his way between the omnibuses and coal wagons that creak and crunch and raise up clouds of street dust. Joshua Jeavons dodging a brewer's dray, eyes alert, keen, seeing no impediments to his progress that he cannot swiftly overcome. Joshua Jeavons, his young man's beard short and pointing sharply ahead from his chin, pulling forward, as if in representation of some greater propellant within. Joshua Jeavons, now striding past a newcomer from the country who is halted by the never-still hooves and wheels before him. Joshua Jeavons, pressing on past the fellow. Joshua Jeavons possessed by strange eagerness, as one set on outpacing an electric storm.

The task I had chosen myself had been to inspect the possible site of one of the Effluent Transformational Depositories. According to my scheme these would be established all across the metropolis at locations of low height, so the fluids would flow into them by gravitational process. The valuable elements would then be removed from the rest by sedimentary separation, and drawn out by steam engine, to be transported away in specially designed carts to rural areas, where they would be sold – at a wonderful profit – to farmers.

The spot was in an area of small roads to the east of Covent Garden. It had seemed simple enough to locate when I sat in my study inspecting my map of the metropolis; so much so that I had not troubled to bring the bulky plan with me. Once in the district, however, the streets proved quite a maze, and for some time I wandered, unhappily aware of the roar of Strand traffic – echoing mischievously from the high brick façades so it was hard to say from exactly whence it came – growing fainter behind me, telling that I was venturing even further from my quarry.

I paused to ask the way of a clean-chinned fellow

selling apples, who pointed me in a direction quite unexpected. 'Through that way, mister, though it's a bit of a step from 'ere.'

Onward I hurried, through narrowing lanes, urchins emerging from alley-ways, yelling and pestering until I scattered them with a raised hand. This was no place for the unwary. Even at this hour the bricks of the walls seemed to murmur faint warnings, and my glance darted ahead, alert for some over-swift movement, perhaps a flash of metal. Indeed, I pondered, such streets – stench and decay rising up from the defective sewers they were built upon – were an aching instance of the need for improving work by engineers such as myself. The effluential evil should be plucked out. Nor only here; half the metropolis required urgent attention. A giant cleansing, a renewal. That the nation might embark upon a new and sanitary road.

I rounded the corner and, with a start, found myself in a chasm-like alley that seemed familiar. No, there was no mistaking it; the clean-chinned apple salesman had utterly misdirected me, whether by accident or from malicious design. I quietly cursed the fellow, glancing up at the shabby houses that seemed to be elbowing one another for space, as a parade of drunken giants, divided by a passage so narrow that wooden rails stretched across from window to window opposite, from which washing flapped idly in the gloom.

I was close to the Seven Dials, fifty yards or so from the rookery of St Giles, a nest of all manner of criminality and vice. My chosen site for the Effluent Depository had, of course, been left far behind, and I reluctantly accepted that I should not attempt retracing my steps; after all, I might only become lost again.

'I'll give you a good time sir, nice gent like yourself.' The speaker was coarse-featured, her face and neck red from exposure to the weather. She clutched at me with her grimy hands and I warned her off with a shout. Other voices murmured their entreaties.

'Any way you like, mister.'

'Just five shillings.'

I was surprised to see so many at such an early hour; usually they gathered only as the light faded, taking their places in doorways as the abusive children seeped away. Perhaps they hoped that, this being a holiday, they might win extra trade.

'Katie'll give you a good one, like you've never had.' This last was quite pretty in a blank, drink-dazed way. Seeing me glance at her, she stepped out. 'Just six bob to you. Yer won't never regret it. Time of your life, you'll have.'

'Is that so?'

'Come and find out, why don't you, eh?' She took my hand and guided it nearer. The material of her dress was coarse, oily to touch, but the breast within was warm and soft.

It was hardly the moment. Unless, perhaps . . . 'You have some place near here?'

''Course. Katie 'as 'er own room, she does. Just six bob. Five and six if you'll get us a brandy first.'

I looked at her hard. 'You'll be wasting your time if you try any cheating.' In the past I had suffered several attempts to rifle my pockets, while once, in a vile den in Borough that I should never have visited, a ruffian burst in and tried to steal my trousers. 'I am not one to be taken in.'

'Who said anything 'bout that? You's safe enough with Katie.'

The poor creature was desperate for drink and so, warning her of my hurry, I took her to a nearby gin palace; a loud, gaudy place, all mirrors on the walls and gaslight thrown here and back in quivering reflection. She drank the spirit in quick swigs, and we moved on to her lodging room. Naked of her cheap clothes she was much improved, her body a little skinny perhaps, and hair lank and in need of a wash, but her face pleasing. I lay down beside her on the bed, touched her between the thighs and felt a greeting warm moistness. The brandy seemed to have had a beneficial effect and she displayed a liveliness rare in her profession.

'Just you lie back,' she urged. 'Katie'll give this gent sich a time as 'e's never 'ad.'

But in my enthusiasm I toppled her on to her back, eliciting a shriek of laughter.

You must understand that the drainage of the metropolis was not a mere question of work, of professional advancement. It was as a mission to me. A passion.

I had long been concerned with the question of sanitary reform. The middle and later 'forties were years when all the nation was growing outraged at the state of its cities, and great public organizations were springing into being; including the Society for the Cleansing of the Poor and, larger still, the Association for the Promotion of Health in Cities. In the company of so many other angry Londoners I joined this last, attending its public assemblies – as busy as Ladbroke Grove race meetings – signing petitions, witnessing discussions and cheering the speeches of its leaders, instilled with the enthusiasm all about me.

It was not long before the Association's pressure bore fruit. A reluctant Parliament was goaded into action, and a new authority created: the Metropolitan Committee for Sewers. Its ranks abounded with fine names – even two lords – and men well versed in the great problems to be tackled, including, as leader, none other than Edwin Sleak-Cunningham, hero of the sanitary movement. A new public body to fill us all with hope. London, greatest city of the planet, vaster than Paris, even than far-away Pekin, to be wondrously free of effluent.

It was after the Committee had been established – about the time of my own marriage – that my views began their alteration. Until then I had, like most other members of the Association, been little more than a concerned spectator, shouting for the cause he favours. Then, gradually – and for reasons I was not certain of myself – I found the issue had become something altogether closer to me; an open wound.

Thus, when I walked through London streets I found myself fiercely aware of the vile smells rising up from gulley holes, of evil deposits piled up in the gutters. Not that these were new phenomena, far from it. Rather it was that I had grown more sensitive to such horrors, until they were a constant affront. I found myself glancing up to the sky with concern, watching for the miasma; the cloud of effluvia gases hanging above the buildings of London, disgorging sickness. I began to discern it quite clearly, and see its shifting evil.

The new Committee produced its first public announcement: it called for rival schemes for the drainage of the metropolis to be drawn up, by an engineer or other member of the public interested. Projects would have to be submitted within five months, after which they would be judged by the Committee members, that one could be chosen and made into reality.

How could I not rise to meet such a challenge? Setting my engineer's training to work, I pondered and planned, then finally devised the notion of Effluent Transformational Depositories; a system quite original and, I confidently believed, utterly answering the needs of the matter. Indeed, I saw it as little less than a double salvation for the metropolis. Not only would the streets be cleansed – the wound healed – but the sale of the effluent to farmers would bring in a substantial income, reducing the burden upon ratepayers, and so adding to the wealth of the citizenry.

Then followed disappointment. My father-in-law and also employer, Augustus Moynihan, refused to take up my scheme for his engineering company, claiming drainage was too much of a departure from his earlier projects, which were most of them railways. Other companies then also proved reluctant, no doubt influenced by the thought that Moynihan – my own relative – had chosen to reject the idea. A great setback. Still I remained undaunted. I had faith in the scheme and determined, if necessary, to work quite alone. I would carry out my own researches in what little free time I could secure for myself, hiring servants such as Hayle from my father-in-law's company, while, for my livelihood, I would continue also to work there. A hard regime, perhaps, but one well justified.

The honourable profession of engineer. That was my vocation, my training, and still it is. If my writing seems sometimes simple I make no apologies. Never was I taught the art of words in the way others show such clever skill; to devise sentences that meander back and forth in interwoven clauses until, without a halt, they have occupied a page and a half and, along the road, twisted meanings beyond recognition.

Nor would I wish it so. Why embellish events when they require no such doctoring? I seek only to set them down truthfully, to call them into life, that they may exhibit their own natural strangeness. I will not cosify that hot summer; if my own character and actions are not always pleasing, so be it. Only by setting down the harshest of details may I hope to comprehend them better. And perhaps exorcize them from my soul.

And what is my story? Most of all it is of the search for my wife. And where I eventually found her.

My first sight upon waking was Katie lying on the bed, watching me with dim curiosity. She was aligned exactly towards me, so that, as I raised my head, her buttocks seemed almost to emerge from the lank curls of her hair, while her feet – kicking the air with vague restlessness – stretched up behind them in the shape of a Vee, toes probing the air.

'How long have I been asleep?' I did not wait for an

answer, but reached for my watch. It was past one o'clock. 'Why didn't you wake me?'

'Seemed a shame when you looked so peaceful.' She rolled upon her side, as a cat exposing its belly, amused by my panic. 'An' there was nobody waitin' his turn outside.'

It was hardly her fault. I tugged at my trousers, angry at my own weakness. To have fallen asleep at such a time.

She rested her hand on her chin. 'What's yer hurry? Why don't you stay a bit.' Eyes watching me, she slipped her hand behind her back until her fingers re-emerged through the crack between her thighs, where they waved in a kind of greeting. 'Might be nice.'

'No, I must go.'

She shrugged. 'Well, come visit Katie again, won't yer? It's nice to see a gent for a change. Don't get many gents round here, yer don't.'

I dropped the coins on the bed.

'What's yer name, anyway?'

My patience was leaving me. 'Does it matter?'

'Only asked, didn't I.' She drew her knees up to her chin, encircling them with her arms, as if to reclaim her parts. 'I told you mine happy enough.'

I picked up my hat. 'Henry Aldwych.'

She seemed pleased with the false name, unlikely-sounding though it was, and released her legs, stretching them out before her. ''Enry,' she repeated to herself. 'Come again soon then, will yer, 'Enry?' She let out a laugh at her own remark which pealed behind me as I left. 'Come again.'

I hurried down the stairs, pushing loose flaps of shirt into the band of my trousers as I went. If I could find a cab on the Charing Cross Road I might not be so late. And I would be able to tidy myself up a touch on the way. If I could find one . . .

'Want a good time, mister?'

'Just six bob to yer.'

Emptied of passion as I was, the women's harsh,

grimly routine voices awoke in me a shame. To have allowed myself to be led by base urges, no better than an animal. And in such a place; a threatening slum. The troubles I had brought upon my own head seemed only too just. I should even consider myself lucky not to have brought some greater catastrophe upon myself; robbery and permanent injury, perhaps, with the further shame of having to be rescued from such a den, and explain. Not for the first time I determined never again to fall to such lowness.

A smell of effluent hung in the air, rising up from some badly built drain, seemingly stronger since my unintended arrival in the district. I sensed the odours as in some way feeding the criminality above, acting as a fertilizer of evil, luring me to misadventure. I held my handkerchief to my nose.

'Got a cold, 'ave yer love? I'll warm yer up.'

It was then, of all moments, that I remembered my dream.

The man had been greyly anonymous, a mere enemy form. My wife, by contrast, had been clearly detailed, clothed – puzzlingly – in her finest Sunday dress. Her face I could not see as it was buried against his chest; she entwined him as a creeper about a tree, absorbing the very flesh.

The touch of the knife in my fingers.

'Only six bob to you.' The woman had misread my hesitation as interest and stepped forward towards me. 'Time of yer life, I'll give yer.' When I walked on she clutched at my coat-tails until I shooed her away.

Of course I knew the inspiration for the nightmare clear enough. The letter I had been sent.

Our rented home was in Lark Road, a street close by the new district of Pimlico, that giant construction yard of fine tall buildings still in their making. Lark Road, by contrast, was neither modern in design nor grand in proportion, but a survival from the age of Queen Anne, the houses it contained most dull and old-fashioned –

sad to say we could afford no better – with rooms that were modest to the point of pokiness.

Our home was, at least, wonderfully clean. My wife kept it so, with fireplaces swept, tables polished, and windows freshly wiped; free of all but the most lately arrived film of soot. It was her fancy to do so. In fact more; it was her passion. She had evidently been working particularly hard in preparation for the luncheon party, and as I walked into the parlour the room seemed to gleam.

'Joshua, at last. We were beginning to wonder if you'd fallen down one of those awful drains.' Though she uttered the words lightly enough, her eyes showed her relief, as well as something like anger at the distress I had caused her. She hated my being late, as it would never fail to make her fear some accident had befallen me.

'I'm so sorry. I quite lost track of time. You shouldn't have waited.'

The two guests, Gideon and Felicia Lewis – brother and sister – watched me with vague curiosity.

'We didn't wait.' Though she smiled, my wife spoke with sharpness, still angry. 'The dinner's not yet ready.'

Isobella Jeavons, turning with a smile to attend to her guests, a sight to behold before me, elegant hostess of a London luncheon party – formal occasions seemed to call forth all her grace and composure – filling me with pride, and a sense of my own clumsiness. Also something like trepidation. It was a rarity to see her so animated, and always I wondered how long it would last, before dissolving into something more brittle.

That day, of course, I had also other concerns. I hung back from kissing her for fear that, were I to venture so near, she might detect through the fabric of my clothes the odours of my recent lust.

The mere thought of it . . .

'I hope you'll excuse me if I change from my work clothes.'

Passing through the hallway I caught a glimpse through the kitchen doorway of the bulky form of Miss Symes, our servant, wrestling with a joint of lamb. Grasping it with one padded hand, she was endeavouring to poke the thing with a long knife, testily, as if to be fully sure it was dead. The meat was pale, and looked still only half-cooked. A relief as it reduced my embarrassment at being late. The bathroom afforded me further encouragement; the mirror revealed my efforts to tidy myself in the cab had been more successful than I had feared. Who knew, perhaps I might, after all, survive the day without suffering disaster.

What my wife saw in the Lewises I could not comprehend. They were a plain pair. Gideon seemed to be lacking in weightiness, troublingly so, his head forever bobbing about, as if he might at any moment quite float adrift from the ground, in the manner of some escaped hot-air balloon. Felicia was more firmly anchored; fiercely correct – so covered up with clothes that scarcely a speck of hand or throat showed – with something of the manner of a trap, ready to spring shut upon the unwary. And yet my wife attended Felicia's bible gatherings with regularity, and invited her and Gideon to our home, in determined preference to other, far less odious acquaintances. When I once asked about the matter, she grew annoyed.

'Joshua, I'm most fond of the Lewises. You mustn't criticize them so. It's not fair of you.'

And yet . . . I watched as, the meal having been so delayed, she embarked on passing round a bowl of burnt almonds. First to Felicia, then – more surprisingly – to myself. Finally she took one with her own delicate fingers, and placed the remainder on the side table. Gideon, abandoned, made a poor attempt to smile.

'Those do look delicious.'

Isobella's cry of dismay was almost too rich. 'Oh Mr Lewis, how could I?' Had I not known of her devotion to them both, I might have imagined she had deliberately contrived to make the fellow look foolish.

She sat back in her chair, feet gathered up from the ground, pressing tight against one another, in a way that made her, all at once, look youthful, even childlike. Why not indeed, when she had barely reached her nineteenth birthday; fully seven years younger than myself. At times she could possess an innocence that quite stole my breath from me; that made me feel as much a parent to her as a husband.

What kind of person could send such a letter, filled with poison towards a soul of such simple purity? The writing had been quite unfamiliar, formed in a style resembling printed script, no doubt to better disguise the hand.

SOME HUSBANDS SHOULD KEEP A
CLOSE WATCH ON THEIR WIVES

Someone from work, jealous of my having married the daughter of Augustus Moynihan, owner of the company? It was the most likely possibility, and yet no candidate sprang to mind; among the faces were none I could imagine desiring to carry out an act of such malice.

Several times I had intended discussing the matter with Isobella, but then had found myself unable. How could I? It would be like teaching brothel slang to a saint.

Brothel slang to a saint. After this interlude of years, I wonder if there was not, perhaps, also a second reason. One protective not of her but myself; a motive barely glimpsed. Fear of what I might discover.

'It's certainly a most colourful room.' Felicia uttered the words in a tone of disapproval, correcting her brother's earlier enthusiasm. The conversation had hobbled and stumbled as a one-legged man on stony ground, until plucked up by Gideon – a touch desperately – and deposited on the subject of 'things on the mantelpiece', which he endeavoured to praise. His sister's puritanical nature evidently saw little that was worthy of congratulation.

'A most bright arrangement,' she continued, in the manner of one who has stumbled upon a minor colliery disaster.

Gideon glanced awkwardly at the carpet.

'We like it so,' I answered with firmness, looking Felicia straight in the eye with a smile. How dare she. I was most proud of our parlour – our display to the world – though we rarely ventured thither except when we had guests. I glanced about at the furnishings, regarding them with a sense of rediscovery.

It was a finely modern sight. The dark green wallpaper and fiercely scarlet french stool were sufficiently strong of colour as to be little affected by accretions of soot from the air and fireplace, while our most valued possessions – the majority wedding gifts, as we had never been in the position to go purchasing pretty things – were cunningly protected against the ravages of dust. Thus the tiny stuffed tropical birds of all colours of the rainbow – nestling on branches with astonishing realism, as if each had set down from flight just that instant for a short rest – were encased in a smooth dome of glass. Likewise encapsulated in two smaller and matching domes were our busts of Queen Victoria and the Prince Consort Albert, executed with suitable dignity of expression, and lodged proudly on the piano.

Probably Felicia was offended that the legs of the chairs and tables were not modestly concealed behind hangings. Certainly she appeared annoyed by something; from the first she had been in a mood of unusual sourness – even by her own severe standards – darting withering glances at her brother, and also at Isobella. How could my wife endure such people?

My ruminations were interrupted by the arrival of Miss Symes, without knocking, as was her way. 'About that ham, missus, that you thought of havin' on the side. There's only the two slices left, see.'

She was a weightily formed woman, built of the kind of flesh that seems always faintly reverberating, as if containing bags of thickened liquid. Persons thus shaped are held in the popular imagination to be of a warm-hearted disposition, but Miss Symes was proof of the weakness of such theories. She was sulky and complaintive, also lazy, and, I was sure, of limitless appetite, as our larder seemed constantly in need of replenishment. We had chosen her only for one reason: she was cheap. Even then we could afford her for only seventeen days in a month, sharing her with the family of a Highbury legal clerk. She had insisted on board, though the arrangement was only part-week, and slept in a room hardly larger than a cupboard, into which it was a mystery to me how she managed to fit herself.

Despite her inexpensiveness, her ill-manners had several times led me to suggest to my wife that we try and find somebody else. Isobella had surprised me with her insistence that the woman stay. The only explanation I could see was that Miss Symes's indolence gave her unrestrained opportunity to throw herself into her passion – so admirable – of domestic activity; cleaning and polishing every object until it shone.

'There were a good eight slices of the ham last night,' I insisted. 'Where's it all gone?'

Miss Symes put on a look of studied indifference. 'Must've just went, mustn't it sir.'

'It's of no matter,' my wife suggested, before I had time to remark further on the matter. 'We're better off without it, I'm sure.'

'Very good, ma'am.' As Miss Symes manoeuvred her person back through the doorway there was a scrabbling about her feet and Pericles, my wife's terrier, scuttled into the room.

It had been my idea that she should have a pet, so she would have a companion to brighten up her hours in the house. Indeed, in some ways the dog might have been viewed as a success; Isobella took to him from the first, embracing him whenever he appeared and inventing all manner of affectionate names for him: 'Peridog', 'King Peri', 'Little Naughty' and many others.

I, however, found myself unable to stifle a growing loathing for the creature. There was something vile about the way he would lick her face so keenly, even her very lips, how he nuzzled the cloth of her dress just where it thinly contained the soft roundness of her bosom. He must have somehow discerned my dislike for him – animals can be surprisingly sensitive to human feelings towards them – for he soon regarded me as his foe, yapping at me with his small dog bark whenever the opportunity arose, growling, and occasionally attempting to nip my ankle with his teeth. Isobella would reprimand him, but without great severity, still referring to him as 'Little Dog' or 'Perikins'. I sometimes retaliated when the creature was out of view of his mistress, with discreet kicks to his person.

'Peri, Peri, Peri the Bad, where have you been?' she almost sang to him as she plucked him from the ground, and allowed him to lunge with his mouth towards her ear. 'Were you playing in the kitchen?'

With small-animal impatience he sprang from her grasp and darted across the room, pausing to stare at Gideon, who reached out, with the idea of patting his head. 'Hello my fine little fellow.'

The dog growled audibly, then snapped, jaws not quite reaching the proffered fingers.

'Pericles,' my wife scolded him, without great feeling. 'How bad he is.'

'He's charming.' Gideon manufactured a smile.

The creature had already moved onwards, now leaping up at the edge of the table, overhanging which was my wife's embroidery. Embroidering was a hobby of hers, and one which she pursued with the same restless perfectionism that she exhibited towards the domestic arrangements of the house; this was already the tenth such creation in eight months of our marriage; an astonishing pace of production. The nine so far completed – now framed and displayed on the walls, fast diminishing in unused space – all took the same form; of a biblical quotation framed by flowers. This latest had not progressed far, and as yet read only, DOEST NOT . . .

'Little dog, really now.' She got up from her seat to reclaim the animal, grasping him firmly on her lap.

It was then I saw the knife.

To look at, it was hardly remarkable; a slim piece, more ornamental letter-opener than cutting blade, with a delicate mother-of-pearl handle. It was on the table among Isobella's embroidery things, and she must have been using it to snap the threads cleanly. Probably it had lain about the house since the day of our marriage, and I had never given it a thought in all that time. Until it had featured in my dream.

In my distraction I had, I realized, been staring directly at Gideon's weak chin for some moments. The conversation having moved onwards from the parlour to the question of work, he had embarked on an interminable description of the duties of an architect of church buildings; his own profession.

'We have the chance to look back over church styles of all ages and nations, take the best from each, and so create such a design that none other will ever be needed again. Think of it. An epilogue to the whole great volume of ecclesiastical architecture. Responsibility indeed.' He paused, regarding me kindly, appearing to assume my blank glare had told of a fascination with his words.

A thump outside the door warned of Miss Symes's return. 'It's ready now, missus.'

'Thank you, Miss Symes.'

An idea came to me. As the others rose from their places I lingered, allowing them to chatter their way out of the room before me. Then, when I could hear all had made their way across the hall and to the dining-room, I plucked up the knife. The very touch of the metal was troubling; almost as something so cold that it threatens to stick fast to one's skin.

I saw a pair of eyes staring at me. Pericles, lodged beneath the table, uttered a growl. A neat tap to his backside with my foot elicited a yelp and caused him to scurry from the room.

'Is something wrong?' called out my wife.

'Just coming.' There was no time to do more than open the front door – as noiselessly as I was able – and hurl the thing into the street slop dirt, grinding it in deeper with the toe of my boot.

At last the Lewises had left us. I closed the door and we made our way back into the house. Miss Symes was clearing plates and such from the dining-room to the kitchen – sporadic thumps and crashes reverberating through the house told of her labours – and so we took refuge in the parlour.

What a relief that they had gone. Only my unwillingness to spoil an occasion into which my wife had invested such effort had prevented my directing some sharp remarks to the two guests. Gideon, in particular, had been infuriating.

The fellow was, it seemed, a keen amateur painter and, during the roast lamb, had embarked on an account – both dull and fairly lengthy – of the lives of Italian Renaissance masters; while the plates of the rest of us grew empty, his remained all but untouched, and the dessert was greatly delayed. Worse was the man's smugness. He talked of Guido Reni and Michelangelo as if both were his personal acquaintances, and described their works with the knowingness a schoolma'am might employ when detailing the efforts of her more able infants, beaming all the while – doubtless at the pleasure he imagined he was affording his hosts.

Isobella perched herself upon the french stool and picked up her embroidery that she might resume her work. She seemed not to notice the knife's absence. For my part, the panic I had felt earlier seemed now painfully absurd; the delusions of a man weakened by tiredness and hunger. I had half a mind to retrieve the object and replace it, at some moment when my wife was busy elsewhere in the house.

Where to sit? Normally I would have chosen one of the upright chairs. Perhaps it was my pleasure at the Lewises' departure that persuaded me otherwise, or the two glasses of wine I had had with the luncheon. Or the bright smile I had watched earlier on my wife's face. Whatever the reason, I sat down beside her on the french stool. It was quite a squeeze, true enough, but still her response distressed me; she fairly jumped, edging away so we were not touching.

One action, one instant, and so much seemed changed. Already I could sense the quiet – that quiet I knew so well – beginning to descend. Speak before it could encircle us both. Say anything.

'The apple and meringue pudding was most tasty. Did you make it yourself?'

'I did.' She did not so much as look up from her work. Though I could not see her eyes I knew, from the very tone of her voice, how they would be changed; animation vanished. Her lips, too, would be altered; taut, as if unwilling to form words. So often it was thus. She resented my absence – complaining of my long hours of work – and yet my presence in the house seemed to make her hardly less uneasy. And of course . . .

The busts of Queen Victoria and Albert glowered down from the piano, as if saddened by the scene before them.

'I thought it must have been yours. Much too good for anything of Miss Symes'.' I struggled on against the hush. 'I'm sure I detected a small tot of rum.'

'I put in a couple of teaspoonfuls.'

Still not so much as a glance. It was all the more galling after her bright cheerfulness during the meal.

Did she prefer the company of the Lewises to my own? I wanted to pluck her up from the french stool, to stir her up – as some mixture left too long, in which the worst has floated to the surface – to shake her in the air, until the brittle silence was gone.

If only there were something . . .

Then I remembered the advertisement I had seen in *The Times* a few days earlier.

Why not? An expedition might do much to blow away the staleness. At least I should try. I made my way up to my study to seek the edition in which it had been.

> MONSIEUR TOULON'S CONCERTS MONSTRES
>
> A third Concert Monstre and musical ballet, in the style and scale for which M Pierre Toulon is so justly renowned, to be performed on Easter Monday at the Surrey Zoological Gardens. Programme entirely changed from M Toulon's great five-hour concert of 1847, held before an audience of 12,000 persons. Meyerbeer's music from the Camp of Silesia to be played for the *first time* in this country. M Toulon's famous Corps of Dwarves to perform a *ballet d'action* entitled *Pompey and the Deserter*. Also M Toulon's own arrangement of *The Grand Triumphal March* of Julius Caesar, complete with Double Orchestra, Four Military Bands, and Roman trumpets. Finally M Toulon's own rendering of *God Save the Queen*, each bar being marked by the report of an eighteen pounder cannon. Admission only . . .

Just the thing. I hurried down to the parlour. 'Come along, my dear. We're going out.'

She frowned. 'Whatever d'you mean?'

'Just what I said. It's Easter, half London is enjoying the holiday, so why not us too?'

Though she protested at first, she seemed not altogether displeased to find herself in an omnibus, streets flashing by outside. My spirits began to rise.

Perhaps it had been just such a notion that had been required all along. For all these months. I simply had not thought to try.

The concert was quite as popular as Monsieur Toulon's previous visit of two years before, judging by the throng of metropolitan citizenry we found gathered in Kennington, joining the queue to the gardens. Once inside, ambling with the crowd past grottoes, classical statues, an ornamental lake, the sight of such a multitude of excited souls took me back to my time as a follower of the Association for the Promotion of Health in Cities. Splendid days.

Best of all, the liveliness of atmosphere seemed to have infected Isobella, causing the smile of lunch time to return to her face. Success. And who knew where it might end.

'But it's lovely. How is it I've never been here before?' She paused, detaining our progress with an outstretched hand, her expression one of almost child-like intensity as she listened. 'What are those cries?'

'The animals.' We were approaching the seats – a veritable ocean of them, enough for an entire army, freshly returned from some Easter battle – behind which rose up the circular glass building that contained the zoo's creatures. I had briefly visited the place some years previously, and inspected the collection – not a poor one – of lions, camels, monkeys, bears, parrots and other tropical birds, as well as a rather scrawny giraffe, and a single giant tortoise on which small children were invited to ride for a small sum.

'But can't we see them? Perhaps after the concert is finished?'

'If the animal house is still open to the public at such an hour, then certainly.' Though most doubtful it would be, I was unwilling to risk forfeiting my wife's newly re-found good humour.

I had bought good seats, despite the extra expense, and our places were close to the front, from where we had an excellent view of the conductor, Monsieur Toulon, as he stepped upon the rostrum. Bespectacled, and with a hairless dome of a head, he was surprisingly clerk-like in appearance for one responsible for so giant an event, and with the huge assembly of players ranged behind, he seemed quite a speck. I glanced up at the sky; though the day was not a cold one there was a stiff breeze and ranks of clouds were chasing each other across the sky, eastwards towards Greenwich. Brave indeed to hold an outdoor event at so early a season.

Isobella seemed to read my thoughts. 'I hope it won't rain.'

'At least we have the umbrella.'

The concert began splendidly, with *The Grand March of Julius Caesar*, a finely furious piece. To be seated before the whole ensemble of double orchestra, four military bands and twenty roman trumpets – strange instruments that produced a sound not unlike a donkey's braying much amplified – was as being perched before a kind of musical hurricane.

For some time thereafter, however, the programme – though noisily diverting in its way – was of less interest. In fact I found myself struck more by the brief intervals between the music than by the items themselves. After Monsieur Toulon brought down his baton with a flourish, and the last great crash of noise of the double orchestra faded away, one would hear – through ringing ears – the strange cries of the tropical creatures, as if they were offering their own retort to the earlier din; the harsh screeches of birds – conjuring up imaginings of fiery plumage – the questioning whoops of monkeys, perhaps the growl of a lion. The effect was most pleasing. Then Monsieur Toulon would raise his hand, abruptly drowning their exotic voices, as the players began work on the next monumental piece.

The concert also offered other delights. It may seem strange, but I do not believe I had ever spent so long a time in such close proximity to my wife until that afternoon. The seats were narrow, and placed tightly together, so it seemed only natural to find my knee gently pressing against her thigh; pleasantly soft to touch even through the cloth of my trousers and her dress. Encouraged by her cheerfulness – she appeared to be enjoying the performance – I made a few experimental movements of my knee upwards and downwards, in a manner that might merely have been considered precautionary against cramp.

Her response was puzzling. While she did not glance in my direction, but stared somewhat fiercely at the orchestra, nor did she shrink from my touch, leaving me uncertain as to whether she was shyly enjoying such attentions, or simply could not move her leg away, being so tightly wedged beside me. Perhaps she had not even noticed. Whatever the truth of it, the sensation had a most agreeable effect, and I was obliged to place my top hat on my lap, that I would not risk scandalizing the venerable lady seated stiffly to my right.

It was a long concert. After four hours, with only one brief interval, the audience began to show signs of restiveness, and also cold – the warmth of the afternoon was fading – with people shifting in their seats, and adding, during the interludes between pieces, their coughs to the cries of the tropical animals. The music, too, had assumed something of a noisy monotony. Consequently Monsieur Toulon's announcement of a quite different kind of item was greeted with some relief, and much clapping.

'I now will like proudly to present the very famous Corps of Dwarves.'

I had been looking forward to something in the nature of a rough and tumble comedy – what else would one expect from a dwarf act – but it was not to be. Though the players looked sufficiently comical in their tiny togas to raise a faint ripple of laughter from the audience, their sombre march on to the stage proclaimed the piece to be a serious one.

'How dull,' I murmured.

The drama took the form of a mime, accompanied by the double orchestra in a quieter but more emotional mood than before. The players' expressions and gestures being so difficult to see, the narrative proved elusive, but I managed to understand the gist of the story. Pompey – played by a dwarf smaller even than his fellows, and clutching a sword as tall as himself – had had brought before him a soldier, his head hooded, who was accused of deserting. Inclined to be harsh at first, the great general then – for reasons I could not quite comprehend – felt pity for the man, and ordered him released. When the hood was removed, however, it was not a soldier who was revealed, but a girl dwarf. One whom, moreover, the famous Roman recognized at once, throwing his tiny hands into the air and embracing her with passion.

Though part of the audience evidently found this greatly moving – there was an approving murmur as the little couple embraced – I was not thus affected. 'Absurd. As if his wife, or whoever she's supposed to be, could have been mistaken for a soldier.'

'And besides,' agreed my wife, 'why did she not cry out from beneath the hood?'

As if in answer to our criticisms an attempt at explanation seemed imminent. The violins moaned effusively and Pompey and the girl dwarf engaged in a dance of reunion, during which she conducted what appeared to be a series of mimes recounting her adventures. Their significance, however, was not obvious, and, beyond her having been violently hurled from a high place, I was still quite as much in the dark as before when the weather so abruptly intervened.

Even as the dwarves first pranced their way on to the stage the sky had darkened with warning suddenness – from somewhere north of the river rolled an unhurried rumble of thunder – and by the time Pompey had discovered the deserter's true identity the leaves on the trees were waving, their rustling just audible above the glad wailings of so many violins. The rain began moments later, commencing with a few ominously large drops, then dissolving into a general rush.

I unfurled the umbrella. We were by no means the only ones to have come thus prepared, and all across the audience and orchestra umbrellas began springing up like mushrooms; above cellists, drummers and tuba players. A servant of some kind even held one above the head of Monsieur Toulon – working feverishly with his baton – though his pate was already glistening wet.

The dwarves, however, enjoyed no such protection. Indeed, they were struggling badly. The rain seemed to have had a pronounced effect upon the surface of their little stage, causing it to grow slippery, and obliging Pompey's guards – engaged in a dance of celebration behind the happy couple, and evidently fearful of losing their balance – to adopt a delicate mincing step, most unmilitary in character. Despite these precautions it was not long before one of their number wobbled alarmingly, struggled to keep balance, only to keel clean over upon his back, tiny legs kicking high into the air.

How could one not be affected by such a sight. A wave of laughter spread across the audience – quite a sound it was too, springing from so many thousands of throats – while I myself was quite doubled over in my seat.

'My goodness,' I began. 'I don't believe . . .'

That I did not finish was because my attention was again captured by the goings-on upon the stage.

The girl dwarf had refused to be intimidated by the wet, leaping about with vigour as she mimed her past sufferings, and it was hardly surprising that she soon paid the price for such recklessness. Her misfortune was that she slid, of all directions, towards Pompey. Seeking, in her extremity, any object with which she might steady herself, her hands found the great

Roman's head, which she grasped by the ears and nose. Alas her efforts proved of no avail, and in a moment she had toppled over, toga flying, and causing a sound resembling a loud slap. He fell too, entangled in his giant sword, which broke asunder with surprising ease.

The audience roared – I with them – and I am sure it was this reaction that was the spark of the incident that followed. The Pompey dwarf – perhaps influenced by the great character he was representing – evidently felt he had suffered indignities beyond all toleration. Clambering to his feet, he turned to the girl dwarf and, without warning, struck her a nasty blow about the face with his hand, then – pushing her to the ground with a shove – jumped astride her that he might deliver yet further punishment.

The laughter of the watchers quite died away. A strangely shocking sight it was, too; this tiny creature inflicting such cruelty to another even smaller and more defenceless than himself. Still the reaction of my wife took me by surprise.

I suddenly realized she was no longer in her seat beside me, but was standing. Her face was pale, her eyes seemingly oblivious to myself and the others sat watching her. 'Stop it.' She uttered the words in a murmur. Then repeated them, shouting out, 'Stop it.'

I had not before detected in her any tendency towards such rash display in a public place. Indeed, she usually appeared to seek only anonymity in a crowd. 'Isobella, whatever . . .' I began. Before I could finish, however, Pompey had produced his own answer to her call, by striking the girl dwarf for a third time. The effect was immediate. All at once Isobella seemed to bolt, like a scared horse in a confined space, trying to force a passage along the row of seats.

'Isobella, what are you doing?' I called out. 'Come back.'

She seemed not to so much as hear, did not pause,

nor even look back. Indeed, she quickened her efforts. Alarmed, I began to follow.

Following, however, proved no easy matter; the gap between the rows of seats was not a great one and I found myself stepping and stumbling upon all manner of umbrellas, legs and feet. The owners, naturally, were far from pleased.

'What d'you think you're playing at, you bloody fool?'

'What's your hurry? Stolen something?'

The timing of our exit could hardly have been worse. Pompey was swiftly overpowered by his own guards, and Monsieur Toulon – determined to have the incident finished with as promptly as possible – gestured, with angry waves of his baton, for the dwarf troupe to depart. The stage cleared, he turned to the audience and, endeavouring to recover his composure, made his final announcement.

'Ladies and Gentlemen, we reach the end of this evening's entertainment. I would like to proudly present my own arrangement of *God Save the Queen*.'

The shame of it. Even now the memory is painful. The whole great ocean of audience rose respectfully to its feet, filling the air with the slow rustling of tens of thousands of frock-coats and fine ladies' dresses. Struggling past the huge family of an angrily moustachioed fellow, I called out to my wife. 'Isobella, you must stop. We cannot possibly . . .'

She paid no heed. Stumbling after her, I saw, from the corner of my eye, Monsieur Toulon raise both arms into the air. At once the whole double orchestra, four military bands and twenty roman trumpets began to play, slowly dignified. The eighteen pounder cannons had been placed on the lawn to either side of the orchestra – long lines of them, pointed, so as not to cause alarm, away from the audience – and were manned by grinning royal artillerymen. The discharges were perfect of time, awesome of majesty, and caused a certain bluntness of hearing, as if one's ears had been dipped in treacle.

We were treated to the most venomous of glares.
'Frenchies, are you?'
'I suppose you take some pleasure in insulting our Queen.' This last was from an old gentleman with a monocle, who threatened me with his stick. Nor could I have blamed him had he struck.

The cab was not a new member of its class and made its way towards Westminster with fearful judderings and creakings of old woodwork. Outside it was growing dark, streets all but vanished into dusk, until, abruptly, a row of lamps already lit would pass into view, revealing in sharp detail the clothes and expressions of Londoners scampering beneath their glare.
'I'm sorry.' Isobella was the first to break the painful silence. 'I just couldn't help myself. I couldn't remain an instant longer. To see him . . .' She turned her head away. 'Do what he did.'
'But why?' I was still full with the shame of our flight. 'One instant you were happy, laughing, and then . . .' I regarded her, but she looked away. 'It was a distressing scene to watch, certainly, but that was no reason to run like that. And at such a moment? Did you not hear me calling you to stop?'
She replied only by quietly crying to herself.
Part of me wanted to preserve my own cold anger – and the rare power it gave – but part was already softening at the sight of her sobbing. 'I just don't understand. It's so unlike you.'
'It was the noise,' she murmured, without great conviction. 'And there was something . . .'
The cab turned a corner sharply, wheels rattling noisily upon the cobblestones, causing us both to be thrown to one side. I looked her in the eye until she met my glance. 'Sometimes I feel I hardly know you.'
She looked down.
'That there is another side to you. Something secret.'
'Joshua, why do you . . .' Before she could finish,

however, she interrupted herself with a sneeze, a light sprinkling of the effect landing upon my frock coat. Shaking her head in the manner of one whose misfortune can hardly extend further, she took the handkerchief from my pocket and began to scrub. 'I'm sorry Joshua. As if I had not already done enough.' Finished, she replaced my handkerchief in the pocket, her head bowed.

The ludicrousness of the moment robbed it of its drama. 'Perhaps you're tired.' Even as I spoke I was annoyed by the note of concern in my words. Where was the cool distance I had wanted to preserve? Already I had half surrendered to her.

'I suppose I am.' She looked up, eyes wider, appealing. 'After preparing the luncheon party. You must be far more so, working so very hard.'

'I dare say.' So tiredness was to be the alibi. Though it was hardly a convincing explanation for the incident, it seemed too late now to try to revert to sternness.

'Joshua, can you forgive me?'

I answered her look with a nod, and placed my arm about her shoulders; she seemed comforted. Feeling her faint sobbing reverberating through her slim body, the last of my resentment drained away. 'You must rest,' I told her. 'You're probably also hungry – it's late – and should have something to eat when we get home. It will do much to restore your spirits.'

'I will,' she agreed, with enthusiasm. 'And you must eat too.' I peered through the window at the London darkness beyond. Turning back, I saw she was glancing at me, close, with a look I had not seen for a long time.

'You're good to me, Joshua. Really you are.' She brushed the back of my hand with her fingers, only for an instant. 'You mustn't think I don't realize how good you are. I do.'

I drank in that look. My arm was still about her shoulders, and she rested her head against me.

Perhaps the day might prove to be a kind one after all. Better than kind; a landmark.

By the time we walked into the house, however, the moment was already slipping away.

It began with her frown, as she looked about the hallway. 'I'm so tired. And Miss Symes has gone to Highbury.' She sighed. 'Joshua, I don't think I'll have anything to eat after all.'

A mere question of food, but it seemed something much greater was at stake. 'I'll find something for you.'

Another frown. 'I don't feel hungry.'

'Just have a little. We can eat together.'

'No, really, I must go to bed.' Her voice was changed now; more matter-of-fact in its tone, growing annoyed at my persistence.

After all that had gone before . . . I could feel anger growing in me. I would not have it end thus. 'I'll light your way.' I took the lamp.

Now the look was back upon her face; tautly silent. 'There's no need.'

'I want to.' I strode from the room, leaving her no option but to follow or be left in darkness. Up to the bedroom; Isobella, I could hear, just a few steps behind. Stepping inside – into her territory, smelling the smells of her clothes and perfumes – my sense of righteousness flagged slightly. As I hesitated, she slipped neatly past, to station herself by the mantel-piece; an outflanking movement that left me on the door-wards side of her.

'Thank you for seeing me up.' While I had grown less certain, she seemed now more sure of herself. 'You'll need a candle.'

I placed the lamp on the table behind me, where she could not reach it. 'Isobella, don't be like this, please. In the cab, the way you looked at me . . .'

She seemed not to have heard, but glanced around the room, seeking something. 'Where did I put those matches?'

I stepped forward and took her hand, causing her to

turn, her body stiff now, on her face something like a smile, but wrong. I looked her close in the eyes. 'Won't you let me embrace you? Only that. You cannot be so hard.'

'I need time.'

'I know, but . . .' Her hand in mine was as a kind of bridgehead, and from it I began drawing closer to her. 'Can't you try to grow accustomed to these things?'

'It's too soon.'

'You don't sound sure.' I progressed again from her hand, hearing her breathing, so quick. 'I only want you to be happy.' I gently touched her waist.

She pulled suddenly back, wrenching free the hostage hand. 'Don't force me to . . .' Her voice was quite altered, containing no nervousness, no apology, only undefined threat. She stared at me, cold now. 'Just don't force me to . . .'

All at once I hated her, for the fear she could conjure up in me, of things that could be lost. 'Mr and Mrs Jeavons. A fine couple we make.'

'I just need time.'

'Will you never stop saying that?'

Her eyes seemed to grow glazed, as if she did not see me.

I wanted to hurt her, cause in her the same suffering I felt myself. Above all to escape the role I had slipped into, of the forever appealing suitor. 'As if I care. As if it troubles me in the slightest.' I half turned. 'I have more important things to think about than you.'

Striding from the room on to the landing, her door swinging shut behind me, I realized my foolishness at having left the light behind me. Unwilling to go back, I fumbled my way forward in the darkness, arms outstretched, in search of my study door.

In the street below carts and omnibuses rattled through the night, and scatterings of drunks sang away the last few hours of their holiday. I lay on the couch, unable to sleep. Already my anger had quite gone.

From her room I could hear her softly crying.

She was so young, after all. Barely nineteen, hardly emerged from childhood. Was it not her innocent dignity that I so admired? How could I have behaved so, clutching at her, no better than some sailor fresh off ship claiming his harlot. Her disposition was not ready for such base urges, just as she herself had said. All that was needed was patience.

Unless . . .

The thought was too awful to entertain, even for a moment.

Chapter Two

> THE CHOLERA NEAR LIVERPOOL
>
> An outbreak of Asiatic Cholera among labourers working on the Runfield railway tunnel near Liverpool has claimed three lives, while fourteen more have lately been taken sick with the malady. One of the dead . . .

Close by Liverpool. I rested the copy of *The Times* on the table beside my cup of breakfast tea, stilled for some moments.

There had been such hopes we might be spared. The disease, after its years' long journeyings, from India across the great land mass of the Russian Empire, to Scandinavia and the German Principalities, had finally reached Britain the previous September, first striking the port of Sunderland. London remained for weeks in a state of fearsome expectation. Only gradually did it become evident the malady was, for the moment at least, confining itself to Scotland. Then, with the arrival of colder weather – Asiatic Cholera being much wedded to the summer months – a great relief spread across the metropolis; a wonderful sense of disaster escaped, and services of thanks-giving were held in several churches.

We were pleased too soon. In January, as if as a warning, a sudden and unseasonal outbreak occurred among the pauper orphans of Tooting – who, to public outcry, were found to have been lodged close to drains in a dreadful state of disrepair, exuding noxious odours – the attack carrying away several hundred of their tiny souls but, to the momentary gratitude of all, spreading no further. Then the epidemic in Scotland, which had appeared all but ended, resumed with ferocity. More lately, beyond the Channel, Paris had been struck. And now the vicinity of Liverpool. Most worrying, however, was the timing of the attack; it was now late April, with the whole summer ahead.

I glanced up through the window. Today at least was cool and rainy. It was hard exactly to discern the miasma against the dark clouds above, but I was sure I glimpsed its brown swirlings. Did it already contain, I wondered, a kernel of Cholera poison, fed from evil neglect below, now spreading, readying itself.

> One of the dead, Hugh McAllister, who hailed from Glasgow and was in his fiftieth year, succumbed ony six hours after he first grew sick. In the belief that a change of atmosphere may prove vitally invigorating to the spirits, the labourers have now been moved . . .

Only six hours. It was the speed of the affliction, combined with its deadliness – scarcely half those struck seemed to survive – that made the disease so feared.

I had been a child when London had last been visited by the Cholera, then an evil previously unseen in Europe. In the event my home district of Clerkenwell was little affected, at least directly. Fear of the disease, however, came to call on every dwelling in the neighbourhood; I saw it clear enough on the faces of customers in my father's shop, heard it in their over-earnest chatter – as if all were combined in some already losing conspiracy, seeking futile reassurance from one another – as they discussed the suddenness of attacks, the bewildering similarity of symptoms to murderous poisoning.

There was talk, too, of happenings in those parts of the city that were badly struck, of huge crowds taking to the streets in their distress, seized by the maddened notion – one that spread faster than the ailment itself –

that it was doctors who were the cause of the affliction; a belief that led mobs to attack medical men, halt hospital ambulances, so they might snatch out their stricken comrades and, as they were convinced, rescue them.

One could only hope that London might somehow be spared. It was not impossible; during the last epidemic the city of Birmingham had remained all but unscathed. Perhaps strong winds would blow the miasma from our midst.

I swallowed the last of my tea with a gulp, then plucked up my hat and coat; potential horror was, after all, no excuse for lateness. Stepping into the hallway I found my way blocked by Isobella, standing in the open front doorway, peering out at the street. She turned without quite glancing me in the face, still awkward after our words of the night before. 'Little dog's very excited. He seems to have found something. I'd just let him out for his – you know – and . . .'

She made room that I might see. There was no mistaking where the vile creature had chosen to dig. It was as if he were acting deliberately. 'He shouldn't do such a thing. He'll bring dirt into the house.' I gave the creature a firm tap with my boot. There was no stopping him, however; he merely rolled his eyes defiantly and continued his work. In a moment he had plucked the knife from the mud and was holding it proudly in his teeth.

'My poor letter-opener.' She took it from him. Some wagon must have over-ridden the thing, as its blade was buckled into a blunted right angle. 'How could it have got there?' She lowered herself more to the level of the animal. 'Peridog, would you do such a thing to your mistress?'

I took the knife from her hand, the touch of it troubling, as something not quite dead. 'I'll get rid of that.'

Isobella rose to her feet. 'But it's mine. I'm fond of it.'

'It's of no use now.' I held it briefly before her eyes.

'Quite broken, I'm afraid. I'll bring you another when I return from work. Something altogether better.'

Some moments away, through the din and dust of the half-grown buildings of Pimlico, I gladly hurled the thing into a water-filled ditch among the foundations of some grand house of the future.

The office of the company of Augustus Moynihan – my father-in-law – was a fine place to behold; a sunlit, dusty, giant of a room, filled up with draughting desks, cupboards stacked with surveying devices, and a noisy crowd of engineers, keenly at work. Adjoining was a smaller chamber that Moynihan himself inhabited, possessing – as did its larger neighbour – a noble view across George Street. To the leftward side could be seen the Palace of Westminster; a jumble of masonry as it rose, phoenix-like, from the ashes of the building destroyed in the fire of the previous decade.

Seated that morning amid such splendour, I found myself engaged – as now was so often the case – in a battle to curb my own impatience. Speed yes, haste no. Thus, deliberately slowing the very movements of my hands as if engaged in some form of French mime acting, I marked out the limits of the building with a pricker – the incision of a needle being more exact than a mere pencil dot – then linked together these points with lines of ink, to begin the ground plan. Already, however, within just a few moments of forming such fine intentions, I found my hands grasping hungrily for bisectors, and causing a small tear to appear in the corner of the paper.

There was so much to do; here was the difficulty (or, as I viewed it in my better moments, the fierce challenge). To both earn my livehihood at my father-in-law's company – where I had been set to labour on the design of a dock warehouse – and in those spare hours I could muster, to devise a drainage plan of my own, required me to summon all the determination I might.

I stretched my arms into the air, as if to catch energy in my opened hands. I had slept poorly the night before – rarely was it otherwise – and was aware of a lurking tiredness, as if close behind me, waiting for some slackening, some weakening of spirit.

I would outpace it.

'Mr Jeavons, is it, sir?' A useless-looking lad had appeared and stood loitering in front of my desk, restlessly twisting about, as if eager to divest himself of his own arms. 'A message from Mr Sweet.'

From the envelope he presented I took a note written in Sweet's clear, strident handwriting, requesting I pay him a visit that day. More time eaten away. Still, there was nothing to be done. Harold Sweet – the fellow whose warehouse I was designing – was not a man with whom to trifle.

'Tell him I'll visit this afternoon.'

The boy had just slunk off when Moynihan emerged from his office, causing a muffling of the room's chatter as he strode among the desks, inspecting work. Augustus Moynihan, Isobella's father, consultant engineer – a status few enough managed to attain – on nodding terms with important Members of Parliament, with giants of wealth in the City of London.

'The work is progressing well, I hope?' He stooped over my desk, regarding my draughtsmanship; an unusual occurrence, as of late we had had something of an unspoken agreement that each should steer clear of the other; I rarely heard from him except by way of his personal secretary.

'There seem to be no great difficulties.' I wondered if this was some attempt at making peace. It seemed hardly likely.

'I'm glad to hear so.' He scrutinized the lines. 'Take care to keep your drawing clean and neat. You have left, I presume, generous space between the structure and the landing sheds? No precautions should be omitted against the danger of fire.'

'It's a concern I'm most alive to.'

'Good.' With a nod of his head he moved on, a tall man, all the more so for his military bearing – he had learned his trade in Wellington's Engineering Corps in the late wars with France – and handsome, even aristocratic in his features, though his expression was often marred by a look of dissatisfaction.

He was not greatly liked. There was to him a kind of charged silence, so that even when charming – and he could be most charming when he chose – he possessed an aura of things unsaid, of unspoken criticism, which afterwards left many uneasy, wondering if they had not blundered into uttering too much, into some clumsy self-betrayal.

This character could hardly have been more untypical of engineers of the day. Most were lively, wide-open fellows who worked like demons, swore to match, and would have a try at anything proposed to them, whether it was a railway to China or a bridge to the moon. Moynihan could be energetic enough in his work, and was undeniably capable, earning full respect from others in the profession, but his reserved manner left him out of tune. The office chatter about him – in which, naturally, I no longer joined, the man now being my own relative by marriage – was rarely kind.

His refusal to support my drain plan had hurt deeply, all the more so as it was but the latest in a series of displays of little confidence in my abilities. There had been the man's reluctance to give me any real role in the workings of the firm; even now the task of designing Sweet's warehouse was a dull one, hardly worthy of an engineer. Most of all, there had been the matter of his dealings with myself and Isobella.

I had thought of seeking work with some other company, and even made some quiet enquiries. What with the difficulties within the profession at that time, however, these had met with no success. Still I was far from resigned to continuing to work for my father-in-law.

I glanced about the dusty expanse of the room, at the figures stooped, like myself, over giant sheets of paper, labouring on the design of some railway bridge or station building – elements of the new railway line that the company was constructing in the far North of England, the Elfield to Gizbee – chattering as they drew, and filling the place with noise. A cluster of sunburned fellows, fresh back from field work examining the course of the new rail route, engaged in lively discussion of the merits of different contractors. Other subjects, too, were in the air that morning. I heard the word 'Cholera' repeated a good few times.

Lucky men, they could count themselves. They had work; a harder time for engineers had not been known for two decades or more. Lines were in the process of construction up and down the country but, strange though it may seem, this did nothing to reduce the number of young engineers seeking employment.

The moment when the whole land seemed to be crying out for one of our number – for any creatures who could hold a sextant, whether expert or charlatan – was not during the actual building of railways but before, during Railway Mania: a mad season of too much money, when the public jingled with sovereigns, was drunk with hope of profit, and would invest in any railway scheme, however ludicrous. Engineering companies did their best to keep up with the demand for projects into which money might be hurled, and plans for new routes were conjured up as fast as you could count – enough to link every lost and sleeping village in the land with every other – speedily attracting brigades of shareholders.

For each project that might actually be completed, half a dozen sank, their engineering companies often with them, and those not lucky enough to be attached to a line actually attaining construction found themselves left high and dry. By now matters had reached such a point that one often heard of good, experienced men taking their chances with a sailing ticket, and the hope of finding livelihood on the great railways being built in Europe, Russia or America.

My eye passed across the many faces. Did there lie concealed within the breast of one of these noisy, work-drunk people, the malice to send a poisonous letter, seeking to set me against my own wife? A smouldering envy, perhaps, of my having married the daughter of the chief of the company? What of Coast, for instance, Moynihan's secretary – a grey-faced, lopsided man, who was always finding fault with my work. In observing him I found I had caught his eye. He met my own squarely, with no sign of shiftiness.

My pencil having broke, I made my way across to Albert Farre's desk.

Farre glanced up at my request. 'How's the Prince of the Sewers?' His head was long and narrow, giving him the look of an attentive hawk. He and I had been apprentices together, having both joined Moynihan's company at almost the same time. Lately he had been all but unable to resist making foolish jokes concerning my drainage work, seeming to find almost limitless amusement in the matter, until, fond as I was of the fellow, I was beginning to grow weary of his chatter.

'Well enough. But in need of a pencil.'

'So I gathered.' He sat back in his chair. 'What've you done with your own? Dropped it down some gully hole?'

Another time I would have enjoyed wasting a few moments joking. Another time. 'Does it matter? I'm sorry, but I've a lot to do today.'

He looked at me for a moment, frowning. 'So I see.' He took a pencil from his pocket. 'There. I'll delay you no more.'

'Much obliged.' I turned to retrace my steps back to my own desk. What my foot struck I do not know – some stool leg or such thing – but it was sufficiently anchored to trip me thoroughly. I could hardly have been better propelled had I been cannon shot; arms spread forwards before me, pencil flying, until I came to a noisy halt on the ground. The buzz of office chatter vanished away into rich silence. Several gathered about to help me up, Albert Farre first among them. 'Are you all right?'

'Of course.' I clambered to my feet, suffering less from bruises than the absurdity of having fallen.

'Are you sure?' Again Farre was looking at me strangely, as if he was not certain what he saw.

'Why ever should I not be?'

'You don't look well, you know.' He hesitated, seemingly unsure whether he should go on. 'You haven't for some time.'

'Don't be absurd.' His remark annoyed me. 'I feel full of health. Better than ever.'

The day I first met my wife was . . .

Backwards by more than one year I jump in the space of a couple of lines. But you must know these things if you are to understand my story.

It was, of all things, the Railway Mania that introduced us. It sounds strange, perhaps, but I am well certain I could have met her by no other means. In these last months, beneath the richly blue Piedmontese summer sky, I have found myself wondering not a few times what different fate might have been mine had the mania not thrown us together. And hers.

That January our company was as busy as ever it had been, the office a scene of phrenetic activity as we laboured to devise a route from Elfield to Gizbee. Elfield to Gizbee: the names occupied our thoughts more thoroughly and constantly than a priest's musings on the deity. Good fellows, however young and lacking in experience, were hurled into icy rural nowheres in the hope they would discover where a railway might be made to go. In the office in London their reports were stitched together as best could be, blank miles painted in with conjecture.

The moment was fast approaching when we would be required to submit proposals to Parliament –

further progress was impossible without approval from some yawning House of Commons committee – and the office was alive with the drawing of overdue maps, descriptions of stations, enumerations of lately conceived cost figures. I was working with Moynihan that day, helping him write an account of the route of the line. It had been going well enough, too, until he began impatiently shuffling through the pile of documents on the desk before us.

'Where's Hall's field book? We can't go on without his notes on the Kingsfell section.' He scoured the papers twice more. 'Damn the thing. I took it back with me last night to look at and must have left it there.'

Hayle and the other servants were all out on last minute errands. Moynihan himself could hardly leave the office at such a time, and would trust nobody else to continue drafting the route description.

'I'll fetch it,' I volunteered.

Moynihan's unforthcoming nature was nowhere more evident than in the way he rigidly separated his work and private life. While most of the leading engineers of that time were known for their generous sociability – dining and drinking and talking into the night on any subject that took their fancy, whenever their work gave them time – Moynihan had never been known to invite anyone, whether employee or colleague, to his home. Likewise it was rare indeed for one of his household servants to be seen at the office.

He scrutinized me, reluctant. 'Very well.' He scribbled a note. 'You know Trowbridge Street? It's not far. Give this to the butler and he'll fetch the thing for you. Then get yourself back here without delay.'

All across the world nothing excites curiosity and speculation more keenly than secrecy, and it was no different in our office. Moynihan was a widower, and there had long been rumours amongst his workforce that he possessed a daughter. Nobody being able to glean any firm facts on the matter, however, the able minds of so many young engineers and clerks had resorted to imaginative slander, and with time the boss's daughter had grown into nothing less than a scurrilous tradition of the place; as a progeny in some way strange or deformed, and quite beyond presentation to the public world.

'Talks to trees, she does, like old King George.'

'An hunchback fit to scare horses.'

'. . . black as India ink.'

'. . . grabs at every pair of legs she sees in trousers.'

'. . . drinks a gin palace dry and spat in Queen Vick's tea at a Buckingham Palace party.'

Understandably I felt more than a little curiosity as I strode through the streets – there was no cab to be had – towards the famously unvisited house. It was a thorough-going winter's day and the street slop-dirt was part frozen, treacherous to traverse. House roofs were covered with soot-darkened snow, sheets of which – softened by the warmth of the buildings – were liable at any time to slide down in avalanche upon the unwary pedestrian below, instantly begriming him.

It was only a short distance from the office to Trowbridge Street, adding to the strangeness of its seeming removal from the alive world. I glanced up, watching for faces at the windows, but seeing none. Certainly it was no home to be ashamed of; the building was a grand one, fronted by a splendid white-painted façade, and lying within only a few dozen yards of the greenery, now dulled in hue by the winter season, of St James's Park. Most men would have been proud to invite their fellows to such a place.

I waited a while at the door, stamping my feet against the cold, until a sour-faced butler appeared, examined Moynihan's note and ushered me inside. A glimpse of fine stairway lined with portraits, and then I was deposited in a small waiting-room. A disappointment. During my swift departure from the office I had managed to tell Farre and the others of my errand, and it was little less than a matter of honour that I should have some tale to relate on my return.

'Mr Jeavons.' The butler had reappeared. 'The book Mr Moynihan requires is not immediately to sight. Probably the maid's tidied it away.' His manner was pompous, no doubt to distract from his failure to find the thing. 'May I suggest sir, that you yourself look, as you'll be more familiar with its appearance.'

'Very well.'

He led the way again past the grand stairway. The library was not a large one, and contained little except works on engineering and related subjects. I was still scouring the shelves for Hall's field book, when into the room floated the sound of bustling skirts. Turning, I found myself looking at a young woman.

She was fair and very pale of complexion. Beautiful, yes. Her age was that of earliest womanhood, and in her movements, her speech, there remained hints of childishness, of skills employed with such careful concentration that one had a sense of their being practised almost for the first time. What struck me most forcefully, however, was the aura of tension about her; something like nervousness, half concealed beneath her fine manners, almost as if I were the confident host and she the unknown visitor.

She glanced at me only for an instant. 'Barrett, why was I not told we had a visitor?'

The butler looked far from happy, stepping forwards to meet her before she could advance into the room. 'Mr Jeavons has come on an errand.'

'He's still a visitor, is he not?' Her words were calm enough but her voice sounded a touch shrill for a daughter of the house addressing a servant. 'I should've been informed at once.'

Barrett stood his ground. 'Mr Jeavons has been sent by your father's office. He came to . . .'

I interrupted, unwilling to have my situation described on my behalf. 'I came to collect a book.'

My speaking thus seemed to add to her sureness, and she stepped round the butler into the room.

Already I was intrigued. The expression on her face seemed almost to pull in two separate directions; the tautness of her smile – as if she were wary of something just out of view – at odds with the proud look in her eyes. Indeed, my own feelings towards her were no less contradictory. At the same instant I was struck with both awe at her fine young lady's manners – my own Clerkenwell upbringing had left me with more than a little nervousness of any event requiring social niceties – and also an urge to embrace and comfort her.

'Mr Jeavons, I fear you'll have a poor view of our hospitality.'

'Not at all.'

She introduced herself – firing a quick look at Barrett, who had failed to do so – and the word Isobella rang in my head for the first time. 'Perhaps we may tempt you to stay a while, Mr Jeavons, and take some tea. Then you won't deem us a household utterly neglectful of its guests.'

Her invitation excited but also puzzled me. Was it prompted by mere politeness as she had implied, or was there some other reason? Had Moynihan spoken of me – it seemed most unlikely – or had she perhaps confused me with somebody else.

Barrett interposed before I could reply. 'Mr Jeavons is required back.'

The fellow seemed keen indeed to have me gone. His coolness served only to strengthen my desire to stay. 'A moment or two will make little difference, I'm sure.'

By the time I had located Hall's field book all had been made ready. Joshua Jeavons taking tea with Isobella Moynihan, secret beauty, subject of years of ignorant speculation. A maidservant, plump and silent, carefully juggled the fine crockery and a cup was in my hands, heavy to hold and threatening to clatter, making me feel clumsy in front of Isobella, balancing hers quite still in the air above her knees.

I had never seen such a fine room. It was so well

furnished with windows that even the smoky winter light seemed heartening. Every object was full of splendour; the mounted fireplace with a brass lion and lioness prowling above; the rich red curtains; a giant tripod candlestand formed into a subtle likeness of goat heads, its lower portions supported by three delicate feet, with talons. Feet, indeed, seemed to be everywhere, supporting the table, the chairs we sat on, the fire-guard. It was a most modern sight.

'I imagine you must have visited your father's office in George Street?' I asked. The conversation had come round to the present work on the Gizbee line.

'No, I never have. Really I ought to, I know.' Isobella was adept at evading questions she chose not fully to answer – especially for someone so young – and had given away almost nothing about herself except that, like myself, her mother had died when she was very young. I, on the other hand, felt quite interrogated, and was sure I had caused disappointment as I admitted my junior position. Calmer now, her expression had grown brightly unreadable and there was no telling what was in her thoughts. Perhaps she was already regretting having invited me to stay.

The conversation reached a pause, and I drank the last of my tea. 'Miss Moynihan, if you'll excuse me, I fear I should not be too late back.' I got to my feet. 'I thank you for your kindness.'

'So soon? You'll not stay a little longer?'

'I only wish I could.'

She also stood. 'Well, now that you've visited us, you'll do so again I hope, and before long.'

'I'd be delighted.' If the conversation had ended then, I would have left much affected by her aura, but doubtful that I had witnessed anything more than the game-playing of a rather strange and fascinating young woman, perhaps fretfully bored on a dull winter's afternoon. I would have been most uncertain of taking seriously her suggestion I return.

The conversation was not ended, however. As I was

turning to leave, she touched my sleeve with her finger, so lightly that it was a thing hardly felt.

'Do you promise?' The look in her eyes surprised me no less than the question.

For a moment I hesitated, but only for a moment. 'Yes, I promise.'

Her voice sank almost to a whisper, too quiet for the ears of the maidservant. 'There's no need for you to tell my father of your intention to call again.'

It was an extraordinary remark, enticing and troubling. 'Would he disapprove?'

'No, no.' She glanced at me again. 'It would just be better.'

In no more than a moment the temperature between us had risen so high. 'Then I'll not mention it, of course.'

I left the house in a strange state; exhilaration mixed with misgiving. To deceive Moynihan, even by omission, would be to risk losing my employment. Indeed, to be in any way placed between daughter and father was certain to be dangerous. I disliked the position she had so swiftly put me in, requiring from me a kind of dishonesty; I felt no great love for Moynihan but he was my master – I owed him for that alone – and had done me no ill.

The brief taste was strong, however. I do not believe I seriously considered, even for a moment, going back on my promise.

Moynihan was in his place at the far end of the office by the time I returned, and I glanced towards him uneasily. Farre and two others swiftly gathered about, greeting me with hushed curiosity.

'Were you let inside?'

'Any signs of the daughter?'

'Hunchback, was she?'

The faces – laughing, expectant – heightened my sense of a gulf freshly opened, of the new loyalty I felt.

* * *

'Do you mean to say, then, that you had no awareness of the state this drain was in?'

The slum landlord under questioning was hot and red of face. 'I had no awareness that anything was greatly amiss.' He glanced unhappily towards the public area, where a couple of shabby types – journalists – were taking notes.

The Metropolitan Committee for Sewers was nothing less than a Parliament in miniature. A large house had been converted for the purpose, the chamber fully equipped, with places for Committee members, a secretary to keep notes of the proceedings and seats for visitors and journalists. No elements of legislative procedure were absent, and quite a sight it was to watch, as justice was meted out against those who were, by their negligence, polluting the skies with effluential poisons.

The Committee met in Crete Street, on the way to Mr Sweet's yard, and I had decided to pay a swift visit en route. I had alerted a minion of the place to call Mr George Hove – my connection among the members – and, standing by the door to the debating chamber, I could see the servant point me out. Hove nodded importantly, without getting to his feet.

'You have not observed, then, that the drain was blocked and quite filled with deposits of a most offensive and dangerous type?' The interrogator of the slum landlord was none other than Edwin Sleak-Cunningham himself; leading civil servant, in close contact with high government figures, and one who had contributed greatly to the sanitary movement. Sleak-Cunningham was a fellow who seemed to attract enemies – not that this had obstructed his efforts – a fact which I was inclined to ascribe at least in part to his appearance. A thin figure, almost ghostly with pallor, he exuded intense determination, belief, at times resembling a kind of frozen priest. His critics claimed him to be secretive, a dictator of committees.

I felt respect for him, and was pleased that a soul of

such abilities had been drawn to the sanitary cause, smiting the sinners of defective drainage. Indeed, when Moynihan spurned my drainage plan I had had hopes of eliciting Sleak-Cunningham's help. On the one occasion I had managed to talk to him, he had even showed some interest in my notion. In the event, however, I found him to be so busy – possessing other duties in addition to his sewerage work – that it proved all but impossible to meet again. After many failed arrangements, he had written – apologizing – and suggested I instead speak to Mr George Hove, a colleague of his on the Committee who was less pressed for time.

'You were, then, unaware,' Sleak-Cunningham continued, 'of the putrid stench that so blighted the neighbourhood that many were unable to sleep at night.'

I glanced at the fellow. Probably he had two dozen appointments lined up for that very afternoon.

'I don't remember.' The landlord glanced again towards the journalists.

'Is there a history of amnesia within your family, perhaps?' Sleak-Cunningham's remark brought laughter from the other members of the Committee. Hardly had it died away when the questioner's expression regained its seriousness, eyes fixed sharply on those of his prey. 'I suggest you search your memory well, Mr Feines. You realize, I hope, that you can be prosecuted over these matters.'

George Hove emerged from the chamber. 'You wanted to speak to me, I believe.'

'I hoped I might call upon your help in a few matters connected with my researches.'

'I see.' He uttered a faint sigh. 'Is it urgent?' Though he was of much the same age and build as Sleak-Cunningham, Hove could hardly have been more different; quite absent was Sleak-Cunningham's intensity of eye, his strong presence in a room. Hove had the closed nature of a minor mandarin; regarding the world with prim suspicion, his demeanour as stiffly upright as an old piece of charcoal, seemingly in danger of breaking into parts were he asked a disrespectful question or required to give a direct reply.

'It is urgent,' I told him. 'I'll be unable to continue long without some assistance, that's certain. Nor would the help I require take much of your time. There are a couple of sewer outlets which are not easily reached, and also I believe you have some figures on flow of . . .'

He cut me short with a wave of his hand. 'Mr Jeavons, I'm much occupied presently. Perhaps you could be so kind as to send a list of what you need? I'll do my best to attend to the matter as soon as I can.'

An obvious tactic of delay and inaction; two of Hove's favourite weapons. The truth of it was he loathed doing favours. He was the sort who is happiest dealing with his fellow men through the medium of lengthy forms – I sometimes imagined him communicating with his wife by such means – and it had only been by persistence that I had managed to extract any usefulness from the fellow; embarrassing him by constant harping.

Persistence. A slow and tedious game, but what other choice was left to me? 'I'll send a list to reach you by tomorrow,' I told him. 'I'd be grateful if you could act promptly as the matter is, I assure you, of urgency.'

Outside, the rain had grown heavy, and I glanced about for a cab. The frustration of it all. As if the value of my notion – the benefits it could bring – were not obvious to see. At times I felt as if I were a beacon of sanity on a dark night.

Harold Sweet's yard was in a poor district, not far from the Seven Dials, where I had encountered Katie only the day before. I stared out from the cab window at London flying by, a London of ragged figures: some reckless in the downpour, others glumly loitering, glowering at the wet. They should be pleased with such weather. Did they know what favours would drop upon them when the season turned hot? Probably not. Most were children or little older, with few grey hairs to be seen among the throng; a city of fast-ageing young, of persons barely half-grown in height, resembling midget adults with their quick looks, the swift-found hardness of their eyes.

Every day more tramped in to join them, from villages and small towns all across the country. For the last years they had come, most of all, from Ireland; a stream of displaced humanity fed, seemingly without limit, by the bubbling catastrophe of the potato failures. All drawn to the great metropolis, a city already heaving with the weight of its people, struggling still to digest arrivals of ten, twenty years ago. All come to test their ingenuity, their stamina, and their luck.

Behind lurched a disjointed skyline, buildings seeming to lean on one another, as if ready to fall at any instant. Thus had the capital grown: wildly, like some hungry forest, quite without plan. Only when the pressure of clattering vehicles so blocked the arteries as to threaten to halt its very life might the building of a road be considered, as, recently, New Oxford Street, tumbling to dust grand houses and nests of vice alike.

Some claimed to see a grandeur in the way the city had spread, without any visible logic. How admirably different, they claimed, to the despotical capitals of Europe, where kings redrew all as they pleased, subjugating at once both architecture and citizen. I was as patriotic as any other man, but saw no cause for pride in a system that supposed matters only deserved to be righted when they had lurched into catastrophe.

Harold Sweet had the unusual distinction of having invented his own name. 'What's it matter to me what people call me, as long as it's not "You lazy so-and-so",' he had explained at our first meeting, talking with lively energy that had left me impressed. 'In my book it's what you do with your life that counts, not what you were born with. I came into the world Harold

Oaster, and what usefulness is there in that? Better to have a name that people will easily remember, that it may help trade. Yes, put your own name to work, why not? I sell molasses, so what more suitable than Harold Sweet.'

It had to be said that Oaster fitted him a good deal better. Sweet, with its longer tapering vowel, struck me as being a thin man's name, and there was little that was thin about this fellow; he resembled nothing so much as a grinning bear with clear eyes.

Consuming of time though the warehouse project was to me, I always found pleasure in visiting his yard. It was a place of such splendid activity; carts being loaded and unloaded, barrels of molasses stacked into piles or opened up that their contents might be inspected, the substance itself filling the air with its sickly scent, and causing the ground to be sticky underfoot. The spot seemed to breathe enterprise and the creation of wealth. It was a true reflection of its master.

Sweet spotted me as I walked in through the gates, waving cheerily for me to join him in his office; a wooden box of a thing, with deep windows that he might always keep a good watch on his men. 'How prompt, Mr Jeavons. I hope it's not been trouble for you to come at such short notice, but I had to talk to you without delay.' His broad smile, though encompassing eyebrows, cheeks, lips, dimples, and even his beard, always seemed to miss the eyes themselves, which regarded me studiously. 'All last night I was thinking of the warehouse, and whether we're planning it right.'

'I see.' His words struck me as ominous. If the warehouse required redesigning I would be further deprived of time to research my drainage scheme. 'What were you concerned with?'

He tugged thoughtfully at his beard. 'For a start these fire-dousing machines. Surely two would do rather than four.'

At least that would not be a great change. 'Is that wise? Molasses can go up in a mighty blaze.'

A man who relished a dispute, Sweet grinned, seemingly enlarged behind his desk; fuelled by the prospect of argument. 'It'll light, certainly, but it's no tar or hemp. Thorough precautions would surely be adequate. Or do you disagree?'

I shrugged; it was his warehouse, his molasses, after all. 'If you're sure.'

'I am, Mr Jeavons.'

To be in the presence of the man was to be struck by the compelling nature of his character. The fellow was well known as a self-created success. He had begun with his father's grocery business, a modest enterprise no larger than my own father's watch repair in Clerkenwell – like my own, his speech still possessed a remnant of shopman's twang – but had managed steadily to increase sales, until able to open a further shop. By then he had begun specializing in molasses above other goods, and, on opening a third shop, found himself in a position to make his own arrangements with importers; leasing the yard and himself distributing to other traders. Now he intended to go further still; to take up an interest in a small dock in Rotherhithe, build a warehouse, and import molasses in his own right, direct from the West Indies.

Nor did he apply his talents only to molasses. He had become quite a figure in the government of Westminster, having taken on the duties of a Poor Law Guardian for the parish; overseeing local medical arrangements, and the workhouse for the paupers. Admirable achievements, without doubt. Indeed, he had the reputation of being no less zealous in his management of the poor than he was in pursuing his own business concerns.

'Another question, Mr Jeavons.' He had placed before us a sketch I had done of the likely frontage of the building. 'Have we enough windows here?'

It was hardly an enquiry I had been expecting. It also

threatened a considerable amount of extra work as I had all but completed my fair copy of the design. 'You feel it will not be sufficiently imposing?'

'Imposing?' He smiled at my foolishness. 'Mr Jeavons, you should know me better than to say such things. No, my concern is that it will be too dark inside.'

'Too dark for the labourers to see?'

This guess amused the fellow hardly less than my previous one. 'Not at all. Too dark for them to be seen.' He rested his hands upon the table. 'It's not a little important in this business. Have the building full of dark corners and they'll be up to all manner of tricks. Slipping molasses into their pockets to steal, or just swallowing it down their throats on the spot. No, the structure must be properly light.'

I glanced at the sketch, trying to think of objections that would deter the man. 'It would add to the cost.'

'How much? No more, surely, than I would save on the two fire-dousing machines.'

I shook my head. 'That I couldn't say. I'd have to study the whole matter in detail.'

He was not so easily put off. 'When can you let me know? Tomorrow?'

Tomorrow I had more than a full day's work already planned, as well as a determination to visit the Committee for Sewers that I might again apply pressure to Hove. 'I'd say it'd take at least a few days.'

'A few days?' He frowned. 'Mr Jeavons, I can't afford to have this project delayed.'

I shrugged. 'I'm sorry but I can't see a way of having it done sooner. I'm very busy at the moment.'

'Busy?' Again he seemed to swell at the prospect of battle. 'Are we not all busy men, Mr Jeavons. I administer this company – not such a small one, you may observe – I have a family, and lately I've also taken on the task of Poor Law Guardian for the Parish – I'll be busier still if the Cholera comes – but, as far as I'm aware, none of my duties has been neglected.' He studied me for a moment, as a general anticipating an easy campaign. 'Now let us examine how busy you are. You're not, I believe, engaged on any other project for Mr Moynihan.'

I met his look. 'Not for Mr Moynihan. But I'm working on a scheme of my own. A new system for the drainage of all London, to present to the competition of the Metropolitan Committee for Sewers.'

'Drains?' He frowned, surprised. Perhaps he had imagined that, as Moynihan's son-in-law, I was of a lazy disposition and had won my place through nepotism. 'And Mr Moynihan's not involved?'

'Not at all.'

Having suffered this setback in his original campaign, he changed to a new line of attack. 'A scheme for the Committee for Sewers, eh? I imagine they'll be all for increasing the burden on honest ratepayers to pay for the business.' He regarded me knowingly. 'But then perhaps you see no harm in working for such people?'

'You're mistaken.' I corrected him not without pleasure. 'If the Committee takes up my plan the rates will not be increased by a penny. In fact the opposite will be true. My system is designed to create a profit – and a not insubstantial one – through sales of effluent to farmers. Within only a short time of construction parish rates should be appreciably reduced.'

Sweet opened his mouth to retort, only to pause, the look on his face changed. 'To farmers. Well why not, I suppose. And you believe this would be practicable?'

'I don't doubt it.'

He pondered, tapping the desk with his fingers. 'Mr Jeavons, I believe this project of yours interests me.' He smoothed his beard. 'And you say you're pursuing it quite alone?'

'Indeed.'

'What of the noble Metropolitan Committee for Sewers?' He made little effort to disguise a note of scorn in his voice as he recited the name.

'They're helping me as well as is within their powers. Their time is much occupied.'

'Of course, of course.' He waved his hand in the air dismissively. Then sat back in his chair. 'I wonder if I couldn't help you.'

A surprising suggestion. I learned, however, that the man had quite a number of connections within the labyrinth of metropolitan government, including the world of sewers; connections won through his work as a Poor Law Guardian. I listened with no little interest as he hinted at what help he might be able to supply in terms of favours and information.

He regarded me with a faint smile. 'Of course I might hope that, were I to assist you, you'd find yourself in possession of a little more time to deal with these little questions concerning my warehouse.'

A businessman to the last; it was not simple charity that was being offered. Still his suggestion was enticing, especially in view of Hove's irritating delayings. 'Of course. I could have an estimate of the effect of your proposed savings completed by tomorrow.'

'Excellent.' He smiled broadly. 'Now what exactly do you require?'

Just when I had needed it most sorely, succour had come, as a gift from providence. I glanced up at the sky as I strode from the molasses yard, and could have laughed at the miasma. Best of all, I had won the support of an avowed anti-governmentalist. It occurred to me – not for the first time – that therein lay the beauty of my scheme. Though it had been called into existence by a committee of the state, it offered profits enough to satisfy the most determined of entrepreneurs. A meeting of state and enterprise, nothing less. I would have Messrs Sweet and Sleak-Cunningham shaking hands yet.

Isobella I found in the dining-room, hard at work polishing candlesticks.

'Careful,' she told me, before I had greeted her. 'Have you wiped your shoes?'

I had, but I did so again for good measure, then took from my pocket the small wrapped package.

She examined the thing, puzzled. 'What is it?'

'Open it and find out.'

She carefully untied the bow and freed the wooden box from its wrapping, then extracted the paper-knife.

I had chosen it with care, and was pleased with its appearance. The handle was bone, with – painted in wonderful detail – a depiction in miniature of two Ships-of-the-Line, of the type involved in the last war with France, both under full sail as they blasted each other with all cannon. The scene was repeated, all but identical, on the reverse side.

'It's lovely.' She examined the design. 'So finely decorated. Far prettier than the old one.' She placed it with her embroidery things. 'Thank you.'

I woke perspiring in the darkness – startled – then slowly took in, by the faint glow from streetlamps beyond the window, the calming sight of my study all about me; desk and chair, my books, the familiar patterns of cracks in the plasterwork upon the ceiling.

My fingers were painful. It was prolonged clenching that had made them so; real clenching of an imagined weapon. I recalled the look of it, all too clearly; the bone handle with its painted warships, grappled in battle.

Chapter Three

Joshua and Isobella Jeavons, shoes squeaking on the floor, clothes rustling and brushing against the pews, part of the collectively hushed din as the congregation rises to its feet. Joshua and Isobella Jeavons, each taking a lungful of candle smoke scented air, that they may join with the others in singing the next hymn of the morning.

It had been among Isobella's first requests of me – one that had puzzled me at the time – that I take her to church for a Sunday service. This had been back in the era of our engagement, a tense, waiting season, when splendid triumph then fear of looming catastrophe seemed to chase each other back and forth through my thoughts. Isobella Moynihan, beautiful, graceful, to be my very own. But so many weeks till the wedding day, and every hour nothing to prevent her from changing her mind. Not that she gave me grounds for such doubts, but the fear persisted, of its own accord.

I visited her as frequently as I was able, usually in the afternoons – a time she herself preferred – when we had tea. Though I never ceased to thirst for these meetings, they often proved something of a disappointment, frustratingly absent of intimacy. Present throughout was the plumply silent maidservant, juggling with the china and obstructing my urges to embrace Isobella. Traditionally we would sit by the window, the green of St James's Park – now bursting with spring colour – just visible to the right, and the life of the street passing below.

'A dog seller,' Isobella might announce. 'See? Over there by the lamp-post. What lovely spaniels. D'you think they mind being carried in that way, under his arms?'

'They look content enough. Probably they're used to it.' I was happiest when she felt in a mood to comment on the menagerie of humanity striding and loitering below. I felt close to her, felt I was being admitted into something secret. There was an almost child-like quality to her delight – delight in wickedness – at observing the world from this place of concealment.

'And what of that one, so small, with his eyes working hard. D'you think he's a pickpocket?'

'Very likely.'

It was on such an afternoon, with an abruptness quite against the flow of the earlier conversation, that she enquired if I were a regular Sunday worshipper.

'Not regular. I'm a believer, of course, but a poor church-goer. My father was the same.'

'You dislike to go, perhaps?'

'On the contrary.'

'Then . . .' She threw me a glance. 'Will you take me?'

She explained that Augustus, though a firm adherent of the Church of England, was usually too busy for such things. They rarely went except at Christmas and Easter.

'It seems cruel of him not to take you,' I remarked.

'I'm sure he would were he able.'

The conversation left me impressed by what I saw as her quiet devotion to her faith. But later, as we began to attend Sunday services at a nearby church, I found myself surprised at how little interest she displayed in the sermon, the prayers and the hymn singing. Indeed, she seemed to find no pleasure in any of these, but be waiting for the moment when they would be over. Only later, as the congregation gathered about the porch, chatting and gossiping, did she come to life.

Then, gradually, I came to realize her true purpose was not one of worship at all, but rather to collect about herself new acquaintances; to assemble a social world.

She began with the vicar, then, with his assistance, quickly became introduced – I with her – to other church-goers. Despite her youth, she showed quite a talent for politely friendly chatter. Her progress was swift – I had had no idea that church attendance could be such an efficient means of growing to know strangers – and with every passing Sunday we learnt the names and professions of ever more Westminster Anglicans; of lawyers, traders, schoolteachers, retired officers, minor politicians, all their wives. As we walked back from the church, she would recount, with triumph, her discoveries of the afternoon.

'Mrs Whitcomb says Mr Clement has the gout.' 'Did you see how grey that Mr Fielding looked – he's a drinker, surely.' 'Mrs Diamond is expecting – I believe it's already her third.'

I was surprised by the fierceness of her interest in these people – many of whom were on the wrong side of dullness – amounting, as it did, to little less than a hunger. Nor was she any less determined that they should know about ourselves. In particular she would relate – in fiendish detail – the arrangements of our approaching wedding, until even the most chatter-loving among them began to show a certain glassiness about the eyes.

It was a new and unsuspected side to her. Thereafter I found I could not but view differently her love of observing the world from her upstairs window.

Also I became subject to a new concern. If she had – through her father's negligence – been so removed from the world as to be thus starved of society, then was it not possible that her interest in myself had stemmed only from my having, by chance, stumbled into her life, rather than any firm and enduring attachment? It was a fear I kept to myself.

Then, hardly less abruptly than she called this new world of acquaintances into being, she abandoned it.

It was a change that coincided exactly with our wedding, although what connection might lie between the two I could not guess. From the first she had been most eager that we should marry in the church we had been attending, and that her new friends should be invited. Nor was it otherwise; quite a gaggle of them came, despite their foreknowing – in such fearsome detail – the planned agenda of the occasion.

Yet, even after this ample show of loyalty, when the great day was over Isobella seemed suddenly changed towards her church friends. Gone was her fascination with their lives. Gone too was the desire to tell them all her news; indeed, when questioned she would give only the most arid and meagre replies, causing, at first, surprise, and later, resentment. She even ceased to show any enthusiasm for attending Sunday services, finding lazy excuses to remain at home; she was tired, or Pericles would be lonely in the house without us. That we continued to go, if erratically, was the result only of my insistence, as I felt it was wrong to cease worshipping so abruptly.

'Why are you so altered towards these people?' I asked her one morning, after she had hurried us from the church door with hardly so much as a hello to her old friends.

She seemed surprised. 'I'm not.'

'You treated Mrs Whitcomb as if you hardly knew her.'

'I didn't feel like talking. Is there anything so wrong in that?'

Joshua and Isobella Jeavons rising to their feet with the congregation, filing out into the nave of the church at the same steady pace, dressed with the careful, sober finery of those shuffling all about them, negotiating their way through the eye of the needle of the church doors. It had been some weeks since our last visit – I had been so busy with my drainage research – and I hoped we would not receive disapproving glances from the vicar.

I watched the faces all about. What did they see, these noisily chattering ratepayers, when their eyes chanced to rest upon the Jeavonses? What conjecture did they volley back and forth amongst themselves? A charming young couple? An ambitious young engineer who had managed to marry his employer's daughter; his coldly proud wife who would appear so friendly, only to cut and ignore as if she never knew one. Some still more scandalous appraisal, perhaps?

Whatever their conclusions, they were, I had no doubt, far away from the true history of Joshua and Isobella. We were as a passing carriage with blinds drawn, at once seeable and closed from sight. And were they not the same, these stoutly proud parents, spinster sisters, bachelor uncles, withered grandparents, cocooned in their privacy, unknown behind their public display.

The day was a dry one – though, blessedly, the season still showed no sign of working itself into heat – and the current of worshippers emerging from the porch eddied into small chattering groups. The greetings and polite witticisms of that morning, I did not fail to observe, seemed altered from those of other Sundays; a touch stilted, hinting at nervousness concealed. It was hardly surprising considering the sermon. The vicar, the Reverend Michael Bowrib, was not usually one to subject his flock to harsh moral warnings, but that day he had changed his tack, preaching on times of looming peril; citing biblical instances of sinners who had saved themselves from various vile fates by constant prayer, dynamic reformation of their decadent lives. His words were received with a discernible hush. Only Isobella seemed unaffected by his delivery, sitting well back in her pew and yawning several times, as if she could not have cared less if the Good Lord gave her the Cholera that very afternoon.

'How lovely to find you here.'

We had been discovered, I realized unhappily, by the Lewises; Gideon was bobbing along beside us, his sister Felicia close behind.

'Thank you again for that splendid lunch.'

'Don't be foolish. I should thank you for the splendid letter you sent.' Isobella treated them both to a bright smile, of a kind long denied her other church-going acquaintances. The Lewises. Her choice seemed to defy all reason.

Gideon jabbed a finger into the air, struck by a thought. 'If you're not dashing off anywhere, then why not take tea with us? Bowrib's coming. We're waiting for him now.'

Tea with the Lewises and the Reverend Michael Bowrib. My response was swift. 'I fear we ought to be on our way home. Miss Symes has been preparing Sunday dinner.'

'The house is near,' he insisted keenly, more to Isobella than myself, then glancing round to his sister, perhaps hoping to enlist her help. If so, he was disappointed; she remained a yard removed from the rest of us, emanating faint disapproval. In honour of the church service she had clothed herself even more thoroughly than usual, and yet those small pieces of body showing maintained a disturbing presence; spongy neck and padded wrists seeming somehow unhappy sprouting from a dress, giving her the look of a boxer in a frock. Was it my imagination or was there an awkwardness between her and her brother? Perhaps they had had some domestic disagreement.

'We don't need to rush back, Joshua.' Isobella, to my annoyance, was already at work undermining my objection to taking tea with the pair. 'Miss Symes is always late with dinner. I'm sure we'd have time.'

'But that's splendid.' Gideon's head bobbed with delight.

I saw no escape.

Though my wife had been to the Lewises' home many a time, attending Felicia's Bible afternoons, I had successfully evaded paying a visit. Walking inside, I found it much as I had imagined; the dark dullness of colour and the hangings that modestly concealed every table leg reflected amply the prudish natures of its inhabitants. Bowrib – out of his pulpit a small and rotund fellow with a loud laugh quite out of scale with himself – was most surprised I had not visited before. 'Then you won't have seen Gideon's paintings. You should take a look, really you should. The man's nothing less than a genius, believe me.'

'Take no notice, Joshua,' retorted the artist himself, fidgeting with delight at the compliment. 'It's nothing more than a little pastime of mine. I'm sure you'll find my efforts very poor.'

He spoke more truth than he knew.

To see his works entailed nothing less than a full tour of the house; the man was no miniaturist, and his canvases measured a good six feet across, some far more, causing them – of necessity – to be placed in every place where the walls were spacious enough. Thus we passed through the sitting-room, dining-room, study, a bedroom, even a bathroom. Throughout I racked my brain for phrases to sacrifice to Gideon's hungry smile; phrases neither so outrageously offensive that they would anger my wife, nor so dishonest that they would offend my own pride.

Not that the fellow was wholly without talent. He showed a certain full skill in depicting buildings – hardly surprising in view of his profession – which, though they tended to resemble giant boxes drawn upon with ink, were always recognizable for their function. It was in the little matter of the human form that he ran into trouble. Unfortunately the subject he had chosen for his inspiration – biblical episodes of sublime heroism, suffering and strength of character – required more than a small dose of humanity to be present.

His men were a particular problem. While his women, if fibrously Felicia-like, were always convincingly discernible for what they were, this was not so of their biblical fathers and brothers. These seemed lacking in any certainty, even of their own gender, a difficulty which their beards – a universal and, I suspected, desperate addition – did little to overcome.

Most troubling of all, however, were the expressions upon the faces. These were awesomely wide of the mark. Thus Moses discovering the stone tablets displayed not the sombre enlightenment one would expect, but a disagreeable smile, worthy of some old miser perusing the begging letter of a little-loved nephew. Likewise Adam and Eve, in the midst of their expulsion from the Garden of Eden, seemed possessed not of the regret one would imagine of two who have just stained humanity for ever, but rather a lively eagerness, as young waifs on their way to Greenwich Fair for Easter. And Mary the Virgin watching over the baby Christ in his crib – a poor sort of fellow, more likened to a punctured football than a child – emanated not divine contentment, but a shocked stare, as a cook who has left the goose too long in the oven.

The maid caught up with us in Gideon's study. 'The tea's ready now, sir.'

At last.

Gideon seemed put out. 'We've hardly seen half of them.'

'It would be a shame to have it grow cold and waste,' I suggested.

'True enough, I suppose,' he agreed, reluctantly. He began making his way back towards the parlour, Bowrib and my wife close behind. Nor, as you may imagine, did I have any wish to linger. Before I had had a chance to escape the room, however, I found myself detained, by Felicia's voice.

'Perhaps you'd be interested in seeing my brother's depiction of the Crucifixion, Mr Jeavons. I believe it to be one of his finer attempts.'

For her to address me at all was a surprise. Though we had never exchanged more than a few words, Felicia and I had seemed to have a kind of understanding; a mutual knowledge that each held not an ounce of liking for the other, and should leave him be. Until today.

'The tea's ready,' I reminded her.

'It's just here, in the passage.'

I found myself regarding Christ upon the cross surveying the heavens, and suffering alarming resemblance to a fairground bearded lady faintly troubled, perhaps wondering where she might have left her doorkeys.

'Very striking.'

There was an awkward silence.

'Mr Jeavons . . .' Another surprise. Felicia began, only to hesitate, caught on the edge of further speech. Most unlike her usual barging self.

'Yes?'

'I wanted to speak to you . . .'

Another halt. What was she trying to say? The alarming thought occurred to me that she might be about to utter some expression of romantic intent. It was unlikely, true enough; what of her fierce prudishness, and her having in the past treated me only with distant distaste? But one never knew. And she was regarding me with a strange intensity. The thought of touching that spongy neck . . . I turned away, and found myself looking up at the Mary Magdalen, watching her Saviour upon the cross with a look of concentrated discontent, worthy of a midwife picking her corns.

'The others will be wondering what's become of us.' I tried to inject into the remark a light-heartedness, as if I had observed nothing unusual in her behaviour.

Rather than answering in a like spirit, she shifted her form to better obstruct the stairway down, studying me with seriousness, even a look dimly threatening. 'Mr Jeavons, there's something you should . . .'

This time it was not her own awkwardness that restrained her, but – to my great relief – the sound of footsteps drawing near on the stairs. She made way for the vicar.

'Must've left my jacket here.'

It was an opportunity not to be missed. 'I'll fetch it for you, Mr Bowrib.'

Felicia seemed to snap back to her old self. Throughout our taking tea she resumed her tightly stiff persona, treating me to not so much as a glance, and speaking on no subject beyond biblical matters and the poorness of the weather.

I was even a little regretful of my own escape, curious now as to what I might have learned.

> THE CHOLERA: A SPANISH CURE
>
> *Dear sir,*
>
> In view of the current public discussion of the Asiatic Cholera, I felt it my duty to inform your readers of a little known and invaluable cure for the malady. During a visit to the city of Seville in Spain I was introduced to an eminent local physican, Dr Rios Montero, who informed me of a remedy he had found most effective during the last great outbreak of sixteen years ago. The sufferer should be administered three small cups of olive oil – no other oil will serve – with a period of eight to ten minutes allowed to lapse between the consumption of each. After the last has been taken, warm water should be drunk in abundance, and a wonderful improvement will be seen to occur in the patient's condition. This cure . . .

Pelham had observed my standing still, listening. 'Something up, Mr Jeavons?'

I took a step forward towards the flow of effluent, trying to ignore the odours, and peered into the sewer outlet. The sound – a splashing – had seemed almost to come from within the drain, but I could only discern dank darkness. 'No, nothing.'

What a finely productive day it had been. Indeed, a productive week. Sweet had possessed more connections in and about the world of drainage than I had thought possible, and through his agency I had now visited a whole series of sites, including the higher reaches of a sewer – at a point close by the Ball's Pond Road – where I had been given a tour by one of the inspectors, and had gained valuable insights into possible incorporation of elements of the old system within my Effluent Depository scheme; a useful means of reducing costs.

Presently I was working on the Essex shore, just eastwards of the City. Already I had been shown round several sewer outlets by Samuel Pelham, district sewerage officer; a solid and dependable fellow, if rather lacking in neck, so his chin seemed to spring directly from his collar bones. He had answered my questions concerning variations in effluential flow so fully that many of the measurings I had intended to carry out were rendered unnecessary, and I regretted having elected to hire Hayle for the afternoon, and thus being burdened by the sight of him loitering uselessly at my expense.

Truly the river was something to behold. The black hulls before us seemed to sprout quite a winter forest of masts and spars, the nearer ones – growing from ships beached high on the mud – piercing the sky at demented angles. Such was the quantity of boats anchored in the stream that it seemed hardly possible any sailing room remained, but, from the higher parts of the bank a narrow waterway could be seen, somehow kept free, along which managed to creep all manner of traffic.

Thames barges floated with the flow of tide, broadsides first, their crews wrestling with long thin oars to keep within the stream, causing their craft to resemble waterboatmen insects of a gargantuan species, accustomed to a mad sideways and sliding method of propulsion. Other barges – battling against the force of the tide – had raised their grand, flapping sails, warm-brown in colour, speedily hauling them down, mast and all, whenever a bridge rose into sight. Smaller vessels dodged between the barges; Spanish schooners laden with fruit, a raft of timbers towed by a lonely soul in a rowboat, ugly Dutch eel boats, and more.

'Measure the depth over there,' I called out to Hayle, as much to see the man do something for his shillings as to enhance my own knowledge. Were there further questions I needed to ask Pelham, touching the sewer we were stood before? I could think of none.

Following the line of the muddy bank, my eye lit upon a group of fellows, half a mile distant, just discernible between the hulls. They were stood before the next outlet, the Ancient Walbrook, and, as I studied them, seemed to be inspecting the site, measuring the flow of effluent, just as we had been doing. Curious indeed. What was more, I saw they bore more than a faint resemblance to ourselves – though they numbered twice as many – with some dressed in the frock coats of professional men, others in the scruffier garb of servant helpers.

'That party in the distance,' I asked Pelham, pointing out the group. 'D'you know of them?'

He followed the line of my outstretched arm, eyes squinting in the sun. 'I can't say I do, Mr Jeavons.'

'Puzzling.' I picked up the measuring stick on the ground beside me. The Ancient Walbrook was the outlet we had planned to inspect next. 'Perhaps we should pay our respects.'

'As you wish.'

I turned to the loitering servant. 'Hayle, we're continuing along the shore.'

But then, while we were still in the midst of collecting together the measuring devices I again became aware of the sound I had heard earlier. A light splashing, sharpened with echo. This time I had no doubts to its source; it was indeed coming from the mouth of the sewer. An animal, perhaps, that had strayed thither? It seemed unlikely. I peered inside – it was one of the larger of its kind, half as high again as a man – but saw only darkness.

Pelham, too, had heard, and stepped down towards the outlet, casting me a glance.

'What can it be?' I asked. 'Some creature?'

'Human creatures, I'd say.' He stared into the outlet with his wide, watery eyes. 'No-one up to any good, that's certain.'

Hayle had also stopped to listen. The sound would one moment grow loud, then all but fall silent again, as if those responsible were trying not to be heard.

'I'd know of any official group visiting the sewer,' Pelham continued. 'And the public aren't permitted to go wandering free about the place in case they do damage, whether to the drains or themselves. No, they shouldn't be in there.'

'But who would want to go into such a . . .' Before I completed the question, my eye was caught by a flickering within the sewer; seemingly the effect of a weak lamp playing upon the green-stained brick-work within. 'I see their light.'

Pelham's voice sank to a whisper. 'The tunnel curves round. They'll be on us soon enough.'

'We should arrest them?'

'I dare say.' He looked none too sure; nor did I feel otherwise. But we could hardly do nothing. Backing away from the entrance that I should not be seen, I turned to Hayle. 'The people within,' I told him in a hushed whisper. 'We're to overpower them as they emerge.'

The servant pouted, unimpressed. 'Says who? I'm not being paid for fighting, am I? I'm here to measure that filth. That's the job I bin . . .'

I waved my hand to quiet him; there was no time to argue the matter as the splashing was fast growing as noisy as if a small army were about to march out of the London drains. 'Just do as I've said.'

He opened his mouth to retort, but had not the chance. At once the sound was altered, its sharpness lost, and the figures strode out before us.

The echo within the drain must have greatly

exaggerated the din as, rather than a great force, there proved to be only three, one no more than half-grown in size. Even as I jumped forward, I found I recognized their garb; the greasy coat with dark lantern attached to the breast, the bulging sack carried on the back, and long pole, taller than the carrier, with an iron hoe at the end. They were just as the four who had run from me that evening, shouting 'spy', leaving me so puzzled.

The battle was short. The poles they carried could have proved dangerous weapons had not – fortunately – their owners been taken by surprise, and been much weakened by the effect of daylight upon their sight, causing them to blink and shade their eyes as they were set upon. In a moment all three had been felled, their hoes wrested from them and used to pinion them on to the mushy ground, where they struggled angrily.

Victory, and a quick one at that. The three of us cheered 'Hurrahs', none louder than Hayle, who, though he had tackled the runt of the trio – a mere lad – shouted out all manner of dangerous war cries, as if he had conquered a whole regiment of Bonapartist Frenchmen rather than a single child.

Then a kind of quiet set in; the three sewer men still, so they might take in their captors. Pelham, lacking in neck as he was, resembled, as he crouched on his foe, nothing so much as a nervous toad; he glanced at me, evidently unsure what to do. My captive was no midget and had only one eye, which gave him a sinister air. His clothes stank abominably, and were vile to touch, but, for the moment, I could see no other course but to stay as I was, keeping him pinioned, until . . . Until what?

'Who are you?' I demanded fiercely of the man. 'And what manner of roguery were you committing in the sewers?'

'Who are YOU?' he answered with spirit. 'And what's YOU doin' assaultin' poor folk as 'as done no harm.'

Pelham put a tone of regality into his voice. 'We're

representatives of the Metropolitan Committee for Sewers and it's our duty to deal with criminals destructively tampering with Metropolitan property.'

I was surprised by the seeming healthiness of the three. All were pallid of face, but otherwise strongly built, quite lacking the sickliness one would expect of men who had endured such long proximity to effluential poisons. 'What's the proper way of dealing with such fellows as these?' I asked Pelham, in a voice as fierce as I could manage.

'Proper way, yes.' He seemed unhappy with the words.

'You've found such people before?'

'Not exactly, but I've heard tell of them. They're professional scavengers.'

'Heard tell of us, 'as yer?' called out the one-eyed fellow beneath my grip. 'An' I've heard tell of the King of Prooshia.'

The remark, though it was of little meaning, seemed to delight his companions, and they burst into fierce laughter, even the lad regaining his spirits.

'Perhaps,' I suggested to Pelham, 'we should take them to the police.'

He nodded. 'I dare say.'

'Why do it?' One Eye twisted his head about, that he could regard me, relative to the discomfort of his position, with a kind of nonchalance. 'Why go to all that trouble and, I might say, danger.' His eye managed a thoughtful inspection of the afternoon sky. 'Just over some poor unfortunates as 'as done no wrong.'

'You've caused damage to the sewers,' I told him.

'Damage to 'em?' Pelham's captive, a lean sort with long sideboards and giant ears, seemed to find the idea appealing. 'Where's the need when they're dropping to bits all of their own.'

'You were stealing,' Pelham retorted. 'You're scavengers of the worst sort.'

'Shore workers,' One Eye replied, correcting. 'Shore workers is our trade, although there's them as calls us

Toshers, and without disrespect.' He twisted his head towards Pelham. 'And where's the harm in picking up stuff as'ud just go to waste t'otherwise?'

'It's illegal,' Pelham insisted.

'See what we've got, why don't you?' One Eye glanced across to the lad. 'Show 'em what y'ave in your sack, Jim.'

Hayle was uncertain whether to let the boy move, but I was curious. 'I suppose there's no harm.'

Released, the lad scrambled to his feet with outraged dignity, removed the sack from his back, and emptied the contents on to the mud in a heap. It seemed of a piteous nature: ends of junk metal anonymous from wear and breakage, pieces of wood, strands of old rope, and a single ha'penny.

A moment of silence. My captive observed me thoughtfully with his solitary eyeball. The idea of trying to propel the three into the hands of the law was hardly enticing, nor, I suspected, necessarily just. 'I suppose,' I said to Pelham, 'if we had them promise not to go into the sewers again . . .'

'I promise,' One Eye shouted, before I had a chance to finish, his companions adding their pledges in an instant chorus.

Pelham glanced at the sad heap of detritus poured on to the Thames mud, then at the form of Giant Ears, larger than his own. 'There's no need, I dare say, to be unnecessarily harsh.'

'Quite.'

'Especially now they're promised.'

The shore workers did not dally. No sooner had they been released than they scrambled to their feet, plucked up their hoes and were striding off between beached barges, at a pace only thinly short of an outright dash.

It was not until we were walking over the slimy Thames bank, towards the outlet of the Ancient Whalbrook that I began to wonder if our action had been of kindness to the shore workers, or if we had done them the opposite of a favour. Had the three been delivered to the courts, I reasoned, they would likely have spent several months in gaol; by the time of their release the heat of the summer would be past, and with it the worst of any Cholera. However, by allowing them to go free, and – almost certainly – to return to their scavenging among the poisonous substances, had we not made them strong candidates to be the very first victims of the looming epidemic?

The urges were within me and, not for the first time that evening, I found my eyes fixed upon the smooth shape of my wife's breasts filling out the silk of her bodice. She was working on embroidering, the words of which, amongst emerging roses, now read, 'Doest not that w . . .' and I fancied I could discern, even through her dress, a light ripple in the softness of her bosom as her arms flexed to and fro with the needle. Pericles, as if reading my thoughts, faintly growled.

I resumed study of the piece in *The Times* which, when I had first glanced upon it, had quickened my heartbeat: 'NEW DRAINAGE PLANS FOR LONDON'. The article, I was sure, explained the identity of the group of fellows I had briefly observed in the distance that afternoon, working below the Ancient Walbrook sewer outlet. Almost certainly they had been labouring on one of the two schemes *The Times* described.

Like my own, the plans were to be presented to the Metropolitan Committee for Sewers. Both were still in a state of research but both – to my envy – were backed with the wealth and might of engineering companies. The names of the two engineers involved were dimly familiar, but no more. Mr Gerald Herbert offered 'A System of Grand Artificial Rivers', while Mr Clive Danby proposed a 'Giant Under-Thames Tunnel'. Here in print before me: details of notions that would be competing against my own drainage scheme.

As I examined the article more closely, however, my concern abated. Though the piece was not a long one, and the descriptions simple, I perceived serious flaws.

Mr Danby's plan was the most open to criticism. *The Times* had quoted at length his own description of the 'Under-Thames Tunnel', which he claimed to be a sweeping answer to London's urgent needs, possessed of a grandness of vision with few equals in history.

> Ponder if you will Sulla, Cicero, Augustus himself, brought hither from their own glorious age, to stand, awe-struck, before the Under-Thames Tunnel, silenced by the great enterprise they see – pipes thrice as tall as themselves, and of a most modern design – silenced by the economy and daring of the design, outshining even the famous Cloaca Maxima of their own fair city . . .

But why, I considered, build a giant sewer *beneath* the waters of the river, when this was bound to cause overwhelming difficulties of construction. One had only to think of the history of Marc Brunel's Thames Tunnel – merely extending crosswise beneath the river, from Wapping to Rotherhithe, and thus a mere midget in comparison with Mr Danby's proposal – which had been subject to repeated inundations and disasters of all kinds, finally reaching completion no fewer than fifteen years after it had been begun.

Mr Herbert's scheme was a more practicable one. It had also the appeal of a greater stylishness of appearance, attributable no doubt to Mr Herbert's being – as *The Times* mentioned – in addition to a trained engineer, a keen amateur architect and art historian. His 'System of Artificial Rivers' was to be a network of open drains that would spread down across the metropolis from both north and south, as the roots of a gigantic tree. All would flow down to the Thames where – and this was to be the magnificence of the scheme – they would join two huge open sewers, one on each bank of the river, and each riding atop raised embankments containing also roadways, railways, and fronted with mile upon mile of marble colonnades, one above the other, in gothic style.

> The open sewers upon raised embankments – or 'Artificial Rivers' – are intended to grace the Thames, and all London, not only with great practical advantages, but also with all the noble elegance befitting our leading city. The colonnades will call to mind the soaring splendour of our cathedrals, the finery of our great country houses. Indeed, these constructions will be the envy of the modern world, raising London, at one stroke, to the status of not only the largest and cleanest, but also stateliest city of this earth . . .

Grand intentions, no doubt, but what of the question of expense. Mile upon mile of marble would not be lightly accepted by the ratepayers. In addition, by carrying the effluent downriver – to a giant processing station – a great part of the valuable elements would, to reach the rural hinterland, have to be transported all the way back from whence it had come, adding to costs and reducing profits.

Surely the Metropolitan Committee for Sewers would see the advantages of my own Effluent Transformational Depositories over these lavish and ill-conceived designs. By placing the depositories all across the vastness of the city, transport to farms surrounding the capital would be reduced to the minimum. The scheme would not be unduly expensive to create and, once established, could be administered locally; each parish would oversee the running of its depositories, and claim, without danger of divisive argument, those profits earned. The inhabitants, indeed, would have the daily pleasure of seeing their own depository, in their very midst, and of witnessing its quiet work; their own parish gold mine.

While the report did not alarm me, it nevertheless suggested action I realized it would be unwise of me to neglect. These rival notions would now be under discussion, and, consequently, it was proper that I should try to bring attention to my own idea.

I would write, I decided, a letter to *The Times*, briefly setting forth my proposal. The time was ripe, after all, as the successful research of the previous few days had done much to answer possible difficulties. It was a long shot, of course. There was no certainty that it would be printed, nor, if it were, that it would chance to catch the notice of men of influence.

If only I could explain my notions directly to Sleak-Cunningham. It was he, after all, who would be the main judge of the contest.

The man was so infernally busy.

I had a thought. I recalled he had, despite his thin form and pallid face, quite a reputation as a *gourmand*. Perhaps he could be enticed. A dinner. If I were to have printed some grandly formal invitations, they would give an impression of splendid dishes and wines. Certainly it was worth attempting.

Nor would I invite only Sleak-Cunningham and his wife. The Hoves, too, should be asked. And why not Sweet as well. Both were involved in the matter, after all. Sleak-Cunningham and Sweet; they might even be surprised how much – through the medium of my scheme – they had in common.

Isobella, I was pleased to discover, seemed taken with the notion, putting down her embroidery to listen. 'A dinner? But what a good idea. We've never held one before.'

I realized it was true.

'I'd need to clean out the house thoroughly. And we'd probably have to hire a servant to help, at least for the evening.' As she spoke, thoughts running ahead of her words and causing her moments of bright confusion, I again found my glance lingering on the soft protrusions of her breasts. My attention must have troubled her, as her excited planning soon died away.

* * *

Katie's skin was as pale as could be, except for those parts exposed to the light during her long hours loitering the streets – her hands, face and neck – which were sun-burned with an exactness as if dipped in dye of a light red-brown.

'Katie does like t'ave a proper gent visiting.'

She had become almost a habit in the preceding weeks. Although after each encounter I decided – as that afternoon, reaching across for my shirt – that I should never return to her squalid room, a few days usually proved enough for the remembrance of her skinny form to regain, in my imagination, an alluring enchantment.

She stopped the progress of my arm, opening up the fingers that clutched the shirt so it almost fell from my grasp. 'You 'as ever sich soft hands, 'Enry. So smooth an' that. Doctor, is yer?'

'Engineer.' I freed my fingers, that I might slip the garment over my head.

'Ingineer?' The discovery seemed to please her. 'What a lark, eh? All them rileways an' that.' She lay back, drawing up her legs and resting her hand casually – temptingly – beside the curls of her lower hair. 'Sure you wanna take yerself off in sich an 'urry, now?'

'I really must go.'

'As you like.' She watched as I attached the collar. 'Work round 'ere, you does, I suppose?'

'In Westminster.' Even from where I sat I could detect the fine scent of her parts.

She nodded approvingly. 'Very nice. Seein' all them prime ministers goin' past an' sich.' She mused for a moment on the notion. 'Live round there, too, does yer?'

'Further away.' I pulled on my trousers.

Rolling herself on to her front, kicking her legs idly in the air, she glanced up at me with a playing look. 'Where?'

'Pimlico.'

She uttered a squeal of recognition. 'I bin down there. Which street then?'

Her questions were growing irritating. It was not the first time I had found myself annoyed by the endless chatter. 'Does it matter?'

She shrugged, a touch put out. 'Only askin', weren't I.' Climbing up from the bed, she stretched, arms high in the air, extraordinarily naked. 'Sure you don't want to stay a bit longer?'

I was not sure.

It was only later, after I had finally left, that it occurred to me to wonder at her curiosity. Merely my over-tired imagination? Perhaps. Still I was pleased that I had thought, during my visit, to give her a false name.

> THE CHOLERA: A CHLOROFORM CURE
>
> *Dear sir,*
>
> I find myself in a position to recommend to your readers a most valuable means of overcoming the horror of the Asiatic Cholera. A wine glass should be filled to the brim with brandy, to which should be added ten drops of chloroform, this mixture to be administered to the sufferer without delay, and repeated, in identical quantities until the symptoms of the malady have quite disappeared. The type of brandy used is not of great import, although a French variety, of quality, is naturally to be preferred . . .

I sat up sharply, pulse racing, skin moistened with perspiration. Slowly the study furniture came into view all around, surprising in its familiarity, reassuring.

The dreams had become ever more regular in occurrence; indeed, of late I had sometimes been troubled with several in a single night. This last, however, had been different from its predecessors. Though the weapon had been the same, the victim had not been my wife. This time the nightmare – still haunting me with its lingering alarm – had been my murderous assassination of Albert Farre.

I got to my feet, pondering the change. An improvement? Perhaps, though it hardly seemed a great one.

Stepping across to the door, I found it fastened shut. Foolish of me to have forgotten. Lately I had been subject to such strong fears that I might sleep-walk – though never had I done so before – and might, in unconsciousness, do some terrible deed, that I had omitted no precaution.

I lit a candle, retrieved the key from its hiding place beneath a chunk of coal in the fireplace, and made my way downstairs. To be out of the study had a calming effect, and for some time I sat at the kitchen table, munching at carrots left over from dinner. Would a sleep-walker be outwitted, I wondered, by devices he himself had taken when awake? Would I have known where the key was hid? Quite a philosopher's riddle.

Whatever the case I could hardly allow this state of affairs to continue. Thus I thought as I crept back past my wife's door – as silently as I was able, that I would not wake her – to my study. Mere nightmares they might be, but they were interfering with my sleep, even threatening to dislocate my concentration upon the drainage plan.

If I could only discover the sender of the malicious letter, surely the whole problem might be overcome.

This thought remained well alive in me the next morning. Sat at my desk at the office, I scrutinized the faces all about, watching for anyone acting strangely towards me. Several times I caught the eye of Farre, and found myself embarrassed by his beakily friendly nod. How would he look if he knew of my dreams of the previous night?

At least my work on Sweet's warehouse was progressing well enough. My plan of the building might not have been the neatest of its kind – a failing I set down to my troubled sleep – but it was approaching completion, while Sweet had been well content with my costings of the project with more windows.

Glancing up, I saw Gerald Prowse rapidly looking away, as if in pretence at not having been observing me. This was the second time I had caught him doing so. I waited, keeping my head bowed, as if in deep study of the plan before me, while my eye kept watch on his part of the room. Sure enough, after only a few moments he was again peering at me. With a strangeness of expression, too. I looked up and once more his gaze sped away.

Gerald Prowse? It seemed hardly likely that he would be the perpetrator of such vicious behaviour. He was no more than a lad; still in the midst of his apprenticeship, and – being a little lacking in sharpness – frequently the butt of jokes and deceptions by his elders.

But could one be sure? I would keep a close watch on the boy.

Always to press forward, countering each obstacle in one's path, never to look back or falter; this was the only way to conduct oneself. At least so I believed that summer, with the fervour of a fanatical Mohammedan.

A wind-blown day in late spring, the breeze chasing clouds across the sky, one moment throwing houses, pavement, passing carriages all into shadow, the next lighting them up with a brief taste of warming sunshine. Thus I recall the afternoon when, with much trepidation, I approached Trowbridge Street, that I might ask Moynihan for his daughter's hand.

It seemed as if the whole world were somehow apprised of my intention, my feelings. Was there not a knowingness in Barrett the butler's glance as he ushered me inside? And was it chance that, as I fidgeted in the waiting-room, the footman happened to be striding past carrying a pot and peered in, and the silent maidservant happened to be creeping by clutching a tea set and also peered in?

And Moynihan himself?

On my second visit to the house there had been no sign of him, though I thought I heard his step, echoing from some recess of the house. When I asked Isobella if it were indeed her father, she had been vague. 'Possibly. I'm not sure if he's at home this afternoon.'

The encounter had proved a disappointing one. After all my hopes and trepidations of previous days, I had found Isobella distant, even formal, speaking – often with that glimmering agitation I had observed before – only on subjects of general interest, and always in a voice loud enough for the maid to hear every syllable. I wondered if she had come to regret her earlier enthusiasm, and it was with some uncertainty that, rising to my feet, I asked if I might visit again.

She reduced her voice to hardly more than a whisper. 'The weather's growing so much brighter now. Perhaps it would be nice to walk in the park.' It was with her eyes that she suggested I should not tell her father.

Thus I found myself leading a strangely divided life. On Sunday afternoons I would meet Isobella at the end of the lake in St James's and we would take a stroll. These occasions could not have been more proper – she would not even allow me to grasp her hand – but possessed a finely charged quality nevertheless. Likewise, though we spoke little except of light matters, the very secrecy of our rendezvous implied an intimacy between us, a sense of decisions silently agreed.

During the week I continued to work phrenetically on the plans of the Elfield to Gizbee, often in the company of Moynihan. Neither he nor I made any mention of his daughter, but I was all but certain he knew something; the servants would surely have commented on my second appearance for tea. Also I was sure I sensed subtle changes in his behaviour towards me. His manner, though still distant, seemed more intense, the heaviness of his silence more weighty.

Twelve Sunday walks. That was all that it took. With each my pleasure at her arrival – always a few minutes late – grew deeper. With each I found enhanced my wonderment that such a graceful – and head-turning – creature should choose to spend time with me. Ever more urgent was my desire – resisted – to embrace her, and dispel that nervous tautness about her lips. Greater, too, was my fear that, next Sunday, she would not come.

Our twelfth Sunday. She was late, far more so than before, and it was the alarm this caused in me that prompted my proposal; tipping the balance between fear of asking, and fear of not. She too seemed agitated; perhaps she guessed my dilemma. For a time we walked in silence. Then I led her away from the promenading crowds beside the lake, and we stood beneath a horse chestnut tree, raining fresh-grown leaves and white explosions of blossom. I took her hand, hardly able to look her in the eye.

'Isobella, will you marry me?'

Her reply took me aback. She almost laughed. 'But of course.'

It was she who suggested I write formally to her father requesting a private interview. She would hardly listen to my nervousness of Moynihan's response.

'My father was a watch-maker. That may not matter to you, but . . .'

'Just do it, Joshua. Have trust in me.'

The next day I wrote to Moynihan. My apprehension abated somewhat when, the following morning, I received a reply inviting me to visit him at home the following Saturday. Then he must know, I reasoned. Doubtless he had known all along. Much pleased that the air could be cleared at last, I sought him out at the office that I might accept his invitation and offer my thanks. He silenced my effusion with a raised hand.

'We'll speak on Saturday. Now I'd be grateful if you'd address yourself to the matter of the gradient of the line at Silmoor.'

Most of all I wanted to speak to Isobella. Our weekly meetings allowed for no such spontaneity of arrangement, however. Thus my life at work continued for some days within the same tight atmosphere of things unsaid and uncertain that it had before. Until, on that wind-blown afternoon, I found myself being deposited in the waiting-room by Barrett the butler, his face so knowing.

'Mr Moynihan will see you in the library.'

Strange of him to choose the same room where I had searched for Hall's field book, which was neither grand nor comfortable. I found him standing behind the single table, so that I had to step through the narrow gap between it and the wall to shake his hand, causing a chair to scrape upon the wooden floor.

'You wished to speak to me, Mr Jeavons?'

For the previous few days I had thought of little except phrases I might use at this moment. Now it was come upon me, I found myself robbed of any suitable means of broaching the subject. How could one, when, except in my own near-certain suppositions, the man did not even know I had met his daughter. Should I begin by admitting I had been regularly seeing her, deceiving him by omission? All etiquette seemed to run short of the situation.

'You did wish to speak to me?'

'I did.' The words came at last. 'The truth of it is, the matter concerns your daughter and . . .' A vain final search for some proper phrase. 'I'd like to marry her.'

'You would?' He showed no surprise, more an exasperation. 'Mr Jeavons . . .' He recovered. 'I thank you for your offer, Mr Jeavons, but I'm afraid I am unable to accept.'

The reply caught me quite off balance. 'May I ask why?'

'I do not see it as a suitable match.'

'But sir . . .' I stared at the man, trying to comprehend his thinking. His words had given away so little. 'I know this is a momentous step in the life of your daughter. I realize the concern you feel for her welfare, all the stronger, no doubt, for her being your only child, but . . .'

He interrupted, shaking his head. 'Mr Jeavons, I've given you my answer.'

I could not stop. 'Have you talked with her? D'you know her views? I'll be as good a husband as could be desired, you must believe me. The affection I feel . . .'

He turned towards the door. 'Please don't go on.'

'You disapprove of my background? Is that not it? You worry I'll not be worthy of her? But I'll make myself worthy of her. I'll work hard, I'll . . .'

A fierce glimmer of restrained anger showed through the man. 'I have no doubt you will, Mr Jeavons, but that's not the issue. I have spoken. This interview is over.'

The hallway was empty – the footman and maid-servant had doubtless made themselves well scarce when they heard raised voices – as I strode towards the front door. Barrett darted out from some recess with my hat and coat and abruptly I found myself in the bright spring afternoon once more, still half numbed to what had occurred. I began walking, my pace slowing as the consequences of the interview began to make themselves properly felt.

All lost in a single moment. All those months of hope, of mad excitement. Already it seemed worse than foolish to have imagined any other outcome were possible; to have led myself down a path towards such pain.

I was some hundred yards down the street before I heard footsteps clattering behind me. It was Isobella. 'Joshua?'

'You know . . . ?'

'Of course.' She looked, more than anything, scared. 'Wait here for me. Don't leave, whatever you do.'

I can only say I have never known such waiting. Joshua Jeavons, bubbling as a pot with the lid too tight, trying not to let himself hope, trying vainly to force his thoughts into some kind of blank doze. Joshua Jeavons, unable to help himself constantly staring at the house, from tapping the railings beside him with the frequency of an operator of the electric telegraph.

Finally the front door opened and she stepped again into view, alone, hurrying up the street towards me. She spoke not a word, answered none of my faminous questions, but simply took my hand in her own, led me back through the front door – past the staring butler – and into the library.

Her father was still there, even in the same spot. He looked changed, however, looked as I had never seen him before; there seemed an emptiness to his expression, as if the charged silence within him had imploded.

Isobella did not so much as glance at him, but stood, face flushed, breathing fast. With excitement, or exertion from having run to fetch me? Her eyes were wide, with what looked more like anger. A raw anger I had not sensed in her before. At her father's objections, I imagined. Indeed, she seemed possessed of something like power, sudden and dangerous.

'I feel that my decision may have been . . .' Moynihan, speaking at last, in a flat voice, faltered, as if lost of the moment he was in. 'May have been over-hasty.' The way he stood, too, was altered from his usual self, not quite straight. 'I have therefore decided to assent . . . to your marrying my daughter.'

I strode towards him, hand outstretched. 'I thank you with all my heart.'

He nodded with a kind of smile and allowed his hand to be shaken.

Afterwards, hard though I tried, I never could induce Isobella to explain how she had caused him to change his mind. Indeed, she quietly declined to discuss the matter in any way.

Chapter Four

THE CHOLERA: A WARNING

The National Council for Health urges the population of London of the likelihood of imminent outbreak of the Asiatic Cholera in the capital. All precautions should be taken. Landlords should deal at once with any blocked drains or noxious deposits on their property which might be a source of effluential gases. Parish authorities and Poor Law Guardians should take steps to ensure they command adequate numbers of medical staff, and inspectors to visit afflicted areas. Additional dispensaries of medicines and houses of refuge should be established where required, while . . .

The warning was not unexpected. The malady had been spreading slowly but steadily southwards from Liverpool, striking several Midland towns, while a handful of cases – fortunately all seemingly isolated – had occurred in Whitechapel and around the London Docks. Also the weather was changed. For the last three days the sky had been cloudless, the sun strong enough to transform the slop dirt of the gutters into dust, so fine that it would be set flying in the air by every passing carriage; a salty veil that blinded the eyes.

One comfort, albeit a small one, was that I was as well prepared as I reasonably might be; I thought with satisfaction of the supplies I had acquired – not without difficulty – of olive oil, brandy and chloroform.

Glancing further into the newspaper I found the

edition had quite a number of items on the Cholera, including a long piece on possible causes of the malady.

> What subtle influence passes by, what blighting cloud overshadows the world, when thousands thus fall death-smitten; one moment warm palpitating organisms, the next a sort of galvanized corpses, with icy breath, stopped pulses and blood congealed, blue, shrivelled up, convulsed. All the while the mind remains clear – so strikingly far from the case with Typhoid Fever – lucid, shining strangely through the glazed eyes, with light unquenched and vivid to the last; a spirit looking out in terror from a corpse.

Fine prose, certainly. The essence of the piece, however, I found disagreeably misleading, insisting, as it did, on describing all theories, however ill-founded they might be.

Thus it gave a full account of Liebig's Zymotic or Fungoid Theory – one of the most unlikely of notions – which claimed the cause of the evil to be minute fungi in food and water, attacking the blood in the same way yeast works upon wort, and thus, Liebig conjectured, explaining the blood's thickened consistency.

Here in print, too, was the Telluric Theory, which argued the disease to be an emanation from the very earth – a kind of a volcanic phenomenon – and which had for evidence nothing more than the mystery of Cholera never having broken out aboard ship. Also the Ozonic Theory of Monsieur Quetelet – a scientist of doubtful reputation – who maintained Cholera to be the result of a lack in the atmosphere of that newly discovered gas, ozone, excess of ozone causing influenza. As proof the man offered only the strange fact that Birmingham had escaped the disease; a blessing he claimed to be the result of the city's many great chimneys, and the ozone they generated.

Present, too, was the Specific Volatile Poison

Theory. A belief I felt to be particularly misleading, this claimed the malady was carried in people, in quite the same way as the Smallpox virus, lurking within their bodies and being transmitted from one to another. But what, I thought as I read, of the numerous and well-documented instances of doctors who had spent weeks in close proximity to Cholera sufferers, without themselves contracting the disease. Such was not at all the case with Smallpox. Also why the erratic course of the last epidemic – striking one district while leaving its neighbours untouched, then vanishing so quickly away after just a few days – if it were not issuing down from a malevolent cloud passing above?

Only at the end did the article finally come to the Miasmatic Theory. The idea was described, accepted as the most likely candidate for the truth, but – to my annoyance – nothing more. It seemed astounding the paper could so under-describe the vitality of the proof. Had not the great majority of Cholera outbreaks occurred near criminally ill-constructed sewers? What of the miasma cloud, fed by these abominations, hanging above the rooftops, poisoning city dwellers? Had not many men seen it? Had I not seen it with my own eyes? What doubts could there be?

My irritation abated only when I turned the pages further. There it was, my own letter.

DRAINAGE OF LONDON: THE BENEFITS OF A SYSTEM OF EFFLUENT TRANSFORMATIONAL DEPOSITORIES

From Mr Joshua Jeavons of 17 Lark Road, London.

So the world now knew. I was heartened by the sight of the words – so familiar to me – firmly inscribed in black print, and my own name written clearly below. All across the capital at this very instant there could be men of note pondering and discussing my proposal.

Gerald Prowse left the building housing Moynihan's office, strode with his loping, young man's step past the giant building site that was the Palace of Westminster, then entered a beershop to seek some lunch. He was an easy sort to follow unobserved, certainly, and I was well able to keep up with him and even overhear him order his lamb steak. Next I bided my time, waiting until he was hard at work with his knife and fork before seating myself down at the table, just opposite his place.

'Prowse, tell me why you have taken to staring at me as you are at your desk. And pretending otherwise when I catch you doing so.'

'Mr Jeavons . . .' The suddenness of my attack caused – as I had hoped – startlement upon the fellow's foolish, faintly moustachioed face. He reddened, and his fork – supporting a cargo of potatoes and strands of lamb in a united mush – hung in the air above his plate. 'I wasn't doing anything.'

'You were doing exactly what I've described. Why?'

The fork came to rest on the uneaten portion of lamb, its load slowly sliding back from whence it had come. 'It was no more than silliness.'

'What silliness?'

Fidgeting with his fingers – mentally wriggling – he glanced behind him, as if in hope of discovering some saving distraction. 'Just on account of stupid talk.'

I regarded him coolly. 'What talk?'

'Does it matter?'

'It may do very much.'

'Mr Willow said you were going mad in the brain, like old King George.' Hardly had he uttered the words than he seemed regretful of the admission. 'It was just his joking. Nothing more. He said that's as why you're so short with everyone nowadays, and why you fell over with such a crunch. Nobody took him serious. Honest, Mr Jeavons. But Davy Hope, who's working on the Kidderbridge junction behind me, kept saying I should see, as you were afoaming at the mouth and such.' Again he grew embarrassed. 'I knew it was just foolishness, of course, but I couldn't help having a look.'

A ludicrous business. Or was it? Willow was a beery, noisy fellow – a soul I had never quarrelled with before – but if he had been spreading such stories about me then what else might he have been doing? And Prowse himself? I studied the lad's face for a moment, watching for any signs of deceit. I saw none, but one never knew. His entire story could be invention; an attempt to divert suspicion from himself. I would keep a close watch on them both.

'I shall expect you to keep this discussion to yourself.'

'I will, of course.' He nodded earnestly, relieved the interview was ended.

The glory of that sound; the rushing of water, sharpened into a roar by the echo within the drain, as it burst headlong into the daylight, cleansing, carrying away the vile substances, dashing towards the Thames.

'Flushing started already,' Grant – my sewer guide for the afternoon – observed cheerily. 'Look at it go, eh.'

'Indeed.'

The wave of liquid – a surge close on a foot high – flowed from the outlet below us towards the river, filling the air with a most cruel stench, that caused me to cover my nose with my handkerchief. Still I regarded it with satisfaction. What firmer evidence could there be of the Metropolitan Committee for Sewers' determination to act decisively?

The machinery for flushing the sewers had long been in place, and was simple enough to operate. In the upper reaches of the main drainage arteries had been constructed walled reservoirs, where river water would collect during high tides and then remain, held by a type of door or penstock. When this was unfastened all the accumulated water would be discharged in a rush, utterly scouring clean the sewer – or so was the intention – and speedily removing the noxious deposits into the Thames.

A simple enough procedure it would seem, and one that should, surely, have been regularly carried out. Sadly this had been far from the case. The criminally idle nature of earlier metropolitan government had allowed the maintenance of the drains to be wholly neglected, until many were not so much conveyors of effluent, as elongated cesspools. The situation had become desperate. Only three years earlier there had been such an accumulation of rancid gases in the old Fleet River (long covered over and, to all purposes, transformed to a grand sewer) that a tremendous explosion had occurred, bursting through the street by King's Cross, and causing such a tidal wave of filth that three poor houses in my native district of Clerkenwell had been carried away, and a Thames steamboat smashed clean against Blackfriars Bridge.

The new authority of the Metropolitan Committee for Sewers, by contrast with its predecessors, had acted with dynamic promptness. Hardly had the threat of Cholera been officially declared than the Committee was sending out gangs of flushermen to effect a thorough scouring. Flushing was, of course, by no means a complete solution to the city's troubles; many drains were now too clogged to be improved even by a wild rush of water, while the whole system was so pitiably defective that it required not cleaning but replacing. However, flushing remained the only measure that could be undertaken in the short time remaining before an outbreak of the disease was likely to begin. The Cholera-creating effluviential poisons lurking beneath London would be, if not vanquished, at least reduced.

'Come on mister,' called out Jem. 'Make the old bloke do the trick with the red bits of wood.' The urchin must have been in the habit of loitering about the river as this was the third time he had appeared, seemingly from nowhere, to watch us working. He never showed surprise at his rediscovery of our party, behaving as if no time had elapsed since our last encounter.

'You be quiet,' Hayle brayed, glaring at the boy as he stooped to lay the measuring stick along the edge of the drainage tank. 'Afore I decide to throw you in.'

This was quite a threat; the tank was a deep one, the bottom a good forty feet below them. We were on the Southwark bank of the Thames, where the level of the land was so depressed that the effluent could only be discharged into the river at low tide. When the tide was high the drain outlets had to be sealed shut – to prevent the Thames water from rushing back into the sewers, and inundating the lower-lying neighbourhoods – and the effluent left to accumulate in such drainage tanks. Now the tide was out, the river was empty as could be – all the more so for the enduring warm and dry weather – and the tank held nothing but a residual ooze.

'You leave the boy alone,' I told Hayle. I would have given further encouragement to the nascent interest the lad had shown in our work, but we were too pressed for time. Grant had only two hours to show me four outlets.

'He's trying to throw me over, he is,' Jem's piercing voice rang out, and he clung on to Hayle's bony frame like a cat panicked on a high branch.

'You get away,' Hayle retorted, adding, in my direction, 'I didn't touch the little bugger. It's just his fibbing.'

I had little interest in which of them was right or wrong. 'I thought I told you to leave the lad alone.'

Jem disengaged himself and ran nimbly along the very edge of the precipice to where I stood, at once tugging at my jacket. 'Make him do the stuff with the stick and the red bits of wood. I want to learn it proper, see?'

'A model pupil,' Grant murmured dryly. He was a lean, bemused sort of fellow, who seemed to derive a calm but deep satisfaction from his work in and about the sewers. He had been giving me a most informed account of the idiosyncracies of the Southwark outlets.

'Another time,' I told the urchin. 'We're too busy today.'

'Go on, go on,' he yelped, all at once quite changing tack. 'Give us a shilling. I'll hold your jacket for a shilling. Go on. Hot day and all.'

In the end I gave him the thing to carry, just to quiet him, choosing the less begrimed of his arms to place it upon.

The district where we were working was surely the most fantastical and sickly in all the metropolis. Jacob's Island, close on Bermondsey, was a haunt of crazed wooden houses – so ramshackle that a stiff breeze would seemingly have had them tumbling – all vying with one another for space, as old men arguing on their death beds. Many had tacked to their sides precariously overhanging galleries, extra sleeping rooms, and rickety bridges connecting them with other houses, so they altogether resembled residences in some medieval painter's imagining of hell.

Flowing beneath were a whole set of creeks and sewers, giving the neighbourhood the name of 'The Venice of Drains'. We had earlier crossed one of the most notorious of these, the Dock Head Creek, its water – much affected by the dyes of the leather dressers – coloured scarlet, and covered with scum resembling a giant cobweb, through which loomed the patterned carcasses of animals that had tumbled in, as so many ill-wrapped packages.

Glancing up at a row of toppling-over houses beyond the drainage tank where we were working, I observed a bucket being lowered by a rope from one of the upper galleries. Slowly it descended, into the very ooze itself, where it tipped, filled, and then, wobbling with the weight of its contents, began its journey back upwards. When it finally reached the gallery a hand darted out from shadow to claim it. I pointed out the sight to Grant, and he shook his head with a kind of grim amusement.

'There's some of them who drink it.' It was a thought not only vile but seemingly impossible, but Grant was insistent. 'Those that can't get themselves Thames – that are too sickly or hemmed in from the river to be able – generally haul up what they can from a creek or such, straight below their houses. 'Course they let it stand for a day or two first. Some boil it even. Still I can't think it tastes too sweet.'

The notion left me feeling sick in the stomach. 'What of the water companies?'

'Place like this isn't worth their while.'

Hayle had completed his measuring of the tank perimeter and I felt I had seen more than enough of the outlet. 'Let's continue along to the next.'

It was only as we turned to walk along the river bank that I observed a figure picking his way over the mud towards us. His step was energetic yet careful, as some large creature that has trained itself to dwell among far smaller animals without crushing them underfoot. Behind him a Thames boat – those hansom cabs of the water – lay beached, its commander drooped listlessly over his oars; evidently the vessel from which the man had sprung. As he drew nearer I recognized him, as much as anything from his beard, as none other than Harold Sweet, molasses trader.

'I thought it was you I spotted up here.' He seemed proud of his intrepid arrival, cheerily waving his hand towards the boat with the air of one posing, without great success, as a dangerous pirate. 'How're you progressing?'

'Very well, I'm glad to say.' I shook his hand.

Grant, whose assistance had been secured through Sweet's agency, greeted him respectfully.

'We'll come to this dinner of yours.' Sweet smiled at me with the air of one distributing favours. 'I wrote to say so just this morning.'

'I'm most glad.' Nor was I otherwise, although, of

course, it was Sleak-Cunningham I was most eager to hear from.

He regarded me keenly. 'Lucky I should find you like this, it is. Why don't you come along with me to the warehouse site for an hour or two. It could be useful for us to look over the place together. Take in the lie of the land.'

So that was it. I had rather guessed he had not strode up from his boat only to exchange pleasantries. 'I still have quite an amount of work to do here.'

'When you're done then. It's not far, and I'll be there all afternoon.'

More time taken up, and I had been hoping to do some work on my diagram of an Effluent Depository. How very like Sweet to secure every ounce of return on his help to me; the sense of payment owed that marked a good businessman. But I could hardly feel resentment in view of the considerable assistance he had provided. 'I'll join you as soon as I'm finished.'

'Good, good.' He was turning to leave when Jem tugged at his sleeve. 'Give us a shilling, mister, give us a shilling.'

I would have expected a man such as Sweet to brush away the urchin with no more ceremony than he would an insolvent eager for molasses. To my surprise he paused, bent down and examined the lad's face with a certain interest, as a clever-eyed bear discovering the puzzle of a succulent creature hard to extract from its hole. 'And why do you ask me for a shilling?'

Jem's face took on a look of piteous woe. 'For to eat, mister, for to eat some poor morsel of some'it.'

Sweet glanced up at Grant and myself with a knowing look, as a showman to his audience. 'But if I give you a shilling,' he continued to the boy, 'would I be helping you?'

Jem seemed to regard the question as hardly worth answering. ''Course you would.'

'What would you do after you had spent the shilling, eh? More begging, I dare say.'

'P'raps.'

Sweet regarded the boy with lively benignity. 'But if I give you nothing, you'd be forced, from need, to find yourself employment. Once working you could find yourself somewhere to live. Then rise to a higher position, perhaps, and altogether better your miserable life.' He glanced from Jem to myself with the air of having conjured up a white rabbit and several doves. 'So it's kinder by far, you'll agree, if I give nothing. That way I'll not further pauperize you.'

Jem regarded him sullenly, with the look of one who has wasted good time. 'Too late, i'n it? I been pauperized already.'

'Tchaa, tchaa.' Sweet shook his head. 'There's a lesson for you here, boy. An important one, that you'd be wise to study well. Charity is a dangerous thing. It's a belief I . . .'

Further enlargement of his views was interrupted, however. Hayle, whom I had dimly observed from the corner of my eye fumbling in his pockets, uttered a shout. 'Two half-crowns clean gone. He's had them, the little bugger.'

'I never did, I never did.' Despite his words, the urchin took the precaution of dropping my jacket on the mud and stepping nimbly back several paces.

'Catch him, catch him,' Hayle demanded, striding after the boy.

There seemed little other option, and Grant and myself joined him in giving chase. Indeed, I did so with some spirit, more than a little angered that the boy – whom I had tried to encourage, to educate in the important world of drainage research, in which he had feigned interest – should now reward me by stealing from my servant, by showing me up in front of my most useful helper. I felt nothing less than betrayed.

In the event, however, catching him proved no easy matter. Jem proved well adept at traversing the slippery surface of the Thames bank – no landscape for speed – and while Grant, Hayle and myself found ourselves sliding and falling in the vile slime, the boy managed to spring lightly away. By the time we had reached the shore he had quite vanished into the maze of leaning houses beyond.

We trudged slowly back to the sewer outlet. Sweet had not joined in the pursuit, and seemed magically neat and clean compared with the rest of us, caked as we were with grey-green Thames mud. 'What was I saying, before we were interrupted?' He regarded us with rhetorical knowingness. 'I think it was how charity can be a dangerous thing.'

As I worked on the Great Drainage Map of London, inking in black circles to represent suggested locations for the Effluent Transformational Depositories, my eyes several times lit upon the four letters lodged so cheeringly on the edge of my desk. Four acceptances. Sweet's, of course, was no surprise, and likewise Albert Farre – whom I had decided also to invite, that I might have present another soul close to my own age – had already told me of his intention to come to the dinner. But what of Edwin Sleak-Cunningham? The great man of drainage reform to come to my own house, to take his dinner in my own dining-room, and learn of my ideas. A wonderful triumph indeed. Ever since his letter had arrived I had been filled with restless hope, with impatience at my having chosen as the date of the event an evening still some days distant.

In addition to Sleak-Cunningham, Hove had also written to tell of his acceptance, though his message arrived after that of his senior, leading me to suspect his bureaucratic soul had been guided by a spirit of emulation rather than a wish himself to attend. All would bring their wives except Farre – who had none to bring – and it promised to be a large occasion indeed, with nine at table.

I hoped they would not be taken aback when I began delivering my account of the System of Effluent Transformational Depositories. I had not over-stressed the lecture element on the invitations, adding merely a handwritten postscript on each, to the effect that I hoped to use the evening to explain a little about the scheme. Probably there would be a certain surprise when I stood up to speak, notes in hand. I comforted myself, however, that the subject was such a lively one that, once embarked upon, the guests would be too swiftly captivated by the dazzling notions to disapprove of my methods.

The formalities of the evening also troubled me a little. I had no great knowledge of dinner etiquette, but supposed the best time to begin the lecture would be after the meal had been consumed, when the ladies retired to chatter amongst themselves. Indeed this was the only possible moment, as the matter was hardly suitable for female ears. I worried, however, that this would allow me little time properly to explain my ideas. There was so much to tell, and it would be nothing short of catastrophic to misuse such a God-given opportunity. If necessary the ladies would simply have to wait rather longer than was traditional before again joining us. An hour or two. Longer even.

The early summer dawn had just begun to break outside, and the house opposite my study window, normally coloured a smoke-darkened grey, was lit a deep and splendid blue. I had not intended to stay working all through the night, but now that it had happened I wondered if it were not a cunningly good way of arranging things. I was tired of course – I could feel the weariness in my limbs, the fogginess of thought as I rose from my desk and stole quietly from the room – but had I not progressed some distance, if slowly and a shade untidily, on the drawing of my Drain Map? Also, by remaining awake I had avoided the risk of further troubling nightmares.

A faint growling emanated from Isobella's room – Pericles had heard my passing – followed by a rustling sound, and I hoped I had not woken my wife. In the kitchen I prepared myself coffee, and collected upon a plate several large potatoes, a swede, and the remainder of a leg of pork. Really I should not eat so much, I knew – lately my stomach had begun to swell, as if I had become a keen drinker of beer – but the hunger within me never seemed to abate. In addition, eating helped keep me awake.

I felt myself relax as I reached the parlour, lay back on the easy chair and began devouring my dawn meal. I wondered if I should not spend more time in this room, perhaps even work here. The study was growing increasingly uncomfortable to me; even when I had no intention to sleep there was always the risk that unconsciousness would steal up on me. Thus only the previous night I had come awake slumped at my desk, hot with perspiration at having stabbed to death both Moynihan and Sweet.

Indeed, there seemed no limit as to whom I might now murder, having variously done to death Miss Symes, Gerald Prowse, Mr Willow, Hayle, both Gideon and Felicia Lewis, Hove, the Reverend Michael Bowrib, Barrett the butler, and even several people whom I had never even met but only read of in *The Times*, including William McReady the actor, Carlyle the great historian, and Prince Metternich, deposed helmsman of the Habsburg Empire. Only the weapon remained constant – the knife I had given my wife – causing me to wonder if I should try to remove it as I had the last. There was little opportunity; Isobella had of late been much engaged upon her embroidery, and seemed to carry it constantly with her. Also she was bound to be most curious at a second such disappearance.

The light filtering by the curtains told of sunrise well under way, and I could hear the first stirrings into life of this new metropolitan day. Pulling the curtains back, I watched a nightsoil cart clatter slowly past, doubtless just finished with emptying some household cesspool. The sight called to my mind a finely motivating piece I had read – it had been only the morning before, although it already seemed several days distant – in one of the monthly journals, in which a writer by the name of Dr Kelvin had conclusively proved how, were London not rapidly provided with a proper sewerage system, its central areas would vanish quite away beneath a rising tide of effluent.

The logic Kelvin had used had been the unalterable laws of economics. The drainage of the metropolis being presently so defective, he had pointed out, a great part of metropolitan nightsoil was removed in carts, such as I had just watched pass by, in which it was carried to rural areas to be sold to farmers. As London grew, however – which it never ceased to do – the distance these vehicles were required to journey would increase, until a point would be reached when the substances would have to be transported too far to offer profit. Nightsoil traders would be forced to abandon their work, and at once evil deposits would begin to build up in the streets. Logically, such a process could only lead to one result.

> Contemplate, if you will, the creeping catastrophe that will be brought thus upon ourselves. Day by day the vilenesses will grow in slow accumulation; first rising in depth upon streets until vehicles and horses find themselves ever mired; next blocking stairways and the doors to houses that their inhabitants cannot enter or depart; finally reaching so high that the central parts of London – the hub of enterprise and government of our great city – will be as some desert, palaces, Inns of Court, offices of great companies, the architecture itself, all vanishing from sight beneath the tide of evil.

Powerful reasoning, I considered, getting up from my seat, the potatoes and swede dealt with and the leg of pork reduced to bone. In the light of such argument could even the most fanatical anti-governmentalist seriously resist the call for revolutionary rebuilding of the sewers? I shook my head as I left the parlour and retraced my steps towards the kitchen, catching sight, en route, of Miss Symes's unexpected form, perched at the top of the stairs, clothed in a billowing nightdress and brandishing in her hand a candlestick.

'Oh, it's you, sir,' she called out in a hoarse whisper. 'Whatever are you doing about so early?'

'Just sorting out a few things.'

She regarded me, disapprovingly. 'At such a time of night? I thought you must be some murdering robber.'

I had no intention of pandering to her fussing. 'Don't be so foolish, woman.'

Murmuring some under-breath criticism, she turned herself about and retired clumpingly away.

The air was still cool outside the house, the sunshine – weakened though it was by the smoke and the miasma haze – sharply restoring. As I strode down the street a tramp began following close behind, his face and clothes equally dark-stained, so he might all of him have been lately dipped in tar. He tugged at my jacket, calling out for money in a flat, remorseless tone. I recalled, for some reason, Sweet's philosophy of pauperization, as addressed to Jem the miniature criminal. Charity can be a dangerous thing. 'Away with you,' I called out to the fellow, 'before I fetch the police.' The threat proved effective, and with a scowl he trudged off to seek some other victim.

An early morning breakfast stall gave out an enticing aroma and warmth, and I sat for a while, watching the owner working at the charcoal fire pans, boiling up saucer after saucer of coffee, enough for the stream of bleary and poorly washed early birds, stopped on their way to begin their labours. I had several saucers myself, and felt their enlivening qualities battling away my weariness.

Next I strode along Whitehall to the near end of the Strand, and one of my favourite parts of London. Hungerford market, that elegant construction upon two levels – fish, fruit and meat stalls now just stirring into life, filling the air with fine smells – was built in the same style and with the same Tuscan granite columns as nearby Covent Garden. From the upper terrace on the river side I stepped out on to the younger Brunel's pedestrian bridge, springing from the very market itself, and busy now with souls hurrying across from the Surrey shore. The crush was a tight one, and it was with some difficulty that I lingered for a moment beneath one of the Italianate towers, to admire the outline of St Paul's, rising up through the swirling, smoky London haze.

Proud buildings of this great city. How few of the metropolitan citizens scurrying past would, I pondered, have any knowledge of the peril in which their capital now stood; of the danger that those fine façades would – without a proper system of drainage – quite vanish from sight beneath a remorseless tide of effluent.

Invigorated by my early morning walk, I decided to make my way back to the house. The prospect of a further day's hard work was burdensome, perhaps, but not impossibly so. Indeed, such sustained wakefulness and labouring gave me a strange sense of heroism, as if I were the first human ever to have attempted such a thing. Even the unexpected sight of Katie did not subdue my spirits.

She seemed to have observed me from the far side of the road, through the gathering traffic, and darted across with agility in the moment's gap between a coal wagon and a brewer's dray. 'Mr Aldwych. You're up early.'

'You too.'

'It's different with Katie, i'n it. With Katie it's late.' Bleary in the sunlight, she glanced up at me with a tired coquettishness. 'Coming to visit soon, are you?'

'I dare say.'

'That's my 'Enry.'

It did not fail to occur to me to wonder, as she strode away, what she could be doing so far from her own domain, and so near my own. I even followed her for a while, until convinced she was pursuing a course away from my house. She might already know its location. I imagined her knocking at the door. Arriving on the very evening when the dinner was to be held, with Edwin Sleak-Cunningham within.

Too much to think of. And such quantities of work remained to be done. To stride forward was the way, dealing, one by one, with all obstacles in one's path.

That wondrous moment, when the vows were said and Isobella was suddenly, indisputably mine. I can recall it exactly; the delicate church scent of candle smoke and damp stone; the pregnant hush of the congregation; the faint summer singing of birds outside, struggling to be heard above the clatter of morning traffic.

I inspected her, delicate features half seen through the white veil. How tempted I was to lift up the material, reveal her face, open her up. To capture her, draw her to me, until – there and then, in the very church, regardless of shocked convention – my lips would meet her own (an action which, extraordinarily, I had never accomplished before). Joshua Jeavons, stood before the altar, imagining himself kissing his bride Isobella. Kissing slow, slipping his tongue wickedly deep into her mouth, secretly, before the whole congregation of respectable Westminster Anglicans. Kissing Isobella, long and fine in delicious triumph. Kissing her, best of all, before the very eyes of her father.

I had hoped the man had overcome his disapproval of my status. His manner, after all, had seemed improved; distant but not unfriendly. Then, only a few days before the wedding was to take place, came the incident of the dowry.

I guessed, even before Isobella spoke, that something was wrong; her manner, I observed as I greeted her in the upstairs room at Trowbridge Street, was grown stiff, almost haughty.

'My father says he does not approve of dowries.' Though she uttered no opinion of his view, I could sense the anger hidden within. 'He sees them as an outdated convention, likely to undermine the independence of a young couple.'

'I see.' It was devastating news. Also astonishing. One would have expected it to be a matter of pride for a wealthy and successful man to ensure his daughter lived in a state of finery reflective of his achievement. Usually it was so. How humiliating to have all the world see his own progeny endure shortage and discomfort. Yet, I reflected even then, Moynihan had shown little enough concern for the views of his fellows. Never had he troubled to show off his grand house. Indeed, he had steadfastly resisted the curiosity of his engineering colleagues to witness his splendours.

'But why should he do such a thing?'

'That is not for me to say. It is his decision.' Isobella took refuge in distance, closing herself away as if I was little better than a stranger. Infuriating. Of course I could guess the fellow's reasons. His decision was, I strongly suspected, nothing less than an attempt to sabotage the wedding. Though Isobella and I had never discussed the subject, we had both been quietly assuming some assistance in our new lives, and, indeed, had built it into our conjectured plans for the future. Of course it was his right, but . . . I resented the thought of being in the man's house, his guest. Even now he was likely no more than a few dozen yards distant, separated by only a plaster and brick wall or two.

'You are silent.' Isobella regarded me questioningly, less remote now.

'It's a great pity. A pity indeed.' Our lives would not be impossible, but on my salary alone they would be far from sumptuous.

Her face grew tense. 'This changes your views, of . . . ?'

'Of course not.' Her question surprised me; had she

suspected I was some kind of fortune hunter? If her wealth had been an influence on my infatuation it had been only of the most innocent kind; the pleasure of seeing her clothed so beautifully, possessed of such fine manners. 'Did you need ask?'

'I wanted only to be sure.' She closed her eyes for a moment, visibly relieved, and my heart was quite warmed, even at this unhappy moment. I took her hand.

'And what of you? It's for you that the change will seem harsh, after the life to which you're accustomed.'

She shook her head as if surprised. 'It's as nothing to me. You must know that.'

At the time, though I did not say so, I was by no means certain she would adapt to a more meagre way of life with the ease she foresaw. But she was to surprise me. Not once, after we were married, did I hear her complain of the small size of the rented house, of Miss Symes, or the dull nature of our meals. Such matters were never the issue between us.

Capture the scene, seize it, petrify it, as in a daguerreotype, figures immortalized in a living moment; title: 'Afternoon of Triumph'. Joshua Jeavons opening the door to his carriage and helping inside his bride Isobella, picture of innocence in her flowing white dress, a swan of a creature. Joshua Jeavons, young beard pointing forward sharply from his chin, jutting ahead in dynamic expectation. Joshua Jeavons, one foot inside the carriage, turning, with a gesture almost aristocratic, to offer a calm wave that is received with loud cheers by the watching guests. His father seems to stretch up on his very toes to wave back, grinning like a madman at this seen conclusion of his son's good fortune. Beside him Albert Farre, a little drunk, brays wishes of good luck.

Joshua Jeavons inside the carriage, propelled rudely back into his seat as the vehicle jolts forwards, to carry him to Waterloo Railway station, and an uncharted future.

The wind was up at the seaside town we reached that night, stirring the waves into an angry foam. During the train journey I had sensed Isobella's nervousness – wholly natural on such an evening – and, accordingly, I loitered for some time by the harbour, watching the fishing boats rise and fall with the swell – a faint echo of the wild movement beyond the quay – so that she would have a little time to herself, to rest her thoughts and prepare.

The house had been recommended to me by a friend of Farre's, and had proved pleasing; a small, attractive place in the newer part of the town, run by a widow who, sensible to our situation, had been admirably discreet and invisible. All was quiet when I returned.

I knocked lightly at the bedroom door, my wife answering with a phrase I did not discern but which, from the unhurried tone of voice, told of her readiness. The bedroom could hardly have been a finer picture; fire burning contentedly in the grate, Isobella lying in the grand wooden bed, facing modestly away from me, golden curls decorating the sheet, a hint of neck bared.

'Isobella.'

The abruptness with which she sat up surprised me. Pulling the sheet with her, so she was covered almost to her chin, she did not speak, nor look towards me. The action stole the momentum from me, and having wanted to embrace her, I found myself slowed, wondering how I might calm the moment.

'What a day it's been.'

'Indeed.' Her voice sounded brittle.

I turned the lamp down to a glow, that she would not be in some way shocked by my undressing, then began removing my tie. The air about the bed smelt of brandy, and I wondered, surprised, if she had been drinking.

'Is the room to your pleasing?'

'Oh yes.' She spoke the words quickly, fending off the enquiry, innocent though it was, as a batsman might a difficult ball.

Still clothed in my shirt and trousers, I sat upon the bed beside her. 'Mr and Mrs Joshua Jeavons.'

'Truly.'

I reached out to embrace her, but she flinched. I could see and hear her breathing, so fast. 'You're troubled?'

'Really, I . . .' She closed her eyes for a moment, as if in concentration, then stared at the bedclothes.

I felt there was something she was trying to say, but could not utter. 'What's wrong?'

Her eyes seemed to go blank. 'Nothing.'

'Tell me.'

'Really, there's nothing.' All at once it vanished.

Just wedding night nerves. I felt them too. I glanced at her, at once so familiar, so prized, and at times so unknown as to seem a stranger. 'This is all so new to you.'

Oddly my remark seemed to increase rather than calm her unease, the tautness about her mouth.

'Don't be frightened,' I urged. 'I'm nothing to be frightened of.' I reached out for her hand. 'Besides . . .'

There was no warning; that was the shock of it. One moment she was lying quietly beside me, the next she was lurching, tumbling from the bedclothes. A glimpse of a giant nightdress, billowing as the sail of some storm-tossed ship, covering all but her shapely ankles – ankles that would remain long after, painfully alluring, in my memory – and she was gone.

She fled of all places to the luggage room. By the time I reached it she was inside, had closed the door, and even blockaded it with some bulky article.

'Isobella, what on earth's wrong?'

She was crying and, it appeared, also piling more heavy objects against the entrance. 'I'm sorry. I just . . .'

'You can't stay there. You'll catch your death.'

'It's all right.' The banging finally ceased. 'There are our coats and things. I'll be warm enough.'

'But this is absurd.' I leaned against the door. It did

not give at all. 'Come out. Please.' I tried to think of words that might move her. 'There's no need to be frightened. If you like I shall even sleep on the couch. But come out, so we may at least talk.'

She gave no answer.

'This is our wedding night. We must be together.'

'I'm sorry.' The sobbing stopped. 'It's just all too soon.' Her voice took on a certainty, even a hint of threat. 'Don't try and . . .' There was a rustling from within, as if she had sat down. 'We must wait a while, that's all. Just wait.'

> THE CHOLERA: AN AMERICAN CURE
>
> *Dear sir,*
>
> I have recently been in correspondence with an eminent physician from the great city of New York, who has recommended an American cure for the Asiatic Cholera which proved of great effect during the late outbreak on the far side of the Atlantic. The sufferer should, as promptly as possible, be administered quantities of ice and salt, while simultaneously being given, and with the greatest energy, an external application of friction and heat. The combination of contrary temperatures is most invigorating and stimulating to the bodily functions, and this method . . .

It was Miss Symes opening the front door that woke me. Her voice sounded grumpy. 'Bit early, isn't it, to go knocking people up and pestering them with letters?' A shrill child's voice uttered a reply I did not catch and the door was slammed shut.

The strong light glimmering through the curtains gave promise of another warm day. I discovered myself to be wearing my shirt and trousers of the night before, with a dressing gown draped about them and, sitting up, I could feel the stiffness in my arms from having remained slumped over the dining-table, using the Great Drainage Map of London as a kind of pillow.

I had been asleep for as many as several hours; the pen lay close by my hand, and I must have nodded off in the very act of inking in the likely placement of sewers that would feed the transformational depositories.

'. . . pestering people with letters . . .' Miss Symes's words came back to me as I stretched, but changed in significance, prompting an uneasy curiosity. Tying the belt of the dressing gown, I opened the door to the hall. The servant was gone but, on the small table close by the front door, I saw an envelope. Even from that distance of several yards I seemed to know it – the size and pattern of the words, perhaps – and, sure enough, as I drew closer I recognized the hard, print-like handwriting.

I hardly troubled to comprehend the message but strode straight on to the kitchen, where I found Miss Symes wrestling with a giant fish – jaws gaping as if in angry surprise at such indignity – that was one of the courses of the imminent dinner party. The preparations were well under way and fruits, vegetables, meats and other ingredients were spread all about her; over tables and chairs, lolling on plates and bread boards, filling tureens and baking tins.

I brandished the letter before her.

'Who delivered this?'

'Mister Jeavons.' She regarded me with disgruntled surprise. 'That little girl it was, as just knocked on the door. Something fresh from the gutter, looked as if she'd not have said no to a bit of stealing.'

'You've seen her before?'

She shook her head indignantly. 'I'd have told, wouldn't I.'

'Didn't you ask who sent her?'

She glanced at the still-sealed envelope. 'Say in there, I dare say.' By now her curiosity was awoken. 'Something up, is there?'

I did not answer, but strode back to the hall. Pulling open the front door, I went outside, over-visible in my dressing gown and slippers, but undeterred for that.

Around me were a tramp, a lad carrying a bucket of eels, and two more respectable types on their way to work, but no little girl. I hurried on to the corner, glancing up and down the street that adjoined our own; here a cab, a brewer's dray unloading barrels into the basement of a beer house, and a handful of people tramping past, springless of step at this early hour. But no little girl.

I sped on, to the street beyond, and the one further still, now broadening my quarry from small girls to any adult I might recognize – Prowse, perhaps, or Mr Willow – but all I saw were strangers. At another corner – another useless vista – I reluctantly concluded she must have taken an altogether different direction and, more conscious now of the stares of passers-by, I began retracing my steps.

In the hallway once more, I picked up the letter.

DO YOU NOT CARE WHAT YOUR WIFE DOES WITH HERSELF? ISN'T IT TIME YOU STOPPED HER DISGRACING YOU BOTH? KEEP HER LOCKED UP AT HOME, BEFORE EVERYONE KNOWS.

A FRIEND

I stared hard at the letters, but gained no revelation. Should I go straight to the office, and confront Willow with the document? Perhaps catch him off guard? But what if the whole matter was nothing to do with him? After all, the malice might be from a foe not of mine, but my wife's. Strange though it may seem, it was a thought I had little considered. A member of the church congregation, for instance, angry at being snubbed. My wife might even recognize the handwriting, and thus solve the whole mystery at once.

Still I hesitated, reluctant to subject one so innocent to such poison. And . . . was there not also that half-heard fear within me, of what might be discovered?

Tentatively I climbed the stairs, and knocked at the bedroom door. 'Isobella, I need to speak to you.'

'I'm not ready.'

Waiting, I thought with pleasure of her uncomplaintive nature, dressing herself without fuss when, until our marriage, she had always had a maidservant to help. She soon opened the door, allowing me inside to take in the delicate, feminine fragrance that habitually filled the room.

'Well?'

I stood before her, awkward. 'Nothing really. A piece of evil and ludicrous slander. I'd not even trouble you with the thing, but I thought you should see.' I handed her the letter, and she examined it, eyes widening. 'There was another like it, some weeks ago. I thought you might know the writing and so we might discover the scoundrel responsible.'

She sat for a moment in silence. 'It's so absurd.'

'Worse than absurd. It is wickedness.' Glancing at her, I found her less puzzled than I would have expected. 'You don't recognize the writing, do you?'

She shook her head in slow thought. 'But of course I do. It's Felicia's.'

Now it was my eyes that were widened.

Felicia Lewis? That prudish, garment-encased trap of a thing? I had no more thought of her than of the Emperor of China. Indeed, it had never even occurred to me that it might be a woman. Felicia Lewis? What sense was there in . . . ? But it would explain the incident at their house, when she had behaved so strangely, taking me aside with the pretence of showing me her brother's rendering of the Crucifixion. And I had thought she was flirting.

'But why would she do such a thing?'

'Why not? You've seen what she's like, forever seeking out other people's sins.' Isobella crushed the paper into a tight ball and threw it to the ground. 'How dare she? When I had thought her my friend.'

'Wicked indeed,' I agreed.

She seemed hardly to hear. 'It's just because she's so strange about Gideon. She can't stand him paying attention to anyone else, almost as if she were his wife, not sister. Probably she's scared of him running off and leaving her to herself, an ugly old spinster.' She grew flushed with anger. 'All those Bible meetings I went to. The shame of it. Never will I venture near her house again.'

One among her phrases had snagged my attention. 'Gideon?' He had seemed nothing more than a bobbing-headed fool, but then . . . I felt a faint tightening about the throat. 'What attention was he paying?'

She glanced at me, for the first time, a shade uneasily. 'It's so absurd. A mere nothing that his sister has maliciously lit upon.' She looked away towards the window. 'The poor fool believes he's in love with me.'

'I see.' The discoveries seemed to creep through me slowly, gripping me more painfully with the passing moments. A world of secrets, unknown, unsuspected. I was surprised by the calmness of my own voice. 'And you?'

'Nothing.' She glanced at me, insistent, beginning to realize my own feeling. 'What on earth d'you think? I just felt sorry for him.'

I was numbed by curiosity to know the extent of the disaster. 'You've been meeting together?'

'Of course not.' For a moment she looked absurdly young. 'Only by chance, when I went to the house. I had to tell him how impossible it was – it would've been cruel not to – but he just wouldn't listen.'

I watched her face, trying to believe. 'Why didn't you tell me about this?'

Her voice rose. 'It would only have troubled you.'

Silence seemed to rise between us.

'You should've, rather than keeping it secret.'

'There was nothing to tell.'

Quite what happened within me at that moment I still cannot quite say. It was almost as if something had slid from my grasp and fallen far away. I no longer trusted her. Suspicions half-formed, barely kept at bay all those past weeks, buzzed in my head with a growing din, drowning calmer thoughts.

'Why should I believe you?'

She looked suddenly scared. 'Because it's true.'

'So say you?' I took a step forward, pushing her back. 'What else have you been keeping from me?'

'Nothing.'

Her hands, secretly touching . . . 'All those times you said it was all too soon. Too soon for me, but not for Gideon Lewis.'

'That's not . . .'

I toppled her on to the bed. I am not by nature a harsh man, but that instant it was as if something foreign had found its way inside – though little compared to what was to possess me later – and I wanted only to hurt her, to use her. I forced my lips upon her own, hard, until she twisted her face away.

'Get off.' She struggled to free herself, but I held her down with the weight of my own body, her arms flattened beneath my elbows. Pericles was yapping furiously outside the door, and scrabbling at the wood, but I paid him no heed.

'Let me go.'

I hardly heard her voice, but tore at her bodice with my hands. The material was strong, however, and gave not at all.

'Leave me be,' she yelled, piercingly, into my very ear. I wedged my legs between her own, through the layers of petticoats and dress, driving them apart, only to feel a stinging pain in my hand. She had bitten it.

I might have struck her, but something stopped me, recalled me. Turning my head about, that she would not be able to sink her teeth into my face itself, my eyes lit, by the purest chance, upon her embroidering, lying upon the bedside table, and – jabbed into it – the knife with painted battleships. Sight of the thing froze me.

I drew back, at once winning a sharp poke in the eye.

I staggered from the bed.

Isobella was crying. 'How dare you? How could you?'

My original anger was fading, leaving me high and dry, weary of spirit. All at once I felt sorry for her, reaching out a hand to help her from the bed.

'Don't touch me.' She spat the words. 'Get out of my room.'

Joshua Jeavons walking through thick smoky fog that has his eyes watering, through London streets half vanished away. Dusk at midday, consuming perspective, swallowing more distant pedestrians, causing a desertedness as if the metropolis had lost the greater part of population; inhabitants stolen up from its gutters without the faintest sound. Joshua Jeavons stepping forward, knowing his way even in the soot-filled grey.

But is there not a change here, as he approaches the entrance to the graveyard? A new expression on his face from the usual hungry impatience; a thoughtfulness, even doubt.

Joshua Jeavons staring for a time into the fog, seemingly searching, questioning. Answers there are, too, beyond that gauze; solutions to mysteries known, to problems still unthought of. But not yet. Joshua Jeavons has a long road yet before the summer will have yielded him the last of its revelations.

The sight of my father's grave always inspired in me resentment of Moynihan, anger at his refusal to have given a dowry. Indeed it was the only matter over which my lack of wealth truly hurt. I had so wanted to honour the man with the grandest of occasions; carriage with four horses desporting the finest black ostrich feathers, twenty mutes all decked in black crêpe, and a place in one of the fine new cemeteries outside the centre of the town – Kensal Green, perhaps – where he would have a giant of a headstone, inscribed with lines of fondest remembrance.

I had done everything I could. Thither went all my

few savings, as well as the small sum he left behind, but it did not procure much. Funerals are so costly. A handful of mutes – in that state of wretched drunkenness that pervades their profession – clutching black ostrich feathers, a carriage with only two horses, and for a destination a cramped churchyard not far from Clerkenwell. It was this last that distressed me most; a churned-up mire of a place, with headstones wedged so close together it was hard to see how there could be room enough below. I myself had seen the vilest of goings-on at the paupers' end of the yard, and once, close by my father's plot, had caught a sexton breaking up one of the older headstones and hurling the pieces away. Indeed, I dearly hoped one day to be able to move my father to a finer and more peaceful home.

I regarded his resting place, recalling the purpose of my visit; I had hoped to conjure up advice, wisdom he might have offered. Staring at the stone, I tried to form in my mind a detailed picture of the man – not so easy as one might suppose – and achieved an impression of quick eyes, half-moon spectacles, gnomishly domed head, and two tangles of hair above his ears, rising quivering into space.

As soon as the picture became properly recognizable, however, I realized he would have been the last person from whom I might have gained advice. Had I not tried once, just a few weeks after the wedding – indeed, only a few short weeks before he passed away – when I was still impatiently eager to find an answer. I had visited my father at his shop in Clerkenwell, just as he was closing, and he had given me tea.

'Isobella's well, yes,' I told him. It was such a thorny, awkward business. 'The first weeks of a marriage, I dare say, are not the easiest of times. So much that is new. Especially for the wife.'

My father nodded, but as if he had hardly heard my words. 'Such a wonderful creature, Isobella.'

I tried again. 'There have been worries between us.'

For some moments he left the phrase hanging thus,

then, with a faint shrug, plucked up a piece of watch to study. 'Mere nothings, I dare say.'

'Well . . . A difficulty has arisen . . .' I wondered how I could possibly broach the subject. Such matters can be so much more difficult to explain to persons close to one – especially family – than strangers, 'arose in fact on our wedding night.'

He frowned. 'What are you trying to say?' He shook the watch piece in the air, almost angrily. 'You'll be quite fine, d'you hear. I won't hear such fussing.' He peered closely at the desk top, plucking up a minute spring. 'When I saw you both walking into the church, I knew you were right together. Everyone knew.'

It was the first time I fully grasped the strength of his determination to see my life as somehow complete, firmly on the path to happy conclusion. As if any life can be so. I had not the heart to pursue the matter further.

A relief it was, too, that I had not. How could I have lived with myself if, during what were to be my father's last weeks in this world, I had selfishly clouded his thoughts with my own troubles.

Through the mist I could see the greyed outline of a man – the sexton – at the poorer end of the graveyard, hammering at the ground with a spade, causing a sound harder than that of earth; a 'chock, chock, chock', faintly numbed by the fog.

I strode out of the churchyard, observing that the trails of smoky vapour seemed to be lifting slightly, filling the street with strange light; a luminous dusk. With a clattering of hooves an omnibus hove into view and I clambered aboard, taking my place on the open upper deck – damp in the mist – squeezed beside two keen young types, legal clerks by the look of them. Sitting back, with no paper to occupy me, I found myself overhearing their chatter.

'The Whitechapel Poorhouse, it was,' said one, relishing his own account. 'Seven gone already, and ten more sick. One came down with it after supper, so I heard, and was topped by breakfast-time.'

'And there's no mistaking what it is?'

'Certainly not.' The first was indignant at this slight on the drama of his news. He lowered his voice a shade. 'Vomiting fit to burst, they were. Turned near blue, too. And when they opened up the veins, the blood was thick as molasses. Almost black it was.'

The other stared down at the floorboards of the vehicle, evidently affected by what he had heard. 'Seven gone, you say.'

The first sat back, basking a little in the power of his news. 'And that's just the start of it. Mark my words.'

So it had begun at last. Strange to say, I felt almost relieved by the discovery, after the long weeks of waiting. If it were to come, let it come now.

Chapter Five

THE CHOLERA: A CHINESE CURE

From Father Joseph Rizzolati, Vicar Apostolic, Hou Kouang, South China.

Dear sir,

I have had Cholera morbus and should have been a dead man in four-and-twenty hours had not the malady been taken in time to a good physician. The ordinary and most convenient treatment is this: the tongue of the patient is punctured in innumerable places with the point of a table knife or crystal blade, so as to provide an abundant effusion of blood. Then, whilst some of the attendants stretch the principal nerves by main force, others give the patient severe blows to the chest, the back, the thighs and the hips, until torrents of blood gush forth. When the crisis is over the patient recovers, at the cost of numerous scars and bruises and skin as black as a negro's. Thus . . .

What an assemblage of grand persons to behold, gathered in all their fineries beneath the roof of none other than Joshua Jeavons; waited upon by his servants, seated at his dining-table – indeed tightly wedged about it, as the room was barely large enough to hold them all – and eating the food he had provided. I was all but dazzled by the honour, and the opportunity.

I was also concerned whether my display of hospitality was sufficient to impress these guests – having never seen their homes I had little idea of the splendours to which they might be accustomed – or whether they secretly despised what they saw.

The table at least was no cause for worry. At the last moment Albert Farre had kindly suggested I borrow the dinner service of his aunt – an offer that explained the closeness with which his eyes followed the other guests' hands as they plucked and replaced the delicately thin-stemmed wine glasses – this last proving to be a splendid collection, with plates depicting rural scenes in subtle blues, as well as glittering silver cutlery and candlesticks, and a giant tureen so polished that it seemed to illuminate the room.

The smallness of the building, however, was troubling to me; in particular the dining-room was so cramped we might have been taking dinner in a Royal Navy frigate's Ward Room rather than in a modern London household. I had not failed to observe the way Edwin Sleak-Cunningham, when he arrived, had glanced about him dubiously, casting looks towards his wife, and then – greetings barely done with – lamenting how he feared he would be unable to stay for the whole evening.

'What with the Cholera started up, we've quite a crisis brewing at the Committee, and I promised I'd be in at some lunatic hour tomorrow, almost before the birds are singing.'

An annoyance indeed, when the whole event had been planned to entice the fellow.

Harold Sweet, too, seemed disappointed, regarding me with brusqueness, as if I had in some way let him down, while his wife – a noisome and discontented woman with an accent straining to impersonate the sound of elegant wealth – expressed fierce interest at the discovery that we had been living there for as long as ten months. 'So clever of you to find the space enough to put everything.'

I wondered if they had assumed Moynihan had housed us in some urban mansion; if they had been looking forward to an evening of fashionable entertainment. Perhaps they had even hoped my father-in-law would be present, and they might talk with that great man of engineering. As if it would have been fitting to invite the very one who had turned down my scheme.

Only Hove and Albert Farre seemed to regard the proceedings without criticism. Hove was too preoccupied hanging on to Sleak-Cunningham's coat tails, that he might not miss one single of his superior's words, his wife – a dumpy, crushed creature – hurrying after him. As for Farre, being a close acquaintance of mine he had something of the status of an honorary member of the household.

The mood improved when the introductions in the parlour were done with, and all wedged themselves into their places around the fine gaudiness of the dining-table. The first course, though only soup – a concoction of red cabbage and apple of my wife's – seemed to be a success, and my thoughts ran ahead to the other dishes prepared, trying to assess likely responses to each.

More pressingly urgent to consider was the question of the timing of my lecture. With Sleak-Cunningham threatening to leave early I could not, I realized, delay until the ladies departed to the parlour for their gossip. A pity. It meant I had no means of removing them from my lecture on drains and effluent; hardly proper subjects for female ears. But the alternative was to make no speech – hurling away the whole purpose of the evening – and that was something I was not willing to consider.

I would detail my scheme after the main course, I decided, when all were still firmly seated about the table; if necessary well delaying the dessert. The grandeur of vision of my plan would surely prove captivating enough for Sleak-Cunningham to forget his thoughts of an early departure. He would want to hear more.

The servant we had taken on for the evening – a slight girl by the name of Jenny, who charged little but had troublingly uneven teeth – arrived to collect the soup bowls. We should have hired several such persons, as befitted such an occasion, but what with the great expense of the food and wine it was more than I could afford. Her ungainly leanings over guests brought distraction from the proceedings, and, perceiving this was a useful chance to slip away from the dining-table, I rose to my feet. Edging my way behind the guests, my eye caught for a moment my wife's glance, causing her to look away.

Matters had been more than awkward with the two of us no longer on speaking terms. Of course it could have been worse still; Isobella might have refused to assist with the event, might not have attended, or acted coldly and without welcome to the guests (in the event she had been distracted, but not without a withdrawn hospitality). Still I found it hard not to feel a resentment towards her. What of her dogged failure to apologize, her sulky behaviour, as if it had been I who was to blame? Also there was the humiliation of having to direct every remark through the malicious medium of Miss Symes – now posted in the kitchen – who showed a disagreeable delight at her position of new importance, even commenting on the messages I gave her, with surly nods, or disapproving grunts, that always implied clear partiality in favour of my wife.

The soup bowls had been cleared by the time I returned, endeavouring, as I negotiated the passage back to my seat, to hold the scrolls and maps of my drainage scheme high in the air, that they would not scrape against the heads of guests I passed behind.

'What d'you have there, Joshua?' called out Farre. 'Some revolutionary petition to Parliament?'

'You'll see soon enough,' I answered mildly, though his remark annoyed me for its poor taste. There was little room to place the bulky documents – on the floor they would be vulnerable to the faint grime of soot drifted from the fireplace – and I chose in the end to balance them, somewhat precariously, on the mantel-piece, beside a large china dog with tears in its eyes, that had been a wedding present.

'But you want to interfere with the whole balance of the economy.' Though Sweet uttered the words quietly enough, his clever eyes sparkled ominously.

'You entirely miss the point.' Sleak-Cunningham was warm of voice, quite unlike his usual self. I had placed them at opposite ends of the table, but they appeared to have manufactured themselves a noisy disagreement even at such a distance. 'Look no further than the flushing of the sewers we're now undertaking. Even aside from the vital benefits against the Cholera, the savings are remarkable. Effluent removed at six-pence per cubic yard. A mere fraction of the price required to be rid of it by cart.'

Sweet regarded him darkly, as if his words had been somehow slanderous against himself. 'Savings, you say? To whose profit? You just discharge the sub-stances away, robbing the nightsoil men of their honest livelihood. It's against all the logic of economics. Nobody benefits, except perhaps some parasitical committee.'

'Gentlemen, gentlemen,' I interposed, concerned at the way the dispute was speeding towards personal rancour. The sooner I brought amongst them the unifying device of my drain plan, the better. I glanced impatiently towards the door, wondering what might be delaying the arrival of Jenny. She should have brought us several dishes by now, including the game pie, the potatoes with parsley, and the pork with orange. The huge roast fish was to come later. 'Don't grow so serious that you'll spoil your appetites.'

The two combatants were too well embarked on their quarrel to be so easily distracted; indeed they showed little sign of having heard me at all. Sleak-Cunningham waved a bony finger at his opponent, directing towards him the same cold stare I had seen him hurl at the slum landlord at the session of the

Committee for Sewers. 'You, I suppose, would have no committees. You'd have them done away with, and the fate of our cities left solely in the care of . . .' He jabbed his finger towards the other's eyes. '. . . Of blind entrepreneurs, who, if they see no glint of profit before them, would happily leave our metropolis to turn to a mere swamp of defecation.'

Such words caused me to glance towards the ladies. Mrs Sweet and Mrs Sleak-Cunningham, however, were hardly listening. Spurred on by loyalty to their spouses, they had embarked upon a separate fracas of their own, hardly less fierce, concerning the merits of a leading hat and bonnet merchant. Only Hove and his wife, Isobella and Farre were unembroiled in the spreading war.

What could Jenny be doing with her time? Her arrival with the meat dish – now well overdue – would likely mute the dispute, or at least smother it of vilificatory remarks, unsayable in front of a servant.

'When the need is there,' Sweet retorted, 'a market will spring up. D'you really think the great banks of the City would sit back and let their premises be engulfed in effluent? Of course not. They'd pay well to prevent such a thing happening and, under a system of open competition, good men will vie with one another to do it cheapest. Better, by far, have the fate of the nation in the care of free men of enterprise . . .' he regarded the other accusingly, 'than in the hands of mere committee men, holding back others to their own stagnant pace of life.'

'I would have you know . . .'

I did not take in Sleak-Cunningham's reply, as my attention was captured by the door opening, and Jenny at last stepping into sight. Her arrival, though amply welcome, was also puzzling. Her arms hung by her sides. Why, I wondered, was she not carrying the meat?

She did not cast so much as a look towards the heated disputants as she squeezed behind their chairs, but hurried towards my own place. 'Mr Jeavons, somu't's up.'

'Whatever is it?'

'Best you come see yourself.'

The arguers seemed hardly to notice my progress from the table. Something up? In my mind's eye I saw Katie knocking at the door, requesting to speak to me on a matter of urgency; her look charged with silent purpose, brimming with invented tales of injury. I saw her being led to the parlour, where she sat, waiting her moment.

It was not, however, to the parlour that Jenny led the way, but to the kitchen. Nor was there any Katie to be seen. Instead, sprawled upon the floor, surrounded by vilesomely reeking ejections – as I walked in she vomited up a little more, then groaned – was the hulking form of Miss Symes.

So there it was. So sudden, so unexpected. Thus I regarded, with black wonderment, this premature arrival of the great foe, come to my very kitchen. Joshua Jeavons, head spinning with drains, with lectures to give, with important figures to persuade, staring at the stricken figure of a servant woman who never inspired in him anything but dislike, but for whom, now, he cannot but feel reluctant pity. Joshua Jeavons juggling urgencies, furious at the timing of the affliction, swearing to himself in a low murmur.

I stooped down to feel her pulse, which was still strong. 'How d'you feel?'

She glared up at me, face glowing with perspiration. 'What d'you think?' She surprised me by the powered malevolence of her words. Then, with a loud grunt, she heaved again, this time expelling only a belch.

'How long has she been like this?' I asked Jenny.

'Not so long, I dare say.' The girl stood awkwardly, nervous of the crisis about her, leaning forward on her toes. 'I would've told you sooner, Mr Jeavons, but I didn't rightly know if to call you out of your dinner and that.'

I glanced at the sufferer. 'We'd best get her up from there.' As I pondered how I might put these words into action – by no means a simple prospect considering the woman's weight – my attention was, however, distracted by the sound of footsteps, then the appearance in the kitchen doorway of the bird-like form of Albert Farre. Miss Symes's groaning must have been heard from the dining-room, the din of the governmentalist dispute had died away. He glanced about the room.

'My God.'

'All's well in hand,' I told him, a little impatiently; I had had some vague notion – perhaps foolish – of keeping knowledge of the crisis from the other diners, at least for the moment. 'The matter's being well attended to.'

'Don't you believe it,' accused the patient with energy. 'He's done nothing but ask if I felt well. Imagine.'

Before I had a chance to reply, more footsteps were audible drawing near, and I watched unhappily as Sleak-Cunningham's pale face peered into the room. 'I heard a shout and thought . . .' He looked on in grim fascination. 'It can't be, surely . . . ?'

'Why ever not?' Sweet, close behind him, though more businesslike, was not unaffected by what he saw. 'The first case in the parish.'

'That we know of,' corrected Sleak-Cunningham, unforgetful of their recent rivalry.

'It's quite all right,' I told them, struck by an unsettling sensation of events sliding even further from my control. I gestured to Farre. 'Can you give me a hand getting her up to her room?'

Farre acquiesced, if with a certain squeamishness at actually touching the woman – who was, admittedly, more than a little stained by her sickness – and we helped her on to her feet. Hove raised his hand, with the air of a prim pupil who has the answer. 'I'll fetch a doctor.'

'Good man,' approved Sleak-Cunningham. 'I know of a fine practitioner close by our house. We can take a cab together.'

His reply jarred. I stopped, bringing a halt to Miss Symes's slow progress across the room. 'You're not leaving, surely?'

Sleak-Cunningham frowned. 'I don't see what further assistance I might usefully give.'

'But what of the dinner?' My remark may seem strange, perhaps, but you must understand my passions of expectation had been raised to such a pitch during the previous days that I could not contemplate the evening being so quickly, so unexpectedly lost.

The guests regarded me with surprise. The scene before them had evidently driven their thoughts far from the planned agenda of the night.

'Dinner?' Sweet cast a grim glance across the room, lingering on the dishes to be served that were ranged on the table. Miss Symes's first salvoes, I now saw, had struck a number of glancing hits upon these, including the roast fish, the potatoes with parsley, the parsnips and beans, and the splendid apple meringue and cream cake that had been bought, at no little expense, from one of the better shops near the Haymarket. I cast her a glance, wondering, with feeling, if she could not have made more effort to aim her expulsions.

'There are matters I want to discuss,' I urged. 'Important matters.'

'This hardly seems the time.' Sleak-Cunningham was impatient to be away from such proximity to sickness.

'Quite so,' added Sweet, for once agreeing with him.

As it was, further discussion was halted by Miss Symes herself, who, still propped up by Farre and myself, coughed twice, then disgorged a mouthful of substance from her gut, terminating the matter more effectively than any words could have done. After offering brief thanks, well-wishes, promises of imminent doctors, and vaguer forms of help, the Sweets, the

Sleak-Cunninghams and the Hoves were all gone.

What remained now, of the evening that I had inflated with such hope. A woman I had never liked struck with sickness. It was a low moment indeed. Still I tried not to despair. One battle lost did not mean the war could not yet be won. I must look ahead, think of other means of publicizing my notions.

'I suppose it may be some time before Hove's doctor arrives.' Farre had stayed, the servant Jenny too, and we had managed to convey the patient to her box of a room, a bucket lodged by the bed.

'I dare say.' My thoughts were too distracted to much attend to his meaning.

'He could be out on call when Hove gets there. For all we know, quite an epidemic may be started, and doctors could be hard to catch.'

'True enough.' The whole neighbourhood might be engulfed, and we might both be breathing in the miasma poison even as we stood before Miss Symes lain upon her bed. Still, I could not see what Farre's remarks might achieve, beyond fuelling the glowering distress of the patient. 'What of it?'

Farre stooped bird-like above Miss Symes. 'We should try and do something ourselves, at least until help arrives. It could make all the difference.'

He had a point. My thoughts turned wearily to the matter. 'It's possible, I suppose.'

'I have heard opium can be most effective. D'you have any in the house?'

'Not opium. Though there are a few things that I put by for such an occurrence as this one.'

Farre rummaged through the collection of newspaper cuttings with interest. 'What about this one? Olive oil – you have a bottle of it here – and warm water.'

'I dare say it may do as well as any.'

He again examined the print. 'The instructions are clear enough.' He turned to the patient herself. 'What d'you say we give this a try, Miss Symes. It could clear up the whole thing in a moment.'

She was unsure. 'You're sure it'd work?'

'Says here it never fails.'

She shrugged. 'Then I suppose so.'

Jenny was sent down to warm a good quantity of water, while Farre found a cup of correct size to administer the olive oil. I found myself slowly warming to the thought of testing a cure; it was at least a welcome distraction from the failures of the planned evening. And what a triumph if we were to discover, by scientific method, a reliable remedy.

Miss Symes swallowed the first cup and, encouragingly, kept it down for the full eight minutes before the second dose was taken. This too she retained, and our hopes were fast growing as the time for the final swallowing drew near; this to be followed by copious quantities of warm water, which Jenny had standing ready. The third cup of oil, however, proved too much for the woman's constitution, and was barely swallowed when it came back, together with – judging by quantity, the two earlier successes, and a substantial remnant of her dinner.

'It was so close.' Farre frowned; the experiment had quite captivated his interest. For that matter, it had mine. 'We should try again.'

'We certainly should not.' Miss Symes had, it seemed, been thoroughly put off the olive oil and, despite our combined urgings, would not be swayed. 'I ain't touching another drop of that foreign muck. Good enough for Spaniards, it may be, but not for proper English folks.'

Farre again searched through the cuttings. 'What of this?' He held up two bottles. 'A cure, Miss Symes, made up of two substances well known to these shores.'

She shrugged. 'All right. I dare say.'

The written description of this second cure, however, proved to be by no means adequately specific. The dose – ten drops of choloroform in a wine glass of brandy – was to be repeated every ten minutes until the symptoms disappeared, but as Miss Symes insisted on instantly expelling the first glass into her bucket, we were left unsure whether we should then wait for the required interval, or whether this failed attempt did not count, and we should proceed again at once. In the event we compromised and delayed five minutes, but with no greater success. After a third failure Miss Symes again grew obstinately uncooperative.

The Chinese cure, we both realized, was sadly inapplicable. For a start we lacked the 'attendants' who were 'to stretch the principal nerves by main force'; the exact meaning of which process neither of us was quite clear of. Also there was the difficulty we would face trying to persuade Miss Symes to embark on the great letting of blood required.

This left the American cure, which she greeted with interest, even enthusiasm. 'Leastways with this one I don't have to swallow nothing peculiar.' Jenny was despatched to heat bricks in the oven and bring ice – fortunately we had acquired quite a quantity, for preserving the apple meringue and cream cake – which she mixed with salt, while Miss Symes began – with surprising absence of shyness – to divest herself of garments that she might be more easily given the 'External application of friction of heat'. Both Farre and myself watched, not without a certain trepidation, as her ample form was revealed to sight. In the event, however, the question of who should apply friction never arose. Before Jenny had brought the hot bricks there was a loud knocking at the door.

It was the doctor sent by Hove.

He was a serious man, who seemed to match the heavy black leather case he carried. Marching up the stairs, led by Jenny, he absorbed the sickbed scene with sombre but deep-rooted astonishment. I realize now it may have looked out of the ordinary, with Miss Symes nakedly recumbent in the tiny room, strips of newspaper all about her, as well as a bottle of olive oil, brandy, chloroform, and a tureen of salted ice.

'What on earth's going on here?'

'We're attempting a well-known cure,' I explained, handing him the relevant cutting.

He glanced over it with growing displeasure. 'This? But it's quackery of the first order. As if such practice has any sound basis.' He surveyed us with the disdain a schoolmaster might employ upon two pupils caught spitting upon one of their fellows. 'You are dabblers. Dabblers, what is more, who may have caused this lady serious harm.'

Then, however, looking to the patient – her face showing fierce dissatisfaction towards Farre and myself at such scathing utterances – he seemed to grow distracted from his own words, sinking into silence for a moment. He stepped forward to examine her. 'Wait . . .' Stooping over her, he peered at her lips, her eyes, then the skin on her arms and stomach, touching this last in several places. 'How d'you feel?'

Miss Symes shrugged, glancing away almost shyly at his proddings. 'Not so bad now, I suppose. Better than before, anyroads.'

'Perhaps the cures we attempted earlier had a beneficial effect,' Farre proposed.

The doctor replied with nothing more than an exasperated 'Hmmph', at once turning back to the sufferer. 'Tell me what you have eaten today.'

'Everything?' Pausing for recollection, Miss Symes itemized what she had consumed, listing a veritable banquet of snacks and meals, the ingredients of many of them well familiar to me, as they had been obtained from our sparse everyday larder, or from the preparations for the failed dinner.

The doctor pondered. 'Anything else?'

She thought. 'There was one thing, I s'ppose. In the afternoon I went out to get some apples as were needed, and on the way I had a few cockles from a stall.'

'Cockles?' The doctor clapped his hands with sombre triumph. 'There we have it.'

'You mean . . . ?' I began.

'A clear case of poisoning by food, from that most common of all causes, shellfish.'

Miss Symes uttered a kind of vengeful wail. 'You mean it ain't the Cholera?'

'Of course not.'

I have to admit it was not a happy moment. Our mistake, though understandable enough, was unfortunate. Miss Symes, angrily pulling her clothes back about her, quite revelled in the misjudged treatment she had been given. 'And all evening these two were feeding me the most poisonous foreign stuffs and substances, having me strip meself bare, till they came close to killing me clean away.' Her accusations were directed, of the two of us, almost exclusively towards myself. 'Evil-minded, deliberate murder, it was.'

Though I insisted we had been acting with the best of intentions, the physician proved obstinately sympathetic to her plight. Indeed he went so far as to sharply criticize Farre and myself for, as he termed it, 'Playing doctors'.

'As if the practice of medicine is a mere matter of collecting cuttings from newspapers.' Writing out a bill charging me for the pleasure of being thus denounced, he helped his patient down the stairs. Farre – eager to be swiftly away from this scene of his embarrassment – was close behind, Jenny also, regarding her evening's work, I dare say with reason, as well complete.

'Don't think you'll have me working in this house again,' Miss Symes challenged, in the drama of the front doorway. 'Not after what's gone on this night. I'd not come back if you begged me.'

I made no attempt to convince her from her resolution, grateful that some slight benefit might be won from the evening.

The first glimmer of early summer dawn was visible in the sky above them as they went. Turning back into the building, I stepped into the pronounced quiet within. The dining-room table was still covered with the debris of the halted dinner which, after the long and wearying night, seemed as if preserved from some earlier era. I stood for some moments, suddenly weary, pondering sleep.

It was only then that I began to wonder where Isobella could have been all this time. I had not, I realized, seen her since Jenny had hurried to my place at the head of the dining-table, to tell of Miss Symes's illness, all those hours ago.

I climbed the stairway to the bedroom door, but it was closed, with no glint of light from beneath. She must have crept quietly up to retire early, I decided, ignoring all the din of cures and doctors outside. Still it seemed strange. Reluctant though I was to wake her, and so perhaps further aggravate matters between us, I tapped lightly at the door.

Silence.

I tapped again, and softly called out her name. Still nothing. Heart beating more quickly, I turned the handle. All within was quite as usual; everything in place, all faintly lit by the dawn light shining in through the windows. Except that my wife was not there. Examining her bed, I saw it had not been slept in.

Chapter Six

Two days ago I woke to find the Alp mountains that curve about Turin transformed, their sharp outlines a freshly glaring white. There are other signs, too, that autumn is well advanced; the noonday sun still has the power to burn scarlet an Englishman's nose, but after nightfall a chill spreads through the air, summoning forth smells – finely alluring – of woodsmoke fires. Yet my memoirs have barely reached the true start of matters. Slow progress, perhaps, but I will not be hurried; I refuse to allow any such thing. In my days in London I hurried enough for a whole lifetime – speeding forth, eyes all but shut – and paid hard for the pleasure.

Besides, it is not easy exactly to record one's actions of two years ago. The urgent nature of my departure from British shores – a leaving that was, indeed, nothing short of outright flight – prevented my bringing any but a few documents detailing events of that awesome summer. I have only my own remembrances and, though my powers of recollection are far from weak, these I treat with caution.

Memory can subtly mislead. It can blind one with a sense of certainty. It can add logic to events when in truth no logic was to be found. It can even have knowledge oozed back before its proper time, insinuating into one's remembered thoughts discoveries not yet made – waiting in the future – when in truth one was in confusion; bogged in quagmires of the moment.

What was one thinking on this given day? What did one feel? How much did one grasp? Such questions are not always easily answered even on the very day itself, let alone eight-and-twenty months later. The picture is cloudier still if, at that distant time, one's own judgement had wandered fearsomely astray.

Though I miss London of course, I am growing fond of this foreign city. I am renting a set of rooms – Piedmontese seem not to think of living in houses, but lodge together of their own choice in chambers within huge blocks, as would the English only if they could afford no better – which overlook on one side a narrow alley crowded with food shops and wine merchants. At night even with the windows closed I can hear voices rising up in the sing-song and somewhat nasal local dialect – greeting one another, arguing, duping a passer-by and more – and, though the sound sometimes distracts me from sleep, still I find it strangely pleasing.

Of course Turin is a small and unimportant city compared with the great metropolis of London, largest on this earth. That hot summer of two years ago one seemed to breathe the very size of the place. Thus it seemed that morning – air already well warmed though it was scarce past ten – as I sat unhappily in a hansom cab speeding its way towards Battersea village.

Most troubling to me was the thought of what surprise might be waiting to be inspected at our destination (though I was impatient to get there). Also there was the matter of Constable Collins; a fellow I had already come to regard as both useful to me, and potentially dangerous.

In build he was typical of his profession – a huge fellow, filling up the cab, so I found myself quite wedged against the door – but with silent, sharp eyes. These last had an unsettling way of fixing themselves upon my own, for only a moment, but with something like thoughtful study; a habit I had observed also in his superior, Superintendent Lisle. It was as if each was re-examining his suspended judgement of my case; perhaps wondering if I had indeed played the part I claimed, or might yet prove more criminally interesting.

Collins peered out from his window, ducking down to bring his head low enough, and I found myself regarding his uniform. I had never before paid much attention to the dress of the Metropolitan Police, but now, finding a specimen lodged at such suffocating proximity, I regarded it afresh. The blue cloth coat, with its seven large buttons down the front, was most unmilitary in manner – perhaps deliberately so, that fears of despotism would not be awakened among the population – possessing instead the style of a respectable citizen, though of one full generation past. The effect of such old-fashioned clothes was curious upon Collins, who – for all his hugeness – was a younger man than I. It gave him the faint air of one pretending to be somebody else.

My eye came to rest upon the fellow's chimney pot hat, sat upon his lap. This was an old one, its outer skin cracked and torn, and revealing a structure within of what seemed to be struts of metal. Metal? Curious, I tapped him on the arm, calling away his attention from study of the hot landscape.

'My hat?' he answered, amenable, though his eyes were watchful still. 'It's made to be strong enough to hold the full weight of a man, see. So if I come upon a wall I need to peer over, but that's too high, I can use my Chimney Pot as a step.'

'Most ingenious.'

'It is,' he agreed. 'Though I can't say I've had cause to put it to use. Not yet, leastways.'

He turned away that he might resume inspection of the view, throwing before me a mass of blue shoulder and shaved neck. At the sight of it I recalled – with weary horror – how I had done the fellow to death only the night before; for company the man had had, among others, Harold Sweet, the Duke of Wellington, and Mr Kossuth, the famous Hungarian revolutionary who had lately been so much in the papers. The blade had sunk in just about there, at the base of Collins's neck, and with great ease, as into semolina pudding.

Four days. For four whole days Isobellas had seemed to float before me, by turns innocent and guilty. Isobellas drowned, or self-poisoned, or leapt from some great height and smashed upon the earth, all of them regarding me with blank and lifeless eyes, accusing. Then Isobellas without conscience, stepping jauntily into carriages, baring shapely legs, or lying desported between strangers' sheets, chirping with laughter at my recounted credulity.

Not knowing; here lay the hardest part of it. I knew not what to think. Should I torture myself with remorse (though I seemed to be doing so already) or burn with plans of revenge (a course, by turns, also embarked upon). Which likelihood even was preferable? A lifetime's guilt, or the humiliation of a cuckolded husband who has never himself achieved a night abed with his own erring wife? I really was not sure.

As a rest from such pleasant thoughts I chose to follow the example of my helper and spy, Constable Collins, and stare out of the window.

It was a London unlike itself I saw. A hot breeze, arrived the previous morning, had brought changes that had quite altered the metropolis from its proper character; wearying its inhabitants – usually so full of spirits – and sapping them of energy to pursue their livelihoods, as if natives of some steamy jungle nation. Partly it was the heat that effected this, and partly the constant distraction of perspiration; one's hands and face would shine with damp, then adhere to themselves street dust from the air, that soon formed a salty crust – filling one with impatience to cleanse oneself – transforming beggars and earls alike into grime-masked savages.

The Thames-damp heat seemed to permeate all. The sun, as it lurked – dazzling but vague of location behind the miasma haze – appeared in one's wilting consciousness capable of swallowing sound itself, movement too. The muffling of the cab's wheels, altered to a duller pitch as the vehicle passed over one of the new wooden-surfaced streets; was this not the heat's doing? So too the stillness of the Monument, looming high above the counting houses and bankers' homes of the City, as some tower of ancient Egypt. Or the placid silence of barges on the Thames, creeping forward, brown sails limply grasping the hot breeze.

We crossed by Waterloo bridge, hurrying near the great new railway station – also to be called Waterloo – now close to completion, with stonework, iron and glass rising high into the air. Then suddenly a glimpse of fierce activity, from Londoners with hunger enough to be untroubled by mere temperature, working upon a dustheap that rose above the low houses all around, so it resembled some urban volcano. The cab swung past the gates of the dust yard, space alive with scampering and half-naked humanity, clutching to the hillock as insects to their nest, sifting through smaller heaps of still unsorted dust – even now a cart discharged a new load, freshly swept up from the streets – into junk metal, into breeze for brick-making, and into the remainder that made up the main mountain, to be sold as manure.

In moments it was lost to sight. Buildings began to diminish in scale, allowing momentary, half-seen views of hills beyond. Then walls, windows and chimneys vanished altogether, and the cab entered the green of the orchards and vegetable plots of the market gardens around Battersea.

'Here we are, sir.' Constable Collins emerged from his silence. Jumping from the cab I followed the man as, with huge and unhurried steps, he approached the riverside alehouse in which our quarry lay waiting. Occasionally he would glance back as he went, doing so always with a nonchalant air; as if concerned only that he might be walking too swiftly for me, and not at all worried that I might try to slip away unseen.

He gave the door a sharp rap with his hand. When this brought no result – the building seemed lifeless at this early morning hour – he struck it with the rim of his chimney-pot hat, the metal frame causing quite a thump upon the wood. This proved sufficient, and in a moment footsteps echoed from within.

'At last.' The door-opener was, I guessed from his pronounced belly and important manner, the landlord. He inspected us, far from satisfied. 'Just the two of you, are there? And in a cab. Won't be easy shifting her off in that.'

'We've not come to take her,' Collins told him. 'This gentleman just wants to have a look.'

'A look? How long am I supposed to wait?' The landlord seemed to grow more paunched with anger. 'One of your lot thumps on my door in the middle of the night – wakes the whole household – saying I've got to store her, then slinks off and leaves me to it. I'll have customers arriving within the hour. How am I supposed to run my business?'

The constable was unintimidated. 'It won't speed things none, us arguing out here.'

Not for the first time during the previous days, I had wished our capital possessed a proper morgue, following the example of that famous institution of Paris. The landlord opened the door wide to allow us inside, noisily, that we might know his continued displeasure. Walking behind, he directed our progress with impatient shouts, 'Not that way, it's left here,' as if it were deliberate carelessness on our part not already to know the building's geography.

I saw the moment we entered the room that it was not her. Isobella was never so tall. The corpse had been placed, of all choices, in the kitchen – it was a small inn, and perhaps that was the only room of size to easily accommodate her – among baskets of new potatoes and spring onions. The table she lay on was too short, and her legs – grown stiff – jutted out over the end, troublingly straight, the blanket suspended upon them, as if by some trick of magic.

Collins and the landlord stood watching; waiting for me to pull back the blanket and deliver my verdict.

Certain though I was that she would be unknown to me, it seemed easier to comply than not. The girl's face was bloated from her hours in the river, but not greatly distorted. I was surprised by her youthfulness; though tall, she was hardly more than a child.

'It's not her.'

Collins nodded, observing, and the landlord uttered a grunt of disapproval, to show his lack of interest in whether I recognized her or not, as either way we would not be taking her off his hands.

I glanced again at the girl. It was not as if she were greatly different from the half-dozen others I had seen; corpses have a sad way of resembling one another, as members of some specialist club. Regarding her, however, I found myself affected, as not before. Isobella, naked in some other unknown place, lain upon some stained and splintering table, being wearily prodded and joked about by strangers. I could see the scene so clearly.

I pulled at the blanket, sharply, that she would be covered.

'Something wrong, Mr Jeavons?' asked Collins.

'Nothing. Can't we just leave her be?'

He regarded me, thoughtful. 'You're quite sure she's not your wife?'

'Quite sure. Of course.'

Joshua Jeavons, very early on a sunny morning, stood impatiently before his father-in-law's house, shadows of the iron railings still long upon the ground, and the chattering of birds in nearby St James's Park declaring the dawn to have been of recent occurrence. Joshua Jeavons tugging at the bell-pull, tugging remorselessly, oblivious to the sensibilities of servants within, to the hopes of Barrett the butler – likely still sat droopingly in his bed – that the din may be nothing more than some small-hours drunk, who will soon be gone.

My first thoughts, as I regarded her empty and unused sheets, had been of Trowbridge Street. It was the house where she had been brought up; the home of her father, who was – however cool she seemed towards the man – after all, her sole remaining relative of closeness. I imagined her fleeing there, slipping impetuously through the door, exhausted by the tensions between us, by the many preparations for the dinner party, or the shock of overhearing the guests' discovery of Miss Symes's apparent attack of Cholera. She might be waiting even now. The breach between us – for which already I felt anguish and remorse – could yet prove reparable. Indeed, I would make it so. I would tell her my regrets, beg her forgiveness in a soft voice.

'Mr Jeavons?' Barrett cut a strange figure before me; stiffly butlerish of pose, though he was attired not in his formal coat and tails but a huge nightshirt, upon his head a nightcap with a red woollen ball at its point – this last drooping curiously on to his shoulder – that gave him a carnival air. His face was bleary.

'Is my wife here?'

His eyes began to show some animation; a faint glow of gossipful curiosity. 'Not that I know of.' He held open the door. 'Perhaps you'd best come inside.'

Not that he knew of. Following him within, already my hopes were fast withering. It was Moynihan who put them to rest, stepping down the stairway, dressed in a fine silk dressing gown. But it was the expression upon his face I noticed most; so worried. 'What's happened?'

'It's Isobella . . .' No need to ask if he had seen her; his unhappy look was answer enough. If she was not here . . . My fears altered to wider alarm. Where then? With whom?

Moynihan frowned darkly. 'When was this?'

My speedy narration of the events of the previous night proved of little cheer to the man; indeed, he grew troubled in a way I had not seen since the morning he had granted me Isobella's hand. He leaned slightly against the marble pillar that formed the base of the swirling bannisters, seeming to sag. In his silken dressing gown, bulging now, he looked somehow dissolute, as an old drunk.

'Where could she have . . . ?'

I could not help but regard the man with some slight sympathy, despite the dislike I had long felt for him. Was he not suffering the same anguish as myself? For a moment we stood thus, both caught for words, the air silent except for the cries of the birds in St James's Park.

'There's not some cousin she might have gone to?' I asked. 'Some childhood friend?'

He shook his head. 'She has no real family besides myself. Nor any close friends of her own age, as she was educated here by tutors and met few other children.' I was struck by the man's absence of initiative; so unlike his usual self. He seemed quite without suggestions.

'A maidservant perhaps?'

'She had little liking for any I employed.'

One thing was clear; to remain here would gain me nothing except time wasted. 'The others who were present last night might have observed something,' I suggested. 'It would be worth seeking them out.'

'Of course,' agreed Moynihan, his voice still numbed. 'I could come with you.'

'There's no need. Really.'

Only as I turned to leave did he begin to recover himself, his speech, all at once, eager. 'You must tell me if you discover anything. The very instant.'

'Certainly.'

He would not leave it thus but followed me to the door, naggingly close. 'The very instant. You promise?'

A strange reversal; he beseeching, I cool towards him. 'I'll do all I can.'

Thus, that sunny June morning, began the investigations that were to occupy me so long, so exhaustively. What did I hope to learn from the dinner guests? I little knew myself. Perhaps that one among them might have observed my wife was distressed. Even that she had spoken of her intentions, her words then becoming forgotten in the confusion surrounding Miss Symes's drama. Anything. Anything that might point away from the direction I was beginning to fear.

To discover each of the fellows proved a lengthy business, all the more so as I could not help but regularly hurry back to Lark Road, in the hope – a vain one – of finding her returned, or at least having sent some message.

Farre I found first, just arrived at the office, grey-faced after the long evening before. Though full of shocked sympathy, he could offer no help. 'Perhaps she just wanted to be alone for a while. Women can be odd creatures.'

'Alone where? It's been all night.'

He shook his head unhappily, his eyes wishful that he had some answer to give.

Sleak-Cunningham, next, I discovered at the Committee for Sewers, fresh from terrorizing a landlord who had left a giant cesspool uncovered. Though not unkind, I found him disappointingly brusque, offering what brief and practical advice his lack of time allowed; as usual another appointment was looming near. 'She must have gone somewhere. Think carefully. Think of anyone she might have visited.'

It was such thoughts that most alarmed me.

Hove I discovered in the same building, though he proved embarrassed by the matter, seeming to regard it as one unsuited to the attention of a government servant. 'I'm sorry, but I don't know how I may help you.' Indeed, he appeared faintly disgusted, as if I had spat upon his shoe and was calling him to help me with its cleaning. His recourse was to the world of forms. 'If anything springs to mind I'll write you a note.'

Sweet, whom I found in his molasses yard, berating two of his workmen for slackness, showed surprise, but also – much to my annoyance – a reluctance to treat the news with seriousness. 'Running off into the night? What a business. I'm sure she'll turn up before long, with all kinds of silly tales to tell.' His eyes glistened, wondering if I might, while in his office, be made to further discuss the progress of his planned warehouse.

Perhaps he was right, I pondered. Perhaps it would prove to have been no more than a passing ludicrousness. Yet I could not convince myself so for long.

None of the guests having had anything of usefulness to say, I turned my step, reluctantly towards the house of the Lewises. Though they had never been far from my thoughts, I had dearly hoped that some discovery would make a visit thither unnecessary. If the answer to the matter lay with Gideon and Felicia it was hardly likely to be a pretty one. Yet any answer, I was fast coming to feel, would be better than continued uncertainty.

Can one smell deceit, sniff out the bitter scent of lies? So I wondered as I waited in the parlour of the brother and sister, though my nose detected only a mix of wax-polished wood and China tea. Above me stretched a huge canvas depicting Samson's day of glory, in which the famous hero – a dithering-faced fellow, resemblant of a bank clerk surprised to find himself equipped with fearsome muscles – seemed, puzzlingly, to be not so much causing the temple to topple as hiding behind the pillars, in an effort to shelter from the falling masonry.

'Mr Jeavons.' Entering the room, Felicia offered a plump-wristed hand to shake. Her eyes, I observed, avoided my own. Was this because she had never held any liking for me, and was surprised by this unexpected visit? Or because . . . ? Might my wife be here even this instant, concealed in some upstairs room?

'Miss Lewis . . .' The awkwardness of things suspected but unsaid caused me to hesitate. Should I begin with a lengthy explanation? It seemed so clumsy. 'Your brother's not here?'

'He's at work. Perhaps there's some way I can be of usefulness?' She regarded me now, meeting my glance. 'Would you like tea?'

'No, no.' I found my eyes resting upon Delilah, loitering in the shadow of a column, her look perplexed, like a young milliner girl wondering if she may pick her nose without being observed. The best course, I considered, was to begin quietly, hinting, and watch Felicia's reaction. 'I have come about a matter concerning my wife.'

But she did not so much as blink. What was more, when I tried again, telling of Isobella's vanishing, she only frowned with concern. 'But how terrible, Mr Jeavons. What can have become of her?'

A disappointment. I saw no course left to me except to take the plunge. 'What indeed?' For a moment I said nothing, allowing a silence to swell in the room, enlarged by the ticking of a standing clock in the hallway. 'Miss Lewis, I know about the letters.'

She half-smiled, as one puzzled. 'What letters?'

'The two you sent me. Telling of goings-on between Isobella and your brother.'

She only threw me a cold look. 'Mr Jeavons, I'm afraid I don't know what you're talking about.'

'His feelings for her.'

'Feelings? If you are joking – and I can only assume that is the case – then I must say I find your humour of a poor sort.'

I waved away the answer as some annoying curtain. 'She's been here. I know it. Is she here now? Tell me.'

Her face grew hard, unrevealing. 'I will not have you slandering my brother's good name.' Her voice rose. 'Slandering him, what is more, beneath my very roof. Mr Jeavons, I must . . .'

I did not trouble to hear her out, but decided to settle the matter myself. Past her padded form I marched, and up the stairs; past the gloating miser Moses, past the Easter Weekend Adam and Eve, past the punctured football infant in his crib, and the bearded lady yawning upon the cross, until – ignoring the flow of threats from my hostess, close behind – I had tramped through the house, top to bottom, and searched through every room.

But found nothing.

It was as I was stepping from the porch – for company a salvo of Felicia's icy promises of legal redress – that it occurred to me that the woman might not, after all, be pretending. I had only my wife's word that the letters had been in Felicia's hand. Even Gideon's described passion might have been mere invention, to shield some other more loathsome soul.

Nothing was certain. Possibilities seemed to slide back and forth as china plates on ice. I felt almost as one in the centre of some giant conspiracy, with scores of fellows energetically employed day and night to enhance my confusion.

One thing, however, was clear. My own attempt at investigations was making little progress. The best remaining course, it seemed, was to try and engage minds more experienced in such matters than my own. I swiftly made my way to a station of the Metropolitan Police Force.

It was one I had passed many times – usually on the top of wind-blown omnibuses – but never ventured inside. Waiting there, among the crowd of blue-coated fellows hard at work, I was struck by a sense of something obscurely familiar. Thus the way the rooms – containing so many neat desks and noticeboards listing objects stolen – were at once open to one another and also snugly cavernous, and all faced upon a central counter. The bow windows, too, were as of some other place, with their tiny panes of glass, resembling melted bottoms of bottles. Then I realized the building must have previously been an alehouse, probably converted hastily to its new purpose when the Metropolitan force had been established, some twenty years before. Its previous life seemed to linger; the constable on duty at the desk taking the place of the landlord serving pints; two desperate-looking arrivals shouting of stolen wallets supplanting hot fellows eager to quench their lunch-time thirst.

Superintendent Lisle I discovered in an upstairs room – probably once the living quarters of some beer-bellied landlord – with a view down upon a narrow thoroughfare, clattering with traffic. He was a lean, stiff type, whose manner – though affable – gave little away.

'You've come to us very promptly, Mr Jeavons.' His words seemed to contain something like criticism. 'You say she's only been gone a few hours.'

'It's so unlike her to do such a thing.'

'I'm sure.' He leant forward upon the desk. 'Perhaps you can tell me a little of the background to the matter.'

Quite a barrage of questions he asked, occasionally taking down a note – jotted so swiftly that his pencil seemed only to dart across the surface of the paper – though usually he wrote nothing, only silently listening. His eyes, I observed, as I endeavoured to answer as best I might, watched me with care, even intensity, in a way I found unsettling. What was he examining? My clothes, true, were in a poor state, as I had been wearing them without a halt since the morning before. My face, too, was quite a sight – I had glimpsed it, with some surprise, in a mirror at the Lewises' only an hour before – with rings of sleeplessness below my eyes. But what was my appearance to do with the issue?

'Have you, perhaps, had any recent disagreements with your wife?' Lisle listened quietly, tapping his knuckles with his pencil, as I recountered the matter of the poison-pen letters and my fruitless visit to the Lewises. He sat back neatly in his chair. 'I see.' That watchful look. 'You must have been angry.'

'I was upset.'

'But not moved to violence?'

'We had a row.' I was beginning to wonder at the man's questioning; wonder at his thinking. 'You are suggesting, perhaps, that I am responsible for her disappearance?'

The pencil danced in the air in light denial. 'I'm suggesting nothing, Mr Jeavons. I'm merely asking questions.'

For a moment I imagined Felicia hurrying hither before me to set the man's suspicions against myself; feigning the concern of a dutiful subject. But how could she have known I would choose this station and not another? Unless, of course, she had visited them all. But then . . . I rebelled against my own train of thought, striking me, as it did, as most improbable.

But could one be sure? I was struck by another possibility; what if I had fallen victim to the machinations of some jealous rival in the world of drainage? Isobella's very disappearance might be explained thus; an attempt to distract me from my precious work. Of course it was most unlikely, but still . . .

'Let us hope your visit here will prove needless.' Lisle spoke now in a concluding voice. 'But if you've heard no word from her by this time tomorrow, then I ask you to come back. There are measures that should be taken.'

'Certainly.'

Tap, tap, tap with the pencil upon his knuckles, as he observed me. 'We have quite a number of unknown persons discovered, many of them female. Drownings and other accidents for the most part.' A frown. 'You must know of course that I hope and believe such things will have no bearing upon this question. But if nothing is heard, and you have no objection . . .'

'None, of course.'

Thus began, the next day, my expeditions with Constable Collins, to hospitals, parish rooms, undertakers' shops and more. Whether it was the corpses' identities that were the subject of Lisle's interest, or whether it was really my own behaviour, I could not have said. Nevertheless I joined these grim expeditions willingly enough. At least they gave me a sense of something attempted. And if Isobella lay pale and bloodless in such a place, then I must know.

In the meantime I embarked also upon a few studies of my own. Three nights running I took my place opposite the Lewises' home, always in the same spot; in the entrance drive to a grand house just opposite, conveniently placed in the shadowy space between two streetlights. Here there was foliage enough for me to stay largely unseen – though I caused occasional startlement to a few more observant strollers – and I was able to keep watch in peace. The most productive hour, I soon discovered, was late dusk, when lamps had been lit within but the curtains not yet drawn.

Not that I saw any sign of my wife. Indeed the only event of interest – which I observed on the first night – had no proven connection with her disappearance.

It was a row – if so one-sided a battle can be so described – and a furious one. Unfortunately it took place in an upstairs room, allowing me sight of the two involved only when they stepped before the window. Gideon seemed all but silent, loitering abjectly – waiting for the next assault – as some spineless child caught stealing from his mother's purse. By contrast Felicia was constantly on the move, marching into view and away, then back once more, jaws working without halt, as if part of some clockwork device.

If only I could hear their words. Despite the warmth of the evening the window was tight closed – an arrangement somehow typical of their household – and I could discern nothing more than faint and meaningless mumblings. Except, this was, at moments of crescendo, when Felicia's shouts carried clean through the glass, offering me a stunted phrase or two.

'How could you have thought . . .'

'. . . any brother of mine . . .'

Intriguing, but hardly of much utility. Darting a quick glance into the street below – though not in my direction – she quickly pulled shut the thick green curtains, and all was hidden.

The house in Lark Road grew much changed in four days. Most of all there was the silence; a hanging quiet – broken only by Pericles' sudden outbursts of barking – that seemed to permeate the rooms, almost as a smell. There was a smell too, and one ever more pungent: of the remnants of the great dinner. A servant of Farre's aunt had washed and retrieved the dishes and cutlery, but the uneaten courses remained in the kitchen, still glistening with Miss Symes's projections, and some of them gnawed by the dog. Really I should deal with them, I knew. But there was so much else to think of.

I had taken to spending almost all my hours in the parlour, as the study had become abhorrent to me. It was a pleasant room, suffering only the disadvantage of looking directly upon the street, so that the steps of those passing were well audible; I could not help myself, each time I heard a light and feminine tread, from glancing through the window, in case the maker might be my wife.

I had brought my desk into the room, placing it before the piano. There, beneath the watchful faces of Victoria and Albert, staring proudly from beneath their glass domes, I continued labouring upon my drainage plan. Laboured hard, too, despite the reverses so lately suffered. Indeed, rather than growing distracted from such matters, I worked harder than ever, late into the night, using every hour remaining to me after my investigations seeking Isobella. I found in the scheme something like comfort; questions of land heights, effluent flows and depository sites offering a rare sense of the ordinary, of matters achieved.

And I made good progress. The field work, fortunately, I had already all but dealt with before my wife's vanishing. This left me only remaining parts of the description, and of these I was, in four days, able to finish the written text, the diagrams of transformational depositories, and even the drainage map of a future London. In other words, the plan was finally complete.

Not that I considered my task done with. Far from it. Two full weeks remained before I was required to submit my notion to the Committee for Sewers and I had determined to use that time to make a full copy of the whole document. Quite an undertaking this would prove, I knew – it ran to some one hundred and sixty pages, with several dozen maps and illustrations – but how well justified. After all, how could I submit a treatise so valuable to the risk of accidental loss – an inefficient clerk, sifting through papers without proper care, perhaps – or fire. Or deliberate sabotage by rival drainage theorists.

'The logic of the Effluent Transformational Depository is the logic of the unalterable laws of gravity. Thus, we may see, the means of . . .'

My copying of the introduction to my drainage scheme was interrupted by a slow rapping on the front door. Could it be . . . ? The thought was instinctive rather than logical. Isobella's knock was different; never so harsh.

I had had only two visitors since her vanishing. Farre had appeared on the evening of the first day, to offer any help he might give; a kindly thought, if one of no great utility. Then Miss Symes had come, twice, though less charitably of motive, claiming on each occasion to have neglected to collect some dismal possession, '. . . that I thought I'd best take 'fore someone makes off with it.' The objects – old dish-cloths and the like – were so foul and valueless that I was sure they formed no more than an excuse, her real purpose being a malicious curiosity to learn the extent of my disaster. If it were her now, I considered, making my way towards the hallway, then I would not so much as allow her into the house. I would suffer no more of her loathsome gawpings.

Opening the door, however, I found before me not the bulk of Miss Symes's person, but the pale and wizened form of the Reverend Michael Bowrib.

He looked flustered. 'Oh Mr Jeavons. I'm so glad to have found you in.'

'Vicar, what a surprise.' I had never greatly liked the man, and wondered what could have brought him. 'Come in.'

'I can't stay.' He ventured no more than a step inside the hallway. 'You see I've just heard about this awful business of . . .'

So he knew; it came as a slight surprise to me, as I had not yet so much as visited the church. But such news travels fast. The same network of gossiping informers of which my wife had formed a keen – if temporary – part, had now been carrying accounts of her own scandal.

'Has she returned?' Bowrib was excited; he seemed even forgetful of uttering the sympathetic words one would expect of one in his profession. I wondered if his motives for visiting differed greatly from Miss Symes's thirst for news of my catastrophe.

'She's not.'

A deep nod. 'Then could I talk to you?'

His eagerness was beginning to gnaw. 'It's kind of you, vicar, but I really don't need any help. The matter will soon be decided, I'm sure.'

'But, Mr Jeavons, you don't understand.' He seemed at risk of bursting quite open. 'I've seen her. Just yesterday afternoon.'

Oddly enough, the thought of her walking freely about, for all to meet, was one that had hardly occurred to me. 'Yesterday?' Three days after her vanishing. Why had she not visited me? Written to me? Something.

The nub of his message out, Bowrib subsided a little. 'I thought nothing of it at the time, but then I had no idea what had happened. I only learnt this afternoon, you see . . .' He wrung together his bony hands, uneasy now at the subject.

I regretted the suspicions I had felt towards the man;

he had been motivated only by concern. 'How did she appear?'

'Distracted, I suppose – she hardly replied to my greeting – but otherwise there seemed nothing amiss about her.'

Nothing amiss? I felt chokingly angry. 'Where was she?'

'Pall Mall. Going towards Haymarket. At a stiff pace, too.'

Perhaps she was in trouble; beset with some horror she could not confide. It was not likely, true, but possible. Or . . .

'Have you seen this woman? Round about here, yesterday afternoon?'

'Should I ought'er 'ave?'

Constable Collins towered over the match-seller, so huge and straight of bearing that he looked – though his clothes were those of a rakish young costermonger – almost more exactly like a policeman than when in his uniform. He regarded his quarry with a certain glumness. 'Then you've not seen her?'

'Certainly I've not, I'm sure, Mr sir.'

The constable ignored the fellow's snide tone, merely taking back from him the locket I had provided, with its likeness of Isobella. As we turned away, however, the other murmured, in an under-breath voice calculated just to be within our hearing, 'And a merry Christmas to you, Inspector.'

Collins seemed faintly to wince. Not for the first time that afternoon.

It was not his fault that he was so visible of profession; if any were to blame it was rather Lisle, who had suggested he attempt such disguise. Collins, for all his lumbering size, was sharp aware that – in the eyes of metropolitan scavengers, and managers of dubiously smart cafes – his civilian dress left him as inconspicuous as a pyramid of ancient Egypt lodged upon Oxford Street, claiming itself a mere lamp-post.

As the hours had passed and we had made not the slightest progress, he had shown increasing unhappiness.

The Haymarket of London; magnet of fashionable wealth and fashionable vice, grand carriages clawing their way up the slope and rattling keenly down, before the most splendid of shops and cafes; where every kind of bauble may be bought, and outside which every manner of beggar, thief, pimp, and seller-of-nothings lurk, in hope. For all my anger I could not help still wanting to catch a glimpse of her. My eye would be caught by some back-turned girl with faint resemblance, capturing – for an instant – all my concentration, until she laughed into the air, showing her stranger's profile.

'I ought to be getting back to the station before long, I s'pose, sir.' Collins glanced at his watch, guilty at his lack of success. 'Perhaps she didn't come this way after all.'

'Perhaps so.' I had observed a change in the fellow, and also Superintendent Lisle, since I had brought Bowrib to see them. Not that their watchfulness towards me was gone; it was rather reduced, their suspended judgements not fallen into firm decision, but leaning less strong against me. Progress? I remained wary of them both. Who knew what was really in their thoughts; they might even be deliberately trying to lure me from my guard.

'The superintendent will be in touch shortly I'm sure,' announced Collins, in the manner of one keen to have some practical suggestion after such a day of failure. 'Or you could come back with me now if you like.'

'I have some other things to attend to,' I answered. 'Perhaps I could have back the locket?'

'Of course.' He fumbled it from his pocket with a huge hand. 'Sorry, sir.'

I watched the fellow leave – winning glances and grins from those he lumbered past – but did not myself step from my place. For some time, as we went about our fruitless work, I had been pondering that, without such a beacon for company, I might well prove more successful than he.

In the event, setting about the task, I discovered it to be no easy one; even without the man at my side I found myself tarnished merely by having been seen in his company.

'Hello, if it's not the copper's friend.'

'And what might I do for you, Mr Peeler?'

I elected to wait, burning away time by walking to that favourite spot of mine, Hungerford Market, then across the bridge of the same name – affording a fine dusk-time view of St Paul's, rising smokily above the ragged City buildings – and on, as far as the huge Lion Brewery in Southwark. By the time I returned to the Haymarket it was dark. The famous street was quite altered, shining with gaudy gaslight, and teeming with life; predators and their elegant prey.

I had shown the locket – lit up each time with the flare of a match – to no more than three fellows before I found myself in hope. It was a dog-seller I was stood before, and something in his eyes told me her face was familiar to him.

'Why you asking?'

'I'm a friend of hers.' I struck a further match, fingers juggling with too many objects; he could not take the locket himself as his hands were both full with King Charles spaniels, mournfully watching the contortions going on above their heads. One made a feint at snapping at my thumb. 'It's important.' Taking back the locket, I held out a clutch of coins.

He eyed them coolly, the dogs too. 'Oh yes?'

I added a couple more, and, with a certain nonchalance – doubtless that he would not weaken his bargaining power by over-friendliness – he gave a nod of acknowledgement. 'Bit older than that now, is she?'

The strange excitement I felt. Though Isobella had given me the locket at the time of our engagement, the likeness had been taken a year or more earlier, and the face depicted, while recognizable as hers, was still girlish. 'She is.'

He gave a slow nod. 'Yesterday afternoon it was. Came over t'have a look at the dogs, cooing and that like they does. Bit funny she looked, I remember.' He frowned, perhaps trying to find words. 'Angry, but with herself, sort of. Like she wanted someone to clout her one. Made me wonder if she was on the gin.'

A curious description. Hardly respectful either, though this was no moment for indignation. 'Was she alone?'

He shook his head, watching me with a kind of grim curiosity, doubtless wondering at my connection with the woman. 'With a bloke.'

Perhaps I should not have been surprised. But to hear it told . . . my wife, whom I had lived with all those months, and thought I knew . . .

Of course I guessed who it must be. 'A thin man, was he? Not much older than me, with a head that seemed to bob about?'

To my surprise the lad shook his head vehemently. 'Naah, naah. Grey-haired geezer he was, what there was left of it up there. Dressed rich, but sort of oily the way he moved.'

Not Gideon. 'But that's impossible . . .'

'True as can be.' The lad spoke keenly, glancing with hard eyes at the coins in my hand. 'See now. Here's 'im.' With this he began strutting before me – causing the spaniels' ears to flap in time with his jaunty step – his chin jutting forward, and tongue licking his lips in a music-hall mime of old man's lechery. 'That sort. Couldn't keep his eyes off her.'

I was disgusted. Also baffled, as the description bore no resemblance to anyone I could think of. 'Did you see where they went?'

'Getting dark an' that, weren't it. Anyways, I wouldn't be sure they stuck together long, what with her bawling at him like she was.'

Another surprise. 'Bawling?'

'Yeah. Fit to scare half the street. After she done with cooing at the dogs they goes strolling off an' I saw him murmur som'it into her ear. But she couldn't 'ave liked it none, as before you could blink she was roaring fit to burst.' The boy's voice took on an aristocratic drawl. '"'Ow dare you suggist sich a thing? 'Ow dare you?"' He grinned, proud of his own mimicking abilities. 'Then she goes storming off, but none too fast, as if she didn't want to lose him. She needn't have worried, as he was close 'nough behind. I think it were off that ways. Into one of the cafes, p'raps.'

His story was hardly reassuring, though it did offer, if one set aside his own vile conclusions, the chance that my wife had been teetering on the brink of catastrophe rather than already lost.

The cafes of the Haymarket. These were splendid affairs – finest in London, and of a kind I had never before thought of venturing inside – with the most modern of decoration and the highest of prices; the cost of a mere brandy was hardly to be believed. Customers were mostly on a par; splendidly dressed fellows, careful in the way they lounged. Alongside the grandeur, however, a darker element was also discernible; thus the young women who sat alone at tables, many of them possessing beauty and dressed in the finest crinolines, but who conjured up a sense of the unexpectedly familiar – recalling to mind nighttime alleys – as they glanced coyly at men passing by, offering them perhaps a greeting, a mistaken recognition, in voices a jot harsh for those so finely attired.

At each cafe I ordered the cheapest item on the menu, whatever it might be, then delayed the waiter with chatter, until I deemed the moment was right to show the locket. After trying five establishments, however, and causing corresponding depletion of the coins in my pocket, I had bought myself nothing except scornful glances at my simple attire. I was beginning to wonder – and hope – if I had been foolish to think she had visited any such place. At the sixth, however, the waiter examined the portrait with more interest.

'I might have.' The man, a smoothly knowing sort, surprised me with his absence of wariness; so much in contrast with the responses of his colleagues in other cafes. Nor did this establishment, the Castelnau, seem to have anything less to hide than its rivals; even as I had entered two finely plumed young women had offered me bright smiles, one asking me if I was not the fellow she had met on Tuesday last.

The waiter hovered beside the table. 'Though my memory can be a little slow at times.'

I held out some coins. He eyed them without speaking until I added to their number.

'Now I recall. Yes, she was in here, I'm sure.'

'Yesterday afternoon?'

'That's right. Something like five, I'd say.'

I swallowed my remaining pride. 'With another?' With a sinking heart I watched the waiter nod. 'An older man? With greying hair, not much of it?'

Here, however, he shook his head. 'Nope. Young fellah, hardly past twenty. Rich by the look of him. Son of some nob, I'd say.'

Different again? My wife seemed to be familiar with half the manhood of London. 'You're sure this was yesterday?'

'Certainly I am.' He regarded me confidently. 'They were in here for a while. Looked like they were getting on close, too. I saw their feet under the table.'

A few short words, spoken to me by a stranger, in a place not known to me until that day. Yet their effect upon me . . . Gone were my last hopes. And I was left with whom? With Isobella the dirty. Isobella the loose, the cheap. Isobella the harlot; except to her own husband, for whom it was always 'too soon'. Isobella the betrayer.

And Joshua Jeavons the cuckold of cuckolds.

'You all right?' the waiter was frowning.

'Of course.' I had to be gone from this place, had to feel a breeze upon me. I threw the coins upon the table. The other plucked them up, swiftly counting their value as he slipped them into his pocket. Getting to my feet I found him raising a hand to delay me.

'Important to you is it, this?'

'What if it is?' If he had more to tell I was by no means sure I wanted to hear.

'This wasn't the first time they've been in. I've seen her before, I'm sure. And as for him, lately he's been almost a regular.'

'So?'

The waiter must have heard the warning note in my voice. 'I'm only trying to help you, mister.' He opened his face, offering a smile of reassurance. 'I'm saying they might be in again. Especially him. If you come evening time, there's a good chance. I could point him out to you.' He slipped his hand into his money pocket. 'Of course it'd be risky for me, and that.'

More bartering; bartering for further poisonously wounding revelations. I shook my head. 'Not now. Perhaps another time.'

Trafalgar Square with its roar of clattering vehicles half seen by lamplight; brougham cabs and heavy wagonettes, brewers' drays and whitechapels laden with vegetables, dog carts and brightly painted omnibuses, all swirling in slow procession. Though I hardly heard their din. The scurrying crowds; every kind of beggar, swaggering young clerks, milliner girls and genteel ladies, fast racetrack fellows and stiffly doleful military sorts freshly loosed from squeezed regiments, all elbowing forward. Had I known my own wife any better than these strangers?

Whitehall with its lurching façades of erratic buildings, hardly two the same; half-timbered inns, brick shops, stone government buildings making a strange parade above such a traffic-crushed thoroughfare. Ahead the masonry of the Palace of Westminster loomed into view, silhouetted against a smoky moonlit sky, the two intended towers still little more than stumps; fists vanishing into gloves of scaffolding.

Even these seemed changed to me. Spoiled.

'I saw their feet under the table.'

All those months of courtship, of engagement, of marriage. Had she simply ceased to care at some moment, some hour? Or had the whole long journey been a deception, from that very first afternoon, when she had found me in her father's library, and asked if I would stay for tea.

'Son of some nob, I'd say.'

Was that what she had wanted all along? A dapper young lord? Then why trouble the life of Joshua Jeavons? Why show enthusiasm to be his wife?

Victoria Street, that new thoroughfare, still in the midst of construction, roadway raised up above marshy wasteland to either side, where the slum of Palmer's village had lately stood. The wide scars of demolition were clothed in mist, a gang of street urchins faintly discernible through the gauze, filling the rare patch of empty space with some ragged game, their shouts muted by the foggy air.

I glared at the scene, almost as if it, too, had done me injury. Past the foundations of great buildings soon to line the new street I went, past Westminster House of Correction, and the Grosvenor Canal Basin – giving forth its stench of oily and stagnant water – and to my own street.

I ignored Pericles' growls and, lamp hissing before me, stepped into Isobella's room. The bedroom of both of us, it should have been. I began with the cupboard. So much had I been a stranger here that I had never seen its contents before, never even opened its doors.

Most of the objects – rather to my surprise – dated from her girlhood; plaster dogs and horses, dolls in pretty dresses – all in a remarkable state of preservation – and a medallion souvenir from Brighton.

The shelf below contained books; quite a little

library, also of her youth. She seemed to have kept every volume of exercises from her studying days, and I found myself discovering the same round, but uncertain-seeming writing describing all manner of things: animals to be found in Sweden, ways of cooking beef, simple mathematical calculations, the splendours of the Magna Carta. In addition she had kept many journals, most of them issues of the same publication, titled 'Household Wisdom', with the description beneath, 'For the useful instruction of young ladies'. Leafing through one such, I found myself studying 'What every young lady should know, for her future happiness'.

> A clean house is a house respected and content. Young ladies, be sure you make your own thus. Objects that may shine pleasantly – silverware, the faces of clocks, and items of china – should be made to do so. All surfaces should be kept free of dust and settlings from the atmosphere, while . . .

Here at least I could find no fault with Isobella. I glanced down the page.

> It is most unseemly for a young and still unmarried lady to entertain a male guest without other company present to join in their cheerful conversation. Most suitable as candidates for this pleasant task are, of course, the young lady's parents, or a female friend. Failing this a servant will suffice; she can be employed perhaps quietly providing tea, and, for the young man, even refreshment of a more solid kind. Thus . . .

I recalled my first visit to Trowbridge Street, that winter's afternoon. Yes, this lesson, too, she had evidently studied. If only she had kept it more presently in her thoughts.

Having finished with the books and magazines, I set to work upon the framed pictures upon the mantelpiece. I had found no diary, but might there not be some letters? Even notes of arrangements made, hurriedly jotted? Something to tell of a secret life. The pictures were small affairs, depicting biblical or moving scenes; a crofter's dog mourning upon his dead master's old chair and suchlike. I prised open the backs, removing the prints themselves before dropping the separate pieces on the floor. Nothing.

'Looked like they were getting on close, too.'

I began to work more swiftly, pulling forth dresses from the wardrobe. Now I plucked shoes, a coat, blouses and stockings and bonnets and more, corsets, her very undergarments, letting them drop upon the floor, throwing them before me.

'I saw their feet under the table.'

At once I found myself gripped as by a fever, as one drunkenly possessed, hurling, tearing the cloth. Pericles made feints at my hands, his head flicking back – eyes rolling with flashes of white, giving him the look of a creature demented – as scarves and hats and corsets flew above him, casting leaping shadows on the walls with the light of the hissing lamp. Until the cupboards were all empty.

I had found nothing.

It was then, my glance passing level with the top surface of the ransacked chest of drawers, that I saw the tangle of cloth and needles of my wife's embroidery. These, somehow, had escaped being thrown to the ground. Sat on top was the knife with the decoration of embattled ships of the line. I glanced at the thing for only a moment. Then slipped it into my pocket.

Pericles uttered a low growl.

Joshua Jeavons crouched in the midst of the wreckage of his wife's possessions, turning the pages of her young ladies' magazines, though he seems not to take in the meaning of the print. Joshua Jeavons absorbed, eyes seeming faintly to burn, as one who has passed round a corner in the road, into a harsher and more ugly landscape, to which he is slowly coming to adjust.

I was sitting there still when I was brought to the

present by the sound of a knock on the front door.

What if it had been Isobella? The question occurs to me not infrequently as I sit in my Torinese rooms, so high of ceiling and window, rich with smells of food and smoke, drifting inside with the cooling evening air. I would have been angry, of course. But – I like to imagine – controlled of myself. Coldly hearing her out, then offering my reply.

I have to admit, though, I am by no means sure.

Fortunately it was not her. Pulling open the front door, I found stood before me the stiff frame of her father. 'Joshua, I'm so glad to find you in. Have you news?'

I had all but forgotten the man, and my promise to inform him instantly of any discoveries made. 'You'd best come in.'

Lamp in hand I led the way to the parlour, littered as it was with drainage documents. I cleared a chair of diagrams of Effluent Transformational Depositories that he might sit, observing, as I did so, a look of dubiousness upon the fellow's face. Probably the house did appear a little strange now, with its jumbled and neglected rooms and the pervading scent of rotting food.

'There is news,' I told him.

He nodded, tautly eager. Looking at the man – the lamp illuminating one side of his head with bright clarity, but leaving the other in darkness – I realized how changed I was towards him. Four days ago I had regarded us as allies in our concern for Isobella. Now I was no longer so sure our interests coincided. I did not want to discover my wife with him at my side. Nor, for that matter, with the lumbering Constable Collins. No, I wanted to find her alone.

'She's been seen,' I told him. 'Just yesterday, by the Reverend . . .'

Though relieved, Moynihan did not seem as surprised as I had expected by the news. Surely it was remarkable that his vanished daughter had been jauntily promenading London streets? Or, I pondered, was this perhaps not the first time she had disappeared? He sat back in his chair, frowning, as might a general puzzling upon unclear reports from his scouts. 'Nothing since then? Have you been down to the Haymarket?'

'With a police constable. We questioned a number of people.'

'And?'

'They told him nothing of usefulness.'

'That's all?'

No. I would not have him know the rest. It was for me alone. 'That's all.'

A slow nod. The way he watched me, I wondered if he had guessed I knew more. 'Joshua, we really must be as one on this terrible matter. It's of such importance.' He glanced at me, stiffly earnest. 'I know we've had differences in the past, but I ask you to put such matters behind you. We must work together.'

The lamp began spluttering unhappily, and I rose to light a candle before it expired. 'And what of you? Have you had any thoughts? Perhaps some person to whom she might have flown?'

He shook his head.

'Has she ever done such a thing before? Or made you suspect she might?'

'Never.'

The lamp finally died. Sitting down opposite the man, observing his features by the flickering candle, I had the strange feeling that he, too, knew more than he was prepared to tell. 'You're sure.'

'Of course.'

The impression lingered, however, remaining strong in my thoughts even when – having taken the names of the two policemen I had been working with – he rose to leave.

'I had hoped to see you at the office, at least to know what had happened.' His tone, as we made our way into the hall, was faintly reproachful.

I had no intention of sounding apologetic. 'I've not had time. Nor will I have for a while, as far as I can see.' I gave him his hat. 'Besides, there's little enough work for me now, with the Sweet Warehouse design complete.'

He nodded, relenting. 'But we must stay in touch. It's so important. Bring me any news, the moment you have it. Come to the office, come to my house, day or night. And I'll do the same for you.'

He offered a hand and I shook it, though by no means convinced of the partnership thus signified. Opening the front door a warm gust of wind blew inside, causing the candle flame to lean frantically, then die, leaving a tiny and short-lived glow at the tip of the wick. There was no sign, now, of the moon, and the darkness outside was as thick as that within, enveloping us both.

'I'll get a lamp,' I offered.

'It's of no matter.'

I could hear the fellow feeling his way towards the door – banging noisily into the coat-stand en route – and, beyond, his tread changed as it found the stone step.

'Don't forget to tell me any news. The moment you hear.' His voice, calling out from the foggy blackness, sounded unexpectedly near.

'I won't.'

I heard his footsteps echoing away, and he was gone.

Of course it was to be the last time I saw him. At least alive.

Chapter Seven

The great globe turns in slow revolution, and turns again, as some giant millstone ever grinding. Grinding upon men's hopes and fears, upon their passions, their hatreds, slowly reducing all to fine dust. Grinding likewise upon the small life of Joshua Jeavons, in ways constantly unexpected to him.

Thirty times the globe revolves. Then thirty again, air and gases – warmed mightily by the sun's glow – sweeping slowly back and forth across its upper half, consolidating the heat they bring to the lands beneath. Sixty full rotations. With each the certainties enjoyed by Joshua Jeavons – mere speck though he is within such immensity – grow a little more battered, as apples in a tumbling box. Yet their reduction, sad to say, has still far to go.

Where may we find him after two months have passed, early upon a Wednesday morning? Not at his house in Lark Road, a cup of tea comfortably before him. Nor at his father-in-law's office, working upon some quandary of railway mechanics. Nor yet in the molasses yard of Mr Harold Sweet – whose warehouse is now fast rising up from its foundations – or the debating chamber of the Metropolitan Committee for Sewers, frenzied with summer accusations. No, we find him before one of the larger London docks, where – driven by no motive beyond simple need – he finds himself, for the first time, seeking a meagre day's wage emptying ships' cargoes.

Joshua Jeavons nervously taking his place among the roughened morning crowd; that mob of every kind of unfortunate, bankrupt and ne'er do well, all of them drawn thither – himself likewise – because there, alone in all London, a day's pay may be won by any man lucky in the morning scramble, regardless of skill or character.

Restlessness in the air as the minutes tick by; shoving matches breaking out, threats of later 'settlings'. Until a rolling, rhythmic din fills the air; the chiming of a hundred clocks across the eastern metropolis, ships' bells too, all announcing the hour. Eight o'clock. The gates swing open and the crowd surges in, segmenting itself into smaller groups before the line of calling foremen – the choosers – who set to work picking out faces already known to them, and favoured.

'Taylor, in you go. Clock Quay. Reeve, you too.'

The crowd is so alive with shouting of the foreman's name, so fevered with arms waved in the air, with fellows jumping on to the backs of others to be better noticed, that it resembles some angrily tentacled sea creature.

'Keith, you're in. Clock Quay. And you, Sturrock. Thomas, Rock . . .'

Joshua Jeavons, shouting as loud as the rest of them. Joshua Jeavons, appearance much altered with weeks passed; shirt collar frayed, frock coat worn and shapeless, and on his back a strange and battered leather sack, fitting so well to his frame that he might have been carrying it since birth. His step may be as impatient as ever, but his eyes also are different; distracted and seeming to stare, troubling to any who catches his glance.

All across the metropolis, too, the weeks had brought changes. The summer heat, once begun, showed little relenting, and grass in the parks and gardens was yellowed, leaves on the trees fading to brown, as if autumn were arrived months early. Street dust was little less than a plague, blinding the eyes as it flew, coating alike window panes, boots of gentlemen, woodwork of carriages, and the foreign vessels riding in upon the river; painting all a sandy beige, as if eager to transform London into some angular desert.

The heat seemed to gain strength from its very endurance, slowly baking the stone, bricks and timbers of the metropolis until they were its allies, strangely warm to touch even at night. The air itself seemed to have caught fever, robbing Londoners of sleep, making snug beds unexpected foes, sheets hot against the skin.

Other changes had come, too; changes less discernible to the eye, though no less awesome for that; changes quietly evidenced by the great number of funeral processions plying the streets. Normally to be seen only in the central part of the day, these bleakly solemn cortèges were now an all but continuous sight, from first light of dawn until after night was fallen, as undertakers – blissfully overcome with employment – found they had barely daylight hours enough to cope with the wealth of trade fallen into their laps.

Most were poor affairs, for tradesmen and the like, with only one carriage, and no more than two or three feathermen, drunkenly parading their black ostrich plumes. Here and there, however, was some grand death, with a splendid hearse – all glass and wood and tiny cast-iron crosses sprouting from the roof – as well as several mourning coaches, and twenty or more feathermen, coachmen and mutes, these last decked out in finest gowns, gloves, and silk hat bands, and dour as could be.

The cause of this sudden thriving of the industry of death was a mystery to nobody. Week by week the toll of victims of the disease was listed in *The Times*, edging upwards with each issue. Coroners' reports on other pages filled in the details behind mere numbers; sometimes the malady would single out a victim, leaving his family and neighbours untouched, if shocked and fearful. Elsewhere a whole street or court might be struck, with dozens taken, and more fleeing their homes in hope of saving themselves. Mostly it was poor areas that were afflicted, though not only such;

among the list was the occasional government official, financier or businessman, while in a Wandsworth terrace of newly built houses and most respectable residents, more than two dozen were taken in a single week.

Again and again the coroners noted, to my interest and satisfaction, that the malady frequently appeared in the vicinity of defective sewers. Worst struck of all the metropolis was Jacob's Island, the 'Venice of Drains'; that slum of crazed wooden walkways and overhanging rooms, close by which I had examined the sewer outlets. Now it was the disease centre of London, and within its black alleys and crowded dens of population the Cholera ranged freely, snapping up victims by the score.

And what of measures taken to counter this evil? The Metropolitan Committee for Sewers – that fine institution, in which I had such faith, and to which I had sent a full copy of my Drain Plan – had, I had been proud to see, put its machinery into motion with admirable promptness. Indeed, every Londoner within pistol shot of the river could smell the evidence of the Committee's determination. Flushing drains into the Thames had been conducted on nothing less than an heroic scale, with noxious effluent expelled by the hundreds of tons.

Yet, strangely, the Cholera had shown no signs of abating. Indeed, it grew steadily worse, confounding all predictions, and striking panic into the surviving population, poor and rich alike. In newspaper leaders there was concern at possible public unrest.

My dearest Joshua,

I write knowing myself to be beyond forgiveness. Nor do I ask any such thing. Rather I seek to tell you that I AM truly sorry for the hurt I may have caused you.

It was never my intent. Know this. Contemptible though I am become, I was not always so. Joshua,

> believe me. It is not my nature. Nor am I to blame alone. My greatest misery is that you, who are possessed only of goodness, should be the sufferer.
>
> It is better I am gone. Forget me now. Remove me from your thoughts as a thing unworthy. I will never trouble your life again. But try, I entreat you, to think upon me not too harshly.
>
> I am not so wicked as I seem.
>
> Sincerely yours,
> Isobella.

Thus it was; the sole communication received by me from my wife. It had arrived a full week after her vanishing, delivered to the house one afternoon when I was out, by hand – if only I had been there to see the face of its bringer – and written upon a strange sort of paper, that might have been used for the wrapping of flowers.

Confusion; this was my soonest response. I was filled with desire to believe the sad humility of her words. Glancing over the letter a second time, however, I grew harder. Had I not believed enough already? Enough for a hundred cuckolds. Why should this be anything other than an attempt to waylay my just anger. She asked me to forget her, to remember her without over-harshness; perhaps she knew of my searchings, and was fearful I might soon discover her.

Not that my investigations seemed so well advanced. In fact, sadly, this could hardly have been further from the case.

Superintendent Lisle had shown signs of losing interest in the matter almost from the moment I became – thanks to Bowrib's sighting of my wife – such a reduced candidate for murderer. Indeed, though he never said it clear, he hinted there was probably now little that could be done.

'We'll continue to put out descriptions, of course. But having heard nothing for so long makes me wonder if she mayn't be staying somewhere quite willingly.' He lightly tapped his knuckles with his pencil, his look politely knowing. 'Perhaps not even in this country. In which case . . .'

I found myself angered by such insinuations. Although there was certainly evidence enough to support them.

And as for my own labouring upon the mystery? Another man might have let the matter rest. He might have endeavoured to forget Isobella, as she herself had urged, or even have left the country; flown to America or Russia to start a new life. To stop? To cease to inflict pain upon myself with hourly needle-sharp ruminations, and instead begin to piece together a new and fresh existence? No, I do not believe I considered doing so even for an instant. Isobella was as an itch that would give me no peace; a potent mixture of mystery and unendurable insult.

Thus I threw myself into the task of further expeditions to the Haymarket; day after day of them. Though, to my disappointment, these evinced only one solitary discovery, and this was more alarming than useful.

'You ain't the only one no more.' The dog-seller had recounted the information only after much negotiation, the two spaniels watching me, one sniffing my sleeve. 'There's another looking for her now.'

For some reason my thoughts turned to the man he had last seen Isobella with. 'The old one? Whom she bawled at?'

'Naah, naah.' He took a kind of pleasure at my wrong guess. 'Completely different. Not posh. A pale bloke, as if there was no blood inside 'im. Pale hair, an' eyes like water. Quite a startler to look at, he was.'

Another description that meant nothing to me. My wife seemed to be keeping strange company indeed. 'He wasn't from the police?'

'Nothing like,' the lad answered firmly. ''E didn't have no nice painting of 'er like you did. Just a drawing, on a bit of paper, rather messy, though it was her right enough. And he was dead keen.' He regarded me a touch scornfully. 'Gave more dosh than you did.'

My concern at this mysterious rival made all the more galling the relentless failure of the Cafe Castelnau to offer up either my wife or the young aristocrat. One of my first actions had been to take up the offer of the smooth-faced waiter, and I spent evening after evening of expensive vigils at a corner table, watching for the man to signal the arrival of the aristocratic son. Watching in vain. As days passed my confederate began to grow irritable at the delay in receiving his sovereigns.

'They've no right to vanish off like that. The fellah should be more regular in his ways.'

With time my declining capital forced me to abandon my table, and instead observe the cafe from a distance; I would stand on the pavement opposite, sometimes for hours at a time, watching all who came and went, and straining to observe my ally within; a regime of seemingly motiveless loitering that caused much bafflement to the match-sellers and beggars I had for company.

'Enjoy hangin' about in the dust all evenin', does you?'

Money. It was lack of it that turned my thoughts to Moynihan, and caused me to reflect – with faint surprise – on his failure to show his face. Strange it was, especially in view of his determination, at our last meeting, that we should work closely together. Though his silence had suited me well enough at first, as my few savings became depleted relief turned to something different. I needed work and, unhappy prospect though a return to the man's employment was to me, I could think of nowhere else where it might be found.

Thus I made my way to the office; strange to me after my long absence. I soon learned there had been changes here too; alterations that seemed to go far in explaining my father-in-law's behaviour.

'He's hardly ever here now,' Farre recounted in a

hushed tone. 'The word is he's engaged on some secret project for the admiralty.' He leant closer, eyes beady with rumour. 'Nobody knows for sure, of course, but Mr Luke claims it's a new quay for Portsmouth, that can be moved open and shut with steam engines, while Ned Harris says it's some new gunboat, small but very fast, with a single but mighty piece of artillery.'

As if such details mattered much to me. From Barrett the butler I learned that the man was now rarely to be found at his home either. Most annoying. There seemed no course left except to write to him.

The reply I received within only a few days. Though most courteous, he answered, to my disappointment, that he was unable to employ me at the moment, though he hoped to do so at some later date. He enclosed three sovereigns. Curiously he made no mention of Isobella.

The sovereigns, at least, were most welcome. Two I sewed into the hem of my frock coat, that they would be preserved, ready for payment to the waiter at the Cafe Castelnau if need should happily arise. The third was my own, and served to keep hunger at bay, at least for some further days. These I used to tour other engineering companies, although without success. It was no time to seek work, and even a visit to Harold Sweet at his molasses yard proved unavailing. The man nodded sombrely as I recounted my difficulties. 'I'd take you on if I could. You know that right enough. But trade's been so slack just of late that I may have to rid myself of a couple of these here.'

Only when all but the last pennies were gone did I resort to selling household possessions. A desperate measure, certainly, but once having settled upon it, I hurled myself into the task with enthusiasm, even a kind of passion. Several times I scoured the house – each shelf, cupboard, drawer – that no object, however paltry in value, might be overlooked. Again and again I journeyed back and forth, carrying weighty articles from pawnbroker to second-hand shop and back, that I might locate, by scientific method, where the highest prices could be found.

The process proved something of a revelation. Treasures of our parlour I had long regarded with soaring pride proved worth far less than I had imagined. Even the busts of Queen Victoria and Albert, whose dust-protective glass domes Isobella had kept so vigorously polished, fetched only a few shillings. Though disappointing, such discoveries offered up a kind of fascination as I recalled the givers – most of the objects having been wedding presents – and learnt exactly their generosity or mean-spiritedness.

I sold everything: chairs and tables, mirrors, pots and pans, my own clothes – indeed, as I realized later, more of these than was wise – and even my wife's abandoned dresses and undergarments. Within only a few days the house was emptied, and the rooms gave forth strange echoing sounds as I walked among them.

As for the sum raised, though not a huge one, it would have likely provided me with a frugal living well into the autumn months. You will doubtless have observed, however, that I use the words *would have*. This is because the capital did not remain in my hand long enough to discover. Within only a few days I had used the bulk of it, on the renting of a slum room.

A slum room? A strange course of action, it may seem, for one who has just rescued himself so narrowly from hunger. At the time, however, I assure you the notion struck me as nothing less than a stroke of genius.

The decision was immediate. Weeks of fruitless traversing of the metropolis, back and forth from my home to the vicinity of Haymarket, had inspired in me more than a little impatience. Weeks passed and the Cafe Castlenau had yielded up nothing. Yet she must be, I was convinced, somewhere within those maze-like streets; must be known to some among the rush of people forever brushing past one on the way. It was as if London itself were some gargantuan lock, for which I lacked the key.

ROOM TO RENT. RAITES FAIVRIBULL.

The sign caught my eye one afternoon as I was striding down a grimy way between the Seven Dials and Leicester Square, not far from Katie's den, and within a few hundred yards of Sweet's molasses yard. Hand-scrawled on a piece of vile paper, it had been stuck on to a door with a rusty nail. I paused, filled with thought.

The landlord proved easy to discover; an old Jew with tired-of-life eyes and a beard as long as his face, evidently puzzled that someone of respectability should show interest in such an area. The room itself was no better than one would expect, with bare, plaster-flaked walls that gave forth a strong odour of damp, and for furniture only a collapsed bed, and a chair well on the road to final extinction. The building containing it was as others of its kind, with a single privy – a spot of unutterable vileness – serving a dozen fiercely populated rooms, and no piped water.

The position of the place, however, interested me greatly. As the crow flies it was no more than a couple of hundred yards from the grand cafes of the Haymarket. Also it possessed a commanding view; in addition to the road below, a second street – one that led up from the very direction of the Cafe Castelnau – aimed itself exactly towards the room's cracked and soot-coated window, providing a vista of all manner of traders and beggars and thieves, vanishing into smallness with distance. The rent, if not cheap, was within my powers, even though the landlord – grown suspicious of my purpose – demanded three months as a start.

My design was to use it as a daylight advance post from which I might observe the crowds beneath;

though I could hardly envisage my wife having any business in such a slum of a district, she might well use it as a route to Covent Garden or Holborn. To this end I thoroughly cleaned the window, and carried up a telescope previously used in my engineering work.

From such a base I could also, I reasoned, become quickly known to the local population, subtly blending in among the poor wretches and winning their trust. If I showed my wife's likeness to everybody in the vicinity – so near where she had last been observed – there was surely a good chance I would find at least one soul with a useful tale to tell.

In the event, winning the co-operation of such people proved more easily said than done.

Thus the fellow who inhabited the room above my own. A large man with a round face much like a gnarled orange, his main interest was in vicious-tempered dogs, which I could often hear barking through the ceiling. From overheard chatter I gathered he entered these in rat-killing contests in East End beer houses. His response, when shown the locket, was to stare at me strangely. 'And who're you then, askin' questions?' As if in answer to his own, he then tugged the lead of the animal at his feet, causing it to bark menacingly. 'I ain't seen her, nor nobody else you're curious 'bout.'

So too it was with the Irish family – too numerous to easily count, though they all of them inhabited a room no larger than my own – who lived just across the landing. When I questioned the mother she seemed somehow alarmed at my face – though I had done nothing more than most politely address her – and hurried away without so much as a reply. Later I overheard her on the stairway, instructing some of her many children in the importance, whenever passing my room, of chanting a prayer of supplication to the Virgin Mary. 'That you'll be safe from spells.'

A most ludicrous reaction. Yet when I attempted to tell her so – through the fastness of her locked door –

she pretended there was nobody within, though I could hear their whisperings.

Of course I did not limit my investigations to the building I inhabited, but soon began exploring the whole area; mercifully it had not yet been touched by the Cholera, and thus was in a state of relative calm. Quite a campaign, I embarked upon. Questioning, and observing too; watching for any suspicious figures who might be in the pay of my enemies, might themselves be drain rivals, come in person – their faces unfamiliar to me – to embark upon their wickedness.

I at first concentrated my efforts upon landlords of beer houses and gin palaces, as these seemed something of an authority as to the locality's population. They were also, I discovered, a dour and tight-lipped tribe, wary of parting with their knowledge.

Another figure of importance, whose role was not altogether foreign to that of the public house landlords – although he would have denied this fiercely – was the Reverend Rupert Hobbes. A fellow utterly removed in character from the wizened Bowrib, he had, from a dingy church of recent construction, taken upon himself the task of reforming the area – in very much the same spirit as missionaries sent to darkest Africa – an ambition that acquaintanced him with many of my neighbours. His face exuding joyless determination, he answered my questions willingly enough, if with a faint odour of disapproval. I suspected he was unhappy at another stranger come to this territory of squalor that he had come to regard as his own; had I been more abjectly crushed and purposeless he would perhaps have welcomed me more kindly.

And then? Smart Jermyn Street shops, gin palaces, dingy hotels. I interviewed scornful receptionists, shop managers, loiterers and more, until the questions rang in my head with the familiarity of prayers.

'I wonder if you can help me. I'm searching for a woman who disppeared close by here. This is her likeness, though it was taken a few years back.'

With time I had a growing sense of being recognized by people I did not know, but who had heard of me by repute. All across the locality I found myself regarded with near identical glances – wary – as if those questioned had heard already of my enquiring. Nor was this an illusion; they HAD heard. 'So you're the one, eh?' I would be told. 'Like asking questions, don't ya?'

A wearying task, the constant accosting of suspicious strangers. It was with some relief that I found myself standing outside a familiar doorway, above which a face known to me was likely to be found. I glanced at Katie's window, considering whether to go up. What harm could she do me now? I was beyond blackmail.

'Why if it isn't Mr Aldwych, come after all this time.' She smiled as she opened the door. 'What a treat to see me gent again. Katie's liked to think sometimes of Henry up on some lonely mountin', buildin' his rileways.' Inspecting me more carefully, she frowned. 'What you been up to? Had yourself an accident?'

For a moment I was puzzled. Then I realized she must be surprised by my appearance. Probably I looked a touch tired about the eyes. My clothes, too, were in something of a state. In my enthusiasm for selling I had rid myself of all but one of each garment – one top hat, one frock coat, one pair of trousers, one shirt, and a single pair of boots – and, though I cleaned these frequently (usually in the small hours of the night, that I might avoid the derisive shouts of passing urchins) I was inexpert at the art of washing, and they seemed to finish hardly cleaner than before I began. Indeed, the constant scrubbing brought new difficulties; none of the garments being in their first youth, shirt collars soon grew frayed, cuffs and elbows likewise, while my frock coat and trousers lost all shape, and would billow and sag like ships' sails in squally weather.

'Nothing like an accident,' I informed her. 'I'm most well.'

She shrugged, still doubtful. 'Coming inside, then?'

'I won't. Not today.' I had no wish to give her the wrong impression, short of shillings as I was. A pity. Seeing her so close before me, her warm form so evident beneath her loose dressing gown, I felt stirrings within. 'In fact I've come to ask you a question.'

'As you like.' Distant at my refusal, she leaned against the wall, examining the locket with something like disapproval. 'No, I ain't seen this one. Who is she, then?'

This I was not prepared to have her know. 'A friend of mine.'

'More than a friend, I'll guess.' My rather transparent deceit seemed to annoy her.

'Try and remember her face,' I urged. 'You might see her in the future. If so, then tell me at once – it's most important. You can find me easily, as I've rented a room close by here.'

'Round here?' Her eyes narrowed as I told her the address. 'That's 'orrible bad, it is. What you doin' with yourself in such a place?'

There seemed no reason to be secretive. Perhaps I imagined I might even win a little sympathy; a commodity I had had little enough of, after all. 'I've rather fallen on hard times.'

My expectations proved wide of the mark indeed. 'You?' She regarded me with something like anger. 'What about your job buildin' all them rileways?'

'I had to stop.'

'Stop? But how can you 'ave?' She spoke as though I had deliberately let her down. ' 'Tisn't right.'

As if it were anything to do with her. I replaced the locket in my pocket. 'You remember my address?'

She was not to be distracted. 'Why should I then? After you've been gone cheatin' an' deceivin' honest folks.'

'I've done no such thing.'

She eyed me coldly. 'Told Katie yer was a real gent, didn't yer? A gin'rous rich gent, an' she believed yer.

Now it turns out you's no better than a common scrounger. I'm not surprised none that you're dressed all ragged and looking so mad.'

It was ludicrous logic. 'I had money, now I don't. I've told you nothing but the truth.'

'Probably you never even built a rileway, did you? Never built nothing. You's nothing but a cheatin' fraud.'

Probably, I thought to myself, she was drunk. Seeing no point in prolonging such a dispute I did not offer a retort but, uttering brief thanks for her help, turned and departed down the stairway. I was pleased I did so. As I descended the steps I heard her cries calling after me.

'Don't bother yerself to come back, you lying bugger. Katie don't want to see yer face no more. Yer not welcome.'

To be bawled at by a tart outside her bedroom. A lowly comic incident. Probably no less absurd, I pondered as I walked into the street, was my earlier fear that the poor drunken creature had been a cunning and scheming blackmailer. Though it was a pity to have fallen out with someone who might have been useful as an ally in my search, I was not greatly troubled.

In the event, of course, the row was to prove more important than I would know.

As my questioning continued, my knowledge of my neighbours increased. I had always assumed Katie was the only person known to me in my adopted district; after all, I had hardly courted the company of such people as beggars, vagrants, loiterers and the other tribes found wandering its ill-smelling streets. The following afternoon, however, I learned I was not quite so bereft of old acquaintances as I had thought.

The day was another hot one and, parched after several hours of keen enquiring, I had stopped at the only source of water close by my room; a street pump whose liquid was discoloured and foul-tasting, though quenching to the thirst for all that. In the midst of drinking, water spilling down my chin, I found myself greeted by a raucous cry.

'The drain man.'

It was Jem. A Jem transformed, however; indeed, only by his squealing voice did I recognize him. Gone was the grime all but masking his features; a beady-eyed face beamed at me, clean of stains. Gone too were the rags of fustian and corduroy held together with string; he now had a suit and waistcoat of fashion, better of cut and cloth than ever I had worn. His boots were of good leather, from his waistcoat pocket hung a watch chain that looked real gold, while in his hand he grasped a stick – short, as his changed appearance had not extended to growth in height – with a fine brass knob at the end.

'What a friggin' lark meeting you here, eh?' His manner of speech, too, had altered; he had adopted an important way of uttering phrases in one quick-fire delivery, even if they bore little connection with one another. ''Ow's ya drains then – still runnin' round them sewers with the baldy bloke, is ya – what you doin 'ere anyways?'

I was aghast. Also, to be honest, a little envious at this unjust transformation – dishonestly won I was sure – so grotesquely differing from my own. 'At least I've not resorted to thieving.'

Jem was not in the slightest put out. 'Per'aps you've bin missing out – come up an' see me rooms, why don't ya – just round here I lives now – grand place as you've never seen with two fireplaces an' a real chandelier on the ceiling – got me own gal too as is called Sal – almost fifteen she is, that's a yer older than me an' she's got tits like you'd never believe – come up an' see why don't ya – 'ave som'it to eat – look like you need it – what you bin doin' with yourself – bin livin' in them sewers of yours or som'it?'

'I've been leading an honourable life. While as for you . . .' The fellow's latter pronouncements I found especially hard to digest. 'Your own girl?' He reached up hardly higher than the water pump. 'You're no more than a child.'

He merely grinned, swaggering all the more. 'I's old enough I can tell ya – stop bein' such a snoot – you should git some fun into ya.' He turned about in a kind of pirouette. 'Meet me partners.'

At his wave two wan adults who had been lingering a few yards back stepped into view; doubtless his accomplices in some pickpocketing racket. Though both were twice him in age and height, they were strangely subordinated to the boy, watching him quietly, as if awaiting his next utterance. Their clothes, too, were noticeably cheaper than his. Evidently it was Jem's talents that were the source of the gold.

'Slim Jimmy and Robbo,' he introduced them – both looked a shade unhappy at having the names recited to this stranger – with a certain pride, as if they were his own creation, cleverly assembled from small parts. 'This is the sewer bloke I told you 'bout,' he added, for their benefit. 'The one as let me boss round his old death rattle of a servant.'

'I was trying to give you a little well-needed learning,' I told him sternly. 'A thoroughly wasted effort, by the look of it.'

He waved his hand in denial. 'Don't be such a snoot – a good lark it was – what a thought meeting you here – come on, drain man, come up and see me rooms and me gal an' 'ave a bite of som'it why don't you?'

Nothing could have been further from my wishes and I told him so.

He merely grinned, as if this too were some joke. 'As ya like, mister – it's your own loss.'

Costermongers' stalls, pawn shops, cheap lodging houses, even dingy courts reachable only through covered passages half blocked with street dirt. Pure finders, beggars, bird-duffers, thieves, vagrants, madmen. Until, finally – with the exception of those places from which I was rudely driven forth with shouts and hurled filth – there was not a nook or cranny of the neighbourhood left to visit. Short of extending my enquiries outside the district – a notion that seemed of little purpose – I had reached the end.

And what had I learnt? The answers given had varied enough in style; from the polite, 'Sorry sir, I can't say I remember seeing that'un,' to the wary, 'Certainly I 'aven't,' through to the abusive, 'Who'er you, staring so hard and poking your nose where it's not wanted?' and finally the yelled, 'Git outa here yer snot nosed bugger'. In essence, however, all were the same; uniform in their uselessness to me. Nobody had seen her. Or, at least, nobody was willing to admit so.

Was this chance? Mere coincidence? That every single soul I addressed denied knowledge of the matter? The uniformity of their utterings seemed to me to point rather in another direction. Felicia, or some agent of hers, hurrying through the streets – watchful for my step – darting into doorways, whispering threats, offering coins? The balding lecher seen by the dog seller? The one so pale of skin, who had been seeking her? Even some creature of the aristocratic son? Or, of course, unknown drainage enemies. In my watchfulness I had, after all, seen more than a few suspicious characters. In fact so many that I had been quite at a loss as to which to consider most likely candidates as spies upon me. Perhaps all of them.

Whoever might be involved, the result was the same. What choice did I have – dispiriting though it was – but to accept the campaign of questioning as a failure? I must again concentrate my hopes upon the Cafe Castlenau.

The slum room, then – my vigils at the telescope having proved no more effective than my interrogations – had proved of little usefulness. Still I felt no regrets; indeed I grew ever more attached to the place. Squalid though it was, it at least had none of the deafening emptiness of the house in Lark Road, with its rooms that echoed one's every step, as if to better point out people and objects absent. To wake in the now bare parlour was to wake very alone. By contrast – the walls of the slum room being thin – I was never remote from the company of shouts, of bustle, and every kind of life.

Though I had intended it to be only a daytime haunt, I thus found myself spending nights there; at first infrequently, then more often. I even grew accustomed to the vileness of the privy, and to washing myself from a bucket filled at the streetpump; this last was near by, in a road named Boot Lane. Little by little I carried thither useful possessions – among those few that remained to me – from the house. Mostly these were tools of draftsmanship – ruler, pencils, quills, trisectors, great quantities of paper, and even a large table-top to draw upon – for my continuing work on the Drainage Plan for London.

'I'm most sorry but there's nothing we can do.' Hove seemed to grow more awkward and unwelcoming with each news-seeking visit I paid the Metropolitan Committee for Sewers; the way he blinked and fidgeted it was almost as if he were fearful I might grow suddenly violent. 'What with the Cholera everything's been much delayed. I asked Mr Sleak-Cunningham about the drainage competition only yesterday, but he still couldn't give a date.'

I suspected his embarrassment was worsened by my having invited him to dinner; Hove was that very English kind of soul who suffers agonies if he has to say helloa to the same fellow at a drinking table and from behind his own office desk. Certainly I found it increasingly difficult to reach the man.

'Mr Hove says the matter will be dealt with as soon as possible, of course. But he reminds you the Committee is struggling with a great crisis.'

Not that I had any wish to distract the Committee from its pressing duties. I simply wanted to know the result as quickly as I might. The thought of my plan, so neatly described and illustrated, lodged in the Committee's offices, was finely warming to my spirit. Indeed, having achieved so little in my search for Isobella, it was a rare source of hope.

I felt it was only wise to add further to the number of sets of the plan I had, that I might keep them in quite separate locations; places where no jealous rival could possibly anticipate their being stored. Only thus could I outwit some onslaught of malevolent fate. Two full copies I completed, three, four; the increasing number lodged in my possession seemed only to add to my enthusiasm to manfacture more. Thus I worked on, through the nights, copying and copying again, until the phrases written became as some epic poem to me. One set I kept in the fireplace – concealed in the flue – and another in the mattress of the bed, which I tore open and carefully sewed together again. A third I dangled from the window at the end of a thick piece of string; an experiment I came to regret as, during a heavy summer thunderstorm, the lettering dissolved into strange blurrings, as if representing the language of some sea creature. As hard as I laboured upon duplication I racked my brain for more ingenious places where copies might be hidden.

My visits to Lark Road became rare. The rent on the house was paid for several months to come, but this was as nothing to me; the place served to depress my spirits so. The building grew more distant even in my thoughts, all the more so after the last living reminder of my wife's existence there – Pericles – chose to go.

The animal kept up his lonely guard on his mistress's room for a remarkably long time, it must be said. Weeks after her vanishing he still lingered, barking furiously when I passed by the door to her room. I never fed him myself – my liking for the creature had not altered with time – and was never certain how he survived, though I suspected he left the house through a small window in the kitchen – one low enough for him to reach, that had long been stuck half open – to maraud about the area, scavenging.

What canine notion caused him to so suddenly abandon his place is hard to say even now. A wild change it certainly was. One afternoon I came to the house to collect any remaining preserved food; jam, sugar and the like. Having found precious little – probably Miss Symes had made away with it without my noticing – I was on the point of slamming shut the door, when the dog hurtled after me. At first I thought his purpose was simple escape from the building, but then I observed his path was not towards the open street but to my feet. Without so much as a warning bark he sank his teeth into the toe of my boot; not actually drawing blood, but leaving a most unfashionable mark upon the leather. The difficulty of kicking at a creature that has attached itself to your toes. Doubtless those practised in such matters have devised subtle techniques, but I was obliged to resort to mere hopping and cursing until – having come close to toppling over – I managed to catch the animal under his front legs with my free limb, distracting him enough to send him into a graceless arc through the air.

Though he did not resume attack, instead vanishing into the din and scamperings of the street life, I had not rid myself of his attention. Even as I walked back to the rented room I thought I heard a low growling from close by – so quiet as to be half lost among the clatter of carriages – as if the creature were deliberately following. The impression was not a false one. Only a few days later, when making my way to the water pump, the animal sprang out at me, barking and lunging until I threatened him with the bucket I held.

Thereafter I kept a sharp watch for him – regretful that I had sold my walking stick with its lead knob – and sighted his sharp eyes more than a few times. He seemed to have established a kind of home for himself; a nest of evil-smelling vegetable refuse, rotted wood and mixed abomination, whose colour he himself quickly came to assume. The spot was only a few dozen yards from my new lodgings, and I had a strong sense that he was quite deliberately keeping watch upon my movements. Perhaps he wondered if I might lead him to his mistress. Or he hoped to catch me unawares, and exact some canine revenge for the slights he believed he had suffered.

With time I adapted my room to offer the little comfort I required. The bed had collapsed without delay – perhaps suffering from the additional weight of the drainage plan within the mattress – and I left it so, finding it more stable than when raised up upon its legs. It mattered little anyhow, as I used it seldom enough; I had not regained the gift of easy sleeping, and spent many of the sultry night-time hours not even attempting rest, but seated at a kind of desk I had rigged up by the window, fashioned from all manner of broken bricks and pieces of scrap wood, precariously supporting the table top.

There I would work, copying my drainage plan by candlelight, sometimes pausing to peer through the telescope. I had arranged this on a tripod, so it was never far from my eye, pointed at the street corner below. Even in the darkness I would sometimes stare through the instrument, in the unlikely hope of seeing her face – lit perhaps by some lamp she might be carrying – pass before the glass, brought into clarity.

It was with little enthusiasm that I found myself embarked, after an especially long absence, upon the way to Lark Road, one sultry afternoon. Conscience had driven me thither, that I might be certain no letter lay waiting there for me; an unlikely prospect, in view of her last communication, promising to be gone from my life for ever. I expected to find nothing except the empty blankness that was so familiar.

I was to be surprised. Not by some envelope lain upon the hallway floor, my name upon its cover, but by a discovery of quite another order.

Somebody had been living there.

The kitchen was the room the intruder had chosen as dwelling place. A number of anonymous rags had been formed into something like a bed while the oven fire was made up and ready to light. Inspecting this last I saw the grate had been filled with all manner of pieces of wood – more was stacked in piles, each formed with remarkable neatness – much of which I recognized. There were the legs of an old stool – one so rotten it was far beyond selling – as well as the cracked headboard of Miss Symes's old bed, and lengths of picture rails and skirting-boards, these last torn from the very fabric of the house, Irish fashion. Glancing about I saw the wounds left by such vandalism, and the tool with which it had likely been achieved; the iron handle of an old pot – one long been severed from its vessel – that had a flattened end where it had once been affixed, sharp enough to gouge wood from plaster.

The landlords from whom I had rented the house would hardly be pleased. Though it was of little enough concern to me now. My thoughts were drawn, rather, to the mystery of what soul had been there, and whether they would return.

The poverty of life pointed towards some tramp who had found the house empty. He would have gained access with ease, as, the house containing nothing, I had long ceased to lock the back door. A strange kind of tramp, however. The leavings were so tidy; not only were the piles of wood arranged with care, the rags that made up the bed were drawn up into a perfect rectangle, with the old hallway rug – a ghastly old thing – rolled up to form a kind of pillow.

It was not long before I found evidence of a more instructive kind. Beside the sink were four written lists. A literate tramp, then. Examining them, I found myself wondering, with a beating heart, if the writing was not Isobella's. Certainly it bore more than a slight resemblance. But though the style was familiar, it seemed more hurried than hers; the letters wilder, and less carefully formed.

Besides, I reflected, how could it be? She was not sleeping on beds of rags. She was away gallivanting with some son of the nobility. Indeed, with half the wealthy lechers of London. Surely.

Each list was dated at the top and, between them, they covered some ten days, the most recent being of less than one week passed. All described only foods, and these always of the cheapest of kinds and in the smallest of quantities. With them were also calculations, whose purpose was not exactly clear to me, although they seemed always to be juggling with the same meagre sums. The pencil with which they had been written still lay near by; little more than a blunt stub.

The paper was in the form of mere scraps, formed, it appeared, from some larger piece I had myself discarded and left; probably because some blemish left it unworthy of imprinting upon it my drainage plan. The letters and figures were so small that it was only on a second inspection that I discovered the messages hidden among them; messages doubtless intended only for the writer's own eyes. Tight wedged between a long division sum of days, shillings and pennies, and amounts of potatoes and swedes, was spelled WHY CAN HE NOT LEAVE ME ALONE? Nor was this the only one. Lodged in a corner, beneath four ounces of potatoes and three carrots, I discerned, in letters uncertain and tiny: KILLING THING.

There was no sign that the visitor might return; in fact quite the opposite was true. Perched high upon a cupboard I found a sad collection of vegetables and such that exactly corresponded to those of the final list. They must have been left there in the warm air for some days, as already most of them were discoloured and spoiled; a great loss considering the care with which their purchase seemed to have been planned and recorded. Nor was this the only indication that the intruder had left in a hurry. The back door stood open, swinging in the hot breeze.

Some miserable vagrant, almost certainly. Still I resolved not to again leave such a long interval before my next visit. And I took with me the strange lists.

Joshua Jeavons, striding triumphant into the London Docks. Joshua Jeavons, chosen from the yelling crowd of ne'er-do-wells for a full day's work emptying ships' cargoes. Joshua Jeavons, feeling fortune has at last shown him some favour, if of a most modest kind. Just in time, too; the coins in his pocket total only ha'penny farthing, while his belly – unfilled since breakfast time the day before – bubbles with a gnawing hunger.

Behind, the calling foreman's droning of names came to halt. 'That's all there is.' Others had not been so lucky and were already trailing gloomily away, perhaps to wait longer, in the thin hope that some ship might drift in late.

The glory of the London docks, depot of all the planet, destination of goods from all countries, whether frozen or tropical, whether populated by Mahommedans or Hindoos or worshippers of bears. Though it was hardly the best of mornings for me – an experienced engineer reduced to working as a casual dock labourer – still I could not but be impressed by the drama of the place.

Thus the sheer variety of goods collected all about; here a giant stack of cork, there a yellow bin of sulphur, or a small mountain of lead-coloured copper ore. As I strode along the stone quay my feet trod one moment upon the stickiness of West Indian sugar, next on the slipperiness of Spanish oil. The air itself told of far off foreign lands; now sickening with the stench of hides from the wildlands of America, next warm with fumes of Caribbean rum, then sharp with the tang of vast stores of Mexican tobacco, or scented with the light fragrances of a shipload of coffee and spices from the Orient.

I was directed to the rearmost part of the dock,

below a large clock tower, where the foreman – an angry, skull-faced soul – barked and pointed down a stairway descending beneath the quay itself. 'Them as is marked with a letter "O" on them is the ones. For those of yous as can't read, that's like a fish's mouth, wide open. I want the lot brought up within the hour, d'you hear. Remember, like a fish's mouth.'

Below was a kind of misty subterranean palace of vaults, air dank with grapey spirit and dry rot. Stretching away into the distance were acres of wine hogsheads, some of which it was our task to move to the surface; I joined forces with a bearded fellow and set to work, wrestling one of the things – as awkward of shape as a lead midget – up the stairs. We had just brought it into the daylight – both perspiring in the river-damp heat – and were rolling it to join others already brought, when I heard the foreman's voice call out.

'That man, shoving the hogshead.'

I saw he was pointing at myself.

'What's that on your back?'

He meant, I realized, my leather sack. It had become such a regular habit to carry it with me that I had picked it up without thought as I left my room that morning. Only now did I wonder if I might have been wise to bring it to a place of work. 'It contains some documents.'

'Documents my arse. You're a thieving rascal.'

'It's the truth.' I peeled the sack from my shoulders and pulled open the straps to extract a thick sheaf of papers, each marked with fine ink lines; the fifth copy of my drainage plan for London. What safer course, I had reasoned, than to carry one set constantly with me, wherever I might go. 'It's an engineering scheme. My own. I'm an experienced engineer.'

Some of the other casuals had stopped to watch the entertainment, pleased that the day should have so promptly provided excuse for a few moments' idling. One called out 'Fight', suggestively.

The foreman plucked the plan from my hands, glowering hard. The fact that I claimed to have written it seemed, for some reason, to aggravate him rather than otherwise. 'I don't care if it's the Bible in bleedin' Hindoostani, nor if you're King of Japan. Bags ain't allowed, thieves neither.'

'I've stolen nothing.' I guessed it was already well too late; the way the man stared at the pages, eyes angrily unseeing, made me all but sure that – despite his proud descriptions of the letter 'O' as resembling a fish's mouth – he could not read. A piece of bad luck for me.

'It's got no business bein' on this 'ere quay. And neither 'as you, mister.'

Sure enough, try as I might, there was no arguing with him. The matter was decided.

I was not allowed to leave through the main gate, but was flung out, without ceremony, through a small side exit that led directly on to the river bank, my sack – laboriously searched lest I had already smuggled into it some exotic tropical goods – hurled after me on to the mud.

Thames slime. My shoes squelched nastily upon it, seemingly in reflection of my thoughts. To be thrown out thus, after all my struggling in the morning crowd. A lowering moment indeed. Ejected from a day's employment I had not even wanted, but had resorted to only from hungry desperation.

The river bank was littered with beached boats, and it was hard to discern the best way out of the quagmire. Light-headed with hunger, I clambered on to the rotted skeleton of an old skiff, that I might peer down from a point of higher vantage. Beneath the hulls to my right – rising up so steeply they resembled sleeping whales – I discerned the ground was of gravel rather than mud, and, accordingly, I stepped down in that direction.

Hunger. Should I abandon the two sovereigns sewed into the hem of my frock-coat, I wondered. A grim prospect. Or sell the telescope in my room, carefully aimed at the life of the street below. To discard either amounted, in effect, to the same change; the beginning of a surrender of hope of discovering Isobella.

Picking my way among the boats I caught brief glimpses of the river beyond, barges floating slowly past with the tide, silent except for the cries of the crews wrestling with their long oars. It was some time since I had been so near the Thames. The stench of effluent expelled into it by the efforts of the Committee for Sewers was indeed overpowering; clear evidence of that body's energetic labours of the previous weeks.

Or should I write again to Moynihan? I had been unwilling before, on the grounds that to do so would amount to little more than transparent begging. Now, however, I was less troubled by such niceties. But how long would it take? I doubted I could well endure more than a couple of days more of hunger, and, what with the delay before a letter could reach him – I did not even know how often he returned from his secret work – and before his reply could come back to me . . .

I had progressed some way along the river bank, still without having discerned a way on to firm land, when, stepping out from the shade of a barnacled hull – thoughts lost in dismal questions and eyes blinking in the sharp sunlight – I walked clean into a fellow marching about the far side of the boat.

The collision all but knocked the breath from me. Regaining balance, I focused on whom I had struck; a grubby, burly sort with unusually large ears. Also winded, he clutched a stick of some kind, whose point he had stabbed into the mud to help steady himself. He glared at me with suspicious recognition.

'The drain copper.'

Behind him were two others; a towering fellow with a patch over one eye, and a flimsy-framed lad with an irked, pugnacious look upon his face. It was only seeing the three together – all wearing long greasy coats with lanterns hanging from the breast, and carrying identical poles with hoes at their ends – that I recalled their identity. They were my foes at the battle by the sewer outlet.

'You're still alive.'

Giant Ears uttered a kind of growl. 'Had other plans for us, did'ja?'

The other two, close behind him, regarded me with hard stares, the lad planting the end of his pole into the mud with measured violence. Aware of the cool breeze of threat blowing, I hastened to make clear the meaning of my words, spoken so incautiously. 'I was only worried you might've been struck by the Cholera.'

One Eye watched me warily. 'That so?'

Remarkable. I regarded the three, as if to be sure they were indeed stood before me, and not some hallucination of hunger. How could they have survived the long season of epidemic? Did they possess, I wondered, some resistance to the poisonous effects of the miasma cloud? If so . . . The chance meeting could be the beginning of important discoveries.

'You've been working the sewers all these last months?' I asked.

'What'cher want to know fer?' demanded the lad accusingly. 'Want to go snitchin' on us, does yer?'

'Drain copper,' repeated Giant Ears in a murmur.

I held up my arms that they might see the frayed cuffs of my frock-coat. 'Do I look like police?'

They seemed none too sure.

'I'm only an engineer, a scientist if you will, eager to find ways of combating the Cholera. You could help greatly.'

'A signtist?' Giant Ears regarded me, far from convinced. 'Why d'ja jump us that time, then?'

I regretted having done so. 'We let you go quick enough, did we not?' I decided to change tack. 'You don't realize. Your survival this summer is remarkable. The world has much to learn from you.'

'What's so remarkiber?' Giant Ears, though he uttered the words fiercely, betrayed in his eyes a certain interest at the thought of being essential to science. 'Shoremen ain't never bin took by the Cholera. Not this time, nor the last, twenty year ago.'

Another surprise. The whole profession unaffected. I was more sure than ever that the key could lie with these people. 'But that in itself is important. If it's possible to discover why you've not been struck by sewer gases, we could gain new understanding of the malady, even find a cure.'

'Oh yeah?' The lad jutted his chin into the air. 'And what'd we git out'a all that?'

I struggled to think of a reply. 'You could become famous. Your names could be quoted in a hundred medical books, in twenty languages, all across the world.'

'Our names?' One Eye shook his head knowingly. 'Then they'd 'ave it writ down we'd bin in the shores – sewers as you calls 'em – which ain't allowed. We'd all be hauled off ta gaol.'

A ridiculous notion, but somehow the discussion seemed to have reached a point of hingeing on nothing else. The three of them glanced at me, expectant, and I searched my thoughts for some solution. 'You could give other names,' I suggested. 'And only tell the truth to those you trust.'

'Jest tell them we likes?' The notion seemed to appeal to the three, and they exchanged glances, if not thoroughly won over, at least satisfied for the moment. 'Well then,' pronounced One Eye, who seemed to be senior amongst them. 'So what d'ya want?'

The answers to questions; legions of them. Where did they work and for how long, their ways of traversing the tunnels, the garments they wore, whether they used some special means of breathing, and more. To give them credit, the three replied freely enough, and I soon gained a most detailed picture of their habits. Nothing I learned, however, brought me any closer to feeling I had solved the mystery.

A disappointment indeed. Especially after all my sudden hopes.

'When we gonna be faimis, then?' demanded the lad, with the air of one who has already been kept waiting too long. 'How come we's not all dead then?'

I shrugged unhappily. 'I'm sorry. I just don't know.'

The lad scowled, while Giant Ears yawned in the manner of one who had guessed the matter would be of no purpose. One Eye plucked up his pole. 'Come on lads. We've spent enough time playin' at this. Let's be on our way.'

A thought occurred to me. 'Are you going on an expedition into the sewers now?'

One Eye frowned. 'What if we is?'

Despite my hunger, it was an opportunity not to be missed. 'Can I join you? I'll surely discover something if I can watch you at work.'

The three were doubtful, and it was all I could do to assure them they could suffer no harm from my presence. 'Even if I was a spy – which I'm clearly not – I could hardly arrest the three of you by myself.'

'All right,' One Eye agreed, cautiously. 'But if yer cross us, don't think yer won't be looked for, and found, and smashed right proper.'

Thus I found myself an apprentice scavenger of the sewers, walking with my new – and strange – teachers in the warm summer morning air. The river was low with drought, the sun had baked much of the sliminess from the mud, and the going along the bank was not hard; before long we reached the outlet chosen.

'You'd best take your boots off,' One Eye suggested as we stood before the entrance. 'Easier, it is.'

They were each of them barefoot, so his advice was doubtless sound, but still it was not without squeamishness that I removed my boots and socks – hiding them beneath a beached log – and placed my bare feet in the ooze.

Worse was soon to come. Stepping into the sewer itself, it took all my concentration not to think of where my toes were treading, nor what glass or rusty nails might be lying concealed beneath my next foothold.

The stench defied description, causing in me waves of nausea – even though I breathed through the cloth of my frock-coat sleeve – while drips of vileness constantly fell upon my clothes; my only clothes. What if the gases in the air should ignite in a fearful explosion, as they had in the Fleet River sewer? Altogether I came close indeed to changing my mind, and marching out there and then, whatever the wonders of discovery that might lie ahead.

With time, however, my attention became distracted – at least in part – by what I saw. Indeed it was a surprise to me that I had never thought before of exploring the sewers, but had been satisfied with mere inspection of river outlets and flushing penstocks in the upper reaches. The state of the brickwork was shocking; my fellows' lanterns playing upon cracks of great size, while in places the ceiling had fallen clean away, leaving holes that seemed to murmur with threat of further collapse.

Gradually the dripping and splashing sounds all around became displaced by a sharper din – the rattle of carriages, voices shouting – and, turning a corner, the sewer became illuminated with shafts of daylight filtering down from a line of what I guessed must be street gully holes.

'Quiet here,' warned One Eye, and I observed the three of them place hands above their lamps that the glow could not be seen from above. Through the gully holes I glimpsed parts of buildings and realized, with strange familiarity, that we were beneath Drury Lane. The sounds drifting down were so clear that one almost expected the carriages and pedestrians to be in the drain itself. I even heard full pieces of conversation; here a droning monologue concerning the heat, there a dispute between the owners of two dogs that had fought. To be so close to these goings-on, yet unsuspected, evinced in me something of a childish amusement.

Such a place was a preferred hunting ground of my

companions and they swiftly set to work, each selecting a spot beneath one of the gully holes and kneeling to examine the sewer bottom – the current was low – for objects that had fallen through. Nor did they have to search long. In a moment the lad had plucked up a couple of coppers, while the others had collected in their sacks various pieces of bone, metal and strands of rope. I watched, fascinated, as the three of them – so healthy looking – laboured in the very effluent, with not so much as a handkerchief over their mouths.

Aside from the two coppers, their finds seemed hardly worth collecting. 'You can live from this alone?' I whispered to One Eye.

'Live well,' he told me, with pride, holding up a handful of bone and stubs of metal. 'This'll fetch more than you'd guess.'

'There's none in Mint Square as flash as shoremen,' added Giant Ears importantly. 'It's not many days I gits home with less than six bob's worth of finds in me pockets. Gals? We 'as ter fight 'em off.'

Six shillings. The amount was several times what I would have earned from a day's work in the docks. At least they must eat well. I wondered if this was important to their resilience, and asked what they normally took as their daily meals. The replies were extensive – my stomach rumbled fiercely at the long descriptions of pies, puddings, sausages, and all manner of roasted beasts – but included nothing that struck me as unusual.

As we strode onwards the tunnel became shallower – though still tall enough for one to walk easily – while the number of drains joining in from the sides markedly increased, filling the air with sounds of dripping water. Every few minutes my companions would pause and search about them, scouring the brickwork and sifting through the ooze, until their sacks grew quite full. Though I studied their every action, still I could see nothing revealing about their behaviour. Was it their very constitutions that made them so proof against the malignant gases, I wondered. Perhaps some family trait (a worrying notion, as it meant I would have no such protection). On asking their fathers' professions, however, I found none had in any way been connected with the sewers. Indeed all had been skilled men; weavers, smiths and such, while their sons seemed to have been drawn to their strange work as much by an unlikely sense of vocation – a fascination with the river from their early years – as from simple need.

'Rats,' called out One Eye. The creatures had uttered no sound, and were revealed only a few yards away, caught by the faint beam of Giant Ears' lamp. At least a dozen of them there were, as large as kittens, running above the ooze – they seemed careful to avoid the effluent itself – at quite a speed. My companions were little bothered, striking out with their hoes in a leisurely fashion until, a couple reduced in number and squealing fiercely, they had been driven back before us.

One Eye noticed my discomfort. 'Never seen a rat before?'

'Never so many.'

'Scared of a few rats, is ya?' He laughed so fiercely I was worried his patch might fly from its place. 'That's nothing you saw. I've met as many as an 'undred, all woppers. There's water rats, too, as is much more ferociouser than yer usual kind. An' up in Hampstead there's a whole tribe of hogs.'

'Hogs?' It was a most extraordinary claim.

'Certainly. I've not seen 'em myself, but there's others 'as.' One Eye seemed proud of the fact, as if the creatures were his own pets. 'Seems one sow as was pregnant got down there somehow, 'ad 'er porkers, and they've been breedin' ever since. An hintire population there is now, all of 'em most wicious. 'Course they never sees the full light of day.'

'Can't they get down to the river?'

The lad, evidently also well informed of the

Hampstead sewer hogs, chimed in with an air of authority. 'They can't. All them shores up there flows into the Fleet, see, which goes by at a good rate, bein' a proper river. Tho' the hogs may sometimes jump in, their natures is so fierce obstinite and contr'ary – a well known feetchur of such hanimals – that they swims violent against the tide, an' so always makes their way back to their 'riginal quarters.'

Illuminated by the weak light of his lamp, One Eye nodded approvingly at the lad's exposition. I regarded it with some scepticism – none of the three had actually seen the hogs – but kept my own counsel, seeing no need in playing heretic over what was clearly a matter of faith.

We did not progress much further than the battle-ground of the rat skirmish. Though the tunnel continued easily high enough for us to march through, we halted before a gush of steam – warm and sharp in the throat – that swirled in from one of the side drains.

'I reckin we's done enough fur today,' pronounced One Eye, regarding the steam with something akin to regret. 'We'd best be gone from here, temptin' tho' 'tis to stay, or we'll all be flat on our backs afore we knows it.'

Giant Ears and the lad murmured agreement, though both strayed some steps nearer the swirling vapour, breathing deeply.

'What is it?' I asked.

'That's Runyon's Distillery right above us,' One Eye explained. 'These is fumes from the gin-making. Hinough to intoxicate a full regiment, I dare say. It's not the first time I've struck such here. T'ain't wise to linger, neither.'

He called to the others to hurry, and in a moment we had left the spot behind. The fumes must have been of great strength, however, as although we had been exposed to them for only a short time, I soon felt their effects. Indeed so did we all. Thus, in the sewers beneath the streets of London, I found myself member of a troupe of subterranean drunkards, lumbering forward, clumsy of foot, cackling at the others' swayings. The lad was struck more than any, and several times went clean over into the ooze, giggling fit to burst, and having to have his lamp re-lit. Nor were we the only ones. I saw a rat stumbling blearily along the brickwork, then tumble off his track like an old soak.

In the midst of it all, One Eye opened his mouth wide and, in a bass voice surprisingly fine, began singing that music-hall song of the time 'The Noblest Orphan'. It is hard to describe the effect the melody and its touching words had upon the rest of us, in our drink-warmed state. Giant Ears, the lad and I joined the chorus with much spirit, filling the tunnel with strange sound – recalling monks yelling chants at the tops of their voices – as our words mixed with their own echoes many fold repeated. By the time we reached the last lines, when the orphan – just found dead of hunger and cold in a blinding blizzard, on account of his having helped a stranger – is realized to be the long lost heir to a dukedom, we were all of us close to tears.

It was a long walk back. As we neared the outlet once more our mood was well altered; sobriety restored, accompanied by gin-fume hangovers. I trudged wearily through the ooze, at once impatient to be gone from the vileness of the tunnel, yet unhappy to leave the place without having discovered the shore workers' secret.

'You better not cross us,' the lad warned abruptly, for no clear reason besides the after-effects of Runyon's Distillery steam. 'Or you'll get proper smashed.'

The sewer outlet had finally come into sight. Still some distance off, it seemed to hang in the air; a circle of light dazzling to the eyes. I caught a faint but refreshing whiff of salty air. 'It's a fool who threatens when there's no need,' I retorted, irked by the boy.

'Just tellin' yer, weren't I. That you'll git smashed proper if yer does any snitchin'.'

I pondered if it would be worth replying again, and what I might say, but, before I had reached any conclusion my attention was taken by something in the ooze just ahead, caught by the light shining in from the outlet. It glinted as metal. Stooping, I plucked up a tablespoon, by the look of it silver. The other three gathered about, woken from their dreariness, to examine the thing with professional interest.

'I 'ad one like that last month,' stated the lad. 'Fourteen bob.'

'Fifteen more like,' countered Giant Ears.

'Never,' insisted One Eye. 'It's seventeen at least, that'un.'

The amounts were several times what I would have earned at the docks. Though it was poor compensation for my having failed to discover what I had sought, the expedition had not then been wasted time. At least I could now eat.

'I tell you what,' I proposed, holding up the spoon. 'I'll take twelve for it here and now.'

The offer was received with interest by all three. One Eye, as senior, had first claim, and extracted from some recess of his clothes a small greasy purse impressively well stocked with coins, including several sovereigns. The exchange was completed in a moment.

'Don't forgit to get us faimis,' insisted Giant Ears as we emerged from the tunnel into the fresher air. 'And as fer me name . . .' he gave me a thoughtful look, as one who had been considering the matter deeply, 'put me down as Ned the Gent.'

'An' me,' added One Eye. 'I'll be 'Andsome Bill.'

The lad regarded me importantly. 'I'm Giant Jim.'

'I'll do all in my power,' I promised, and watched them stride away along the river bank, possessed of as much proud purpose as three City bankers who have just concluded some gainful contract.

Journey after journey I made – now fortified with a pork and orange pie – from the street handpump in

Boot Lane to my rented room, bucket in hand, that I might clean myself and my clothes. The task – one I carried out usually only in the middle of the night – proved quite a spectacle to the local urchins.

'Wash day for the dirty toff.'

'Starin' eyes is havin' hisself a bath.'

Nor were these the only ones interested. As I worked at the pump, eliciting from it a sad squeaking sound, I became aware of a small pair of eyes fixing me with malignant observation. The eyes, in fact, were the only part of the creature that were easily recognizable. It was some weeks since I had last seen Pericles, and I was surprised by the change in him. His fur was now matted with dirt into a kind of blackened rug that disguised his shape, so he seemed anonymous even of species, and could have passed for some over-sized rodent. Indeed, he seemed to have had dealings with such creatures judging by the scars I discerned upon his snout, doubtless won in battle with metropolitan rats.

There was little change, however, in his attitude towards myself. He advanced with pigmy menace, growling and baring his teeth, unperturbed even when I emptied the contents of the bucket upon him. Fortunately my various foes of the afternoon seemed by no means united by their common persecution. Two of the urchins observed the aggressive concentration in which the animal was so thoroughly absorbed, and crept up upon him from behind without his seeing. In a trice one had taken hold of the creature, clutching him in the air by a hind leg. Pericles twisted and turned, barking and snapping, until finally he managed to sink his teeth into his oppressor's elbow. Rather than winning him freedom, however, this action only caused the boy to hurl him – with astonishing violence for a mere child – at a wooden fence, beneath which he then lay, panting.

An ugly moment. Had not the animal shown such constant animosity towards myself I would have determined to help him. As it was I stepped closer, that I might see his state – he looked poorly – and, when he then snapped at my hand, let him be.

Besides, there was so much to do. After all, I could hardly visit the Metropolitan Committee for Sewers stinking of their very subterranean responsibilities. And visit them I must, without delay, before they finished business for the afternoon. Edwin Sleak-Cunningham must know of this mystery of the shore workers' survival. That it had been beyond my own understanding did not mean it would overcome that great man's mind.

The washing of my clothes proved hard labour indeed. Effluent had splashed upwards from the sewer floor in quantity, black drips had fallen upon me from the roof, and it was only after some hours that my clothes, hat and leather sack were free of stink, and returned to their proper hues. The harsh scrubbing required was, sadly, not without cost; one cuff was all but torn away and the brim of my hat became loose for some part of its length. Also there were the effects of drying. Rather than be long delayed, I decided to wear the clothes still in their state of wrung out wetness, reasoning that the hot afternoon sun would settle them soon enough. Nor was I mistaken, and the frock coat and trousers were quickly done with. Unfortunately my cunning method also caused in them something of a loss of shape; in fact one so severe that my frock coat might have fitted a fellow several times my girth, billowing about me like a flag.

The clothes were long dry by the time I neared the building of the Metropolitan Committee for Sewers. My main concern, as I pondered the message I was to relate, was how best to live up to the promises of discretion I had made to the shore workers. After all, it was possible Sleak-Cunningham barely knew of their existence. How might I describe that strange class without revealing details that would put them in danger of arrest? I would have to use only general phrases, avoiding mention of where I had discovered them, or whence we had ventured.

In the event I need not have worried myself.

What signs were there that something was amiss at the home of the Metropolitan Committee for Sewers? First, even before I had reached Crete Street, there was the sight of a carriage hurtling by, horses' eyes white and rolling as they struggled to give the vehicle pace. As it passed I caught a momentary glimpse of the solitary soul within; a fellow who bore close resemblance to the very Sleak-Cunningham whom I was on my way to visit. But Sleak-Cunningham would never, surely, have been sat in such a dismal way; hunched, as if cold.

Next there was the flurry of black hansom cabs before the Committee building, many already moving – as a flock of giant crows – and speeding away in different directions. Each carried an identical cargo; a single fellow, shabby of dress. More such types stood disputing for the few cabs still unclaimed. Every one of them, I observed, carried a notebook.

The third and final sign was the front door to the building itself. This, usually tight shut – visitors were required to ring and wait as at a private house – stood ajar.

Reaching the entrance, I waylaid one of the journalists as he was about to clamber into his freshly-won vehicle. 'What's happening?'

A cheery, poorly-shaven soul, he exuded – as did they all – something of the excitement of a spectator enjoying the horse races on a fine and sunny afternoon. 'Going on?' The question seemed to amuse him. 'Where've you been with yourself? Outer Patagonia?'

Though I asked again, the fellow had time for no more than his own joke, and clambered into the cab, rapping at the ceiling with his stick. His colleagues seemed no less impatient. After final wrangling as to means of escape, the last of them fitted himself into a hansom and, with a clattering of hooves and wheels, was gone.

I stepped inside the building. The silent hall within showed ample evidence of the scene just ended; the marble floor – normally so finely polished – was littered with boot-marks, discarded paper, and cigar butts. I surveyed the scene, aghast and also puzzled.

The man was stood so still that it was some moments before I saw him. There, beyond the mess, half concealed behind a pillar – almost as if he had been hiding himself away – stood the familiar figure of George Hove. I say familiar, but in truth he was barely so. His thin face, usually emanating such an aura of correct primness, was pale and shocked; bleary.

'What's happened?' I asked.

He hardly seemed to see me. 'They have assassinated Edwin. Nothing less.' He glanced at me, eyes now seeming to focus. 'Edwin has been forced to resign.'

It seemed hardly possible. The leading figure of the sanitary movement, the very soul of the Committee?

Hove stared at the ground. 'They have destroyed him.'

'Who?'

He shot me a look. 'Who d'you think, man? Have you not been reading *The Times*?'

I had not, of course, for some weeks.

He shook his head. 'I will never read it again. Never.' He cast a glance about him, at the discarded papers on the floor. 'They couldn't let him alone even now, after they had wrecked him. On the very morning he had to leave us they came to crow and plague him with their vile questions.' Though his voice was flat, he spoke with something of a sense of need, as if to rid himself of the matter. The words began to flow quickly, spilling from him.

It was a distressing account. *The Times*, it seemed, had taken it upon itself to launch one of its famous thundering assaults upon authorities it deemed inept; in this case an attack – and, as I saw it, a most unfair one – upon Edwin Sleak-Cunningham and his Committee for Sewers. Thus its editorials had thundered at him for failing in any way to modernize the drainage system of London – which he had hardly had time to do – accusing him of wasting weeks merely frightening landlords. It had thundered that his flushing policy had done nothing to overcome the Cholera, merely causing a vicious stench. And, lastly and most effectively, it had thundered against Sleak-Cunningham himself, accusing him of being secretive and lusting for power; a manipulator of committees.

Hove shook his head darkly. 'We were made scapegoat. Scapegoat for the whole Cholera. All so that *The Times* might sell more copies of its rag.'

I was hardly less shocked than he. Sleak-Cunningham gone. For good, too, by the sound of it. The Committee in confusion, perhaps tottering also. I struggled to take in the changed view of things, as a man who has sleep-walked and woken in some strange place. It was nothing less than a catastrophe. After all the hard work – the years of work – of the Association for the Promotion of Health in Cities; the meetings, the lobbying of members of Parliament. The great hopes we had had. And also . . . One question rang out in my thoughts above the din of all others.

'What of the drainage scheme competition?'

Hove showed some annoyance. 'What of it? What does such a thing matter now?'

His words enhanced my alarm. 'It won't take place?'

'What purpose would it serve?'

It may perhaps seem strange, but far more important to me even than the Committee, or Hove, or Sleak-Cunningham's career, was the thought of my plan; so significant, not only for myself, but – as I saw it – for the whole metropolis. I would not have it abandoned on some shelf to rot, or to be stolen by talentless rivals. 'Then I must have my proposal returned to me.'

Hove waved his hand dismissively. 'This is no time for such trivia.'

My voice, if quietened, must have shown the determination I felt. Perhaps it even conveyed some hint of threat. 'I will have my plan back. And this moment, too.'

Hove watched me with wariness. 'For goodness sake . . .' He puckered disdainfully, but with less sureness. 'If you're going to make such a ridiculous fuss—'

I was.

Up the grand stairway I followed, and into parts of the building I had never before seen. A mighty grand sight it was too; little less than a palace. We passed clerks at their desks, in that state of nervous talkativeness typical of unfortunates unable to play any part in a crisis that surrounds them. On through a splendid office – Sleak-Cunningham's, I assumed – with a giant double window looking down upon the street outside, cabs and citizenry dwarfed from such a height. Then finally into a dusty closet of a room, walls covered to the ceiling with shelves of documents.

Hove was evidently familiar with these, as he hardly hesitated before reaching up and plucking one among the many hundred files. Into my hands he placed the familiar binding of my original copy of the drainage plan.

'Satisfied?' Having complied with my demand, he became all at once huffily angry, thoroughly offended. 'I hope you are. There must be a thousand matters more pressing than this.' He tapped the binding I held. 'As if your notions were of any value.'

It was the first time anybody had criticized my drainage plan in such a way. Though I had no wish to step into an argument, I was not prepared to quietly stand back and let the man slur my scheme. 'And how would you know?'

'How d'you think?' He spoke with heat; it seemed I had tapped a well of anger filled by the day's bitter events. 'I was given the task of going through all the entries to ensure they were complete. Yours I regarded as the least satisfactory.' He directed a sneering look to the document. 'The excrement of all London to be sold at profit? It's nothing less than ludicrous. Demand is barely enough to take the little that the nightsoil carters collect from the streets.'

As if a convinced governmentalist such as Hove would say anything else. Still his claim annoyed me. 'You know nothing of profit,' I told him. 'Your mind is closed to such things. You want only to squeeze the ratepayers, regardless of the hardship you may cause them.'

What a day. Stepping into the corridor outside, the lightness of head I had earlier observed came upon me again, and I leant for a moment against the wall. With the journalists gone the building was deathly quiet, as if shocked into silence. Passing the clerks, subdued at their desks, it was only as I approached the top of the stairway that I heard sounds of life. From below echoed up footsteps – several sets of them – although they were so light of tread, and so slow and cautious, that they might have been the servants of the establishment, attempting escape.

A dozen or so they proved to be; a strange-looking collection, glancing about the hall as if lost, or nervous that trapdoors might be concealed beneath the boot-marked marble floor, ready to swallow them up. I observed how their garments, though so cheap they were only one better than rags, had been invested with a desperate attempt at neatness; boots bursting with holes but polished black, hats and coats frayed but quite clean. They might have passed for members of an assemblage of model reformed beggars. Except for their expressions: these were anxious, impatient. Even angry.

Puzzling sight though they were, I would probably have stepped by them without further ado had not one – a wizened, stringy fellow – called out, 'Sir, d'you know your way about this place?' He explained they were a deputation from – of all places – Jacob's Island. 'We've none of us been here before, see. And it's most urgent. We're looking for a Mr Sleak-Cunningham.'

What dealings could such people have had with that unlucky man? Were they witnesses to some drainage crime? But only one of them would have been called, surely. And why did they seem so hurried?

Whatever their purpose, their question was now a sad one. 'You'll not find him here,' I answered. 'He resigned from the Committee just this morning.'

My words had no small effect upon the group, passing over them like a frozen breeze, lengthening the fellows' faces, causing them to frown and glance at one another in shared emotion. Their leader was the first to recover himself. 'Well who's taken his place?'

'Nobody. The man only went this morning. The Committee's still in some confusion.'

My answer caused the fellow to regard me with suspicion, as if I were deliberately contriving to keep him in the dark. 'We've no time to waste standing in empty corridors. We must see somebody without delay. People are being poisined.'

So that was it. Cholera hysteria. Probably half of London was rife with it by now. And *The Times* had pointed the finger of blame at Sleak-Cunningham's Committee.

Having started, the fellow could not stop himself. 'People down our end's got nothin' to drink except Thames. Or worse. An' now, with all the flushing of the sewers by this lot here, the river's bin filled up to the brim with poisin. Pure Cholera poisin. Pouring it into the water like they want us to die.'

Others added their voices. 'Half Jacob's Island's sick or dead.'

'They'll be none left if they don't put an end to it.'

Despite their threatening I could not feel sorry for the poor souls. Had they been calmer I would certainly have explained how their alarms were quite mistaken, and their enemy was not in water but in the air. As it was, however, I deemed it wise only to extricate myself. 'I'm most sorry to hear of this. There are still one or two fellows upstairs who may know more than I.'

Deflected rather than soothed, they grunted acknowledgement and began trooping away up the staircase. Hove would have the pleasure of answering their questions.

Raspberries and apple, with sugar too; the former fruit was dominant of colour, giving the contents of the glass a dull resemblance to blood. I saw the drink long before it had reached my table; indeed, when it was barely emerged through the doors of the establishment's kitchen. The sight of it evoked in me a child-like longing for its taste and powers of restoration; a simple longing, unconscious but intense.

I had picked the first of the Haymarket cafes I reached. A smaller one than its neighbours, it seemed to have something of a horse-racing tradition, containing several sharp types, lounging behind their pink racing papers, while the walls, I observed, were decorated with portraits of the animals, forelegs daintily raised. The waiter had regarded me doubtfully, his glance lingering upon my sagging frock-coat, then scanning the other tables; still scarce of customers at so early an hour.

'All right. But first let's see your money.'

Raspberries and apple. The thick sharpness of the drink caused, with each gulp, wonderful relief, and a faint dizziness. I breathed deeply, as one just emerged from a long spell beneath water. The contents of the glass I had done with so fast that the waiter was still within easy calling distance.

'Another. Just the same.'

The second I drank more slowly, observing the taste of the fruit themselves; apple and raspberries made a fine combination; the right balance of sharpness and something cooler. The sugar soon caused in me a raising of spirits. Sleak-Cunningham gone; it was a disappointment, of course – I could not help but feel resentment towards the man, though illogical, for tumbling from grace thus – but it should not be the end of all my hopes. I must not allow it to be so.

Though the governmentalists might be broken asunder there was still, was there not, the world of private finance. After all was not the beauty of the scheme that it would be highly profitable? What need had I of the Committee for Sewers? I would consult Harold Sweet – the man would hardly be mourning Sleak-Cunningham's fall – that I might learn whom to approach. Someone in that financial whirl of the city, perhaps. He would know. Indeed, he himself might be interested.

I was still in such a state of keen pondering – though my fifth raspberry and apple drink was causing me to feel a touch sick – when I discovered myself to be in shadow; that of a fellow stood close over my table. At first I assumed it to be the waiter, come for payment. Nor was I far wrong, in either detail; only in his identity was I mistaken. Glancing up, I found before me the waiter from the Cafe Castelnau, just a few doors down. He looked much annoyed.

'Why in hell d'you have to bring yourself here?'

I misunderstood his words. 'I'll take my custom wherever I choose.'

'No . . .' He leant forward on to the table, impatient. 'You have the money?'

'What money?'

'The two sovereigns.'

My heart grew swift as I grasped his meaning. 'You've seen them?'

'Him. Of course I have. Spotted him almost an hour ago. I've been half killing myself hoping you'd turn up.' He gave a weary gasp. 'Then, when I see you out the window, marching down the very street, you have to come in here. Took every dodge I know to get out without the boss catching me.'

At last. After all this time of waiting . . . 'He's not gone?'

'Not so far as I know.'

I dropped coins on to the table. 'He's in the Castelnau?'

'No, but near enough.'

I hurried out with the fellow, into the din of the street, glancing at the elegant types drifting past. After all these months . . . 'Where?'

The waiter frowned knowingly. 'Dosh first.'

'It's not easy to get at.' To extract the coins from the frock-coat hem, impatient as I was, I had to resort to ripping at the cloth with my teeth, much to the interest and amusement of the nearby tramps. Until they fell free into my hand, both together.

'Over there,' he murmured, calmer now that his profit was seen. 'In the sea-serpent show he went. I'd best show you.'

I hurried to pay our sixpences, stepping beneath the hoarding that proclaimed, in large letters:

LIVING SEA SERPENT.
FIFTEEN FEET IN LENGTH.
SHOWN HOURLY.

Though it was poorly lit within, there was light enough just to discern, in faint detail, the backs of the heads of the audience. We kept to the rear of the place, paying little heed to the goings-on upon the stage – a fellow with too many teeth, stood before a block-shaped object covered with a blanket, boasting of the ferocity of the creature hidden – but studied the rows before us. The waiter murmured a faint grunt of recognition.

'Five towards the right. D'you see? The two next to the woman in the hat with birds. They came in together. He's the shorter one. On the left.'

I studied the slim neck, the fashionably cut hair. A strange moment. 'You're sure?'

'Certain.'

I handed him the sovereigns but he lingered. 'There's another looking for her, you know. Pale bloke. Almost like an albino.'

Again. He seemed my most determined adversary. 'D'you know who he is?'

The waiter shook his head. 'Couldn't say.' Already he seemed less sure as to whether his informing me had been wise; perhaps he had been taking the fellow's money. 'Just thought I'd tell you.' With a kind of smile he was gone.

The many-toothed chatterer – after warning the audience of the perilous creature they were facing, and recounting whom it had lately eaten – whipped away the blanket. The glass-sided tank beneath contained what seemed only a large eel, looking none too healthy and disappointingly short of fifteen foot; the sight of him caused some booing from the audience, then counter-shouts from those more impressed. Though the introducer continued to tell of its exploits, I observed my quarry and his companion get up from their seats to leave.

Outside, pretending to read a theatre poster, I kept watch as they stopped, that they might discuss where they should go next.

'. . . as dull and dead as Henry's dinners . . .'

'. . . a Mr Danby lecture . . .'

From such fragments of their conversation – uttered in yawnlike, bantering voices – I gathered they were university undergraduates, down from Oxford or Cambridge for the summer vacation, and at something of a loss as to what to do with themselves on this warm afternoon. There seemed to be no great closeness between them – indeed they addressed one another almost with antipathy – so I suspected they had joined company not out of enthusiasm, but from a mutual failure to have made any better arrangement for the day.

My quarry seemed keen to visit some cafe – the Castelnau, I wondered, or had he found himself some new haunt – that they might '. . . watch the gals go by and such'.

His companion – a thinner and altogether more

nervous-seeming soul – favoured, instead, a gallery. '. . . that new one, Herbert, off Piccadilly, that has Roxborough's angel paintings.'

Herbert – I now knew his name – was unmoved. 'I'd rather see the real thing.'

He was quite a man of fashion, dressed up in an outfit of some elegance; his waistcoat was of colour and floweriness fit to line a baby's crib. A precious sort, and, by the look of him, wealthier even than I had anticipated; Isobella seemed to be moving in high social circles indeed. Had she known such people long previously, without my ever suspecting? Flitting away, perhaps, when I was busy at work, to rendezvous with some magnate's son?

This one was so young. A mere puppy. Yet he had, in all likelihood, tasted what I, her lawful husband, had been laboriously denied. His perfumed fingers touching what I had never known.

Though the Sea Serpent had hardly been a success, their wishes proved so contradictory that in the end they found agreement only on a further novelty show. Indeed, as the afternoon dwindled they embarked on quite a tour of such places.

My main concern as I pursued them was, naturally, that I should not be observed; a matter by no means easily achieved as the two scurried half across the West End of London and back, from one den of entertainment to another. That I was not seen was probably due less to my artfulness than their lack of suspicion. Neither was expecting to be watched.

Thus I found myself following them into, variously, 'Banvard's Grand Moving Cyclorama view of the Mississippi River' (described on the hoarding outside as 'The Longest Painting in the World at no less than Three Miles'), then 'Admiral Van Tromp the Dutch Dwarf' (Surpassing any Dwarf yet in Stature, Activity and Manner'), Madame Tussaud's exhibition of waxwork likenesses of the famous, and, finally, Cantello's famous Egg-Hatching Machine in Leicester Square

('Chickens seen bursting from their Shells in the presence of visitors, including Royalty').

The Egg-Hatching Machine proved something of a watershed; loitering outside, on the fringes of a crowd drawn by a fellow selling hair restorer, I heard each word of the debate. While his companion appeared to have been delighted by the sight of the creatures emerging from their shells, Herbert was unimpressed.

'What a bore. A lot of chicklings pecking through their nasty shells.' He blew his nose into his handkerchief with some disdain. 'I say it's time we try something in an altogether spicier line.'

The other disagreed. 'I liked the chicks. Anyway, we've still to see Wizard Jacobs on Oxford Street.'

'To hell with the damn wizard.' Herbert gave the other a look. 'Jeremy, don't you think it's time you jacked playing nursery?'

Jeremy found this last remark offensive, and, after some further wrangling, in which neither would give way, marched himself off in a huff. Herbert was left alone. He stood for a while in front of Cantello's place, kicking absently at a piece of loose paving. Then abruptly turned and strode away towards one of the small alleys that lead to Trafalgar Square.

What better chance could I expect? The way was a quiet one, and long enough that I might catch him up without need of running, and so risk of causing him to bolt.

Drawing near, at a point so dark that I was guided as much by the sound of his footsteps as by the sight of him, I took a long stride, reached forward, and pushed him against the brick wall, evincing something like a yelp. Indeed, beneath his fine clothes he was nothing more than a shrimp of a fellow, and offered little struggle as I held him smartly by the lapels; only uttering a kind of scared whimpering.

'Don't hurt me, please. Take my wallet. It's yours.'

'Your money's nothing to me,' I told him. 'The woman you were with at the Cafe Castelnau. Where is she?'

His face was only a vague shape in the gloom. From his tone of voice my question confused him. 'Which woman?'

'Which woman? Which woman? How dare you not remember?' My wife may have used me most ill, but still I would not hear her slighted thus. 'I'm speaking of Isobella.'

'Isobella?' Still no enlightenment, though he seemed eager enough to give me an answer. 'Isobella Farqueson? The duke's daughter?'

She might have given another name. I thought of striking a match that he could see the locket, but decided the darkness was not without use. He would not know who had waylaid him. 'Fair. Eyes very pale. A full figure. It was in mid-June, a Wednesday afternoon.'

'You mean Lucy?' He sounded unsure.

'You were with her in the Castelnau?'

'I met her there.'

'Lucy then.' Probably she had been too ashamed to reveal her real identity. If she were capable, that was, of such delicacy of feeling. My thoughts recalled how his foot had touched hers beneath the table, so immodestly that the waiter himself had observed. 'What surname did she give?'

'Hardcastle. But what's all this to you?'

'Never you mind,' I told him firmly. 'Just tell me where she is now.'

'It's some time since I saw her last.'

A further insult. 'You took up with her just for a short while, I suppose, then threw her away when you grew bored.'

'Not at all,' he whined. 'She went off with another fellow. A Hungarian.'

Foreigners now. 'Who?'

Here he made a belated attempt to stonewall. 'I can't say. I just can't.'

I gave him another shove to remind him of the hardness of the bricks behind him; not, I admit, without some satisfaction. The effect was like shaking apples from a tree.

'Count Nemis.'

A count. Next I would find my wife had opened her legs to minor royalty. 'And where is this man?'

'He's only sometimes in London. But he stays in the Hotel Orleans. In Mayfair.'

'This had better be true,' I warned.

'It is,' he wailed.

I let him linger a moment in the silent darkness. 'You'd be most unwise to make any attempt to tell this man of our talk here.' As my hold over him would vanish the instant I let go of his lapels, I resorted to a little poetic licence. 'You are known, Herbert, and you are easily found. Stay quiet and no harm will come to you.'

'I will.' The fellow whimpered so fearfully – especially at the sudden mention of his own christian name – that I left him, slumped against the alley wall, with some hope he would do as I urged.

The Hotel Orleans was not a name I was familiar with. Nor was it, I soon learned, familiar to many other metropolitan inhabitants; only after a good deal of asking did I find myself standing before its entrance. Looking on to a quiet street not far from Shepherd's Market, the sign and frontage were modest, and gave little hint of the grandeur within. A uniformed boy pulled open the door as I approached, revealing a surprisingly spacious hallway with, as centrepiece, a marble statue of a naked girl staring musingly upwards in classical pose. A discreet establishment. Two porters scrutinized me uncertainly, probably wondering whether I were some wayward-looking guest worth a few pennies' tip, or one who would shortly require flinging out of the door. Behind the desk, the reception clerk – a hairless sort whose skin possessed a pink, putty-ish look to it, as if he had applied theatre make-up – glanced towards me with disapproval.

'I have a message for Count Nemis.'

The man showed no surprise. 'Give it over then.'

So Herbert had been telling the truth, at least thus far. 'There's no note. It's a verbal message.'

A frown, tempered by the thin smile of one in possession of an insuperable obstacle. 'He's still off abroad, isn't he. Won't be back for two days.'

'I'll return then.'

I had to be sure. Accordingly I did not leave the neighbourhood, but made for a beer house lodged close behind the Orleans. Sure enough, within the hour I spied, stepping in through the door, the thirsty face of one of the hotel porters. Nor were his reddened features misleading; he proved far from averse to accepting the offer of a drink from a stranger, nor prejudiced against a few unexpected shillings.

'The count? Yes, I know him all right. Carried 'is bags a few times. A good tippin' man. When it comes to yer pennies these foriners is often freer than our home grown nobs.'

He had been staying, it seemed, only a couple of weeks previously. I asked if he had been in company.

'With 'is cousin.'

Disappointment. But then I saw the knowing look on the other's face.

'As much 'is cousin as is meself, she was. And as 'ungarian as good Lord Palmerston. Nice bit, mind. If I was a bleedin' count, I'd have myself a few cousins like that, I can tell you.'

Shouts and animal cries breaking the late night stillness of Mayfair; walking along a narrow street, I found before me a shopman's cart, one wheel splintered upon a lamp-post, a cascade of onions and potatoes fallen into the street muck. Before and behind other carts stood caught, their owners cursing as they tried to turn them about in the stifling place. The shopman himself was beyond such efforts, merely striking his horse repeatedly with his whip – in slow vengeance for nothing – and causing the poor animal to neigh and bellow in pain.

An ugly commonplace scene. I strode past as quick as I might. Then, reaching an avenue of fine villas, their front gardens filling the air with rich, summer-night smells, I felt myself caught by sudden faintness. I leaned against a gate post until my head cleared, my breath grew even.

Two days only to wait. Walking onwards, I felt – coming upon me no less abruptly than my weakness – a reanimation. Though light of head still, I was filled with eagerness; a kind of pale energy. I felt as one in control, possessed of power. Striding down the wealthy street it was as if I might – should I choose – command the very bricks and timbers of buildings to stir from their places, the clouds in the sky to scatter and dance.

Two days. And what would I do when I found her? One moment my thoughts were dark; my hand would clench in my frock-coat pocket, touching the thin blade of the knife emblazoned with battling warships. Next I would conjure up in my head impassioned scenes; Isobella weeping distraught on the ground before me as she repented, I – haughtily dignified – hearing her out, sometimes choosing to forgive her, sometimes casting her into the night.

The truth was I could hardly imagine what might occur. All possibilities were as some dreamed fiction.

Regent Street was lifeless except for a solitary drunk bawling at a shop window, and a few tramps crouched in doorways. Beyond, in the rubbish-strewn lanes of Soho, more signs of humanity were to be found. Tarts peered out from their places, cooing to me to stop. 'Give yer a good time, mister.'

'How yer doin', lonely?'

It was some time since I had been the subject of such interest. I was pleased, feeling it to be, somehow, a further sign of my improved fortune.

When I reached the rented room, however, exhaustion

returned, as swiftly as it had departed. I did not trouble to light the lamp but, seeing my way by the faint light of the moon drifting through the window, slumped upon the bed – the copy of my drain plan, concealed in the mattress, a touch hard to fall upon – and closed my eyes.

Weariness flowed through me, yet I could not sleep. After a few minutes I sat up. Probably, I considered, it was my overtiredness – the consequence of weeks of exhaustion finally catching up with me – that prevented unconsciousness.

I rose, more from habit than design, and crossed to my desk, peering through the telescope into the darkness. It was then that I felt the nausea. So sudden that, for a moment, I almost imagined – illogical though it was – that the device might somehow be to blame. But then, rising to my feet, I felt a threatening sense of looseness in my bowels.

I was much relieved to find the privy was unoccupied; an advantage of returning at such a late hour. My stomach was in quite a turmoil. Though concerned, I still imagined I might be suffering nothing worse than had Miss Symes. Something that had been left too long in the hot sun. The pork and orange pie, perhaps. Or even the raspberries in the drinks. I would make camp until it was passed.

It was only later, when the diarrhoea changed to fits of vomiting, that I acknowledged to myself what had actually struck.

Chapter Eight

The Piedmontese possess fine skills indeed in the arts of food. The country being a poor one compared with my own, dishes contain only meagre quantities of meat – reflected in the feeble physique of the inhabitants – but are flavoured with ingenious use of herbs and spices. Though I am careful to keep up my strength with frequent resort to beef steaks, I am also most partial to many of the local offerings.

A staple dish here is pasta; wheat cooked by boiling, often taking the form of long strands named 'Spaguetti'. At first I found its texture unsettlingly slippery, but with time I have grown used to its foreign nature, and now I consume it often. It is especially good with a sauce called 'Pesto', which, though created from nothing more than ground nuts, cheese and leaves of the Basil herb, is most subtle and distinctive in taste.

This popular love of flavours is reflected in the great number of food markets to be found in Turin. These, indeed, are my favourite feature of the city, especially where fruit and vegetables are sold. The stallholders show something akin to artistic talent in the way they display their wares, in patterns of colours finely catching to the eye. Customers make their choice only after careful inspection of the fruits themselves, and much noisy disputing as to the price.

Though the weather is now grey and icy, with a cutting wind blowing down from the Alp mountains, in August the sun is hot indeed here. Accordingly street pumps and drinking fountains are to be found in most of the market places; features that never fail to win my glance. The water is usually of good quality and all but absent of lurking vilenesses, much of it carried hither via ancient water-courses, from streams freshly emerged from the hills. Still, after that long metropolitan summer, I cannot watch the stallholders and their children as they drink their fill, or playfully cause the water to spray upon one another, without remembered disquiet.

The singular feature of the Asiatic Cholera is its utter lack of fever. How different from typhus, influenza, scarlet fever, smallpox, and most of the other fearful maladies that afflict us. These reduce the sufferer to a state remote from the world, whether in dream-like delirium, or the blankness of a sweated coma that may endure for days and nights. Cholera, by contrast, leaves its victims alert, rational – if ever weaker – almost to the very end.

Not that my lucidity made the ordeal easier to endure; quite the opposite was true. Fever, though it can effect nightmarish delusions, at least dulls the senses, and speeds the passing of time with sleep. By contrast I was all too aware of the rising nausea that warned of further attacks of vomiting, the sharp pains in the pit of the stomach that followed each assault.

The privy was an outhouse behind the main building; a shack built upon a hole. It was late as I crouched there in the darkness – hand pressed against the wall that I might keep balance, waiting for the next fit of retching – but not so late that all neighbours were asleep. I heard one pace across the yard, push at the door – a poor piece with no lock, that could be kept closed only by pressing upon it with a foot – then knock more rudely.

'What'cher doin' hin there? Writing an hincyclopedia?'

Though I was reluctant to tell of the nature of my affliction – I feared I might be blamed for having brought the malady into the district – the risk had to be taken.

'I have the Cholera.'

The other ceased thumping at the door, but uttered no reply.

'Can you get me a doctor?'

I heard nothing but his footsteps fade away.

Silence. I regretted not having been firmer with the man. I should have shouted. Demanded he do as I asked, this moment. Or at least required he bring me some water.

This last was the one that occupied my thoughts most as the hours passed.

The process of ejections worked me into a state of parched thirst, mouth dry and foul-tasting, and tongue feeling as swollen as an orange. In my room, I remembered, was some water I had collected in the bucket – if only a small amount – and twice I tried to venture across the yard to the building that I might reach it. The disease, however, allowed no expeditions; I stumbled only a few yards before weakness and further spasms sent me back.

The foolishness of having rented a slum room, of isolating myself from the world I knew. In that oozing darkness any face would have been welcome. Miss Symes herself would have been as an angel.

With time the vomiting and diarrhoea worked upon my body like great hands squeezing dry a cloth; my arms, legs and gut became subject to sudden fits of cramp, while, with my fingers, I could feel the surface of my skin strangely altered. When the dawn light filtered through the cracks in the door, I observed, with revulsion, how wrinkles had broken out across most of my body, while in places I could perceive an ominously blue tinge.

Morning. People, surely. Finally I heard light footsteps and saw a small girl approach, whom I recognized as one of the daughters of the Irish family who lived across the hallway. I leant my head past the privy door and, in a voice so hoarsely feeble I hardly recognized it as my own, told her, 'Get a doctor. As quick as you can.'

Blue and wrinkled, I must have made a ghastly picture; the poor child stared at me as if I were some ghost. 'Doctor?' My request confused her. 'Where is he?'

A simpler demand was at least more likely to succeed. 'Just get me some water.'

She returned with an old stained bottle – setting it down, arm outstretched, on the ground before me, doubtless fearful I might grab her and carry her off to hell – then scurried away as quick as she could. At last. I drank the liquid down in one swig. Unwisely. My stomach churned and it was brought back no less speedily.

Quiet once more, I wondered if word of my affliction had spread through the neighbourhood, and people were deliberately keeping away. As the pale morning light grew brighter, telling of another hot day looming, I felt a weariness spreading within me. A numbing apathy. Though the attacks of vomiting – painful as there had long been nothing left to be expelled – grew less frequent, I found myself becoming almost resigned to the privy; too tired to think of effecting escape.

The Earl of Clarendon's maidservant had eaten gooseberry fool in the evening, only to be carried off in a pitched and sealed coffin next morning. Another celebrated case, much discussed in the newspapers, had been that of Mrs Smith, young and beautiful, who had dressed to go to church one Sunday morning, only to have herself taken direct to her maker by eleven that night. I had been taken ill soon after midnight, so how many hours . . .

A sad end it seemed; Joshua Jeavons, trained engineer, choking out his last breath, slumped in a privy in one of the vilest slums of London. And what of his life? After the long struggle to become trained as an engineer, I had hardly begun to put my skills to use. The drainage plan on which I had worked so hard, in which I had had such faith, would be left with its copies scattered, unknown to any who might put them to use. And as for my marriage . . .

A dark moment. I would never have imagined, as I lay sprawled in that terrible place, that one day in the future, living finely in a distant foreign country, I would look back upon my having been struck with the Cholera, and view it, in some ways, as having been one of the best things ever to happen to me.

You must know that it is possible I would have survived even had nobody come. One of the remarkable qualities of the Asiatic Cholera is that it can depart the sufferer at the latest of stages, though he seems to be toppling on the very edge of the precipice. This knowledge did not, however, diminish the gratitude I felt towards my visitor; indeed, recollection of the moment can still move me close to tears. It was not only welcome, but also so unexpected. Had I been required to guess the identity of who might arrive to assist me in such a dark hour, I do not believe I would have succeeded though I had all morning to try.

The several sets of footsteps must have advanced swiftly, as – weak as I was – by the time I had raised myself to peer through the crack in the door, I could see only pairs of legs, the foremost among them clad in a finely fashionable cut of trousers, polished black shoes, and possessing, beside them, the neat metal tip of a stick.

'Drain man, you in there?'

It was Jem.

A humiliation, perhaps? Joshua Jeavons, requiring rescue from a vile and stinking slum privy. Joshua Jeavons, drainage engineer of the future age, self-appointed saviour of the metropolis, so reduced in situation that he is in need of the help of a child criminal. It did not strike me so at the time, I assure you.

'Slim Jimmy here heard 'em chattering down by the butcher's stall,' he explained, indicating one of the two wan adults beside him. 'Sayin' the toff wot had bin askin' all them questions had bin struck nasty – 'course I guessed it were you – who else could it be – an' I couldn't leave me mate the drain man to go pewkin' hisself to death.'

'Can you find me a doctor?'

'Surely.'

I tried to express my thanks, but he seemed hardly to hear, his attention having already moved onwards, to the task of moving me from the privy. Though I tried to stand I found myself unable, and the lad had his two confederates help me; managing the operation with the same enjoyment with which he had directed Hayle – long previously as it now seemed – my servant during the sewerage researches.

'Take him by his arm, why don't you – an' don' forgit that funny sack there – an' some'un should pick up his feet . . .'

The adults tried to touch me as little as they might – not an easy matter when they were required to carry me bodily out – presumably out of fear of themselves catching the malady. After some shoving and pushing, however, I was extracted from the place.

'My room's upstairs.' Standing now, leaning on the helpers for support, I saw we were leaving the building altogether, and moving into the street beyond.

'You don't wanna stay in this 'orrible slum, does you?' From the scorn in Jem's voice one might have imagined he had never strayed from the most respectable of accommodation, and had slept in nothing poorer than linen bedsheets. 'Come up to me rooms, why don't you.'

A long journey it seemed, along dazzling streets, past street stallholders with their raucous cries; though it could not have been further than two hundred yards. One comfort was that it was bodily weakness that made it so, rather than any further attacks of vomiting. These seemed, for the moment at least, to have ceased.

The rooms were just as Jem had claimed at our last brief meeting; spacious indeed for such a district.

Having sent off one of the adults to search for a doctor, he placed me in the hands of 'Me gal, by the name of Sal'. A sleepy-eyed creature, pretty of face – though she was barely more than a child – she set about giving me a rudimentary wash, as I had been fearfully stained by my ordeal. Then, having me lie down on a couch, she handed me a glass of water.

'Drink it slow.'

Miracle of miracles, it stayed down.

Jem was evidently much pleased to have a guest present, even in such circumstances, and strode about the room, proudly pointing out details of the premises. 'See the chandelier – good in't – this here's me bedroom that I'll show you when you's better – an' I've a wardrobe big enough to put four blokes standin' in line – that's full up with me own clothes – don't think this is me only suit as I've two others jest as good if not better – an' I like to keep Sal pretty – do'n I Sal – and git her lots of bright frocks an' that – some of 'em I even bought in shops – now look 'ere . . .'

Doubtless he would have revealed more. Having managed to swallow a further three glasses of water, however, and so diminish my thirst, a profound weariness came upon me. Though I tried to listen, I soon fell deeply asleep.

I must have slept long, as it was dark when I awoke. Confused for a moment as to where I could be, my eyes first lit upon a face peering at me through the gloom, neck framed by the white rectangle of a dog collar.

'Am I dying?'

'Not you, no.' The voice was that of the Reverend Rupert Hobbes, the urban missionary. 'You're all right.' He spoke with a hint of disapproval, as if I had been feigning otherwise. 'You're among the lucky ones.'

His words surprised me. 'There are others, then?'

'Of course. Two souls carried off already.'

'I was not even the first?'

'I doubt it. One was struck soon after dusk yesterday.'

Though I had been too occupied to give the matter great thought, I had from the first assumed myself afflicted as a consequence of the expedition to the sewers; from some poisoning to which the shore workers were immune. If others in the neighbourhood had also been attacked, however, and sooner than myself . . .

'Is the malady still at large?'

'Certainly it is. Worse tonight than yesterday, with three took sick in the last two hours. People whom I'd best see to, what's more, rather than sitting here chatting.' His grim glance seemed to accuse me of time-wasting. 'As they may be nearing their ends on this earth.'

Jem showed more enthusiasm for my survival. 'Soon be runnin' round them sewers again now.'

'Jest as well you cured yourself,' added Sal, cleaning her finger nails with little girl primness. 'Seein' as the doctor wouldn't come.'

'Wouldn't come?' I was puzzled.

It seemed one of Jem's adult accomplices had been sent to find a physician of the parish, and, what was more, had succeeded. But he had been unable to persuade the man to return and see me. 'Said he weren't 'llowed,' explained Jem. 'An' that it weren't worth 'is riskin' 'is job fer – don't make much sense do it – when I done told 'Obbes he jest shook his head an' scowled.'

A mystery indeed. Though what mattered was that I had survived.

The Cholera had left me in a greatly weakened state, and, at Jem's suggestion, I remained on the couch in his rooms for some little time, resting. His girl Sal had asked advice among neighbours, and I became her patient; first working at sipping quantities of water, then embarking on quite a course of eating. This began with simple foods, such as toast with honey, then extended to more substantial dishes. I could feel the strength returning to me, and after meals – as the effects of the food dispersed through my system – I would grow strangely light of mood, as if from liquor.

This time of recuperation gave me ample opportunity to observe the routine of the household. A shocking routine it would have been, too, in the eyes of any respectable citizen, encamped beside me as a secret witness. The journals of the day would have had no hesitation in choosing phrases to describe such a place; 'A den of vice', or 'A nest of criminality'. Nor, for that matter, would such words have been inaccurate.

'Criminality'? Several times I watched Jem and the two adults stride out to the street in thoughtful concentration, to return a few hours later – noisily cheerful – and lay out their booty on the table; a wallet or two, perhaps a pocket book, or a lady's brooch or purse. Jem was skilled indeed at his new profession judging by the respectful looks on his fellows' faces after each foray, and by the division of the spoils, in which he received as much as the other two together.

And 'Vice'? Even the two adults were sometimes embarrassed by the way Jem would begin slapping or stroking Sal's more intimate parts – quite through her clothes, as if she were naked – though they might be standing close before him, or addressing him in conversation. Also there were the noises. At all times of day and night – indeed, I was astonished by the frequency – there might begin the familiar rhythmic wood creakings, the grunts and squeals, echoing forth from the bedroom. Yet by Jem's own admission Sal was not yet fifteen years old, while he was younger than she.

Vice indeed. And yet, though I was taken aback by such goings-on, I could not find it within me to greatly disapprove.

You are likely shocked, my readers. It cannot be helped. There had been a change – of no small or unenduring nature – in my understanding of things. After all, how much evil was there in pick-pocketing fineries from the fashionably wealthy, or even the rest? Nothing to encourage, certainly, but what of . . . ? One question in particular was much in my thoughts.

'Jem, why did you come and help me? You had no need to do so.'

He seemed surprised, when I uttered this, that I had thought such a question worth asking. 'Like I said, I couldn't leave the drain man to jest go cop it, could I?'

'You hardly knew me.'

He shrugged, eyes already wandering to the window, perhaps seeking some more promising subject for his attention. 'Does it matter?'

Truly there is nothing like an attack of Cholera to shake one's notions from their slumber.

Joshua Jeavons hobbling through the streets of Mayfair, finding himself – after his days of confinement – dazed by the feel of the breeze upon his cheek, by the hardness of cobblestones beneath his feet. Joshua Jeavons, dizzying greyness gathering before his eyes, causing him to lean against a wall, until the moment is passed. Then pressing onwards, towards the Hotel Orleans.

Three days of convalescence and studious eating had done much to restore my strength and, that morning, stepping tentatively from my couch, I had discovered myself light-headed to the point of frailty, but no worse. Jem had been delighted by the sight of me, thus mobile, and had at once used the opportunity offered to press me into a full tour of the house, showing off – with great pride – the splendours of his clothes, his oak bottle chest, the wardrobe large enough to hold four men stood side by side, and many other prized possessions. 'So you can see what a right sharp I's become.'

My announcement, soon after, that I intended to leave my hosts' charge – at least for a few hours – and venture out into the world, brought, however, quite a change. The sitting-room, that had been so serious and adult for all these days, seemed abruptly to alter into a kind of raucous nursery. Jem plucked my battered top hat and, with a shout of triumph, began a game of throwing it back and forth to Sal – she shrieking with delight – so it was ever beyond my reach. I only retrieved it by feigning great anger; indeed this seemed to have been the lad's intention, as it caused him to subside into giggles.

'Drain man the kill joy, drain man the kill joy,' he called out, sing-song. 'Go out and git yerself Cholera agin, why don't you?'

I had almost forgotten the real ages of the two, so mature had they seemed during the previous days, as they nursed me back to health. A strange transformation to witness. And, I may say, the sight of them squealing and playing, children once more, caused my respect for them to be enhanced, not otherwise.

Before I might venture out, I had to attend to the unfortunate matter of my clothes, as these had by no means been improved by my night of sickness. Both cuffs had been torn clean away from my shirt, so the sleeves flapped raggedly, while the front of the garment was fearfully marked with yellow and brown stains that I had been unable to vanquish. Nor was my frock coat much better; the black of the material had begun to fade into greys and discolourations, and the elbows each had a gaping hole. One boot had cracked so that the sole was loosened and my toes peered out at the front, while the brim of my hat – trodden upon by one of Jem's helpers as he tried to raise me up from the privy floor, and further weakened by Jem's playing – hung down, absurdly, as a throwing ring caught about a prize at a fairground game.

Between his childish teasings, Jem went so far as to offer – and most keenly – to buy for me a whole new suit of clothes. I felt I could hardly accept such kindness, as he had already helped me more than enough, but I did ask if he had any materials with which I might engage on repairs.

This process proved no easy one. The discolourations upon my garments proved so ingrained that I was forced to work upon them with nothing more subtle than paint; white upon the shirt, black for the frock coat, hat and the sack containing my drain plans. The holes at my elbows I patched with some spare pieces of sackcloth – though they by no means matched the worn smoothness of the material – while for the hat, I had no choice but to secure the drooping brim with a length of string, progressing downwards from the upper reaches of the garment at a slant, rather in the manner of a cathedral flying buttress. Possessed, as I was, of no cobblers' skills, for my shoes I resorted to the desperate measure of filling the gaping ends with black painted newspaper, and, as my toes were still part visible, of colouring these to match. Altogether, stood before the mirror of Jem's wardrobe, I realized myself to form an odd-looking sight indeed. Though no stranger than many others on the streets of London.

The foyer of the Hotel Orleans looked different by the light of morning; uneasy, and lacking in its night-time slickness. The porters seemed less knowing, more loitering, while the statue of the naked girl in classical pose resembled less a soul seeking the light of inspiration than one fresh emerged from the bath, only to find herself in a room full of interested strangers.

Four days it was since I had stood here last, after my pursuit of Herbert, son of the aristocracy, about the novelty shows of London. The realization came as a shock. Four days. The Cholera had caused such a twisting and turning of the road of my memory that all occurrences prior to my sickness seemed belonged to some other era.

Of what is composed the experience of disease? Suffering, of course, and pain. Also a huge bewilderment of the senses. Lastly – and most important of all – the fear of worse soon to come; a brush with death. A simple enough matter, perhaps, yet the effects can be enduring. In place of mere habit, mere assumption, we may find a surprised excitement at life. Where there had been only haste, can arise new reflection. Anger strangely dissipated.

The truth of it was, though her betrayals still sharply stung, and the mysteries of her vanishing were not at all reduced in their relentless allure, I no longer felt the raw hatred I had for my wife; the wish for undetermined revenge. Something was changed.

'Yes?' The clerk with putty-coloured skin peered at my clothes doubtfully, with something of a sneer. I could hardly blame the fellow; indeed, I was doing my best to conceal from his eye a smudge of black paint that had formed upon the polished surface of the reception desk.

'Count Nemis,' I told him. 'He should be back from abroad by now.'

Inspecting the key racks behind him, he regarded me with bored satisfaction. 'The Count's out. Won't be back till night. Nine at the earliest. You could come back then, though of course there's nothing to say he'll see you.'

An annoyance, I considered, but no giant one. Only a matter of a few more hours. All my forward thinking still focused upon the expected moment of that meeting, and not beyond; strange, it seems now, that I could see no further into the future than an event so unsure and unplanned, yet so it was.

I would sit out the time at Jem's, I decided, where I could resume my rest; he had urged me to return. Nine o'clock seemed no great distance hence. I could sleep my way through to the hour.

How mistaken one can be.

The weather was offering a rare break from heat, and by the time I returned to Jem's rooms a light drizzle was falling. The scene that greeted me was a quiet one, even domestic, with Sal working at her knitting, while Jem and his adult confederates, having enjoyed only a dull morning's pickings about the Strand, were lazily discussing which streets they might 'work' that afternoon. Their voices grew low indeed when Hobbes appeared at the door. Observing the hushed huddle regarding him, he threw them a disapproving look.

'You'll all find yourselves on Botany Bay before you know it. I've warned you often enough.'

Jem only grinned.

It was I that Hobbes had come to see, that he might be certain I had not taken it into my head to die without his say so. Observing, at a glance, that this was by no means the case, he regarded me with dulled interest. 'Better now, I see. Didn't I tell you it would be thus?'

There was no denying he had. 'What of the Cholera? Is it finished here?'

He shook his head grimly. 'Twenty-five more taken from us, and twelve more grown sick only last night.'

'Then it becomes worse.' The numbers surprised me; during the previous days I had observed, from my sick bed, a warm gusty wind blowing upon the windows, that had led me to imagine that the miasma might be expelled from the district. 'I had hoped it might be gone by now.'

Hobbes only shrugged. 'You hoped wrongly.' He glanced at his watch, then regarded me with a look more thoughtful. 'If you're so curious, why not come see for yourself. There's no little to observe, I assure you.' He cast a weary look towards the door. 'Who knows, you might even be useful.'

This last remark told me his suggestion, though sudden, was no less serious for that. To join him on his tour of the neighbourhood; a burdensome offer it seemed. My own brief brush with the disease had left me far from eager to meet with it again, even as a spectator rather than one struck. 'I've no medical knowledge.'

'Neither have I – what of it? You've a pair of arms. And you look recovered enough.' He studied me with a kind of suspended disapproval. 'Or perhaps you don't care to.'

It seemed churlish to refuse assistance when I had been so grateful myself to receive it. 'Very well.'

Walking through the odour-filled ways, still weak of head, my sack of drain plans upon my back – old habits are slow to die – I glanced about me for some signs of the Cholera raging in the district. They were not obvious; the streets were no less bustling than on any other day, the shouts and cries of street vendors selling vegetables or eels all of them quite as usual. But was there not, I observed, something new in the faces; a fearfulness, suspicion. This impression was strengthened when an ageless, red-faced fellow loitering by the roadside fixed us with a malevolent stare, murmuring, in a fashion just audible, 'Cholera doctors, come to finish the job. Cholera doctors come to settle things for proper.'

'Some of them have mad fears and suspicions.' Hobbes had noticed my alarm at the fellow. His tone surprised me; it was protective, as a father defending his children, who have been behaving poorly. 'It's not their natural state. The outbreak has made them so.'

'Has it been bad about here?'

He shook his head. 'Not here. All the cases are near by the building where you yourself were living. Here, though we're only two hundred yards distant, there's not been a single instance. It might be a different continent so far as the disease is concerned.'

And yet the stench of defective drains was far more evil close about Jem's rooms. A puzzle indeed. Was it possible the Cholera could evolve at some distance from its breeding ground, as mosquitoes spreading forth from the pools in which their grubs dwell? But then why should it gather in such concentration . . . I had little time to complete my thoughts, however, as we had soon crossed the frontier between health and death. Hobbes led the way through the gates of a cheap hostel that was close behind the building containing my rented room.

The place was not new to me, as I had visited it

during my great questioning forays. Though populated by young thieves, vagrants and prostitutes, it had possessed a strangely domestic air. The sleeping room being crowded with beds, all had been gathered in the kitchen, where they lounged at long tables; the boys smoking pipes, perhaps reading a Dick Turpin book, while the girls – many of them respectably dressed – busied themselves sewing or knitting. Now, however, the mood was quite changed. The kitchen was all but deserted, except for one poor girl spluttering over a bucket, with another sat beside her to help. The few others present were grouped at the far opposite end of the room, where they chattered noisily, doubtless to drown the sound of coughing.

A painful sight the creature made, shivering with exhaustion and fear. I knew, with such exactness, the sensations she was enduring; watching her I was affected by a feeling of helplessness, little less than stifling.

The sufferer's friend greeted Hobbes with relief. 'Back agin already, Reverind? Can't keep you away, can we.'

We sat beside them, Hobbes offering what help he was able. Though this amounted to nothing more than soothing words, I was surprised by the skill, even warmth, that he put into his task, revealing quite a different view of the man from the dour fellow I had seen before; I could understand now why many in the neighbourhood seemed to have trust in him. For my part – feeling a fierce need to do something of usefulness – I told the girl how I had myself been struck with the disease, and recovered.

'Don't give up to it,' I urged. 'You'll be better before you know.'

Our words seemed to give her some cheer.

If the hostel had seemed a grim spot, our next destination made it seem nothing less than an oasis of calm and comfort. A single room in a tottering house, it was inhabited by at least ten people; though whether they were of one family or two was impossible to say, the confusion was so great. Most of the space was quite taken up with beds, which – despite the lateness of morning and the crisis all around – still had several sleeping occupants, enwrapped in their sheets like mummified Egyptian Pharaohs. The floor was stained with the vilest of spillings, which nobody had thought to clean away, and the air stank beyond description. A poor lank-haired fellow with hopeless eyes – one who, with dismay, I realized I had once questioned in the street about Isobella, and who had answered me kindly enough – greeted Hobbes as if he were some long lost prince.

'Your reverind. Come at last.'

The odours, the suffocating absence of space, the familiarity of the fellow's hopeless eyes; these were too much for me. Only a short while before, walking in the street, I had still been regarding the Cholera as something of a dangerous puzzle yet unsolved. Stood here, I saw it clearly; more clearly, indeed, even than when it had struck myself. It was wickedness, nothing less. 'These people should be in hospital. All of them.'

'True enough.' Hobbes crouched over a child who had been struck; one that, judging by the lank soul's jumbled utterings, was his own. Its mother, too, had been affected, explaining why nothing had been done to remove the mess. 'Except that the parish hospitals are full, and the Guardians haven't seen fit to open houses of refuge.'

To open such places was a usual precaution during such a crisis. 'Why ever not?'

He only shrugged. 'I'm not acquainted with their reasoning. I only know their instructions.'

To do nothing in the midst of such a crisis was not mere indolence, it was . . . 'Whose decision was this? The Guardians', or some higher authority's?'

'I couldn't say.' Turning, he called to the lank-haired fellow to bring up some water from the street pump.

I helped him move the mother from where she lay. 'What could possibly justify such a thing?'

'Perhaps they don't like the smell of charity.'

To open no houses of refuge at such a time . . . The clamour of my thoughts grew louder as we worked upon the dismal room. A criminal act. Greater even than criminal. If it were indeed as Hobbes had claimed. Or might there yet be some less harsh explanation?

We began with those unafflicted who were lying strewn in the beds – one, remarkably, still snoring – evicting them from their places. By moving the beds back and forth we shifted the tiny space remaining, and so were able to scrub at the vilenesses lurking below. Our efforts, gratifiably, were not without effect, and the lank-haired fellow joined us, along with two of those previously sleeping. Before long the chamber was improved, at least within the narrow confines that such a den might reach; we washed the sheets that were soiled, and placed the child and mother on the cleanest of those remaining, that they could enjoy at least some little dignity. Both were in a state of coma – usually the very final stage of the disease – and the skin of each was as wrinkled as that of some ancient crone, but with a visible bluish tinge; it seemed hardly likely either might recover, though the lank-haired man – husband and father – kept up a restless flow of questions to Hobbes, as to his opinion of their state.

'She's got a bit of colour there, on her cheeks. Don't you see? Come an' have a look, Reverind. She's less blue than before, surely.'

The vicar gave no answer, except to promise to return as early as he might, within an hour or two. What else could he say to the fellow?

'Perhaps the Guardians don't realize the seriousness of the outbreak here,' I suggested to him, as we made our way down the stairway. 'Have you spoken to them yourself?'

He shook his head. 'There's been no time. I sent

several messages, but received no reply.'

I have never been one to enjoy the role of mere spectator; of one who takes no action, though the very ground and air seem to be crying out for nothing less. 'There might've been some confusion,' I proposed. 'I could go to them, and try and settle the matter.'

Hobbes only shrugged. 'As you like. Though I doubt there's much purpose.'

I would make it of purpose; I would remonstrate with the fellows, and have them see the matter truly. Indeed, my strength of feeling gave to me a strange sureness in my own powers of persuasion. 'I will go.'

Outside, the drizzle was falling still, working upon the street dust so it formed a powdery mire, much like old dough. The wet was no small relief after the long heat, and did much to steal the salty gauze from the air. Striding through the alleyways, I observed the local women had been quick to make use of this change; on the wooden rails straddling the chasm hung quantities of still-wet washing – heavy in the breeze – doubtless placed there in the hope that it might dry before the dust returned, staining all beige.

'I do'n know you.'

In my haste I at first hardly noticed the speaker. A ragged fellow, crouched on his haunches by the side of the road, his hair seemed to be hurtling all in the same direction, as if he had stood too long in a windy place.

'I said I do'n know you.' When I did not answer, or slow my pace – I was in too great a hurry to dally at the command of some poor madman – he got to his feet, blocking my way. 'Who're you then?'

'What's it matter? Out of my way, please.'

He did not move, however. 'But it does matter. Matters a good lot.' He regarded me, eyes intense, yet somehow un-seeing. 'Snooty voice you's got for one in such rags. Bin sent, have you?'

The remark meant nothing to me. I made to step round the fellow, only to have him block me again.

'In a hurry, in't we?'

'Indeed I am.' The strange gleam in the fellow's eye – unreadable, yet pregnant – made me reluctant to attempt simple force upon him. 'And I'd be grateful if you'd let me pass.'

'Where's you off to then, in yer hurry?' He managed something like a knowing grin through the grime on his face, the effect being most unsettling. 'But I can guess. Off to the wells, in't you?' Having reached this mysterious deduction, he turned, that all loitering in the street might hear. 'Caught one, 'aven't I. Come and see.'

As it was, most of those within hearing – the few pondering melancholy bargains at the stalls – showed no great interest in his announcement to them. Only an old crone and a vagrant child – his face resembling a blackened pancake – stopped to watch.

Though far from certain what manner of fellow he thought he had caught, I felt I had little choice but to try and reason with the man. 'If you must know, I'm set upon a most urgent task, on behalf of the Reverend Rupert Hobbes.'

Though the name caused something like recognition, it brought no change in the fellow's disposition towards me. 'An' I'm good Queen Vick's uncle.' Indeed, he stepped nearer, that he might better obstruct my path. 'Got yer poisin, has you, mister snoot? Yer poisin that you've bin shovin' into our wells, that we'll all drop dead of Cholera?' He stared knowingly at his small audience, and they looked blankly back. 'Show us it, why don't you? Show us your poisin.'

So that was his delusion. An absurd claim, but one also potentially hazardous to me; I glanced about the street, to see if any others were showing interest in the scene. Fortunately none seemed to be doing so. 'The Cholera often strikes hard at a small area. It's nothing to do with poison or wells.'

'In't, indeed?' he asked, with sarcastic surprise. 'So it must jest be coincidince that all them that's bin took's drunk from the same pump, in Boot Lane. But then you'll know it, won't you mister, having jest bin there yourself, pouring your mixings into it till the water's good an' ripe.'

'But that's nothing to do with the matter. That's . . .' Here I hesitated; my thoughts tumbling upon themselves as horses trip in mid gallop. My answer seemed to vanish quite from me; the truth is, I found myself quite stopped by the mad-eyed fellow's words. 'Boot Lane?'

''Course.'

'You're sure?'

'Everyone knows.' He offered me a sneering look. 'Don't try actin' innocence with us, mister.'

It was the pump I had used many times. Used, what was more, during the days just prior to myself being struck down. It seemed hardly possible, but yet . . . In the water, not the air at all . . . The notion caught my thoughts as a scarf snagged upon a thorn branch.

'Stumped, in't he?' the other declared, triumphant, to the old crone and the vagrant child.

My thoughts were spinning. If it were so . . . Gone would be the mystery of why parts roundabout Jem's rooms had been spared; they were served by a different well. And no surprise that the shore workers had been untroubled; only those who drank the vile stuff would be affected – such as the poor souls of Jacob's Island – while One Eye and his friends, on six shillings' worth of findings a day, would never be so desperate as to drink Thames water. They would have beer.

Thus, on that drizzly early September morning, in a slum street, threatened by a wild-eyed madman of a vagrant, I found myself converted. Or at least doubtful of my old faith, which is the first stage of conversion. Thoughts bubbled in my head as some froth, stirred up by the new consequences implied. If it were indeed in the water . . .

Should I return that moment to Hobbes, and confer

with the man? But what of the Poor Law Guardians? I felt like a cat upon a wind-swept branch, unsure whither to leap.

Certainties first, theories later. I would attend to the Poor Law Guardians, dealing with them as quickly as I might. Then, after . . .

'Look at him,' declared my accuser. ''E ain't got nothing to say. Din't I tell yous I'd caught one of them poisiners.'

I had all but forgotten the fellow. 'I thank you for your help.' Reaching out, I took his unsuspecting hand and keenly shook it. 'You've done more service than you know.'

Though it was not intended to do so, I doubt any action could have been better calculated to confuse the poor man. He stared at me, quite as if I had changed myself to a hat stand before his eyes.

The miracle of London. Two minutes walking and I was gone from the land of shadowed alleys and stinking courts, of suspicious glares and fear, and was arrived in a separate world. A carriage flashed past, coat of arms emblazoned on its door and two uniformed footmen perched on the back, blinking at the rainy weather. Elegant loungers whiled away a dull morning peering at shop windows or resorting to another cup of China tea. Faces here showed not the slightest awareness that King Cholera was hard at work so near. But then how many fine folks would venture into such a spot as the Seven Dials? Most likely few had even heard the name.

The Poor Law Guardians, however, would be well familiar with the district. Especially of late. Commanders and dispensers of local government relief, they would have been busy indeed at such a time. Or so one might have assumed. Consequently it was with some concern that, as I approached the building where their meetings were held, I saw no cabs waiting, no messengers hurrying away. In fact I discerned no signs of life at all. Ringing three times, without result, I even wondered if Hobbes might have directed me to the wrong address, until I saw the brass plate beside the bell, title written upon it in fine strong letters. PARISH UNION OF ST GILES AND ST JOHN HOUSE OF ASSEMBLY.

My thoughts turned to the room with its population of sleeping and dying, floors vile with spillings.

Trying the large brass handle, I found the door was unlocked. I stepped inside.

The place was deathly quiet; the only noise within was a faint but persistent scratching, much as some cat idly battling against its own fleas. Closing the door behind me, I pursued the sound, following along a corridor and to a door, ajar. Stepping beyond I found myself in a long-shaped room, all but filled by a mighty table. Around this, presumably, would be found the Poor Law Guardians during their solemn meetings. Now it seated only a single soul, crouched pale and bespectacled at the far end, thoroughly absorbed in writing in a large leather-bound volume, the quill he used causing the scratching sound I had been following. Glancing up to find a stranger stood before him, he gave me – through his spectacles – a hard look.

'How did you get in here? Did I forget to lock the door? Out with you – this is no place for beggars.'

'I'm nothing of the sort,' I answered him, firmly. 'Where are the Guardians?'

He blinked, taken back by my unexpected resolve. 'About their own business, I dare say. They meet on Tuesdays.' He deposited his quill in the pot of ink with an irritable click. 'Today, you may know, is Wednesday.'

'Six more days?' In the very midst of a Cholera epidemic. It was as some wicked joke. Stepping closer, I observed the man was at work transcribing jottings on loose paper into a leather bound volume; his script was one of remarkable tidiness, while the text, by the look of it, seemed the minutes of some meeting. He must be the clerk. Then he should be able to call a meeting. 'They must assemble at once. We have a crisis in the parish. St Giles is engulfed in Cholera – they must be told.'

'You think the Guardians don't know what is at hand in their own parish?' He frowned at my foolishness. 'The Cholera outbreak was discussed only yesterday.'

'And what was decided?'

His face neatly closed itself. 'That's not for you to know. To examine the minutes you must first gain permission from the relevant authorities. As it is, I don't believe . . .'

Permission from relevant authorities . . . 'I've just come from St Giles – I've seen what's happening there,' I declared, with some heat. 'Now tell me what's been decided, before I lose all patience.'

He shook his head, his face emanating the dim glow of obstructive satisfaction. 'D'you have an appointment here, perhaps? No? I thought as much.' He gave my clothes a sneering look. 'I rather think you had better leave this place, before I call in somebody to make you . . .'

He got no further. It was no cunning ploy of mine; I simply hoped that, comprising, as it did, minutes to some meeting, the book in which he had been writing might tell me what I required. The effect of taking the thing from the fellow proved greater than I had anticipated. In an instant his scornful smugness vanished; indeed, his mouth fell quite open, and he stared at the thing – just beyond his grasp – almost as might a mother at her stolen baby.

'Give me that back.' He was on his feet. 'It's property of the Parish Union.'

His interest, naturally, made me all the less eager to obey. Stepping away, I began leafing through the pages of perfectly formed script.

'Stop at once. Your hands aren't even clean.'

So that was it. I picked up the ink pot – quill hanging from it – and held it above the very text.

He turned quite pale. 'Don't. Please.'

'Then show me the minutes to the meeting. They're in here, I assume.' Still holding the inkpot, I handed him the book and watched as, with great care not to crease the paper, he turned the pages. I examined the section he found.

Quite a document it proved. The decisions of assembly – decisions that seemed, from the text, strongly influenced by utterings of the chairman – included all that Hobbes had claimed, and, remarkably, much more. The Guardians had first listened to reports on the extent of the Cholera, seemingly accurate enough, and even including one that quoted a message from Hobbes. Next they had gone on to discuss the matter of houses of refuge, only to vote – and vote strongly, too – against such measures being taken. The same had been true of a proposal that they themselves should meet more frequently during the crisis. Most astonishing of all, however, was the question of doctors. The Guardians had decided, by a large majority, to actually forbid parish physicians from making house calls to those struck with the Cholera.

Doctors prohibited from seeing those struck. It seemed beyond comprehension; the invention of some grotesque satirist of the last century. Yet, staring at the page, I recalled how Jem's confederate adult had been unable to convince a parish physician to visit me, when I had been struck. The man had been scared of losing his place.

I turned to the clerk. 'What's the name of the chairman of the Guardians who led this meeting?'

'That's no secret.' He took the inkpot from me and, with something like petulance, placed it where it had sat before. 'Mr Harold Sweet.'

In one respect I was fortunate; at least the man proved easy to discover. I found him at his molasses yard, standing – keenly purposeful so he resembled some bearded circus ringmaster – before two carts being unloaded of their barrels; efficiently directing the half dozen souls struggling to bring the objects down to the ground. This last was no easy task, as evidenced by one barrel that lay shattered and oozing beside the cart wheel, filling the air with its over-rich sweetness.

'Is it Joshua?' Peering at me for a moment, uncertain, Sweet regarded me with some surprise, even alarm. 'Whatever's happened to you? You look as if you've been dragged round the streets of London head first.'

I was in no mood to be distracted. 'I've not come here to exchange news and pleasantries, Mr Sweet. I'm here because of the Cholera raging in St Giles. I've seen it at work, with my own eyes. Something must be done.'

'St Giles?' He frowned. 'Near the Seven Dials? But what were you doing in such a place? It's a dreadful spot.' He again stared at my clothes.

'It is a dreadful spot,' I agreed. 'All the more so when it's rife with the Cholera. And when the Parish Union Poor Law Guardians – of whom, I believe, you yourself are the commander – choose neatly to obstruct every assistance to those afflicted, even to the point of preventing doctors from tending to their needs.'

Such strong words were not without effect. Sweet looked at me afresh, re-appraising, absorbing this unexpected – but informed – attack, from so strangely altered an acquaintance. Not that he was persuaded by my denunciation; rather he regarded me with disappointment – something like hurt – as if I had betrayed him. 'This, from you of all people. I never counted you among the pauperizers.'

So there it was. The answer to so many questions. The theory of anti-pauperization was now raised into some kind of holy doctrine: unquestionable, requiring nothing short of tribal obedience, to be upheld regardless of consequence. Perhaps I should have known; what of the lecture Sweet had delivered to Jem on the muddy shore before Jacob's Island.

'Charity can be a dangerous thing.'

'And I,' I answered, 'never counted you as a killer-of-men. As one who would deliberately deny assistance to the sick.'

Sweet did not rise to my words, remaining coolly controlled, though his eyes seemed faintly to glow. My claims did not seem to surprise him, and I realized I was likely not the first to have voiced such things. 'You don't know what you're saying,' he insisted. 'You don't know these people. Put them in a hospital and they'll never want to leave. Offer them food and they'll see no purpose in working ever again.' He shook his head, knowing. 'You claim yourself as their friend, but in truth you're proposing to enslave them. Nothing less.'

'But you misjudge me.' I struggled to keep as tight a reign upon my feelings as he did his. 'I *do* know these people. Indeed, I am one of them. You must know that I myself have lately suffered the Cholera and – thanks to your rulings – no doctor would come.'

Probably he doubted my claim, suspecting it to be no more than an over-stretched device of rhetoric. Still he exhibited concern. 'But why did you not tell me you'd been ill?' Regarding my battered frock coat, his glance seemed to soften, perhaps at the thought that he had found a device by which my criticisms might safely be dismissed. Indeed, his voice took on something like enthusiasm. 'You're in a poor state, Joshua. I don't know what you've been doing with yourself – especially in such a place as St Giles – but you've gone downhill fearfully. No surprise you're so excitable.'

I wondered at the phenomenon stood before me. And I myself had admired him. 'Will you call a meeting of the Guardians this day?' I demanded. 'And do away with every one of these rulings you introduced?'

Though irritated, he refused to be so easily swayed from his forgiveness. 'You should take a look at yourself, really you should. You cannot go on as you are.' He reached into his waistcoat pocket. 'Now . . .'

In the legal view, I realized, he had likely committed

no wrong; he was not a man to be caught out in such matters. He might be viewed as over-zealous in his defence of the ratepayers, but nothing more. He might even escape reprimand by his superiors, continuing to be regarded as a good citizen – if a touch stern – hard working, and well deserving of his position. Indeed, for all I knew there might be countless others who had acted just as he.

'Take these four sovereigns.' He held the coins before me. 'That you may feed and rest yourself, and buy some new clothes. Then we'll talk again.'

I could not help but be struck by the proposal. 'You're offering me charity? But surely that is to put me in risk of enslavement?'

'Don't be absurd.' Losing patience, he spoke the words like a dangerous uncle, patting a child gently upon the head when, in truth, he would like nothing better than to throttle his neck. 'This is a loan, and one I have no doubt you will honourably repay. Now take these.' He thrust the coins towards me as if they were some kind of revenge in solid form. 'Then come back when you're properly recovered.'

I did not reply directly but let his offer – and his hand – hang in the air. 'Mr Sweet, I'd sooner take the stolen gifts of a pickpocket than have your gold.'

Hobbes I finally discovered, after some searching, in a dingy room above a second-hand clothes shop. Here he was at work performing the sombre rites of passage over a lifeless figure who – by his dress – had evidently been the shopman, though his selling talents and worries were now past their usefulness. His wife sat close beside the vicar, the look on her face one of amazement rather than grief; her husband's features – though distorted by the squeezings of the disease – were those of a young man, and I imagined the disease had toppled him so swiftly that she had barely had time properly to acquaint herself with the danger. She seemed hardly to hear Hobbes's words, until he reached their end. Then she grew suddenly excited.

'Say some more of it, will you, your reverind. Just a bit.'

'If you wish.'

Later stepping from the room, the vicar received my tale of Sweet and the Poor Law Guardians without surprise. 'I told you there was no purpose in visiting them,' he told me, coolly. The strange meeting with the wild-eyed fellow who had thought me a poisoner awoke a touch more interest. 'Boot Lane? It's an odd arrangement, certainly.'

'You know the well's history?' I asked. 'There was some incident during the last epidemic, perhaps?'

'Not that. But still it's not undeserving of curiosity.'

The spot was only a few yards distance from the dead shopman's door, and we were soon stood before the street pump in question, well familiar to me. It was innocent enough to the eye, certainly. Indeed, it was unexpectedly elegant for such a district, possessing a spout in the likeness of an astonished fish, mouth gaping. In the ground beside it was a metal hole cover.

'The well can be reached by opening that.' Hobbes indicated this last, then gave the handle of the pump a tug, causing a squeaking sound, and a brief gush of water, its colour that of weak tea with a dash of milk. 'There were some difficulties in which I myself became involved,' he explained. 'This was a couple of years ago. The population hereabouts had been growing swiftly and the well began sometimes to run dry, especially in the hot weather. I was asked if I might help.'

I inspected the dribble of water as it flowed over the dusty ground, slowly sinking away. Did the secret lie there? How many drops or glasses-full would be required to send a fellow from this world? It seemed amazing to me now that I had ever been able to drink such vile-looking liquid. Then again, there had been nothing else.

'It occurred to me that it might be possible to have a water company to lay a pipe here, so the well could be topped up,' Hobbes resumed, pausing to try and raise up the metal hole cover; it was firmly lodged. 'They were reluctant to have any dealings with such a spot as here, but finally I managed to persuade one among them to a special arrangement. I agreed to guarantee payment, while the pipe would only be used in times of need, which would keep down the charges. In fact the sums proved very small, and I've never had trouble over the matter. The shopowners pay between them.'

I could see the rounded outline of a pipe beneath the ground, close by the pump. So the avenue of study that had begun with the rantings of the mad-eyed fellow might not, after all, end here. 'Has the well needed topping up of late?'

'Of course. Every week since the heat began, I'd say.'

I would follow, to wherever the road might lead. 'What was the name of the water company?'

The Westminster and Thames Water Company office, filled with rows of clerks sat at splendid desks, was not busy that afternoon; the scribblers were most of them idle, while I found myself to be the only visitor to the shop, and so able to stride directly to the two fellows in authority. These were both young, and of something of a lounging disposition, which – doubtless at the sight of my attire, indicating me to be a most unlikely customer – they made little effort to conceal; as I drew near, one of them, a thin-faced sort with a budding moustache, raised an eyebrow to his colleague, as if I were some fairground novelty.

'Sorry uncle, Westminster Gaol's round the corner.'

The other coughed laughter.

To answer sharply – though tempting – would hardly add to my chances of learning what I needed. 'I've come for information.'

Further raising of eyebrows. 'Oh yes? What exactly? An estimate for your Hampstead Villa, fully piped, perhaps?'

Grinning, the other could not resist chiming in.

'Kitchen, bathrooms and fountain in the garden? Or just the filling of the lake?'

'In fact no.' I spoke as if taking their words as seriously meant. 'It's to do with a wager.'

'Indeed? Ha'penny farthing? Or not so much?'

I pretended not to notice. 'You have a pipe run out to a well in Boot Lane, close by the Seven Dials. I've drunk from there many a time, and have no doubt it's Brentford Thames. I know the taste. Yet there's a fellow across the way from me who insists it's Fulham.'

Budding moustache yawned, growing tired of the game. 'Sorry uncle. Can't help. Off you go back to Whitechapel Poorhouse, or Bedlam, or wherever it is you've sprung from.'

'It's important.'

To my relief, the other then joined in. 'I might even take a small'un myself. Seven Dials? I'd say that's the Chelsea intake.'

'Never. It's Hammersmith.'

'Five bob?'

'Five it is.' Budding moustache stood up from his desk and reached up to the giant maps on rollers that were hung from the wall behind him. 'Let's see how your luck's doing, uncle.'

The Thames at Chelsea. A picturesque scene it made, too, with Wandsworth dairy farms visible on the far bank; cows roaming the yellowed fields between the cottages, and a church spire rising up in the distance. I paid little heed, however, to such prettiness, as my attention was concerned with details closer to hand.

The tide was low and, stepping carefully over the mud by the water's edge, I had no difficulty discovering the long bulge in the slime that marked the Westminster and Thames Water Company's intake pipe; the very pipe that, by some tortuous route, led all the way to the fish-fashioned spout of the Boot Lane street pump. The position of the intake could hardly have been more remarkable. Not thirty yards upstream was the gaping mouth of one of the largest sewer outlets in London.

No doubts were left.

I remained perched upon the slippery river shore for some little time, as barges and rowboats floated lazily by, causing murky waves to spread before me on to the mud and vanish. Above, seagulls hung erratically in the breeze, squawking into the warm sky. A sky which contained no miasma cloud of poisonous gases. Which never had contained a miasma, as no such thing, I now realized, existed. A sky dark with nothing more than the swirling smoke of hundreds of thousands of fireplaces.

Whatever could have put such a notion into our heads? Perhaps the simple stink of the metropolis; a stench so abhorrent it was easy to regard as cause of any evil. Still it seemed extraordinary I had not seen it before. That none had.

None? My thoughts turned to the Jacob's Island deputation – awkward in their patched and polished Sunday best, as they found themselves in the empty corridors of the Metropolitan Committee for Sewers – and the stringy fellow who had acted as their spokesman.

'It's in the water.'

And they had gone there to urge the ending of the flushing of the sewers. The flushing . . . In such a wide and peaceful place, the scale of the disaster seemed to creep through me, as a numbness. Thousands of tons expelled into the Thames, to leave the air cleaner. Except that the air was of no danger, while half the people of London were drinking Thames.

I glanced at the sewer outlet. How much had been shot from there? With the water intake pipe just below, the effect would hardly have been more direct had the stuff been poured straight into people's mouths. And yet so many of us, myself included, had had faith in Sleak-Cunningham's flushings.

Just as we had believed in the miasma.

Sleak-Cunningham. The man had been punished, certainly. Although it was not of this that he had been accused. *The Times* had been as convinced of the miasma theory as everybody else, and had destroyed the man not for having caused the deaths of hundreds – perhaps thousands – but for his slowness to act, his power-loving secrecy. His fall, though just, had been only accidental.

Quite an education I underwent on that muddy shore. Edwin Sleak-Cunningham – beacon of the sanitary and governmentalist movements – revealed as the grand poisoner of thousands, myself among them. Harold Sweet – self-made man, paragon of the creed of political economy – shown to be a giant of inhumanity, prohibiting help to those struck, myself among them.

The process of self-dismantlement; once begun it can run far indeed. Certainties long prized seem to shimmer, precarious and needful of fresh testing. Notions leant upon, as strong crutches, show themselves frail and splintering. Until not a notion remains so sacred that it can linger in its lazy bed of assumption. So it was that distant afternoon.

No, the Cholera had not been the only malady to afflict the metropolis that long summer; another sickness had also been roaming, unchecked and unseen. A fever of belief. Symptoms: restless energy, great swelling of self-importance, impaired powers of doubt and reason. These growing ever more acute, until the patient reaches a critical state, his humanity dangerously diminished, perhaps beyond repair.

Restless energy, absence of doubt . . . Had Sleak-Cunningham and Sweet truly been the only sufferers? Sadly, I realized, it was not so.

Slowly I peeled the leather sack from my shoulders. A scheme so fine that it would answer all needs; that would fuse together the opposed causes of governmentalist and anti-governmentalist; that would both cleanse London of effluent and make its citizens wealthy. That – not least among its attractions – would bring fame and gratitude everlasting to its creator, Joshua Jeavons. That would somehow banish all dissatisfactions, recasting the world, in the manner of some glistening miracle.

Had not Hove, in his plodding way, seen more than I? As if the farmers of England would have need of such a grotesque quantity of nightsoil. And the populations of each district would be pleased to have in their midst a giant and stinking steam-powered mechanism, to process their own vilenesses. No, I too had been blinded by fever. I had barely paused to wonder if my plan was a practical one; I had been too determined that it should somehow answer, at one stroke, to the world's every conceivable need. And to my own.

One swing, a second – wider of arc – a third, and then – arm pulled taut, high before me – I opened my fingers. The sack sailed gracelessly into the air and landed in the water with a light splash. The river was low, and for a moment I wondered if it would remain lodged where it had dropped; as I watched, however, the current gave it a sleepy tug, pulling it from its place. Soon it turned upon its side, water seeping in through the opening, causing its profile in the water to decline, and, doubtless, the ink on so many pages of frantic descriptions and illustrations to run, and dissolve away into the Thames waters, staining them a little darker than before. I was still watching when it slipped beneath the surface and was gone.

What means pure belief? Belief quite severed from the humour and character of its proponent? Answer: all but nothing. It is as neutral and flavourless as pure spirit; as a house awaiting its first inhabitants. It is a thing that may yet be swung towards either good or evil. The most fine-sounding notion (as I was all too aware) can be warped to wicked effect. No, a philosophy is no better than the humanity – or absence of it – with which it is directed; the self-critical intelligence.

Joshua Jeavons quietly emptied of faiths on the soft mud of the Thames bank. A haunting, stilled moment, and one I will carry with me always. Though it was not quite despair I felt. My feet had never seemed to me so solidly stood upon the surface of the earth, my eyes had never seen with such clarity. Small comforts, you may think, but they were to grow within me.

A small crowd gathered to watch the drama. The pump handle proved by no means easy to remove; after vainly trying to smash it with a small hammer, we resorted to using some house-breaking tools of an acquaintance of Jem's, first attempting to prise it out with a crowbar, then, more effectively, striking it with a thick metal pipe. Slowly the iron began to weaken, the handle to bend away, until it snapped free completely.

The watchers seemed uncertain of the usefulness of such destruction, and looked on gloomily. Even Hobbes seemed a touch doubtful. 'Let's hope this'll prove of some purpose, beyond only adding to the walk required to reach water.'

My thoughts were still dark with what I had learned on the Chelsea shore. 'It will. I'm sure.'

The smashing of the pump left Jem in a state of great excitement – he had quite lost himself in the pleasure of shouting out directions to any present – and I felt it best to speak instead to Sal. 'If there's a single case of Cholera close by your rooms,' I warned her, 'then do not, under any circumstances, drink from the well near you. Throw away any water you've collected. And tell Hobbes. Your lives may depend upon it.'

'Aw'right, drain man.'

Young though she was, she seemed to have taken in my words.

Only after I had rung four times did the grand door of the Metropolitan Committee for Sewers deign to open, and then by no more than a crack. The fellow who peered out – regarding me with faint and alarmed recognition – I saw to be one of the clerks who worked in the upstairs rooms of the building.

'I must see Mr Hove.'

'There's nobody here.' He had the unhappy look of a foot-soldier left to defend the fortress single handed. 'There've been no meetings since Mr Sleak-Cunningham left us.'

'One must be held soon, surely?'

He shook his head. 'The minister's out of town and no new chairman's been appointed.' A worried look flashed across his face. 'You're not a journalist, are you?'

A disappointment; if the authority were still unformed, then who might I alert to the discoveries I had made?

I managed, not without difficulty, to convince the clerk to allow me inside, and have the use of pen and paper. The fellow must have assumed I would set down only a short note, and became restless as the minutes and hours passed. I paid him no heed.

Two letters I wrote, one to Hove, one to *The Times* newspaper, though the essence of each was the same. Both recounted the evidence against the miasma theory, and argued the case for the spread of Cholera poison through the water supply. I also urged investigation of all wells, water intake pipes, and immediate prosecution of the Westminster and Thames Water Company. Lurking within the committee building was, I learned, a messenger – idle, needless to say – and, by playing upon the poor clerk's impatience to have me gone from the premises, I had the boy sent off to deliver both missives.

Thus I had done my best to alert the world, floating in confusion though it now was.

Was that all there was left to me to do? It seemed little enough. Stepping into the street outside the Committee building, the air growing warmer now the drizzle was past, I wondered if there was not another little matter I should attend to. Sleak-Cunningham might have been humiliated for the wrong reasons, but at least the fellow had been humiliated, and toppled from his place. While as for . . .

Joshua Jeavons crouched on his haunches by the roadside, oblivious to the dust, waiting for the night to come. Joshua Jeavons pacing through the metropolitan darkness, furtive, his fingers – concealed in his pocket – grasping a small and rattling box. Joshua Jeavons loitering by a street corner, watching for the road to be empty of evening walkers. Then quickly clambering over metal railings, and dropping quietly into the space beyond.

As I had recalled, there were no houses or other buildings adjoining the place. Thus vanished the last possible impediment. Hurriedly I scoured the site for suitable materials, discovering some scraps of wood and a few dry rags. These I placed on a pool of thickly oozing liquid that scented the air, sickly sweet. In a moment I had rolled further barrels to the spot, and broken open their seals, their contents spilling forth. All that was left was to . . . I recall pausing. A strange moment – though it cannot have endured more than a few seconds – of strong flavour; the taste of suspended criminality. Not that I had any serious doubts. My strongest feeling was resentment at having been driven to such desperation.

I struck the match.

My immediate concern was that I should regain the road without being observed. Luck was with me, and clambering over the gates I discovered the lane beyond was deserted. I had only just time enough to regain the main road; even as I joined the crowds my nostrils detected a faint but rich smell, recalling baking treacle cake. Within moments a fierce crackling sound had filled the air, and the street began to lose its night-time murkiness, coming alive with red light and dancing shadows. Others trotted past me back towards the yard, faces bright with excitement at the drama. I went with them, grimly curious.

What a fire it proved to be. Indeed, watching amid a pleasure-yelping mob, I wondered if I might not have caused the destruction of all Westminster. The flames seemed to be as high as a tree. Fortunately there was no wind, while the fire was not so huge as to leap beyond the yard. I stayed until the windows of Sweet's office cracked into splinters – with a sound like gunshots – eliciting a ragged cheer from the watchers.

A dark notion, perhaps? One that may even set your hearts against me and my story? So be it. I cannot reinvent the truth of my past; nor for that matter would I want to do so. My action was rash – and of course criminal – but also just. Justice of a kind new to me, whose logic I was only beginning to grasp.

To think that only that very morning – before the Reverend Rupert Hobbes had paid his little visit, and set me upon my long road of discoveries – I had expected to rest, to sleep away the day. The hope already seemed hazily distant; almost as if belonging to some other man. Indeed, such had been the weight of the day's findings that, for the first time in many weeks, Isobella had almost been banished from my thoughts.

Almost.

An engineer is not worthy of that noble title if he does not possess some good knowledge of the laws of science; thus I am in no poor position to consider the tenacious nature of momentum. Momentum is the sum produced by the speed of a moving object, multiplied by its weight. A livelier representation, perhaps, is that of a coach and horses, in which the creatures cease to tug at their wheeled burden, only to have the vehicle pressing them forward, driving them on with its bulk.

Another instance of the word, though less scientific, might be that of a fellow driven by the restless ache of personal mystery; a soul hungry for relief, striding onwards through the night, though he hardly now has the strength to reason why.

Or, to put it in a more mathematical form:

MOMENTUM × CURIOSITY = JOSHUA JEAVONS
STEPPING (WEARILY) INTO THE HOTEL ORLEANS

The foyer was lively now, with porters carrying in the luggage of late night guests, fresh arrived – most of them couples of which, I observed, the man was usually a decade or three older than his female companion – while others strode in and out through the discreet doors, embarked or returning from forays into the London night. The distractions caused by such activity, together with the growing familiarity of my visits, seemed to do much to reduce the suspicions of the reception clerk with putty-coloured skin. Indeed, he hardly gave me a second glance.

'A message for Count Nemis, wasn't it. Who from?'

'His friend Herbert.' It was an answer I had long had prepared.

Only then did the momentum begin to leave me; the push of the carriage dwindling, leaving the horses strangely deserted. Standing before the desk, watching the purposeful bustle all around, I even wondered if I should not quietly slip away. The matter must be attended to, certainly. But must it be tonight, when I was hardly able to think? I could return tomorrow . . .

'The count will see you now. Room 204.'

Too late. My recollection of what follows grows hazy; perhaps the consequence of my exhaustion, or the seeming unreality of the moment. I remember the shuffling porter, smelling faintly of drink. The gaudiness of the corridors, decorated with lush curtains and occasional musingly naked females in statue form; these last doing nothing to raise my spirits. And the fine brass numerals upon the door.

Also, as I stood waiting, the urge that came upon me;

quite without warning, yet overwhelming of strength. Only to see her face.

The fellow who peered out was young – younger than I – but with a certainty of eye. His spiny moustache, so carefully waxed, proclaimed – as did his thick accent – his foreignness. He inspected me with something of a frown. 'You are from Herbert? Yes? What is this message?'

Of course I found myself utterly unprepared. I had never really thought beyond this point. 'It's . . . A matter concerning your lady companion.'

A narrowing of eyes at this. 'Yes? You talk of Lucy?'

That name again. Observing the man's annoyance, I wondered if I had not struck some raw spot – hardly unlikely in view of what little I knew of Herbert and him – and stumbled into the midst of an old feud. A ridiculous position to find myself in. Yet, to see her face . . . 'Might I speak to her?'

A sharp shaking of the head. 'Certainly no. What is this Herbert's message?'

'It wouldn't take long.'

The fellow regarded me with something like suspicion. 'Why is Herbert not here himself if there is such importance?'

I seemed to be making little progress. It was then, however – between the Hungarian shoulder and the frame of the door – that I caught sight of something. The light movement of a woman; a glimpse of scanty, lacy garments, hurriedly and insufficiently covered with a towel; a hint of bared leg, of slim waist.

Our chatter must have caught her attention. 'Leo, what is this?'

Thus I finally discovered her. Except for one small detail. It was not Isobella.

The remarkable thing was the lack of close resemblance. I do not believe she would have made even a convincing cousin of Isobella, let alone sister; her features, though pleasing in their way, were coarser by far. Foolish, blank-eyed. Had she been at the far end of a distant room still I would not have mistaken her for my wife. Only her hair was similar.

All those dusty vigils among the tramps and match-sellers opposite the Cafe Castelnau. The long pursuit of Herbert the wealthy son through the novelty shows of the West End. The bribing with drink of the hotel porter. And this last mad escapade. All for nothing.

What could the waiter have been thinking of? Probably he had little troubled himself over likelihood, being more concerned with the guineas I had offered. A fraudulent, cheating soul.

But then . . . A thought occurred to me. If it were not Isobella, had never been Isobella, then . . . At once I felt my spirits beginning to lift. Gone was the Isobella shamelessly playing footsie at a table of the Cafe Castelnau. Gone was the Isobella being touched by the soft hands of Herbert, child of the aristocracy, the Isobella lying shamelessly between a foreigner's scented bedsheets.

'What does Herbert say?' The count, having banished Lucy back into the hotel room, was fast growing impatient.

I think I even laughed. The fellow was, at once, so splendidly unimportant. 'Herbert says nothing to you. Nothing at all.'

A mighty frown. 'This is your joke of such things? It is not any joke to me.'

As if I cared. My thoughts were far away as I was led back down the gaudy corridor. I did not deign to answer the reception clerk as – his face gaining, with displeasure, something like a healthy colour – he snorted and weakly threatened police. Only after – as the porters hurled me from the door, into the dust of the Mayfair street – did my ponderings begin to strike a more sombre note.

If my investigations of all these weeks had been, all along, the hurrying of a man down a road to nowhere, then what did that leave me?

What did I know?

* * *

Away to the north a faint red glow in the sky marked Harold Sweet's molasses yard; though the colour was beginning to fade, it had been shining brightly for some hours now, indicating the barrels had burned well; a cause for some satisfaction. My thoughts, however, were more concerned with the sight immediately before me; the house of Felicia and Gideon Lewis.

Though it was approaching eleven, there was still, I was pleased to see, some sign of life, in the form of a solitary illuminated window. This was on an upper floor, just below the servants' quarters, and – as far as I could recall from my knowledge of the building – was that of Gideon's studio. Perhaps he was working late upon one of his biblical paintings, or some commission of church design. The other windows were all of them lifeless, but still . . . I strode forward and rang the bell.

A seller of King Charles spaniels, a lecherous man balding of head, the wizened Reverend Michael Bowrib, Albert Farre, Superintendent Lisle and Constable Collins: these were among the many souls who chased one another through my thoughts that evening. Unravelling; this was the game. Plucking out from the tangle the false strand placed there by the mischievousness of the Cafe Castelnau waiter. Then studying what was left. The remnant, unhappily, seemed to be nothing more than a confusion of threads, lacking, so far as I could see, any connection with one another, let alone taking me in some useful direction.

My first thought had been of Lark Road. Indeed – invigorated by my relief at Isobella's absence from the count's bedroom – I had journeyed there without delay, only to find the place as deserted as upon my last visit; indeed more so, as there was not the slightest sign this time of any mysterious intruder having paid a visit.

Next I recalled the dog seller. Making my way to the

Haymarket – glittering with night-time bustle – I found, however, the fellow was not at work there that night. Perhaps he had sold his day's quota of animals.

Back, and further back, in my thoughts. To her disappearance, to the dinner party. Earlier yet. And so, despite the failure of earlier visits, I became drawn to the house of the Lewises.

One pull at the doorbell I gave – the ringing echoing loudly from within – then another, and yet two more, until I heard stamping footsteps drawing near. Even then the door opened only a crack, held thus by the chain.

'Who is it?' The speaker I recognized as servant of the household, a thin, awkward soul by the name of Betty, spotty of face, this last being the only part of her I could see, the rest being concealed behind the door. I seemed to have woken her from sleep, and her eyes cast a dazed – and troubled – glance at my clothes.

'Joshua Jeavons is my name. I'm come to speak to your master or mistress. It's a matter of great urgency.'

'The mistress is away at her cousins'.' She offered the news with finality. 'And the master'll be in bed by now.'

Felicia away; it seemed quite an opportunity. 'There's still a light burning in Mr Lewis's studio,' I countered. 'The matter is, I assure you, a most important one. Nothing less than an emergency.'

Though she received the news far from happily, her resolve to keep me at bay proved frail. 'I s'pose I should call him. You'd best come inside.'

Doing so, I saw further reason for her reluctance to admit me; she was clothed only in a nightdress, which she gathered about herself with some shyness. 'I can see myself up,' I offered.

She seemed relieved. 'Well, if you don't mind . . .'

There was just enough light filtering down from the studio for me to see my way up the stairs. Finding the door open, and receiving no response to my knocking, I stepped inside.

The lamp was lodged near the entrance, hissing noisily and casting a good white glow upon the room, which was well filled with the smell of paint, and canvases of biblical scenes. I found myself before an easel, supporting a huge rendering – still unfinished – of Moses leading the Israelites across the parted Red Sea; the face of Moses himself calling to mind not so much divinely appointed authority, as a washer-woman impatiently hurrying to the gin palace, fearful she might find it already closed.

As for Gideon I could see no sign. Indeed, I was beginning to wonder if he might have retired to bed, having imprudently left the lamp burning, when, in the quiet of the room, I became aware of a low rhythmic sound, resembling snoring. Pursuing this, I found myself drawn to a collection of canvases leaning against a wooden chest, from behind which extended a pair of bootless feet. Apart from these extremities, the artist – for it was Gideon – proved fully clothed, and slumped most peacefully, his mouth wide open; a ready trap for any incautious summer fly. Most of interest to me about him, however, was the overpowering odour – easily overtaking that of the paint – that hung about his person; that of strong liquor. Sure enough, close by his head stood a bottle of whisky – empty – with another just started close beside.

A most remarkable sight. Gideon Lewis, church architect, friend of the Reverend Mr Bowrib, painter of moments of biblical excruciation, brother of the puritanical Felicia, slumped in drunken insensibility in his own studio.

My foot caught one of the canvases, causing a clatter that saved me the task of waking the fellow. He sat up, eyes open wide, but showing no confusion; he seemed unaware of his having been asleep. Then stared at me.

'Josher.'

For a moment I wondered if he might cry out, or

seek some weapon with which he might defend himself against so unexpected an intruder. I could hardly have been more wrong. His face sagged into a kind of bobbing-headed smile. I realized – with some surprise – the fellow was actually pleased to find me stood before him.

'Josher,' he repeated, clambering up – unsteadily – from the chest. 'Come to see me aafer all this time.' His words were slurred almost to incomprehension. 'Where'f you been?'

It was not a question I rightly knew how to answer. Indeed, I chose not to try. 'I've come to ask if you've some knowledge of what's become of my wife.'

He was not in the slightest taken aback by the question. Rather, he grew petulant; annoyed by my failure to visit before. 'Off course I raven't. That's why I've been so surprise you've not come see me.' He directed to me a wounded look, as one mistreated. 'We're bzozhers, Josher. Nothing less. Bzozhers for our love.'

The remark was puzzling indeed. 'What love?'

He plucked up the full bottle of whisky, and offered it to me; an invitation I declined. 'For Isobella, of course.'

So there it was. All that Isobella had told, at last confirmed: the poison pen letters had indeed been Felicia's. I had hardly needed to wheedle it from the fellow. Indeed, his shamelessness was extraordinary; regarding me now with a look of sombre self-pity, he seemed almost to expect me to applaud him, or offer him an embrace. Perhaps he did.

Strike the fellow down, there and then? It was tempting. Or quietly listen to what he had to say. After some consideration, curiosity won. 'When did you last see her?'

'Not for montss.' He took a large, unhappy sip from the bottle, then, abruptly – the character of his drunkenness seemed very much one of instant changes of mood – grew reflective. 'She's so lovely, Izobella, wreally she is.' At once moved by a new idea, he took my arm that he might lead me across the room. 'Here, I wann show you somesing, somesing spechou. That no-one's seen.' Rummaging – in a lurching fashion – through some canvases leaning against the wall, he plucked out a smaller one among them. 'I had t'keep it hid from F'lisha. If she'd found this . . .' He shook his head grimly at the thought. 'The crying out of an artis' soul, tha's what it iss,' he explained. 'My own artis' soul.'

The painting, in common with his other works, had biblical roots, depicting the Virgin Mary holding the baby Christ. Indeed, I recalled having seen another attempt at this same subject, in which the young saviour had resembled a punctured football. This effort was more skilful, though not greatly so. Most striking to my eye, however, was the fact that the Madonna was a portrait of Isobella. The rendering was a poor one – her face displayed a look of blank stupidity that could hardly have been less like her – but she was recognizable, nevertheless. Nor was this all; as my glance passed across the rest of the picture, and reached the infant Jesus, I realized – with some surprise – that he was none other than a youthful Gideon, grinning cheerfully.

'I wanned to be close to her,' he explained, morose. 'If I couln't in wreal life, then I would in a pitcher.' He sighed, fearfully. 'That's what bein' an' artis's all about. Taking the horrid thingss 'round you an' making them into somethin' you like. See?'

I had had no idea the man was such a philosopher.

Replacing the canvas, he grew changed again, now frowning. 'But she's so cruel, Isobella.' This mood done with, he next glanced at me – for the first time – with something like awareness. 'You's not angry with me, are you Josher?'

I was too drawn to have him stop now. 'Tell me what happened between you both?'

He needed little enough encouragement; indeed –

pausing only occasionally to drink from the bottle of whisky – he embarked on quite a history of the matter. With some revulsion I listened as he recounted – wonderfully untroubled by the thought that he was telling this to the very man his efforts had been attempting to cuckold – how he had observed and admired my wife during her visits to the church, and, later, to Felicia's bible study meetings. It was some time before he had been able to catch her alone – the occasion seemed to have been a morning when she was early for one of the bible meetings – and tell her of his feelings. In response, she had, I had been well pleased to hear, coldly rebuked him. Yet she continued to visit their house, and even sought him out, that she might rebuke him further. Perhaps not unreasonably, Gideon had considered this a kind of disguised encouragement.

'Still I couldn't even get so much as a lil' kissie out'er her.' He regarded me sorrowfully, as if I, her husband, would understand. Nor, for once, was he so wrong. 'Until that night she came throwin' pebbers at my window.'

'Pebbers?'

'Yes. Lil' stone pebbers. To wake me up. It was like a miracu.'

A thought occurred to me. 'When was this?'

He had no difficulty answering; the event seemed so firmly established in his memory that – despite his drunkenness – the date rang out with clarity. 'Monday night, seven'y six days ago.'

The night of the dinner, it had to be. The night she had disappeared.

'I let her in, took her up to my room, happy as could be,' he went on. 'But when I just tried to give her a lil' kissie she was horrid. Wreally horrid. Tol' me I was disgustin' and she would'n have me touch her.' He stared morosely at the table. 'She tol' me I had to sleep on the floor.' The thought brought to his features a wounded look. 'Why'd she do that? Why'd she throw pebbers at my window and then do that?'

Why indeed. It was astonishing. Splendid. For the first time in so many months I felt something like a glow of satisfaction. I had not been the only one.

In the event it seemed the matter of the beds had been little more than academic, as shortly after Felicia had arrived upon the scene, having overheard their chatter. She having – as Isobella had herself recounted – long been suspicious of some liaison between the two, and opposing any such thing with determination little short of obsession, a verbal battle had broken out, with all manner of stinging insults flung. Indeed, it seemed the two women had sometimes broken off from attacks upon each other, and joined in browbeating Gideon himself; recollection of the event appeared painful to the fellow, and the whisky had diminished appreciably by the time he reached its conclusion.

He shook his head gloomily. 'Then she left me. Can you 'magine? Walked out int'se morning – it'us light by then – and was gone. I went after'rer, even though F'lisher was screaming at me to come back. An' you know what she said? Your wife. She said "Gijin, I despise you. Gijin, you're nothing better than a flea." A flea! T'say I, Gijin Lewis, was a flea. And aafer all she did before, too.'

My head was singing with one thought. 'But where did she go to?'

He showed some faint signs of emerging from his self-pity. 'I asked her that. Asked her if she 'us going back to her house, and if she'ud see me again.' He frowned. 'She was strange then – quiet, an' sort of angry at herself . . .'

To my surprise I found myself recalling the words of the dog seller. '. . . like she wanted someone to clout her one . . .' 'And?'

'She said she'd never see me again. She said she wasn't going back, she'd never go back, because all of that had been spoiled. Spoiled long ago.'

'What did she mean?'

Gideon's energy was running low; he leaned

unsteadily against the wall. 'I dunno. I jes dunno.' Eyes half closed, he seemed to be talking as much to himself as to me. 'She looked so miserabu. But when I tried to cudder her, she rouldn't let me. She wen off.'

A last question occurred to me. 'Which direction did she take?'

He struggled for a moment with the matter. 'North, I s'pose.'

It was towards the Haymarket.

An anonymous graveyard somewhere on the fringes of Westminster; thus did I find myself, peering through the iron railings at the scene beyond; drizzle was again falling, giving the metal the look of something sweating.

On the further side of the yard a small group was gathered, lit by flickering lights; the parson holding his lamp high that he might see to read his piece, mourners directing theirs upon the coffin as it was lowered slowly into the ground. A second group stood behind, loitering about a hearse, waiting their turn. A sad sight it was, with mounds of earth thrown up here and there, as if some gargantuan mole had been at work. In one corner paupers' coffins were stacked upon one another, doubtless awaiting the moment when their numbers would be sufficient to warrant the digging of a new grave. From St Giles, I wondered. Altogether the place had the churned-about look of some battlefield, where armies had been fighting too long over the same dismal spot. Nor was it only in the look; a sickly scent hung in the air, as a stifling veil.

At least the place held some usefulness to me. I followed the railings, reaching nearer to the burial group, until I was at a point where their lights shone some proper brightness upon me – just enough to read – then took from my frock-coat pocket the ragged pieces of paper. The hardships and cleansings that the garment had endured had done little to improve them, and the writing upon them was much of it watery and spoiled. Still, enough remained to be studied.

WHY CAN HE NOT LEAVE ME ALONE?

It did resemble her hand, and closely too. Less well formed than was usual of her, certainly; more hurried. But might that not . . .

It was then that I wondered – for the first time, but by no means the last – if I had understood my wife any better than I had the Asiatic Cholera.

Chapter Nine

The remarkable elasticity of time. A month empty of event can pass so quiet in a man's life that – looking back across such changelessness – it may seem hardly a day has passed. Earlier upheavals remain in his imagination still freshly recent, as, through the misleading clarity of frozen winter air, the snow mountains about Turin can appear no more than hills, reachable by a short walk. A whole year can thus resemble an interlude; a thing wasted, or stolen.

Inversely time can grow concentrated – a juice boiled to thickness – causing one day to be as filled as two or three. This is an effect often to be experienced during long travellings, and I observed it myself during my extended fleeing from English shores, across France and Switzerland; each section of that wondrous journey across forests and mountains seeming almost as an epoch of itself. Perhaps it is the savage within us that brings such distortion; the need to remain alert in unfamiliar territory, to set to memory the passing road, so that, if attacked by other savages, a route of escape can be found. Certainly the return journey often possesses the illusion of being far shorter than the outward.

Nor can only travelling effect this. Tumults in one's life, great changes of understanding: these too can cause a day to appear as lengthy as several, vanishing its predecessor behind a fog of distance.

Thus it was that long evening – an evening that, though I did not know it, was to prove my last in the great metropolis of London – as I wearily trudged my way back towards St Giles. The latest hours seemed possessed of their own history, almost remote from my own past. Indeed, the days previous to my struggle with the Cholera were as the life of another, distantly told.

And now? Sleep; this was my great ambition of the instant.

But the evening was not over yet. Far from it.

I had reached quite close to my old rented room when I observed – collected before a beerhouse – the gathering of revellers. There were quite a number, and more arriving – a surprising sight at so late an hour – and thus, though they showed no unruliness, I deemed it prudent to cross to the other side of the road, and keep my glance before me. I had almost passed by them when Jem's voice called out.

'Drain man, come on you old killjoy. Come an' have yerself a drink, an' celebrate.'

'Celebrate what?'

'What d'yer think? Good riddince to ol' King Cholera, of course.'

Thus I learned the news. The attack that had struck the district so viciously – and myself, too – was finally over.

Hobbes, present too, and even supping from a glass of ale, though he looked as tired as death, gave me the details. 'Not a new case since this morning. There are still many sick with it, of course. But since the disease first came there's never been a pause so long as this.' His dour face managed a wary smile. 'We can hope it's done with.'

A relief indeed.

'See here. This is the one broke the pump and stopped the Cholera.' Jem announced the fact proudly, to any would listen, taken with all the enthusiasm of a candidate's canvasser on election day. Indeed, he showed much the same pleasure in showing me off to the crowd as he had in revealing the splendour of the wardrobe large enough to hold four men stood side by side. Faces turned to watch, and, a little to my embarrassment, I found myself the focus of curiosity.

'He's the one done it. Me mate the Drain Man.' Despite his tender years, the boy seemed well steeped in drink – indeed, he exhibited his drunkenness with quite a swagger, as one well accustomed to such things – while Sal, lodged wobblingly upon his arm, was little better. 'An' it was me saved him. It was me fished him out from the pisser when he was a pewkin' hisself to death.'

'You broke the pump, did yer?' Some present had evidently heard of the matter, and regarded me with interest. Thus it was I found myself subject of a kind of drunken congratulation.

'Well, here's to you, mister.'

'Your health, matey.'

Hobbes was less convinced of my role as saviour. 'It seems rather sudden. Besides, the cases stopped breaking out before the pump was broke.'

I was inclined to agree; events did seem to overlap. But it was still possible my intervention had assisted in the disease's decline.

'Well done, mister whoever you is.' A huge fellow with tattoos upon his arms gave me a slap upon the back that all but sent me reeling.

'Yeah, good on you.'

Jem did not leave the matter there, but called out, 'Three cheers for the Drain Man.'

Joshua Jeavons honoured with three ragged hurrahs. Joshua Jeavons, nodded to, toasted in beer, and backslapped some more. I suppose it was my great moment of glory. Though, to be honest, it little felt so at the time. I was pleased, of course, by the approbation of these grinning and ragged strangers. But mostly I just wanted to sleep.

The scene proved a short-lived one; after only a few moments the attention of Jem's audience grew distracted by the arrival of a noisy, straggling group of fellows, intent on attracting notice by seeming as fierce and noisy as they might.

'Where's our free beer?'

'Out of the way, you all. Yer might as well go home now – there'll be none left by the time we're finished.'

For a moment it looked as if a scuffle might break out, but, after only a few scowls and murmurings, the arrivals then filed into the beerhouse, quiet enough.

I glanced at Hobbes. 'Free beer?'

He nodded. 'That's what's brought them here. All of them.'

I had assumed the ending of the Cholera had been the cause of the late night assembly. In fact it was only a focus for the chatter and toastings of the gathering; the reason lay rather in the superstitious character of the landlord of the beerhouse just behind. It seemed the unlucky fellow had been himself struck by the disease and – in a rash moment, upon his sickbed – had promised that, were he to recover, he would liberally entertain the whole district. I caught a glimpse of the man through the open door of his enterprise; a paunched sort, still pale of face after his illness, and looking decidedly nervous.

Well he might. It appeared he had announced his intention to fulfil his vow only a short time earlier, doubtless in the hope that – at so late an hour – few would make use of it. Such scheming showed a misplaced knowledge of the swiftness of travel of the cry, 'Free Beer'. Aside from the gang of noisy fellows, a steady trickle of other thirsty souls had, even as I watched, been making their way to the beerhouse door, and, inside, quite a crush was developing about the bar. The numbers brought their own consequences and a sudden outburst of shouting, only a few yards from us, warned of a likely fight soon to start.

'Don't you shove me.'

'Get yourself away. If you so much as touch me . . .'

Hobbes regarded the scene wearily, and finished the last of his drink. 'I think it's time I was away.'

I felt a wave of tiredness. 'I, too.'

'What d'you wanna go off fer, when we've not told the 'alf of it?' Jem was eager to enjoy further boasting of my – and his own – role in overcoming the disease. 'It's a lark 'ere. Free as well. An' you've not even had yourself a beer.' He glanced round to the crowd. 'Tell the Drain Man he gotta stay, eh? Tell him he can't just go off.' Nobody much answered – all were too intent on the budding fight – but Jem swaggered as much as if he had caused a mighty cheer. 'There you are, Drain Man. Get yerself a drink instead o' being such a killjoy.'

Sal nodded sleepily.

It seemed ungrateful indeed to desert them, after all they had done for me. Besides, as the mood of the crowd grew uglier I was not a little concerned for their safety; they were so conspicuous in their smart clothes. Of course both were well versed in looking after themselves, but one never knew . . .

'I'll stay,' I agreed, and waved goodbye to Hobbes.

Jem grinned. 'That's our Drain Man.'

A beer. I soon regretted trying to get myself one, free though it was. Within, it was little less than a battle; a hot, animal scene, of swearings and sweat and near fights. I recognized some of the others in the crush. Thus there was the fellow who had had the room above my own, his vicious dogs at his feet; barking loudly, and winning him two beers swiftly served. Also, closer beside me, the mad-eyed fellow, who had – only that morning – accused me of poisoning the wells, and put into my thoughts the true nature of the disease. Now he seemed acquainted with my improved status.

'Famis, now, in't you?' he observed, warningly. 'But where'd you be without me?'

Foolishly I imagined there might be some logic to his utterances. 'I thank you again.'

'So you should.' He scratched deep into his wind-blown looking hair, with the air of one fearfully slighted. 'Where'd you be if I'd not calmed that wicious mob, that wanted to string you up? Eh? Answer me that.' There was no need, fortunately, as he answered himself. 'You'd be dead, that's where. Dead as a dead hog.'

There, too, was the mother of the Irish family, who had thought me some kind of dangerous magician; she seemed – by some cunning means – to have obtained a drink for every one of her countless offspring, and they filed out of the room behind her, resembling a parade of virtuous pupils from some school of beer-drinking.

I was even fairly sure I caught a brief glimpse, in the distance, of my friends the three shore workers – now clad in clothes of a kind of wild smartness and fashion, and each possessed upon his arm of a chirping female – though they disappeared too quickly into the throng for me to catch their attention with a greeting.

At last I won the glance of one of the flustered and red-faced fellows serving, and gained myself a glass of beer, together with two more, for Jem and Sal.

Stepping, with relief, from the confinement of the beerhouse into cooler air, I observed that a fight had finally begun. It was a strange manner of battle, fought not between the ones I had observed earlier, but another pair; two tiny, shrimp-like fellows, grey-haired and wizened, and altogether seeming beyond the age for such violence, though they swore with liveliness, for the most part accusing one another – with nothing less than accuracy – of being old.

'That's the last time you shove me, yer half dead, ancient ole bastard.'

'Spill beer on me, would'yer, yer shrivelled up bugger. You'll have yerself inside yer coffin ahead of time, yer will.'

The crowd had gathered about in a circle to watch, chanting their support – for 'New Boots' or 'Green Shirt' – with rising enthusiasm as the combat progressed – if rather woodenly – and the two aged fighters grew marked with sweat and blood. Jem and Sal were as keen spectators as any, Jem much annoyed that his lack of size prevented his obtaining a clear view. Though I felt little excitement at the spectacle –

indeed, the sight depressed my spirits – I took my place beside them, and I was still there when I observed the prim fellow. He must have asked which I was, as he strode towards me with intention.

'Are you the one who broke the handle from the pump in Boot Lane?'

The man could hardly have looked more out of place in such a spot; his clothes were those of an office clerk, carefully attired for a day of inky scribbling, while his face seemed to match. Nor was I the only one to regard him with curiosity; several of the crowd cast winking glances at one another. He himself seemed oblivious to his visibility, regarding me with the air of one of no little power.

I guessed his purpose. Something of this kind had been bound to happen. 'What of it?'

A neat smile. 'You are required to visit the offices of the Westminster and Thames Water Company, tomorrow morning, to pay the full sum needed to have the device repaired. If you do not, then legal action will be taken against you for your destruction.'

Had I been less tired I would have been angrier. As it was, I merely shook my head. 'I have already written to *The Times*, and the Metropolitan Committee for Sewers, urging them to take legal action against your water company. I had every reason to break the pump, seeing as it was your pipe that caused the Cholera here.'

One only had to look at the fellow's face to see he was no man to see reason. Nor did he. Instead he embarked on all manner of self-righteous utterings – how his company's water was pure as could be, and had never caused harm to anyone – then returning to the cheerful theme of legal threats, now for my slandering their good name.

The consequence was perhaps inevitable. Especially with the example of the fight so near to hand. The tattooed giant – who had earlier slapped my back in congratulation and sent me reeling – and another, hardly smaller, showed a lively interest in knocking the clerk down. I tried to dissuade them, but the notion proved too attractive for them to let it go. The prim fellow was still uttering monotone threats when he and his neat office clothes found themselves rolling upon the muddy ground.

A spirited type in his clerkish way, he showed no flusterment, jumping up sharply. 'I'll be back. And with officers of the law.'

The two giants only laughed. I watched him go with less satisfaction. He was a ludicrous sight, true enough, but his words seemed to tell of struggles to come; struggles to change minds, dislodge ideas thoroughly welded in place. Such battles would not be easy.

'Sal's fallen asleep,' Jem observed. Nor was he exaggerating; she was quite drooped upon his shoulder, her mouth open and emitting something like a faint snoring. 'P'raps we'd better go back.'

A relief. 'Certainly.'

Movement caused Sal to be jolted into wakefulness, and she closed her mouth. 'We not gone yet?'

I gave Jem a hand marching her away, and we left the crush of the crowd.

'Still lookin' for that gal o' yours, is yer?'

Perhaps I should not have have been surprised. The cry of 'Free Beer' had, after all, brought quite an invasion of fellows, including – as with the shore workers – many who did not even belong to the district, but had merely been passing near by. Though it was hard in the dim light to see exactly how many were gathered, it felt as if half the vagrants and thieves and sellers-of-nothings of London were present.

'Is yer?'

It was a moment before I recognized the lad. He looked quite different without a King Charles spaniel beneath each arm. Indeed, he seemed restless without such burdens, his hands twitching about his pockets as if in search of something to do with themselves.

'What if I am?'

I will not easily forget the strange gleam in the fellow's eyes. 'I jest seen her, in't I.'

'This going to take long, is it?' Jem, in a drunkenly contrary mood, and confused by our chatter, now wanted to be home without delay. 'Sal wants to get 'er kip.'

'It might,' I admitted, unwilling to let go so fine a chance. 'I could follow you later.' I glanced at Sal. 'Can you manage her alone?'

He nodded. 'Of course. I'll see yer then.'

After the fraudulent advice of the Cafe Castelnau waiter, that had sent me upon such a long path to nowhere, I was more than a little suspicious of this second peddler of information. 'Can you prove it was her?' I demanded. 'What was she like?'

The dog seller, unflustered, answered only by reaching to the back of his muddy neck. 'Got a mole, in't she. Jest there.'

It was not a reply I had expected. Indeed, it caused me much unsettlement. I had myself only seen the mark on a few occasions, as it was usually concealed beneath her hair. 'How did you learn that?'

He gave a kind of secretive leer. 'What's it matter? I proved it was her, in't I.' His look grew more calculating. 'Now, what money you got?'

Money. Indeed, this was something of a difficulty. I felt in my pocket; little now remained of the shillings I had gained for the sewer spoon. 'One and six. It's all I have.'

'You must be joking.' He uttered the words with some disgust. 'One an' six, after all the trouble I'd be goin ter.'

I felt a kind of breathlessness; I could not let this opportunity slip. 'Now wait. There must be some way . . .' Of all the worldly goods left to me . . . 'I have a telescope that's worth two guineas at least. It's in my lodgings, close by here.'

He regarded me suspiciously. 'This ain't some trick o' yours, is it?'

'What trick could it be? I cannot force you to show her to me.'

A wary nod. 'Aw'right. Though don't you think of tryin' no clevernesses.'

To climb those stairs, that led to my old lodgings – so familiar, yet already seeming so remote – was strange to me. Also difficult, as they were unlit at this late hour. I felt my way ahead with outstretched fingers. My main concern was that, my room having been abandoned these past days, the telescope would have vanished. Consequently it was with some relief that, stepping within – the chamber dimly illuminated by the light of the moon – I saw the metal glinting. On the floor near by stood the bucket, still containing the water that had so occupied my thoughts during my night of sickness.

'Here it is.'

The dog seller inspected the thing. 'You're sure I'll catch meself two guineas fer this?'

'Sure as can be. You might get more.' I took it from him. 'Now where is she?'

That leer again. 'I'll show you. It's near enough.'

His words were no more reassuring than his look. We were in the heart of one of the worst slums in all London, so how could she be near by . . . ? Unless . . . Was it here that she had been, of all places? So close to where I had myself been lodging? 'Tell me where.'

He looked now a touch uneasy. 'What's yer hurry? I'll show you right enough.' He gave me a furtive look. 'It don't matter where she is, so long as I find her for yer, eh? I still get that d'vice o' yours, dunn I?'

A discouraging question, but I saw no objection I might well make. 'Very well.'

'Jest follow us.'

During those moments when I feel there might indeed be a deity watching over us – rare now, after my conversion to disbelief – I like to believe I might, that evening, have been the beneficiary of a minor instance of divine intervention. That I was judged deserving of a nudge of help. Because, finally, my notions had completed their changings. After all those months of anger, jealousy and vague notions of revenge, quite a different motive now drove me in search of Isobella. I feared for her.

Nor was my concern diminished as the lad began to lead the way. Rather than take the route that would take us most quickly from the slum, he strode towards its centre.

'It was recently that you saw her?' I asked.

'A few hours ago.' Again that unpleasant smile. 'But do'n worry yerself. She'll be there aw'right. She won't 'ave gone nowheres.'

We soon reached the Seven Dials; an uneasy confluence of such a number of lanes, from which, at any one time, it was impossible to gain a clear line of vision along more than one or two of the roadways, though footsteps and murmurs seemed to faintly echo from all directions.

'Lookin' fer company, boys?'

Even at this late hour a few tarts were still at their posts, voices curling out of the darkness.

'Want warmin' up some this rainy night?'

'Where's yer off ter in such a rush?'

The suggestions were directed mainly towards the dog seller, as, sad to tell, he was the less dismally dressed of the two of us. He gave the women not so much as a glance, his thoughts well fixed upon his reward.

On we strode, past three urchins playing a ragged late night game of kicking a brick. Past a cart loaded with carrots lodged by the roadside, a drunken man lying upon them, singing to the heavens. Past a huge fellow strewn in the gutter, dead to the world – whether from gin or violence – two women crouched upon him, lightening his pockets.

And whence then? To nowhere other than the street – the very building – where Katie had her lodgings. The dog seller stopped before the entrance.

Here, of all places? It seemed hardly possible. 'You're sure this is right?'

That smile. 'Certainly I is.'

Now I hoped for a mistake, hoped that – unlikely though it was – my guide might, like the smooth-faced waiter of the Cafe Castelnau, have merely seen a stranger who resembled the portrait of Isobella. Into the building I followed, telescope in hand. Up the stairs, to the first floor, and higher, to the very level where Katie had her lodgings. Indeed, we hurried by her door. And on, to that beyond.

'Here?'

'That's right.' Though he said no more, the dog seller had in his eye a look of stifled amusement. And so, with something like a spreading sickness within, I realized how he must have come to discover my wife.

Isobella, who had been always so prudish. Who had never let me so much as touch her. Nor even that fool Gideon Lewis . . . With this grimy child, smelling of dogs and street filth. And with goodness knew who else . . . It seemed beyond comprehension.

I stood for a moment, reeling.

My guide, grinning mildly to himself, gave the wood a sharp knock.

But there was silence.

He frowned. 'She's in there aw'right.' He knocked again. 'Must be.'

Still nothing.

He pushed open the door. Following him I saw, from the faint glow through the window, that the room was much like Katie's; peeling walls, a ruffled bed, a stench of damp. And other odours.

It was quite empty.

The dog seller stared about him, mystified. 'I dun geddit.' He peered beneath the bed, as if she might be hiding there. 'She was 'ere before. You believe me about that, now, do'n yer?'

I did not trouble to answer. Isobella in such a place . . . In this room . . . Only a few hours before.

'She'll come back, for certin.' The other was concerned for his reward. 'Not my fault she's gone off somewheres. I took yer where she should've bin, din't I.' He shook his head, annoyed. 'We can wait if you likes.'

Then a thought occurred to me; one that caused me a sudden whirl of anger. If she had been here . . . Telescope in hand, I stepped back on to the landing, and to the door beyond. It was shut, but light shone out from beneath, while I could hear a rustling from within. I turned the handle.

An untimely entrance. Katie was in the very midst of her work, all but vanished – thin limbs outstretched, as some crushed starfish – beneath a huge blubbery sort with a reddened face.

'What the fooch . . . ?' He sounded drunk.

'Out of here.'

He blinked, uncertain as to what dangerous ruse might be being played out against him. Wide-eyed, and murmuring inaudible abuse, he slipped off Katie and struggled to hop into his trousers.

'How dare you come a marchin' in here.' Katie had wrapped a sheet about herself, giving her the look of a dishevelled Romaness.

'How dare you . . .' My anger outmatched her own. 'The woman I sought, here in this building all this time – in the very next room to yours – and you never told me.'

The customer, boots unlaced and shirt hanging loose like a smock, but otherwise dressed, made his escape. In his place the dog seller took the chance to perch himself in a corner, that he might watch his interests.

'What of it?' Katie was cowed rather than repentant. 'What law says I has ter tell you anything?'

'How long has she been here?'

She shrugged. 'Jest a week or so.'

A week. A whole week. And through all that time Isobella had been lodged only a few hundred yards away from where I had been sleeping. 'You knew it was important.'

Her voice rose in sudden defiance. 'What of it? Yer shouldn'ave tol' me them lies, Aldwych. All that stuff 'bout buildin' them rileways an' that. You shouldn'ave led a poor gal on.'

So that was it. A form of lunatic revenge for an invented slight. 'Where is she now?'

'How should I know?'

I detected a wavering in her voice, suggesting she knew more than she cared to admit. 'Where?'

She shrugged, uneasy. 'A geezer turned up earlier lookin' for her. Very pale, he was, like he'd niver been outdoors. She went off with him.'

'A pale bloke?' The dog seller showed interest. 'Why that souns jest like the one came round Haymarket askin' if I'd seen her.'

'But where did they go?'

'I dunno, do I.' Katie adjusted her sheet, without great concern. 'I heard him out on the landing. Making a proper rumpus he was, as she wouldn't open the door and he had to shout through it. Kept sayin' she should come back with him someplace, and see someone – din't say who.' She glanced behind her, as if curious at some detail of the grimy wall. 'For a bit he didn't sound as if he was gettin' nowhere. But then, next time I looked out, there she was walkin' off with him. Quiet, too, like she knew him.'

As if she knew him? 'Did she say when she might return?'

'Naaah.'

That she had left with this mysterious fellow – who had been searching for her almost as long as I – made her disappearance all the more worrying. I could not be blocked again now, surely, when I had reached so close? When I truly had to find her. 'Did she never mention places she liked to visit? Or people?'

'Di'n speak ter 'er much, did I.' Katie's expression took on the look of one unjustly snubbed; it seemed I had struck a sore point.

I stared about the room, caught between abhorrence

and a kind of awful curiosity. 'And she . . .' I faltered over the question. Yet it had to be asked. 'She was . . . as you are?'

'A tart, you mean?' Katie snapped back the words. 'What else d'you think she was doing in here? Having herself some piana lessons?'

A smirking look passed across the dog seller's face.

Still it seemed as a madness to me. How could she . . . ? 'Where'd she been before?'

Katie shrugged. 'Whitechapel I think she said it was. Somewhere round there, anyways. Though I think she'd bin through a few places. Kept moving on.'

I recalled, of all things, the strange message, calling out from among the listed vegetables and fruits. WHY CAN HE NOT LEAVE ME ALONE? A kind of ghastly picture was beginning to form in my mind. Isobella, a fugitive. Seeking sanctuary – I knew not whom from – in a life that could hardly have been more unendurable to her.

'She didn't have much to say to the likes of us gals,' Katie resumed, complaintively. 'Too good fer us, she was, with her little princess voice, and that look of hers, peerin' down her nose like we was beneath her. Niver sink 'erself so low as ter join us fer a brandy or that, would she.' She tightened the towel about herself, petulantly. 'Like that to her geezers, too, she was.' A look akin to relish appeared on her face. 'Not surprisin' she got 'erself beat up.'

'Beaten up?'

'Yeah. Right royal. Nice shiner she picked up a coupl'a nights back, from some poor bloke she gave an 'ard time, tellin 'im 'ow 'e wasn't ter do this, wasn't ter touch 'er there. Askin' fer it she was. Almost like she wanted ter get 'erself knocked about.'

Even here, in this terrible place, she had been the same. But why have ventured near? Why not return to me? I found myself recalling the words of the dog seller, from all those months back.

'. . . Like she wanted someone to clout her one . . .'

But why?

Katie warmed to her subject. 'Got 'erself slapped about thorough. First day here she got knocked right in the gob, so her lips was swelled up like plums. An' soon after, with another bloke . . .'

I could not listen to more. 'That's enough.'

Katie regarded me with something like malicious pleasure. 'Don't yer want to hear such things? Nasty, is they? They's happened to me often enough, I can tell you. And every one of the gals round 'ere, too. But yer not interested in that, is yer, Aldwych? Yer just interested in this stupid snoot bitch o' yers, in't yer?'

I left her there.

The dog seller was close behind. 'Where you going? What about me reward? Not my fault she's gone orff.'

I was in no mood to dispute such a matter, and pushed the thing towards him. Possessing it, he scuttled quickly away. Katie's door slammed shut, and I found myself in near darkness.

And now?

I sat myself in the room, to wait. In the slim hope that she would return. What else, I reasoned, was there left to do?

Unless . . .

Joshua Jeavons, urgency returned to his step once more as he strides towards his old lodging, and beyond, to a heap of refuse piled against a low wall. Joshua Jeavons, sifting through the filth with his hands, but carefully, as if it may do him some injury, softly calling out as he does so, repeating a name. Joshua Jeavons, drawing out some manner of creature – by appearance a mix of rat and rotted dishcloth – clutching it warily, with a firm grip about its neck.

The animal was in a poor way. Indeed, for a moment I wondered if he was alive at all; probably he had barely stirred since his fight with the urchin. Then, however, I observed some faint signs of life; opening an eye he uttered a dull growl and lazily swivelled his head in an effort to apply his teeth to my hand.

Carefully I lowered him to the ground. Seeing a puddle of water he drank keenly. While he did so I took off my jacket, then my shirt, from which I tore away the sleeves – the garment had reached such a stage of frailty that they parted easily – and, tying these together, twisted them into a kind of rude leash. Quickly I slipped it over the animal's head.

Then back, carrying the animal in my arms – I must have seemed like a parent fondly carrying some child of Beelzebub – I hurried back to the doorway. Up the stairs, past Katie's door – tight shut – and to the empty room beyond.

'Don't die on me now, Pericles. Find her and I'll never quarrel with you again.' I placed the creature on to the nest of ruffled sheets.

He only whimpered, causing me to wonder if – a fearful thought – he had quite forgotten his old mistress. But then he hesitated. Sniffed, and sniffed again. And at once there was transformation; his eyes opened wider, exuding something almost like alertness.

'Find her, find her. She must be somewhere in this great city.'

Slowly we made our way out of the room, down the stairs, and into the wind-blown metropolis. The animal was keen enough, certainly, but was fearfully retarded by his weakness. Though sometimes he walked without assistance – even pulled at the leash – more usually I had to carry him, holding him as close to the ground as I was able, with his snout pointing down to the ground that he could sniff, while I would listen for yelps of protest when I took the wrong direction. Naturally this was a most imperfect method of pursuit. Most troubling, however, was his alarming tendency to lose the scent.

Thus in Covent Garden he grew confused, leading me back and forth – yelping and snarling in my arms – among overturned fruit baskets and heaps of discarded plums. Indeed, it was only by ignoring his protests and carrying him quite from the place, back to the last spot where he had enjoyed confident progress, that we managed to resume the search.

Then the same occurred in the Strand. For some time we loitered infuriatingly on that highway that never sleeps while the creature sniffed and wheezed among the dirt strewn on the pavement. Taking him back to an earlier part of the trail proved unavailing, and it was only at a spot further onwards that – with a sudden bark – he again led the way forward.

My confidence began to grow when we crossed Trafalgar Square – as empty now as a parade ground on the day of battle – and descended Whitehall. The route was starting to take a kind of shape. Southwards . . . I wondered if we might be approaching the house at Lark Road. Perhaps she had managed to elude the pale fellow. Although I realized that it was also possible Pericles had quite misplaced the scent, and we would abruptly find ourselves in some anonymous gin palace, he tugging at the skirts of a stranger.

At Parliament Square I almost despaired. We must have tracked back and forth two dozen times – the broken skyline of the half-rebuilt Palace of Westminster glowering down upon us – and then, at such a vital moment, the creature had the gall to fall quite asleep. The details of what followed are now lost to me – dissolved in nightmarish weariness – and I barely recall what method of noise or threat I used to bring him to consciousness, nor how he regained his way. But somehow he did.

Westwards he led. Quite away from Lark Road, then . . . Close above us the windows of the office – my old work place – peered out, blank and dark. And, quite abruptly, I was all but sure I knew our destination.

Nor was I wrong. The animal, too, seemed to gain enthusiasm, demanding to be set down upon the ground and limp forward without help. Through grand residential streets we went, past fine villas, the greenery of St James's Park – gloomy at this hour – ever visible in the distance. Until we reached those iron railings, so familiar to me.

Pericles showed keenness to mark the end of the chase with a display of triumphant – if feeble – barking. He might wake half the household. I picked him up and, though he showed some resistance, managed to quiet him. I have been wondrous glad ever since.

The only sign of life within the house was a faint glow from behind one of the upstairs curtains. Stepping into the porch, I saw the heavy front door shift faintly in the breeze; it was not secured. Strange. Also useful. Fingers about Pericles' snout, I stepped inside.

The sight of the stairway proved too much for the animal; sensing himself so close, he jumped from my arms and, twisting and tugging himself backwards, was able – despite all my efforts to prevent him – to pull himself free from the leash. Away he scuttled, in a brief burst of agility, paws sliding to grip on the slippery marble, up the grand stairway. Alarmed that he might yet alert all to our arrival, I followed close behind. Up to the first floor – he vanishing about a corner of the landing – and to a half-closed door. I stepped into the room beyond.

And thus, in the small hours of a late summer's morning, after all that long summer of searchings, I finally found my wife.

It was she my eyes lit first upon. She was seated upon the bed, back resting against the wall, and, even in the instant that I observed her, I can remember being struck by how strangely comfortable she looked; more so, indeed, than I ever recalled seeing her before. Pericles had lost no time, and was already sat in her lap, licking her hand, while she stroked his head absently, as if she had not fully noticed his arrival. Her clothes were a shock; a cheap scarlet dress – all cleavage and such – of the kind that Katie might have worn. Worse were the marks of bruises on her face.

But most of all I was surprised by the look in her eyes, so unseeing. She seemed no more attentive to my presence than she was to Pericles', staring before her with a kind of unsettling calm.

My glance moved onwards to her father, beside her on the bed. He was not leaning against the wall, but lay on his back; only as I drew nearer could I properly see him. There is something most troubling about the sight of older people in their nakedness, and that was the first shock to me; his dressing gown and pyjama trousers lay on the ground, and he wore only the jacket, leaving exposed a bulk of flesh.

The second shock, of course, was his throat. With his head thrown back this was all too clearly seen, gaping red beneath his jaw; like a second mouth, hungrily open. Though I could see no blood in movement, there must have been quite a torrent, as the sheets about him were coloured for some feet distant. In one direction streaked a long creeping stain.

That stain. Following the line of it with my eyes, I had the feeling of having been pursuing this path all these months, these years. There it crept, over the sheets to the far side of the bed, to my wife – her dress, I now saw, spattered with darker reds – along her shoulder, down her arm, and to the hand itself, elegant fingers still clutching the tiny browning flash of a razor.

She spoke at last, seeing me and not seeing me. 'Have they come? I left the door open.'

'There's only me.'

She seemed disappointed.

I looked from her to Moynihan, from Moynihan to her. So it was he. Had always been he, from the first. Even before I had met her. Strange to say, it was as if part of me had known all along. As if half the summer's madness had sprung from this alone. My fevered work to transform London. All.

Her fingers tightened faintly about Pericles' head, and he glanced at her. 'Will they be here soon?' She spoke the words with directness, like a child who expects one to know the answer to any question she may ask. A clock rang out faintly somewhere in the house, striking five, and she seemed to lose interest.

Months of engagement, a year and one half of marriage, and it had taken this moment, in such a place, both of us dressed in rags . . . I stared at the broken hulk beside her. Only one thing mattered now. The bliss of knowing what matters. 'What of the man who brought you? The pale one?'

'He left. As soon as he had his money.'

He would have been working for Moynihan from the beginning. My father-in-law must have been searching no less hard than me. Searching out of fear of what she might tell? Or simply . . . So much was clear now. Even the business of the secret Admiralty work would have been no more than invention, that he might hurry away whenever he chose.

As if such things were important now.

'You must come with me.'

She seemed puzzled. 'Where?'

'Where you must go.'

I made a tour of the room, pocketing any small valuables that would easily fit into my pockets; sovereigns, golden cufflinks, watch and chain, and more. Jem would know where such items could be got rid of.

The splendour of fine houses; the room had an adjoining bathroom with piped water. Leading Isobella thither by the hand – she followed as quiet as could be – I pulled the vile dress over her head, and rinsed it in the sink, time and again, until it was all but even in colour. Next I carefully cleansed her arms, soothing away the dried brown stains, and vanishing the scab-like lingerings between her fingers. Easing them away. There being no chance of drying the dress, I had to place it over her still wet, hoping we might reach Jem's rooms before she caught cold.

Only as we were about to leave did she lose her

strange calm. The mood came upon her suddenly. As I was leading her by the hand, out of the room, she abruptly pulled herself free, then hurried back, returning to her place beside him on the bed. 'We can't leave him here. We can't.' She looked confused. 'Not by himself.'

'We must.' I took her hand. The fit left her as swiftly as it had begun, and she allowed herself to be led from the room, like a child. Down the great stairway we went. And thus, Pericles trotting at her side, we stepped from the front door. The rain had ceased, and we walked into the steamy grey of a late summer dawn.

THE WESTMINSTER MURDER

Yesterday shortly after eight o'clock, the neighbourhood of Westminster was alarmed in consequence of the mutilated remains of a man being discovered in one of the houses in Trowbridge Street, close by St James's Park. The deceased, who was discovered by the butler, Mr Barrett, was recognized as being none other than the master of the household, the eminent engineer Mr Augustus Moynihan, a figure much respected in his profession, who, among his many projects, designed the Hubert Canal that was opened by the late King.

Several detective police active of C division were immediately employed, including Barton, Barnes and Smith, who at once engaged in making inquiries. Mr Lockwood, a medical officer connected with one of the hospitals, was passing with our reporter shortly after their arrival, and instantly rendered his assistance. He discovered the deceased had been stabbed through the throat at least once, while the absence of the weapon from the scene told the impossibility of the wound having been self-inflicted.

Inquiries during the day revealed the dreadful murder to be a matter of no little mystery. No signs of forced entry were found, and the police are of the belief that the murderer was likely known to the deceased, having probably been admitted into the house by him. The butler, Mr Barrett, explained that recently the deceased had been in the habit of receiving visitors at very late hours, in connexion, Mr Moynihan had explained, with a special engineering project he had undertaken. When questioned, employees at Mr Moynihan's engineering company told of how he was believed to have been engaged on secret work for the Admiralty, although they were ignorant of further details.

The Admiralty itself has been swift to respond to the matter, and at three o'clock this afternoon a statement was issued denying that Mr Moynihan's services had been employed in any capacity. Nevertheless there has been no little speculation as to whether there may have been a political motive for the atrocious deed, especially in view of the strage absence of both Mr Moynihan's daughter, Isobella Jeavons, and her husband Joshua. Mrs Jeavons is reported to have suddenly vanished three months ago, prompting an inconclusive police investigation. Her husband made determined efforts to discover her, but has not himself been heard of for many weeks. Their house was this afternoon found to be quite empty, even of furniture, and there is much concern that they may have fallen victim to the same merciless criminal who caused the death of Mr Moynihan.

Additional Particulars

Other evidence, however, of apparently contradictory implication, has also come to light. A number of valuables were discovered to be missing from the deceased's bedroom, including his gold watch and a number of pieces of his late wife's jewelry. In addition Mrs James Lionel, whose husband is a colonel in the Welsh Guards, and whose house in Trowbridge Street is situated nearly opposite that of the deceased, reported

> seeing at half-past five o'clock in the morning, a man and woman of criminal appearance, walking into the street as if they had just emerged from Mr Moynihan's door. The man she described as a vagrant, the woman as dressed in the manner of a prostitute. Though unable to clearly see their faces, she observed the woman to be carrying some strange animal of hideous appearance, which she deemed to be of foreign origin, perhaps a form of stoat.
>
> It is not impossible that the murderer deliberately employed a disguise. Mr Geoffrey Wilkinson, landlord of the beerhouse in Clarence Road, adjoining Trowbridge Street, reported seeing a group of five or more foreigners loitering near his establishment on the afternoon before the murder was discovered, whom he described as 'speaking French', and 'acting in a furtive manner that excited my suspicions'.
>
> Considerable excitement has been caused by the horrible event, and the house has been literally besieged with persons anxious to see it. The door is guarded by police, whose task of suppressing the public curiosity is anything but an easy one.
>
> Throughout the afternoon and evening a large number of detective police, including some in private clothes, have been actively engaged in watching the departure of trains from the various railway stations of the metropolis, in case any persons answering the description . . .

Despite its southern location, spring reaches Turin hardly sooner than it does England; doubtless a consequence of the city's altitude, and proximity to the mountains. Even now the trees have not progressed beyond the forming of tiny branches, possessed of such a look of detail that, standing out against the bright March sky, they give a sense of one's eyesight having suddenly changed for the better. As for the smaller plants, a few of these have formed small and tentative buds, though at such an early season they put their blossom at risk by so doing; even now the mornings can begin with the sharp chill of frost.

Cold though it can be, the climate seems to suit Isobella. In fact she often . . .

But wait. Perhaps you are angry with me, because of my omission. All this time, and I never told. Well, in my defence I will say that even memoirs are a form of story – or should be – and a wise teller chooses with care the moment of his revelations.

Two years. And good ones they have been, too, although I will not claim all as easy. How could it be so? My wife has been a patient, slowly and fitfully regaining her strength, as the panic drains away from her. Some of it, I know, will probably never be gone.

She has her own room – an arrangement I myself made, that the many ghosts be given a chance to die in their own time – and at first she rarely ventured from within its walls. More recently, however, I have been pleased to see she has begun taking short walks with Pericles in the vicinity of our home, and braving the Torinese dialect to make a few purchases at one of the markets. Indeed, of late she has even shown a willingness to visit me in my study – before she would never venture near – and perhaps stay for an hour or two, reading from a book or sipping a cup of coffee, while I work upon some element of the Fiuli to Nerono railway line, of which I am now chief contractor. A week ago she let me slowly stroke her hair.

How far will she progress along this road? That I cannot say. I will tell you only that I will make her as well as she may become. She is my only project now. And do not doubt, I warn you, the determination of Joshua Jeavons.

Myself? Perhaps it will suffice to report that no longer do I fear waking in the night, damp with perspiration, heart beating from dreams of knives. Nor, though I would gladly see it improved, do I feel any pressing need to single-handedly transform all the world, by cleansing it of effluent.

And the Cholera? I have not ceased my efforts to convince the world of the real nature of the malady, although you will realize the difficulties involved; the great distance, and the poorness of the postal system of this country seem like conspirators against my efforts. Also the need to retain my anonymity – from fancy I chose for us the title of Mr and Mrs Henry Aldwych – prevents me giving exact details of my evidence. Still I have sent out quite a salvo of letters, to members of the reconvened Committee for Sewers, to Parish authorities, and members of Parliament. Nor will I cease such actions, though, sad to say, I cannot report any success to date. The miasma theory seems to hold on to men's minds with tenacity.

The strength of false ideas. If I have learned anything from my summer of discoveries, it is that the more accepted and widespread a notion, the more fiercely it should be suspected. Beliefs have a dangerous habit of creating their own momentum – the momentum of mere fashion – until any who oppose them become the subject of humorous derision, revilement, or worse; a truth that holds as well for small clans as for great nations. Readers, guard yourselves, I urge you, against the toxic slumber of unanimity.

Seek, instead, that most dazzling of prizes; to see through the delusions of your own time. Every generation has its vanity, its scorn of preceding eras, and its determination to be the first – or last – example of humanity of real distinction. Each era and place has its own maddened assumptions, no more evident to their populations than distortions of colour are detectable to a fellow who has from birth seen the world through yellow-painted spectacles. You will not fully escape the influence of your own time – that is an impossible hope – but, if you trouble always to find your own thoughts, you may just rise above the fog of its more ludicrous imaginings.

And that is no small achievement.

Such are the lessons I won from the summer of 1849,

the summer of revelations. An exchange I made – and a most favourable one, as I see it – in which the false comforts of old faiths were surrendered, in return for the noble, if sometimes harsh, clarity of the world seen in truth.

Most of all, however, that long season gave me as its gift my own wife.

THE END

Epilogue

THE REAL END

Some readers may be curious to know a little more about the historical matters dealt with in this novel. And so learn the true end of the story.

The Cholera epidemic of 1849 killed 14,000 people in London alone. As I have told, the scale of the catastrophe was greatly worsened by the measures taken by various authorities to deal with the disease.

First there was Edwin Chadwick, upon whom I based the character of Edwin Sleak-Cunningham; a civil servant of great influence, also an early champion of government intervention in social matters. A man with quite a taste for personal and secret power, he determined to save the capital from the Cholera by flushing clean the sewers, in the belief that the miasma cloud would thus be destroyed at its source. There being no miasma cloud, he caused the disease – which was water-borne – to be ejected into the Thames, which was the main source of drinking water. Thousands fewer would have perished had he chosen to do nothing.

The actions of the Poor Law Guardians, though they caused fewer deaths, were in their way more alarming, not least because the Guardians were ordered to act with greater humanity, but rebelled against their instructions.

The Guardians' superiors, the Board of Health, were insistent that doctors be sent out to help those afflicted, and that they be taken to hospitals where necessary. In addition the Board was much influenced by a new theory; that, in areas struck by the Cholera, those who had not yet contracted the disease could be saved if they were removed to a place of refuge, as they would escape the effects of the miasma cloud. The logic of this idea was false, but the action would have been effective; people would have been taken away from the infected water supplies.

The Poor Law Guardians simply refused to obey. They believed Chadwick to be a man of dangerous ideas, and went out of their way to thwart his efforts. Not a single parish or union made any effort to seek out Cholera sufferers in their homes, as the Board of Health had demanded. Hardly any places of refuge were opened, denying the chance of escape from the disease. Most remarkable, as the epidemic approached, some dispensaries were actually closed down, and medical staff dismissed.

The Board of Health found itself unable to overcome this rebellion, as its powers had been poorly drawn. Only when the Cholera epidemic was all but over was something done. Lord Ashley, that great social reformer, rushed a bill through Parliament giving the Board proper powers, and the Guardians were coerced into changing their ways.

The story of London's drains, if less shocking, was hardly less a catalogue of incompetences.

The famed Great Exhibition can give a misleading impression of London in the middle of the nineteenth century; a visitor from our own era would find it most resemblant to a present-day Third World metropolis, struggling to swallow the stream of migrants arriving each day from the country. The city's population increased many-fold in fifty years. Transport, street cleaning, house construction, drainage, schooling; all these bones of the urban skeleton were inadequate for the inhabitants' ever-growing needs. London further suffered also for being the first such phenomenon; New York, Berlin, São Paolo, Calcutta and others had the advantage, at least, of being able to look back to the mistakes of their predecessors.

By 1848, when a great campaign of public pressure brought about the creation of Chadwick's Metropolitan Commission for Sewers, the issue of drainage was beyond urgency. It was a national scandal. Though some of the drainage ideas of that time – described in chapter three – now seem comical (Jeavons' scheme, incidentally, is based upon the 'Sump's' plan of Mr Henry Austin, son-in-law to none other than Charles Dickens), they were not all so, while the need for action to be taken clearly required one to be chosen, refined until practical, and put into effect. In the end, however, none was.

The first problem was the slowness with which the Commission for Sewers acted; largely because Chadwick wanted to have London surveyed before he came to a firm decision. As a result nothing had been done when, the following year, the Cholera came. *The Times* saw its chance, and, working itself into a state of outrage – its favourite mood – launched attacks that made Chadwick little less than a scapegoat for the epidemic. Ironically the newspaper did not concentrate so much upon his flushing of the sewers (which really had killed thousands) as on his delays, and the secretive and power-hungry nature of his character.

Chadwick was deposed. The Commission never recovered its sense of purpose, and, though the problem became ever more pressing, years passed and next to nothing was done.

It was the dreadful odours themselves that finally broke the deadlock. The sewers continued to pollute the Thames, more thoroughly as the city grew. In 1858 – known as 'The Summer of the Great Stink' – the stench became so bad that sittings in the Houses of Parliament were much affected, with members fainting. All at once the government became wonderfully motivated. Money was found, a scheme chosen, a new body – The Metropolitan Board of Works, that replaced the Commission for Sewers – set to action.

Thoughts of making profit from sewage being now discredited, the scheme chosen – designed by the talented Mr Bazalgette – sought only to expel the substances as efficiently as possible, without polluting the Thames. A series of systems of sewers were constructed, with surprising ease and speed, that met at a pumping station in Abbey Mills – still to be seen – grandly constructed in the Venetian Gothic style. An opening ceremony was held in 1865, attended by archbishops, cabinet ministers, the Lord Mayors of London and Dublin, and the Prince of Wales. Thereafter the British were regarded as experts in this new field, and civic authorities from St Petersburg to the United States sought out their engineers for the construction of their cities' sewers.

The system is still functioning today, expelling London's waste into the North Sea; now, at last, a cause for concern, and challenge to the drain men of our own age. Who knows, a scheme such as that of Joshua Jeavons may yet come back into fashion.

Lastly there was the business of cracking the mystery of the Cholera; no less a story of delays and chances missed.

The remarkable thing is that some had guessed the answer to the riddle as early as 1849; a Punch cartoon of that time shows a child drinking from a water pump marked 'The Cholera'. Yet the hold of the miasma theory on men's minds proved tenacious, and two further epidemics were to pass before it was overcome. During the attack of 1854 there was the famous incident of the Broad Street Pump, the handle of which was smashed – much as by Joshua Jeavons – by the pioneering physician John Snow, who correctly saw the link between drinking water and the disease. Still many adhered to the notion of a poisonous gas-cloud, and it was only after the next epidemic of 1865, when a whole series of cases were traced back to a single polluted reservoir, that the argument was largely won.

By the 1880s London was transformed. Bazalgette's drainage system, together with better constructed houses and improved water supplies, had done much to drive back disease. Underground railways and the creation of new highways – often bringing about the demolition of infamous slums and criminal nests – made journeying across the city greatly easier. Londoners woke to find themselves inhabitants of a city which – though duller than its old self – was almost a pleasure to live in.

Mr Henry Mayhew

This book is in part drawn from the writings of Henry Mayhew. It would be wrong not to say a little about this great man.

A journalistic genius, Mayhew was, within his different field, something of a Dickens; in fact Dickens used his writings as source material for some of his later novels. Working for the *Morning Chronicle*, Mayhew began a series of studies, written as 'letters', of London slumland and its inhabitants, discovering them for his readers much as others might have revealed exotic tribes of the tropics. For, although slums were dispersed all across the metropolis, the 'respectable' population – who made up the great majority of Londoners – rarely ventured into such places, though they might be only a few dozen yards from their own homes. Mayhew's investigations were the subject of much interest, and were later compiled and expanded into the four great volumes of *London Labour and the London Poor.*

Reading Mayhew, one has the refreshing feeling that he was a man above the moral narrowness of many of his contemporaries. His studies of the London poor do not set out to prove where they 'went wrong'. He is more concerned with what sort of people they were, the words they liked to use, their daily habits. This openness of intention seems to have had no small effect on his interviewees and, with only rare exceptions, he seems to have quite won over those whose homes he visited. The accounts are finely alive, and detailed, frequently including long and lively quotations.

Mayhew also offers remarkable pictures of London

at that time. Whether he is describing a Saturday night market lit by hissing gaslamps, the silent Thames traffic, the crowded alleyways of a London slum, or the heroic squalor of the Hounsditch second-hand clothes market, his reports include an almost cinematic attention to detail, including sounds and smells.

The London slums were – as he was well aware – a world fast disappearing, and he himself became something of a victim of their demise. The Londoners of the sanitized and respectable metropolis of the 1880s wanted only to forget the poverty and dirt of earlier times. They chose also to forget Mayhew, and he died poor and unhonoured. Now his writings and the city they portray seem to be the subject of ever greater interest. He is well deserving of such a revival.